EMBERS

ZIVA PAYVAN LEGACY • PART 2

EJ FISCH

Transcendence
Publishing

ISBN-13: 978-1-7334772-1-5
ISBN-10: 1-7334772-1-7

WHAT'S COME BEFORE
FRACTURE: ZIVA PAYVAN LEGACY, PART 1

Four years after Ziva Payvan's disappearance, the Alpha team was approached by a man named Pahl Starcer, a wealthy materials developer from the resource-rich world of Delatori. Starcer admitted that, while Delatori lay within the territory of the Niiosian Mob, the planet was currently under the control of the Ibarra Cartel, a network of arms dealers led by the ambitious Alastair Manes. Having been targeted by Manes due to his ongoing loyalty to Niio, Starcer commissioned Aroska, Skeet, and Zinni to take out Ibarra's assassin, a Haphezian woman named Matia Moryi.

Upon traveling to the primary Ibarra base on the distant world of Panuco, the team discovered that Moryi was none other than Ziva herself. She confessed to them that while she'd had to commit a number of atrocities to prove her loyalty to Manes and the Ibarra Cartel, she was truly there working undercover for Tobias Niio. She'd spent a year with the Niiosian Mob after staging her death, under the care of Tobias's wife, Serenity, followed by a year establishing Moryi's notorious reputation throughout Fringe Space. She had then spent two years working for Manes, quietly crippling Ibarra on Niio's behalf. She informed the team that Manes was aware of their presence in his city and that he assumed they were there to disrupt his operations.

Though pleased to be united with their old friend, the team recognized that Ziva's time undercover had jeopardized her mental and emotional well-being. When she shot Aroska unexpectedly, they feared she had been brainwashed by Manes. But the attack had simply been a last-ditch attempt to maintain Ibarra's trust. To Ziva's dismay, as Manes continued to doubt her loyalty and intentions, he discovered her true identity.

The entire team, including Ziva, was taken prisoner by the Cartel. Just minutes later, however, Tobias and the Niiosian fleet arrived to launch their planned attack on Ibarra, capitalizing on all that Ziva had accomplished during her time on Panuco. She and the team managed to escape in the chaos, but because their presence had disrupted her mission, she was unprepared for the Niiosians' arrival. As a result, Manes eluded Tobias's forces and fled the planet, destroying many of Ibarra's assets to keep them out of Niio's grasp. The team split up, with Skeet and Zinni heading for their HSP ship after a grueling car chase while Ziva and Aroska worked to disable security at the Ibarra spaceport. In the process of gaining access to the port, Aroska shot and killed a young hacker Ziva had befriended during her time undercover, believing him to be a hostile Cartel agent. Then, during the final push to reach Ziva's ship, Aroska himself was gravely injured.

Bracing herself for what was to come, Ziva managed to get herself and Aroska off-world and set a course to rendezvous with the Niiosians...

THE
ZIVA PAYVAN
SERIES

A full dramatis personae and glossary of series terms can be found at
www.ejfisch.com/glossary

For Ziva.

SPECIAL THANKS...

...to everyone who has helped give this story and these characters life, whether via your professional feedback or simply your love as a reader. It has been an honor to share them with you.

Thank you for being along for the ride.

PROLOGUE
4 YEARS AGO - Noro, Haphez

A dull ringing in her ears brought her back to her senses.

She gasped and blinked several times. The scene before her grew lighter and crisper but remained cloudy. It took her just a split second to realize the view was literally of the clouds, and the ringing slowly sharpened into an urgent beeping. She must have only lost consciousness for a few seconds. Blackened pieces of debris shot through the air beside her, trailing smoke and flames. The smell of burnt flesh and clothing reached her nostrils even through the jet suit's helmet, and though the crushing wind dominated her senses, some part of her brain still managed to warn her it was *her* flesh and clothing.

The HUD inside her helmet visor glowed red and the numbers on the altimeter scrolled by at an alarming rate. It struck her that the data pad she carried wouldn't survive the landing she anticipated, and that *she* might not survive if her attention was divided. Struggling against the wind resistance, she reached into the pocket on the front of the suit and removed the device, holding it close to her body to keep it from being blown away. The file containing the three messages she had composed the previous night remained on the screen, prepped for transmission. Without even studying the display, she hit the transmit command and released the pad, catching one last glimpse of it as it tumbled away into the clouds. There'd be nothing left of it after it hit the ground.

Free of that distraction, she directed her focus toward orienting herself and slowing her descent. She considered spreading her arms and legs but didn't want to risk being recognized as something other than a piece of burnt debris. Her mind was beginning to register pain now anyway, and fighting the wind was becoming increasingly difficult. Her right arm, hip, and leg all felt like they were on fire, and the thought occurred to her that they might actually be.

The cloud cover dissolved, revealing Noro below. The city's towering structures rose quickly to meet her, and the disorientation left her momentarily overcome by dizziness and nausea. Another glance at the altimeter revealed they weren't as close as they appeared, but it was unnerving all the same. Keeping her arms pressed to her sides, she took hold of the jet suit's stabilizer handles and prayed the repulsion system hadn't been damaged in the blast. She gave them a squeeze and felt the pack on her back hum to life. The thrust carried her a good distance laterally but didn't seem to slow her fall. That was better than nothing—she had hoped to land as close to her home on the river as possible—but it didn't matter how much distance she covered if she was still moving fast enough to pulverize every bone in her body when she hit the ground. The altimeter told her she'd just passed the one-kilometer mark. The suit should have been working by now; she could already see other pieces of the *Intrepid* striking the buildings below her.

Between the crush of the wind and the high altitude at which she'd ejected, she was left struggling for air. The sound of her own labored breathing was deafening inside the helmet, and she did her best to slow it and quash the encroaching panic. *Come on, come on.* She gave the grips another squeeze and felt herself drift farther toward the river. The thought was morbid, but if she at least managed to make it to the suburbs, the chances of killing anyone or damaging property when she plummeted into the ground would be much lower.

Oh please, oh please.

She squeezed again. Harder. Again. *Harder.*

The repulsion system kicked in and she shot forward, flinching as she came within meters of clipping the edge of a building. She was still traveling faster than she should have been, but at least now most of that speed was on a horizontal trajectory. Lowering her head, she leaned further in the direction of the river and carried herself toward the remains of her home, following the path of destruction the *Vigilance* had carved less than two days prior.

By the time she reached the clearing at the entrance to her neighborhood, the melted sleeve of the jet suit had adhered to her arm and the repulsion pack was vibrating so severely she feared it would explode. As she neared her house, she rose up as vertically as possible, hoping to create enough resistance to slow herself down. She released the control grips in quick intervals, allowing herself to fall for a split second before the repulsors caught her again. Any landing at this point would still be rough, but at least she'd be able to walk. Maybe.

She had just reached the edge of her front yard when the repulsors petered out altogether. Glad she was only a couple of meters above the ground, she flailed to get her legs under her and braced for impact. White-hot pain shot through her body the moment her feet hit the earth, blinding her as she tucked her knees in and allowed her forward momentum to carry her into a roll. Bright shapes danced in her vision, and with the sounds of her own breathing and hammering heart drowning out all other noise, she could only collapse into the grass and lie there numb for several seconds.

Get up, she commanded herself. *Get out of here or this will have all been for nothing.*

She wasn't exactly sure what outcome she'd been expecting when she first came up with the plan to eject from her doomed vessel, but somehow this wasn't it. She dragged herself to her feet and staggered forward, fumbling for the clasps to release her helmet. The air outside could hardly be considered fresh, choked as it was with all the lingering smoke and fumes from the Resistance attack, but it still seemed preferable to being confined within the suit.

If there was a silver lining to all of this, it was that the neighborhood remained practically deserted after so many of the homes had been destroyed. She was also banking on the hope that all the atmospheric infrared probes were focused on the orbiting Federation ships or the explosion site downtown and wouldn't catch sight of her taking off in the *Zenith*. The last thing she needed was to be caught by the Feds after everything she'd just been through.

When she reached the stairwell leading into her underground landing bay, it was all she could do to keep from tumbling head-first down it. To her great relief—and surprise, she had to admit—the ship remained untouched. Truth be told, the agency had probably forgotten she even had it, what with everything else that had been going on. She found herself stumbling up the boarding ramp before it had even lowered completely. Although the interior bore an uncanny resemblance to the ship that had just almost killed her, being inside brought her an indescribable amount of comfort, as she honestly hadn't expected to reach this stage of her plan.

She bypassed the cargo bay and headed straight for the cockpit. There would be time for proper inventory checks later. Besides, she knew for a fact that no one else had accessed the ship since the team returned home from Aubin; all her personal weapons and supplies were guaranteed to still be aboard. Her injuries would have to wait as well. She didn't dare look at them—the adrenaline surging through her body was enough to reduce the pain to an agitated whisper in the back of her mind. She wasn't bleeding, not badly, anyway. The superheated material of the ruined jet suit had helped cauterize the worst of her wounds. Right now, that was all she could ask for.

The *Zenith's* ignition sequence took less time to initialize than the *Intrepid's*, and she found herself lifting off in under a minute. One last thought crossed her mind as she cleared the bay, and she turned the ship's plasma cannons on it. With luck, anyone who investigated the scene would assume the vessel had been stolen by looters, something she was sure would have actually happened if it had sat there much longer.

As the ship continued its ascent, the smoke and haze were replaced by the same cold clouds she'd fallen through minutes before. The city disappeared below her, and as she broke out of the planet's atmosphere, she was presented with the same view of Na she'd seen upon leaving to find Skeet and Aroska just days ago. The thought sent a new ache crawling through her body, something beyond physical pain. Setting the autopilot to take her to the nearest FTL lane, she sat and watched on the rear cam as Haphez grew smaller and smaller behind her. As much as she wanted one last look at the home she doubted she would ever return to, it was probably just as well that the image was totally blurred by the tears in her eyes.

EMBERS

ZIVA PAYVAN LEGACY • PART 2

Chapter 1
PRESENT DAY - Tabaco, Panuco

The *Talon* had already reached an altitude of a good fifty meters before the boarding hatch began to close. Through the opening, massive bolts of plasma sliced through the air, many of which originated from the anti-aircraft guns that had activated at various points throughout the Ibarra compound. Fighters belonging to the Cartel and the Niiosian Mob alike hurtled by just meters away. One took a hit and erupted in a ball of fire; a wave of residual heat rushed into the ship just as the hatch sealed.

The vessel shuddered, though whether it was due to the blast or the continuous plasma fire pelting the shields, Ziva wasn't sure. She risked a glance behind her to ensure Aroska's body hadn't rolled away—there was barely enough space in the narrow cockpit corridor for his prone form as it was. As satisfied with his condition as she could be given the circumstances, she turned back to the front viewport, pushing the ship to its top in-atmo speed as it shot into the clouds. A steady vibration rolled through the frame as it surged upward and passed through Panuco's atmosphere. She reached up and wiped a trickle of blood from her forehead before pointing them toward the Niiosian flagship.

Even up here in open space, the fight raged on. She wove through the frenzy of small Cartel craft that had managed to scramble in response to the Niiosians' arrival, praying the transponder would work. The *Talon's* approach remained uneventful; she sent a docking request and, despite the chaos, received a response code within moments. Gripping the controls with white knuckles, she waited until the last possible second to decelerate, bringing them into one of the battlecruiser's cavernous docking bays while still traveling at a speed she'd probably be reprimanded for later. A nasty, metallic screech filled the air as the *Talon's* landing gear skidded into place in the dock nearest the access corridor. The mag clamps activated with an echoing *boom*, locking the ship into place.

Ziva slammed a fist against the ramp controls, lowering it again just minutes after it had closed. She was on her feet and gathering Aroska up as best she could before it hit the bay floor. Even while still aboard the *Talon*, it was like she could feel every plasma impact reverberate throughout the flagship. The thought had just occurred to her that maintaining her footing might be difficult when a massive jolt sent them both tumbling down the ramp.

She coughed and rolled over, wincing at the resulting sting as she brushed her fingers over the still-streaming cut above her right eyebrow. Aroska's limp body flopped toward her as the floor rocked again, a smear of blood trailing from the gash on the side of his head.

She scrambled to her feet, gasping, struggling for balance, and took him under the armpits. She was vaguely aware of something wet around her eyes, though it was difficult to tell whether it was tears or just sweat. Blood from her brow oozed down around one cheek and gathered on her chin, and she spared a fraction of a second to turn and wipe it on her shoulder.

Frantic docking personnel paid the two of them little mind as they crossed the massive floor. They made it up into the main corridor, and Ziva blinked against the emergency strobes that illuminated the space in bright red hues. She took a long step forward and braced one foot behind a support beam, hoping to anchor herself a bit better. Aroska was dead weight, and so far this was all a thousand times worse than when she'd had to drag him across the harvesting room at Dakiti.

The ship rocked again and Ziva tumbled forward, flinging herself sideways to avoid landing directly on top of him. Pain shot through her wrist and forearm as she caught herself on the floor, mere centimeters from crushing his already-disfigured leg. She rolled away and hauled herself back to her feet, glad to finally hear voices and hurried footsteps approaching. Tobias's soldiers appeared around the corner just as she reestablished her grip on Aroska's arms. They lowered their weapons upon seeing her but didn't slow their advance.

"Get off of me!" she hollered in response to the hands that came to rest on her shoulders. Her breath caught in her throat and angry tears spilled down her face. She pulled harder, plowing through the group and trying not to look at Aroska's head as it lolled limply from side to side. "Back off! Please tell me Serenity is aboard this damn ship!"

"I'm here, Payvan," she heard the woman call from somewhere behind her. The soldiers parted to let the former doctor through.

"You have to do something," Ziva sputtered, reaching out to steady herself against the wall as the ship lurched once more. She yanked Aroska's arm toward her with her other hand, wondering if she'd have to add 'dislocated shoulder' to his list of injuries. "He's been unresponsive for..." She trailed off when she realized she had no idea exactly how much time had passed. "Smoke inhalation, blunt force trauma to the head—"

"Payvan, listen to me—"

"—and a shattered ankle. I don't know what—"

"—me see this cut on your head—"

Ziva gritted her teeth and wiped a hand across her face. "It's not as bad as it looks. I can wait until after—"

"—need to hold still and let me look."

That was it. She released Aroska's arm, pulling the combat knife from the sheath on her thigh as she raised both of her hands. With one, she brought the blade up against the side of Serenity's neck. The other she closed around the woman's throat as she shoved her back against the bulkhead. The sound of firearms being readied echoed through the corridor behind her, audible even above the noise of the alarm, and she didn't need to look to know each of the soldiers now had their weapons trained on her.

Serenity barely flinched, ignoring the knife pressing against her carotid artery and keeping her gaze locked with Ziva's. Aside from the fact that the woman's breathing had quickened and her pulse was hammering in her neck, she exhibited no external signs of fear at all.

"Help him," Ziva said through her teeth, fighting to keep both her voice and the weapon steady. "Now."

A shadow passed over Serenity's face, akin to what Ziva remembered seeing when she'd held the woman in a similar position the first day they'd met. But this was different. There was understanding there, but also anger. Disappointment. Still, she managed a nod.

Ziva released her and lowered the knife to her side, backing away as the doctor began issuing orders and the soldiers gathered to haul Aroska off. They left without another word, with Serenity turning to throw her one last glance before the group disappeared around the corner.

A sharp combination of emotions bombarded her all at once, rendering her numb. She returned the weapon to its sheath and stepped backward until her back met the wall, then sank to the floor with her quivering hands clamped over her head. Part of it was anger. Anger at her team for blowing this mission, regardless of what their intentions had been. Anger at Aroska for killing the one person who had been her friend throughout this whole ordeal, and hardly more than a kid at that. More anger over Aroska's current condition. Then there was the fear that he wouldn't make it. The regret and shame for the way she'd just lashed out at Serenity. Finally, some twisted sense of relief that she was now free from Alastair Manes's clutches. But also apprehension—and again, anger—because after all the work she'd done, he'd still escaped. This wasn't over.

She remained seated there for what felt like eons as the adrenaline that had fueled her for the past couple of hours continued wearing off. The trembling in her hands soon overtook her entire body, and she didn't bother trying to subdue it as she watched the blood from her face drip to the floor. The frequency of the drops slowly diminished until they had stopped altogether, and the combination of dried blood and tears left her skin feeling tight and brittle. With her gaze directed downward, she noticed for the first time how much blood she had on her boots and legs. Very little—if any—of it was hers; the majority was Aroska's, and some might have even been Blain's. The thought sent a new wave of tremors through her body.

She was vaguely aware of the way the echoes of battle had begun to diminish. The impacts against the battlecruiser's hull became less numerous until they subsided altogether. Then came a series of codes relayed over the comm system confirming that most of the smaller Niiosian craft had successfully rendezvoused and finished docking. She ignored the following warning about the impending FTL jump and allowed the jolt to throw her sideways. There was silence throughout the ship for several seconds as all the systems regulated, and then she felt a familiar, relaxing hum within the walls. She pushed herself back up into a sitting position and once again brought her elbows to rest on her knees, supporting her head in her hands.

Footsteps approached and passed by as fighter pilots made their way from the docking bays into the heart of the ship. She sensed some of them stop nearby and wondered what kind of strange looks they might be giving her, but she didn't acknowledge them, and they eventually continued on without a word.

As much as she wanted to let her mind go completely blank, it was impossible under these circumstances. There were too many questions that needed to be answered, and they made her head spin to the point that she almost felt physically dizzy. Most importantly, where was Manes going, and how would they finish this job? But before that, she needed to know whether Aroska would recover, how Tobias would react to the fact that his adversary had escaped, and how she would ever get her only friends to trust her again.

Speaking of…. She caught a whiff of two familiar scents, and without looking up, she knew they were there. Relief that they'd made it not only to the *Saber* but up to the flagship as well took the edge off the pain—both physical and emotional—she was feeling, but only a little. They stopped and watched for a moment just like the pilots, and when it occurred to her that they might be keeping their distance because they hated her for everything she'd done, the trembling set in once more. By the time she managed to raise her head and spare them a glance, she was fighting back fresh tears.

Zinni could always be counted on to show at least a shred of sympathy to anyone she genuinely believed was suffering, and she did so now. Skeet, on the other hand, appeared entirely impassive. On the bright side, it was an improvement over the constant anger and disgust he'd expressed since they'd been reunited. But otherwise, it was just one more reminder of how far the situation had deteriorated.

"Aroska?" the intelligence officer said.

Ziva could only imagine how this must look to them—her, a wreck on the floor, alone. Her response was meager, but it was all she could articulate. "Here. Alive. Barely."

Several more seconds passed before they both moved over and settled against the wall on either side of her. Skeet remained upright, arms crossed defensively across his chest, while Zinni sat down beside her, albeit maintaining some distance.

It was the best reaction Ziva could hope for, and after heaving a shaky sigh, she folded her arms and brought her head to rest against her knees, doing her best to ignore the stench of blood.

NIIOSIAN CRUISER - Deep Space

When the intercom crackled, it felt as though they'd been sitting there for both eternity and no time at all. Ziva was tempted to ignore the announcement, but she couldn't help but snap to attention when she recognized Tobias's voice.

"Would Agent Payvan please report to the bridge."

It came across as a command rather than a request, and he didn't bother repeating himself. She'd spent plenty of time over the past couple of years wondering how this reunion would go, but after Manes's escape and the way she'd just treated Serenity, she doubted they were off to a great start.

No sense in delaying the inevitable. With a sigh, she got to her feet and began walking. Skeet and Zinni said nothing further, but she heard both of them fall into stride a few meters behind her.

Four Niiosian soldiers met them halfway to the bridge. Ziva had anticipated an escort; what she hadn't expected was to have two of the men take her roughly by the arms and shove her forward with the barrel of a pistol jammed into her ribs.

"*Sheyss!*" Skeet exclaimed.

She risked a look behind her and saw that the other pair of thugs had flanked him and Zinni. These men had drawn their weapons as well, though they'd refrained from physically taking hold of the two agents. Both Skeet and Zinni reached for their own sidearms, but a subtle wag of her head prompted them to stand down.

She allowed the soldiers to drag her down the corridor, forcing herself for the second time in as many hours to resist the instinct to fight back. The situation could always be worse; she was still conscious and being allowed to move of her own accord, and despite being under guard, Skeet and Zinni walked unhindered.

An elevator ride and a couple more minutes' march brought them to the command level, where the blast door to the bridge already stood open. A cacophony of voices grew louder and more distinct as they approached, but the scene within didn't match the chaotic image Ziva had formed in her mind. Aside from the fact that nobody wore any sort of formal uniform, it looked like any other bridge and CIC in your average heavy cruiser. Men and women manned their stations, giving and taking orders as they plotted courses, took stock of losses, and gauged the situation. Tobias himself stood at a large display table on a mezzanine a couple of steps above the rest of the floor, surrounded by several other men. One in particular leaned against the wall behind the rest of the group, arms folded as he shifted his attention to the newcomers. He seemed vaguely familiar, and he silently met Ziva's gaze as the soldiers brought her to a stop several meters from their boss.

The man's complexion was slightly darker than most of the people around him, and he had dark, narrow eyes to match. He wore his black hair cut short, and several days' worth of stubble covered his angular jaw. It was clear after mere seconds of studying him that he knew how to handle himself. Despite appearing older, perhaps around Serenity's age, this was a man who could move. To the untrained eye, he almost looked bored, but personal experience had taught her to understand the difference between boredom and calm detachment. In fact, his manner reminded her a great deal of her own as she assessed a new environment or situation. He may have seemed calm and collected for the time being, but his wiry frame was designed for speed. Agility. Precision. Something Tobias himself had once said echoed through her memory: *"Dangerous people recognize these things in other dangerous people."*

A hush fell over the bridge, and she looked away from the stranger to see that all eyes had fallen on her. She wasn't sure if they were really that interested in her or if it had to do with the fact that she'd now drawn Tobias's attention as well. He stepped down from the mezzanine and approached, his demeanor colder than she'd ever seen it. She found herself almost missing the days when she would meet with him in the restaurant on Niio. That had been his turf just as much as this ship was, but the atmosphere had been so vastly different. There, she'd always had some sort of leverage, a way to get what she wanted out of their meetings as well. Now, she was trapped, and she'd never dealt with this level of hostility from him.

He came to a stop a single stride in front of her, jaw set. "Words cannot express how disappointed I am in you right now."

"There were unforeseen circumstances," she replied, putting conscious effort into ensuring her voice didn't falter. "The situation was out of my hands."

Part of her felt guilty for shifting the blame to her team, but the truth was if they hadn't shown up, everything could have proceeded as planned. Then again, they *were* her team, her responsibility. She should have done more to make sure they didn't interfere.

You did everything you could.

Obviously not.

"And was the military-grade anti-ballistic force field one of those unforeseen circumstances?"

"It was."

Might have known about it too, if not for the team, her brain reminded her again.

He wasn't buying it. In a flash, he drew the sidearm from the shoulder holster he wore and leveled the barrel at her forehead. The two soldiers who'd escorted her renewed their grips on her arms, though she'd already opted to hold her ground. Without even turning around, she could tell Skeet and Zinni now had their own weapons drawn and trained on the mobster, and that the other two thugs held them at gunpoint in return.

Tobias kept his focus on her alone. "I took a gamble and entrusted you with a task, one we'd spent months planning for. After all the time you spent on Panuco, how is it that you managed to blow everything at the last second?"

"I told you—"

"I do not want to hear excuses! You have single-handedly botched this entire operation."

For a fraction of a second, she was certain he was going to pull the trigger, but he hesitated when a voice called out behind him: "Tobias."

Movement caught Ziva's eye and she glanced up to see the stranger straighten and step away from the wall. He unfolded his arms, standing loose and poised to react. He'd barely raised his voice when he'd spoken, but it had been no less commanding, and it had been enough to capture Tobias's attention.

The man approached them with slow, methodical strides as though he were concerned that moving too hastily would somehow escalate the situation. "She's right," he said, throwing her a glance that almost seemed reassuring. "There was no way for any of us to predict how this would turn out. Yes, the margin for error was narrow. No, things didn't turn out the way we planned, but we had to know that might happen."

Deep creases cut across Tobias's forehead as he scowled, but after a moment he sighed and slipped his pistol back into its holster, nodding for his men to release Ziva's arms. He turned to face his associate, who seemed just as relieved by the decrease in tension as Ziva was. The stranger beckoned for the mobster to come closer and the two of them stepped away to converse in private.

Taking advantage of her relative freedom, Ziva risked a look back at Skeet and Zinni, who both appeared bewildered. They'd lowered their weapons, as had the two soldiers behind them, but their posture remained rigid. Ready. Frankly, she was surprised they seemed so willing to defend her after everything they'd been through planetside. Or perhaps they were merely acting on instinct and they couldn't care less if someone put a bullet in her brain. The galaxy only knew how much this reunion had complicated their lives as well as hers.

Her attention was drawn back to Tobias and the stranger as they finished speaking. The former approached her again while the latter retreated to his place against the wall.

Tobias slid a hand back over his bald head and adjusted his spectacles. "Agent Payvan, I hope you'll forgive me. As I've demonstrated to you before, these are trying times, and I'm afraid I've been allowing my temper to get the best of me far too often as of late. You've been nothing but a friend to us and it would be wrong of me to compromise that."

The thought didn't bring her much comfort, considering what she'd seen him do to the man who had once been his top lieutenant. While she was pleased that he'd simmered down for the time being, it was unnerving to see how volatile he'd become. He'd always been one of the coolest, most charismatic people she knew, so much so that it was almost disturbing. Now his mysterious friend seemed to have taken on that role. She glanced up to the mezzanine and found the other man suddenly absent.

"What happens now?" she ventured, hoping the abrupt demand would mask the fact that she still wasn't certain whether he planned to kill her or not.

"I would ask that you honor our agreement and stay until this is over." His tone made her wonder whether she had any real choice in the matter. "Your people are free to go whenever they desire."

That was good enough. She turned to leave, though she realized she wasn't sure where she was going.

"But Agent Payvan..."

Of course there was a 'but.' She pivoted back around, bringing her hands to rest on her hips and bracing herself for whatever was about to come.

Tobias moved closer, speaking slowly as if he were deep in thought.

"While Serenity and I do not have what you might call a conventional relationship, it should be evident given the very nature of that relationship that I am willing to go to some interesting lengths to protect her." While not intimidating in stature, that same old chilling twinkle was again present in his eyes, lending his tone an icy edge. "I will say this plainly: you stepped out of line when you came aboard, and I seem to recall you witnessing firsthand what I'm willing to do when people step out of line."

An image of Cole—his former second-in-command—collapsing to the floor with a new hole in his head flashed through her memory.

"I would also like you to be aware of the fact that since your mission is not only over but also resulted in Alastair Manes's escape, you are no longer as valuable to me as you once were."

He paused for the briefest of moments, as if watching for a reaction on her part. She steeled herself, legitimately unnerved by the implications but determined not to show it.

The chilly glimmer in his eyes transformed into one of amusement as he continued. "However, I like to think of myself as a man of principle. I recognize what a personal sacrifice these past couple of years have been for you, and despite the...*unfortunate* outcome we're currently experiencing, I also recognize that the work you've done has ensured we're not walking away completely empty-handed. Consider your slate clean for the moment, but I want to remind you what the consequences will be if you cross the line again."

Ziva ran her tongue across her teeth, still unwilling to let her face betray her thoughts. "And I want to remind you of the same thing I always told Manes: if you want results, you'll let me do things my way. Otherwise, I can walk away at any time."

That amused glimmer evolved into a soft smirk and then a wide smile. "But you won't. You want to see this through as much as anyone else here." The smile vanished as abruptly as it had appeared. "Now go clean yourself up. You look like something that just crawled out of Niio's sewers."

He strode away, departing the bridge through a door on the far side. Those working in the vicinity slowly turned their attention back to their tasks, and the four soldiers who'd escorted her in vanished. Ziva massaged her hands and turned to Skeet and Zinni, who regarded her with confusion, maybe a hint of guilt—*good*—and the same wariness they'd exhibited since she'd revealed herself to them on Panuco. All she could do was shrug at them, unsure what she might say that would help the situation.

They stood in uncomfortable silence for a moment before Zinni spoke. "That could have gone better."

It wasn't reassurance, but rather an objective observation of what had just occurred. Ziva merely nodded in response before looking around the bridge one last time. She turned and took a step back toward the corridor they'd entered from, still not entirely sure where to go. Maybe back to the docking bay and the relative comfort and familiarity of the *Talon*. Despite Tobias's apology, she felt far from welcome here, contrary to how she'd felt when she'd first arrived on Niio seeking his help.

"I don't know what you two want to do," she said, continuing on her way. *I don't know what I want to do, either.* "Watch your backs. I'm not sure how much I trust anyone here anymore."

"I'm sorry to hear you say that, Agent Payvan."

All three of them whirled at the sound of the voice and found the stranger from the mezzanine approaching with a familiar medical bag—Serenity's bag—over his shoulder. He gestured toward the gash on her forehead. "May I?"

Ziva's hand went to her injury, still fresh after the explosions in the spaceport tunnels. Despite the throbbing and the tension caused by the dried blood, she'd completely forgotten about it in the past few minutes. The man studied her, his features verging on kind—for now. Everything about his demeanor reminded her of a snake, appearing harmless enough on the outside but always watching, calculating, waiting. Still, his intentions seemed sincere, and he may have even spared her life by talking Tobias down. That alone prompted a momentary sense of...if not trust, at least cooperation. She nodded and moved back to lean against a nearby console, slouching down to his level.

The man removed a sterile cloth from the bag and began scrubbing at the dried blood and grime surrounding the gash. "Ken Oda," he said, briefly meeting her gaze in an almost cordial manner. "I've heard a lot about you, Agent Payvan. I've been responsible for managing all the Ibarra intel you've gathered over the past two years. Your handler, if you will. It's a pleasure to finally meet you in person."

Perhaps she was still grasping for comfort in an uncomfortable environment, but somehow it felt good to know someone who seemed so operationally minded had been overseeing things behind the scenes. She dipped her head.

Ken's eyes shifted toward Skeet and Zinni; he gave them each a nod in greeting as well before setting the cloth aside. He removed a tiny autoinjector from the bag, touching it to several places surrounding her injury. "This will prevent infection and help with inflammation."

A cool sensation immediately began spreading from the injection sites, reminiscent of Serenity's pseudo caura treatment. "You're a medic?" Ziva asked, almost certain the answer was no. Serenity had combat experience, sure, but this man was different. He may have been perfectly at home in this situation, but the mannerisms she'd previously observed told her this wasn't actually his forte.

Ken offered a faint smile, almost as if amused by the question, and selected a syringe of surgical paste from the bag. "No," he replied, examining her injury with a familiar analytical eye before squirting a thin layer of the clear paste into the wound and pinching her skin together as he went. "Just applying skills from one of several fields of expertise."

He wasn't boasting, just stating a fact. "And is negotiation one of those fields?" she said.

"It can be." His gaze shifted to meet hers again and he seemed to realize she was referring to whatever exchange he'd had with Tobias. His face hardened and he returned his focus to the gash as he spread another layer of paste over the top, sealing the cut.

"So, getting Tobias to deescalate is, what, a hobby?" Skeet piped in when the Niiosian made no move to elaborate.

Rather than respond, the man set the syringe of paste aside and admired his handiwork. "That should hold you together until you can pay a visit to the medbay, which I've been told I should order you to do.

But I've *also* been told you're not one to follow orders, so I can only suggest—strongly—that it would be a wise choice."

She was about to repeat Skeet's question, but it suddenly dawned on her that his demeanor wasn't the only reason he seemed familiar. His facial features were unique enough among Niiosian ranks that they were memorable, and she'd seen very similar features two years earlier as she'd spilled their owner's blood on Zenat. Memories of a conversation with Tobias flashed through her mind.

"There is someone else you'd be well suited to deal with directly. His name is Jerrick Taan, a hitman, an assassin serving Manes in much the same way you'll be serving me..."

"Why doesn't your so-called expert take him out?"

"They're brothers. Half-brothers. Taan used to be one of us."

She was almost positive she was currently looking at that expert. Looking at Taan's brother.

Ken seemed to recognize that something interesting was going through her mind, though she doubted he knew what she was truly thinking. He stepped back and wiped his hands against each other as though satisfied with the state of her wound, then turned to address Skeet.

"I've been a Mob asset for twenty years. Reconnaissance agent. Wetwork expert. I've probably spent more time running covert ops during that period than I've spent on Niio. Tobias elevated me to an advisory role after Agent Payvan began her operation." He glanced at Ziva, his face grim. "You could say I'm Cole's replacement."

Everything was starting to make more sense, and she couldn't help but feel that someone as composed and patient as Ken would make a far better right-hand man than Cole had. "Well, I'm glad Tobias listens to you," she muttered.

The man began packing up the medical bag. "When we arrived in Panucan airspace and it became clear that not only was the Ibarra compound fortified but that Manes was also slipping away, he was ready to kill you outright. I already talked to him once before you even came aboard. I knew something was off when I detected two ships broadcasting the transponder code we gave you when you left Niio."

"Is there some magic word I should know about when it comes to getting the great Tobias Niio to back down?"

Ken once again gave her the impression of being slightly amused without actually smiling. "I merely reminded him that we've already lost too many assets and that we shouldn't throw away another one, especially out of anger." He picked up Serenity's bag and slung the strap over his shoulder. "Now, I'd like to see about making sure your vessels are properly secured in our docking bay, and I will offer another reminder about seeking full medical treatment."

Ziva straightened. "Is there something I could use to get this off?" she asked, indicating the brownish-red pigment she'd worn on her chin and across the upper half of her face for the duration of her charade as Matia Moryi. Nothing about it had changed in the last day, but she'd become hyper-aware of the color in her peripheral vision, though it was difficult to tell at this point what was dye, what was dirt, and what was blood.

"But your cover—" Zinni said.

"Blown. Manes may not know I've been allied with the Mob, but he knows who I am. Knows who Ziva Payvan is. Being Matia isn't going to save me at this point."

The three of them stood around her in melancholy silence for a moment before Ken sighed and turned to leave. "I'll see what I can do."

Chapter 2
NIIOSIAN CRUISER · Deep Space

More than an hour passed before Ziva found herself standing in the locker room lavatory belonging to the nearest bank of crew quarters. She approached the first in a long row of sinks and withdrew the small vial that had been delivered to her in the docking bay only minutes ago, setting it on the edge of the counter before taking a moment to stare at her reflection—stare at Matia Moryi—in the grimy mirror. It took a split second to realize the mirror itself wasn't dirty; most of the grime was on her face. If that wasn't an accurate representation of how she'd lived during the past couple of years, she didn't know what was. She lowered her gaze.

If she was honest with herself, she was having trouble picturing exactly what she'd looked like for the previous thirty-plus years of her life. Relatively speaking, three-ish years wasn't that long to have maintained a disguise, but considering she'd spent two of those years with her very life hinging on her ability to maintain that disguise and cut off any affiliations with her past identity, it was easier to forget her true appearance. She'd imagined having trouble readjusting upon her return to Niio, though a part of her had insisted it didn't matter how well she adjusted given that she could never go home or return to any aspect of her old life. The arrival of her team had been jarring in that sense, akin to awakening from a dream before it ended and leaving her confused, disoriented, and irritable. But now she couldn't help but feel it had been for the best. Despite the unfortunate circumstances, having them here—these people she'd trusted and relied on for so long—was a breath of fresh air. If she wasn't careful, she imagined she might be lulled into hoping things would return to normal. But they never could.

She began by splashing some cool water over her face, clearing away any remaining dried blood. Then, opting to start with the simplest part of her transformation, she carefully removed the colored eye lenses she'd worn for all but a few days over the past three years. They were a harsh yellow shade, turning her crimson irises an intense golden orange. She'd taken advantage of solo missions for Manes and had only dared to remove them in the privacy and solitude of her ship, disinfecting them and allowing her eyes to breathe for a few hours. Still, the extreme lengths to which she'd gone to conceal her identity meant she'd taken poor care of them overall, resulting in eyes that were often bloodshot, watery, and irritated. Despite the discomfort, she'd adopted the haggard appearance as part of Matia's persona.

With a sigh, she abandoned the lenses in the sink and began to work on undoing her braid, separating the clusters of hair that had become matted after months of neglect. Let loose, she was surprised to find that, while ragged, her hair reached most of the way down her back. Bits had been singed throughout the course of her work or had even broken off due to poor health, keeping the length somewhat under control, but still, she'd never worn it so long in her life. It felt disgusting, though she wasn't sure if that sensation was due to the discomfort or the fact that it was legitimately filthy. Probably both.

She bypassed the tiny blade she'd planned on using to remove the colored strings concealing her red streaks and instead unsheathed the combat knife again. She'd killed people with that knife, and who knew how many people Jerrick Taan had killed before she'd relieved him of it and used it against him. Now here she was, essentially killing Matia Moryi. Gathering all her hair into a single fistful, she took the blade to it, sawing straight through the mats and letting the clumpy locks drift to the floor. It would be uneven, but that could be fixed later, assuming she cared more then than she did now.

With their ends sliced and fraying, the colored threads wound around her streaks began unraveling on their own. She merely tugged them loose, discarding them as well. The red hair appeared even more foreign than her red eyes. Before she'd left Niio, she had painstakingly separated her streaks into smaller clusters before rolling them into thick strands and binding them tightly in contrasting colors to conceal them. As her hair had grown, she'd simply added more string, using a variety of knots that only contributed further to the mess. Now, even when released, her streaks remained split and compressed. With her bloodshot eyes, mussed hair, and discolored face, she looked like one of the junkies who had often roamed through the Tunnel in the evenings.

I'm a mess.

As satisfied as she could be for the time being, she raked her fingers through her hair a few times before tying it back into a shoddy ponytail and picking up the vial from the edge of the sink. According to the note—from Serenity, despite everything—that accompanied it, all she needed to do was massage this solution onto her face and exfoliate, and the serum would go to work breaking up the foreign pigments around her eyes and on her chin. She began to squeeze a generous helping into her hand but hesitated when she heard someone come to a stop in the lavatory doorway. A quick glance in the mirror told her it was Skeet; he stood with crossed arms, leaning against the doorframe and studying the mess of hair and string surrounding her feet. He still appeared calm, almost sympathetic, but tired.

"What are you still doing here?" she muttered, working some of the creamy paste into her skin and watching as the reddish dye immediately began to dissolve. It was a stupid question. If he and Zinni had planned on leaving, they wouldn't have bothered coming aboard the ship in the first place.

He lifted an eyebrow in response. "Well, if nothing else, we can't really go anywhere until we have a better grasp on Tarbic's situation. But..." He paused for a moment and sighed. "We stayed because that's what friends do."

His hesitation gave Ziva the impression the words hadn't been easy to say. "I wasn't sure if we were anymore."

"Were what? Friends?" He scoffed. "Ziva, none of this can change what we've been through together."

"Right, but if you can't trust me anymore..." She inhaled sharply as she rubbed a sore spot on the bridge of her nose. It was difficult to tell the difference between dye and inflamed skin.

"I...do trust you."

Now it was her turn to raise an eyebrow. "That's certainly not what it sounded like in the Ibarra cell block."

"I wasn't thinking clearly, okay? I should have known you were on our side the moment I saw you with Aroska."

"You should have known I was on your side the moment I *told* you I was." She felt her chin tremble—something that had happened far too often over the past couple of years, at least behind closed doors—and tried to mask it by focusing her scrubbing efforts there.

"Okay, yes, I should have. But I was angry, just like I was angry when you didn't come to us while you were in trouble with Dasaro, or tell us what happened on that landing pad at Dakiti, or—" he let out an incredulous snort "—tell us you were even a Nosti in the first place."

Heat flooded her cheeks at the idea of being called a Nosti. She gave up scrubbing for a moment and turned to face him, not giving her appearance a second thought. "And I have explained my reasoning for all of those things."

"I know you have. Everything you've done has had a logical excuse. But in each situation, it seems like you've had other options, ones I would have expected you to choose. You've decided against them for whatever reason, and I guess that's what's bothering me. I don't know what to expect from you anymore."

Ziva blinked, unsure what she could say that wouldn't just be repetition of previous arguments. She sighed and returned her attention to the mirror, able to see the faint outlines of her *gesh punti* for the first time in ages as she wiped away some of the dye residue. Even after applying a generous amount of the solution, she imagined her skin would remain discolored for a couple more days, though it would hardly be noticeable with all the bruising that remained around her nose, eye, and the gash on her forehead.

"What I'm trying to say is," Skeet continued, his voice authoritative but not harsh, "I think we both have some valid points. Your arguments have been reasonable, and my skepticism has been well-founded. But I also think we've both been at fault here. I won't lie—it's damn good to see you, especially the real you." He nodded toward her mess and gazed approvingly upon her natural face, dreadful though it was. "I spent most of the past four years confused and hurt, which has made this little reunion less than ideal. But not a day has gone by where I haven't missed working with you, and that makes it all hurt even worse. So, here's the deal: from here on, I will try my best to hear you out and stay rational. So much happened in those last few months before you left that hesitation and suspicion became the default. But you've got to give me a reason to trust you. This has to go both ways, okay? Keep Zinni and I in the loop."

He was right, really. The solution was that simple, yet with circumstances as they were, also that complicated. As much as she wanted to nod in agreement, she couldn't help but shake her head. "I can't make any promises."

Rather than anger or sadness, she only saw exhaustion in his eyes. "Why not?"

"*Sheyss*, Skeet. So much has changed. Look at where we are, what we're doing. Think about the things we've all had to do throughout the past four years. My life consists of nothing but adapting and moving forward. Nothing is constant anymore." Hearing her own words gave her pause. In a galaxy filled with so much uncertainty and instability, he'd always been a constant, something that grounded her, just as she'd been contemplating a few minutes before. He, Zinni, and even Aroska all had.

"I don't know what tomorrow will bring," she continued, "or what I'll have to do, or how I'll have to adapt in order to survive. I can't give anyone a definitive answer about anything. Those don't exist anymore."

He was silent as he considered her words, but it was a silence that gave her the impression he understood. "What do you propose we do, then?"

She turned and studied her reflection in the mirror again. The person staring back at her was, frankly, a disaster: bruised, scarred, disheveled, angry. But it was unquestionably her. In this moment, she was herself again; there was no need to pretend. Matia Moryi wouldn't have tolerated this conversation, but Ziva Payvan had people she trusted. Cared about. Loved, even.

"I guess we try our best and see what happens," she answered. "That's all we can do."

He appeared pensive for a moment before giving her a faint smile and dipping his head, telling her it had been an acceptable response. "Things were easier back when our lives were normal, weren't they?"

She couldn't help but chuckle a bit, considering their 'normal' lives had consisted of assassinations, extractions, sabotage, recon, and the galaxy only knew what else, all of which were mundane by spec ops standards. But the humor of the concept was quickly replaced by a pang of sadness, because while her life still consisted of many of those same things, the circumstances surrounding them were no longer normal, nor would they ever be again. The thought sent a fresh tremble through her chin, and she clenched her jaw to still it.

"They really were," she said.

"What will you do now?"

She squeezed a fresh helping of solution into her hand, noting for a moment how the dye residue on her fingers was almost indistinguishable from the dried blood on her clothes. "Well, I haven't showered in days, so that's as good a place as any to start."

For a second, she thought he might smile, and he watched her for a moment as though considering whether to comment on her state of hygiene. "All of that needed to be said," he finished with a sigh, turning to leave. He paused again briefly. "I hope it was beneficial for both of us."

Ziva could only imagine how difficult these thoughts had been for him to articulate. The two of them had always been alike in so many ways, and despite having been close partners for over a decade, she wasn't sure if she would have been able to open up to him so well. Not right now, anyway.

She took a step away from the sink. "Skeet?"

His head reappeared in the lavatory doorway.

"I'm sorry." The words came out as a choked whisper.

His lips flattened into a thin line. "I know you are."

Once again, it was the best response she could hope for, and she quickly turned back to the mirror before her chin could start to quiver anew. But it occurred to her that Skeet had taken no further steps to leave, and when he made what was easily the strangest sound she'd ever heard him make—some cross between a groan and a sob—she whirled back to face him.

In all the years she'd known him, she'd seen him show genuine emotion on a few occasions. But to her best recollection, she'd never actually seen him cry, so the sight of the tears suddenly streaming down his face was completely foreign. The way he wore his hair high and tight these days made him appear older, more mature, more like a leader, so this current display of vulnerability seemed even more alien.

"*Frouchten hehle*, Z. I...I put my hands on you." He slumped back against the doorframe and looked down at his trembling palms as though he feared they'd developed minds of their own. "I don't know what came over me."

The thought of his fingers wrapped around her throat in the cell block had Ziva massaging her own neck before she realized it. "You were angry," she said.

He scoffed and shook his head, squeezing his eyes shut as fresh tears poured from them. He gritted his teeth. "*Sheyss*, that's not an excuse!"

"Didn't say it was. But it's a reason."

She wasn't sure what to do as she stood there and watched him hang his head. Realistically, it was now her turn to give him the silent treatment. Any attempt to console him was not only far outside her sphere of expertise but also seemed wildly inappropriate given the nature of his actions. At least his current behavior was enough to tell her he was truly sorry for and repulsed by what he'd done.

He finally drew a deep breath and straightened. Damp lines still cut down each of his cheeks, but when he spoke, his voice was steady. "How did we get to this point?" he muttered, shaking his head again.

It was difficult to tell whether he was genuinely asking or whether he wanted her to admit something. When it came down to it, this was all her fault, though she wasn't sure if saying those words out loud would do anything to help the situation. She'd kept things from him, had even actively deceived him, and yet had still expected him to demonstrate the same levels of loyalty he always had. He was right in that there were logical reasons behind her actions, and it was true that he had perhaps responded with less restraint than he should have, but in the end, she had started all of this.

"You were right," she said. "This conversation was mutually beneficial."

He lifted his gaze to meet hers and finally turned to leave again. "Well, enjoy your shower. And...when you're ready, you should go check on Tarbic. I admittedly thought he was crazy, but I don't think I've ever known anyone as tenacious as he's been for the past four years."

The mere mention of Aroska's name sent a new ache crawling through her chest. Was it possible to want nothing more than to see him and simultaneously never want to speak to him again?

Skeet disappeared through the door, leaving her alone in the lavatory for good this time. It was almost unsettling to experience such a raw interaction with someone she'd once shared such a strong bond with. After four years on her own, she'd finally managed to seal off much of the guilt she'd felt about the things she'd put her team through, certain she'd never see them again. Not only were they here now, but they were actively taking a sledgehammer to those walls she'd put up.

Part of her wasn't sure how thoroughly they should bother reconciling at this point, considering things could never go back to the way they were and she had every intention of sending all three of them away from here as soon as was practical. But another part recognized that the reparations were necessary; if nothing else, it would help bring them all a sense of closure before they had to part ways again.

Ziva glanced down at her hand, where the dye solvent had started to dry and become globby. She sighed and turned back to the mirror, using a nearby towel to wipe the diluted pigment from her face. Then, after squeezing yet another fresh helping of solution into her palm, she set about erasing the last traces of Matia Moryi.

Chapter 3
Ibarra Vessel *Oblivion* · Deep Space

The FTL tunnel swirled outside the front viewport of the *Oblivion* as the vessel shot forward through the void. Normally Alastair Manes couldn't have cared less about the view, but at the moment, the rippling silver ribbons of light provided a modicum of relief from the turbulence in his mind. It was impossible to be soothed by it completely; out of necessity, he maintained enough focus to still be seething under the surface. But at least for now, he was outwardly calm enough to stand quietly and reflect. He imagined that state of calm—if temporary—brought a measure of comfort to those around him as well.

They'd made it away from Panuco with barely fifty percent of their available airborne forces. Most of the Cartel ships that traveled through the FTL tunnel behind him were well-armed but not large; despite being considered his flagship, the *Oblivion* itself was only a light frigate. Even if they were at full force, and even if the Niiosians hadn't taken them by surprise, he conceded that they likely wouldn't have fared well against Tobias's bulkier vessels. Perhaps if all his planned retrofits had been completed, they would have had a better chance of defending their primary base, but alas, most of the necessary materials remained on Delatori, and so many of the research and development projects surrounding those retrofits had run into snags or been postponed indefinitely due to setbacks and mishaps. Maybe he was just being paranoid given everything else that was happening, but after the Niiosians had mysteriously gained access to Panucan airspace, he had to wonder if the rest hadn't been sabotage as well.

The mere principle of leaving Panuco behind also stung a bit. The city of Tabaco had always been Ibarra's primary base of operations, their strongest and best-equipped outpost. The Cartel's finest tended to be stationed there, so the fact that it had been hit so hard was more devastating than if any other Ibarra facilities had been attacked. But if there was one thing he had to give his late father credit for, it was instilling in him the notion to never dock all his ships at one port, both figuratively and literally. They may have taken a loss on Panuco, but it hardly represented *all* the Cartel's assets, and if he had anything to say about it, they were far from done here.

Somewhere at the end of this FTL tunnel lay the world of Naris, the location of Ibarra's second largest outpost where he'd been stationed before slaying his father and elevating himself to a position of leadership on Panuco. It lay deep in the Errol sector of Fringe Space, in the opposite direction of most of Ibarra's other resources, including the coveted materials on Delatori. But it was a relatively short trip, and Naris would be most prepared to handle any repairs and restocking of munitions for their small fleet, as well as best able to contribute additional ships to that fleet.

The door onto the *Oblivion's* small bridge hissed open, and without even turning around, he recognized the heavy approaching footsteps as belonging to Kimbra Soto. The Haphezian woman came to a halt a couple of strides behind him, keeping her distance a bit just as she had since leaving Panuco. Part of him regretted treating her so harshly and alienating the one person under his command he'd always felt he could genuinely rely on. But the situation was dire enough that he couldn't afford to have anyone questioning his orders, regardless of how close they were to him. An example needed to be made.

"Final tally is in," she announced. "We have four hundred and three souls aboard two cruisers, ten light frigates, and thirteen freighters. Both cruisers include a complement of twenty fighters and three gunships each, though one only has enough fuel reserves to supply a single squadron."

It was better news than he'd anticipated, having only been aware of a single cruiser that had joined them initially. And he wasn't terribly concerned about the fuel shortage; unless something drastic happened, they'd have no need for multiple fighter squadrons—or any fighters at all—before reaching Naris.

"We'll replenish once we're planetside," he said, prying himself away from the view of the FTL tunnel. He motioned for Kimbra to walk beside him as he turned and departed the bridge, making his way silently down the elevated walkway that separated the fore and aft sections of the ship. Ladders dropped down on either side of him, providing access to the lower decks and crew quarters. To his knowledge, none of those quarters were occupied; the *Oblivion* was operating with a skeleton crew as it was, and if there was a single person enjoying downtime, he'd have his deck officer's head.

The area ahead of them opened into an operations center of sorts, with a large, round table laden with terminals as the room's primary attraction. From those terminals, holographic interfaces were projected, displaying much of the same information Kimbra had just reported to him. A large sphere hovered in the center, a rough rendering of Panuco dotted with an increasing number of red slashes as some of his chief personnel worked to determine which resources had been lost.

He recognized one of the men as the analyst he'd confronted in the Tabaco compound's defensive control center just before departing the planet; he and his staff must have evacuated just seconds after Manes, stealing aboard the *Oblivion* without him even realizing it. He wanted to shoot the man on principle, but his particular skill set might very well make him one of Ibarra's most valuable surviving assets.

"You," Manes said, pointing at him and taking some delight in the way the man almost imperceptibly flinched in response to being singled out. "What's your name?"

"Brady," he replied immediately, snapping to attention. "Brady Tal."

Manes approached, prompting other staff who stood nearby to casually scoot away. "What more do we know?"

Tal swallowed and eyed him curiously, as though unsure how to respond to this casual demeanor after the outburst in the control room. He cleared his throat and returned his attention to the hologram, indicating some of the red marks. "It's difficult to get a solid fix on the situation while traveling through hyperspace, so we'll definitely want to take a closer look once we reach Naris. At least a few of the freighters that escaped were carrying full arms shipments, so we have their payloads at our disposal. Obviously, Operation Recovery by its very nature means we lost resources, but it also ensured those resources didn't fall into Tobias's hands."

Indeed it did. "And do we have any idea where our friends the Niiosians went?"

"The only reports I have state that they retreated from Panucan airspace in the general direction of Niio. Nothing more."

Manes leaned down over one of the terminals, staring vacantly ahead at the hologram as he considered everything. "Once we arrive at Naris, I want a thorough inventory of everything we have on hand. Ships. Weapons. Personnel. Raw materials. We'll regroup with our forces at Naris Base, resupply, and then travel to Delatori together. I want to personally oversee the recovery of the zocrum, carmine ore, and whatever else it takes to make Niio pay for what he has done."

He straightened and addressed Tal directly. "Contact the shipping fleets at Delatori and instruct them to hold. With Panuco Base out of commission, I'm not going to waste time having them bring their cargo all the way to Naris. Assign whatever additional security measures we can spare to them until we arrive."

"Sir," Tal replied, offering a stiff nod. "I also want you to know I'm still working on figuring out what happened with Panuco's planetary defense matrix. Not all my staff made it out so I'm short-handed, but we'll get to the bottom of it."

For a moment, Manes regretted having ever entertained the idea of killing the man. He allowed the softest of smiles to grace his lips, and Tal relaxed visibly in response. "You do that."

He turned, hands clasped behind him, and began to stroll back toward the bridge. Kimbra fell into stride with him, but it wasn't until the two of them had made it halfway down the elevated walkway that he heard her draw a breath to speak.

"Let me guess," he said before she could get a word in. "You're still concerned about Moryi."

"*Payvan*," she corrected him. "I'm concerned about Ziva Payvan.

That's who betrayed you—Matia Moryi never existed."

He came to a stop, grinding his teeth behind clamped lips. He didn't give a damn what the woman called herself. The person had betrayed him, not the name.

"Your point?" he growled, pivoting to face her.

She folded her arms indignantly. "You said you wouldn't let her get away with everything she did."

If the lips spewing these words weren't so enticing, he wouldn't even be permitting them to speak. His second-in-command had her... uses, but *pazska*, sometimes she was insufferable. The state of calm he'd achieved on the bridge was already wearing away.

"Kimbra, we have been over this. In case you haven't noticed, we just lost our primary base. Our sworn enemy arrived on our doorstep without us knowing. There are more pertinent issues at hand."

"And I'm not convinced the two things are unrelated."

He truthfully wasn't, either, but Tobias Niio and his fleet of battleships—however mismatched and unorthodox—did pose the more immediate threat compared to Payvan and her posse of Haphezian agents. "We don't even know if she survived the Niiosian attack. If you had the docks locked down like you were supposed to, she shouldn't have been able to go anywhere."

She bristled visibly and moved her hands down to rest on her hips. "I did," she said with a scowl, "but I never heard from the ground team I sent to intercept the *Talon*. Granted, maybe they were all killed in the attack. Or maybe she killed them and escaped."

Now Manes crossed his arms. "So, what do you propose we do?"

Her gaze shifted a bit and she swallowed. The woman was no idiot; she had to know he was right, but she was clearly unwilling to drop the argument just yet. "I still say we turn her over to the Federation. At least sell her out. Give her something new to worry about."

"I told you before," he said, advancing toward her before the last syllable was out of her mouth. "The only thing contacting the Feds is going to do is put us in the spotlight, and I refuse to jeopardize the structural integrity of this organization like that. It is simply not an option, and you are not to bring it up again. Do you understand me?"

Her mouth twitched as if she wanted to respond but knew better. He stared her down a moment longer to ensure his words were resonating in that thick skull of hers, then turned and resumed his trek toward the bridge, relieved when he didn't hear her footsteps following.

Chapter 4
NIIOSIAN CRUISER - DEEP SPACE

Ziva paused in front of the observation window outside the medbay, a large and pristine space that appeared just as well-financed as the rest of the massive ship. She felt moderately better after having the chance to clean up, though she'd had no choice but to change into a clean set of Matia's old clothes stored aboard the *Talon*. 'Clean,' however, was only relative to the clothes she'd changed out of, which should most certainly be tossed into an incinerator. It was a petty thing, but they made her feel dirty all over again, in ways another shower could never fix.

Serenity was nowhere to be seen, and Aroska appeared to be the only patient in the medbay. His bare torso was dotted with a variety of patches and electrodes. The screens above him displayed favorable vital signs, but he still lay there motionless with his eyes closed. His injured leg protruded from under the sheet covering the lower half of his body, and she saw that it had been fitted with some sort of fast-acting brace. She had to give Serenity credit—the woman may have been abrasive, but she by no means skimped on patient care.

Swallowing hard, she let herself into the room. It was warm inside, and the hum of the machinery had an almost hypnotizing effect. Aroska seemed comfortable enough, though she doubted he was even aware of where he was, and quite possibly of anything that had happened since fleeing Panuco.

As she moved around to the far side of his bunk, she saw that the injury on his head had been plastered with the same blue mesh she'd found on her own arm upon waking up in Serenity's care on Niio. Part of it extended down to cover his bruised and lacerated face, molded to the contours of his brow and cheekbone. His ribs were bound, and an IV line from a familiar-looking cylinder pumped fluid in directly under the dressings. He wasn't hooked up to any sort of ventilator; the rise and fall of his chest was barely perceptible, but he was breathing on his own and that was all that mattered.

The way the sight of him gave her pause made her wonder if he'd felt the same upon seeing her in the med center after she'd been shot in Argall, thus explaining his awkward silence that day. At least she'd been awake and coherent at that point. Right now, she just wanted to find Serenity and determine the extent of his head injuries so she'd have a better idea of when—if ever—he'd wake up. She didn't necessarily regret the things she'd said to him before leaving Tabaco, but after the conversation with Skeet, she didn't like the idea of them being the *last* things she ever said.

She rubbed her hands together, irritated by how embarrassed and vulnerable she felt standing there. "So. We didn't exactly leave off in the best place, did we?" She doubted there was any way he could hear her, but she'd amassed too many thoughts over the past couple of hours and felt it best to get them off her chest sooner rather than later. Besides, it was almost easier to talk to his inert form than have him listening and watching her expectantly. The sound of her voice might even help pull him back to consciousness.

An empty chair sat between his bunk and the next, so she moved over and took a seat, drawing one leg up and wrapping an arm around it. "Leaving home—leaving all of you behind—was one of the hardest things I've ever done. And believe me when I tell you allying myself with Tobias wasn't the most appealing option. Not sure if it has necessarily worked out for the better, but it kept me alive."

She paused and watched Aroska's chest rise and fall for a moment, then propped her elbow up on the chair's armrest and cradled her chin in her hand. She hadn't realized how exhausted she was until she'd sat down. "We haven't known each other that long, but you know I don't always play nice with others. You know I value independence. But after Aubin, and after Salex, and after Ronan...being out here, alone.... Usually I'm good at being alone, but things were different this time, and I'm pretty sure it's all your fault." She clenched her teeth. "And I want so badly to hate you for that."

Several seconds passed as she drew and released a deep breath, steadying herself. "I don't know what you've done to my head, but you're dug in like some sort of parasite and I can't get you out. When I left Haphez, I didn't think I'd ever see you—any of you—again, so I spent the past four years trying to shut you all out of my mind and focus on whatever else I could. Otherwise, I would have just made myself miserable."

She stifled a yawn and stared vacantly down at the floor, realizing she was talking more to herself than Aroska at this point. Maybe that was for the best. "When I saw you in Tabaco, I was angry at first, because it was a reminder of how much I missed you. Then I was relieved. Catching sight of someone you thought you'd never see again? You can probably relate. But I knew I shouldn't be relieved, because I recognized how dangerous the situation had just become for you *and* me. And that made me angry all over again.

"So, I guess what I'm trying to say is...I'm sorry for everything I put the three of you through down there, but I had a job to do. Not finishing that job could have meant the end for all of us. And now that things have completely gone to hell on that front, I'm...I'm going to need help. After four years of trying to handle things on my own, there's no one I'd rather have backing me up." Her voice wavered and her vision blurred for the briefest of instants, and she realized she was once again speaking to him. "So please wake up. I need you to wake up."

She shut her eyes, continuing to rest her cheek in her hand as she listened to the steady hum of the room's machinery. The trance the sounds put her into was disrupted only a second later by an amused snort, and she snapped back to attention.

Aroska's eyes were still closed, but his eyebrows were raised and the corners of his mouth were turned upward, at least as well as they could be with the mesh stretched over half his face. "I'm sorry," he said, his voice hoarse but good-natured, "did I just hear you say you actually needed me for something?"

Heat flooded Ziva's face. "*Huhren shouka souhn,*" she muttered, letting her leg down and turning the chair to face his bunk more directly. She doubted he'd meant to be hurtful, but his words carried a sting that made her regret the two different times in the past day when she'd told him she didn't need him. "How much of that did you hear?"

"Every word." His eyelids fluttered open, though the left one was hindered by the mesh. Broken capillaries in that eye stained the sclera crimson.

"So you're awake."

"Yeah. Regained consciousness an hour ago or so, though I don't remember losing it in the first place. Concussion has been manageable so far with the treatments they've got around here. Guess I got hit just right to knock me out like that. The doctor—Serenity?—said she'd pass the word along, but she must've missed you."

Ziva nodded, leaving out the fact that the woman had likely avoided her on purpose after their little confrontation in the docking corridor. "And you just lay there and let me run my mouth like an idiot."

He managed a crooked smirk. "Believe it or not, I *was* actually dozing. You woke me up when you came in, but once you started talking, I thought it best to let you finish. It was quite the rousing speech, after all."

She wanted to hit him but thought better of it. Instead, she shuffled her feet along the floor and guided the chair up alongside the bunk, bringing her arms to rest on the edge of the thin mattress. "You look like absolute *sheyss*."

"You're not looking so hot yourself." He raised a hand and gently traced her newly revealed *gesh punti*. "Though I have to admit I prefer this classic Ziva look over the Matia Moryi war paint." He shifted his fingers to the freshly mended cut on her forehead, then moved to the puffy, bruised flesh surrounding the bridge of her nose, the result of the blow he'd landed in the prison corridor. She couldn't help but shy away from him a bit, though her discomfort stemmed more from the aggravation of the injury than the touch itself.

He lowered his hand in response and slid it over hers, interlocking their fingers before lying in silence for several seconds. Then he sighed and averted his gaze. "I thought you'd still be angry with me."

It occurred to her he wasn't referring to their scuffle. He was talking about what happened in her apartment after that. "Oh, I'm furious." She pulled her hand away, forcefully enough to prove she was serious, though perhaps more roughly than she'd meant to. "You're just making it hard for me to show it."

"I thought he was going to kill you, Ziva."

"I know you did." She ground her teeth and swallowed as her mind replayed images of the rounds from Aroska's weapon burning through the young man's chest. "I just...it was a bad situation all around." That was putting it lightly. "His name was Blain. I wanted to get him out of that place."

"Words cannot express how sorry I am. I need you to realize that."

She looked down and fiddled with the edge of the bedsheet. "He was always going to be collateral damage," she muttered.

"You don't really believe that."

Well, she didn't want to, but when it came down to it, first and foremost, Blain had been *her* ticket out of there, not the other way around. Historically speaking, people she put in those kinds of positions tended to not experience favorable outcomes, regardless of what her intentions had been.

They sat quietly for a moment before she managed a simple nod of acknowledgement. The shame in his eyes appeared genuine enough, but she still hated the fact that he'd tried to play hero without having all the facts. Then again, Blain's ignorance when it came to firearms had turned him into a target. If she hadn't known any better, she likely would have shot him, too. That somehow made it all worse.

Her attention drifted up to the medication and dosage data displayed on one of the viewscreens above them. "Are you in much pain?"

"They've got my leg numbed up pretty well. My ribs probably still hurt worse than anything." He cautiously placed his hand over hers again, giving it a quick squeeze.

The gesture was likely meant to assure her he harbored no ill-will toward her for shooting him on the beach, though she wasn't sure if she could honestly say it was one hundred percent effective. She grasped his fingers in return and dipped her head by way of a silent apology.

"So, some sort of parasite, huh?" Aroska brought the back of her hand up to his mouth and touched his lips to it; somehow their warmth surprised her. He grinned against her skin. "You're not very good at this."

It was nice to know he was feeling well enough for humor, but she found it impossible to muster up even a semblance of a smile. "I might have used a different metaphor if I'd known you were listening," she muttered as she pulled her hand from his grasp again, albeit more gently this time.

"Don't kid yourself. You wouldn't have even been talking if you'd known I was listening."

"That's probably true."

He sighed and folded his hands across his stomach. "So, did you really miss me?"

He asked as though he thought she was incapable of such a thing, and she would have been offended if not for the fact that she knew good and well she'd always done everything in her power to create that illusion. After all they'd been through and after some of the other interesting insights he'd had about her, she thought he would have known better than to ask. But just as she'd said a few moments ago, she had truly needed to put conscious effort into shutting him and the rest of the team out of her mind in order to function, and as much as she hated to admit it, that had gotten easier as time passed.

"Occasionally," she answered, hoping he'd mistake the truth for sarcasm.

They both looked up when the door slid open. In walked Skeet and Zinni, looking rather glum until their eyes fell on the awake and coherent Aroska. The two of them came to gather around his bunk—though Ziva couldn't help but notice they stayed on the opposite side—with Zinni perching on the edge of the mattress and Skeet leaning against the wall at the head of the bed. Aroska looked up at them and swallowed as though afraid this meeting would turn into another confrontation akin to what had taken place aboard the *Saber* on Panuco, but for a long time, nobody even spoke.

Finally, opting to start things off on her terms, Ziva cleared her throat. "I hope you all realize I was never as far gone as you thought I was. I knew exactly what I was doing, even if it didn't seem like it."

"'As far gone' sounds like you *were* gone to some extent," Skeet said.

His tone wasn't hostile—it had been a mere observation, but it made her bristle anyway. "It's true that I had to...go to *certain lengths* to maintain the Matia Moryi act," she replied, taking care not to raise her voice, "but ultimately that's what it was: an act."

"I think the bigger issue now is what we do about the fact that Matia Moryi isn't real, but we're supposed to have her in custody," Aroska said, looking up at Skeet and Zinni. "We haven't updated Emeri since before you two went back out to find her."

Ziva shrugged. "Just tell him I got away. Or, better yet, tell him I escaped my restraints and spaced myself on the trip back to Haphez. Then nobody will come looking for me again."

All three of them watched her in grim silence, and she was conscious of the fact that they might be wondering whether that was Ziva or Matia talking. But then they all spared each other glances as well, giving her the impression there was more at play.

"I get the sense I'm missing something."

Skeet raked his hand back over his close-cropped hair, a gesture Ziva hadn't realized how much she missed until she saw it. "After you left, a lot changed at the agency. Competition for status among the ops teams is at an all-time high, and sometimes I think it's by pure luck that we've held on to the Alpha title for so long. Evals are supposed to happen this quarter and, well, we've reached the point that we'll be downgraded if we fail our mission."

"And our mission was to bring Matia Moryi in alive," Zinni said. "The exception would be if we had to employ lethal force in a—how did Emeri put it?—'drastic self-defense situation'."

"Even then, they'd no doubt want you to produce a corpse," Ziva mused, leaning back in the chair and bringing her chin to rest on her fist. She should have known better than to think this problem could possibly have a simple solution.

Aroska adjusted his position until he was more upright. "I may just be speaking for myself here, but now that we know the truth about who you are, if it came down to it, I don't think it would be totally unreasonable to focus on protecting you. I...I think I could live with sacrificing Alpha status if it meant keeping you safe."

To her surprise, neither Skeet nor Zinni made any immediate move to disagree, but she leaped to her feet before either of them could get a word in edgewise. "Absolutely not. I'm not letting you sabotage yourselves on my account."

"I think I could live with that, too," Zinni said with a shrug, offering Aroska a nod.

"*Sheyss*, I can't believe what I'm hearing," Ziva muttered, turning in a slow circle with her hands on her hips. "This team is your pride! This team is *my* pride, my legacy. I can't sit by and allow you to lose something you've worked so hard for."

"We may lose it anyway, Ziva," Skeet said quietly.

"But you can still give yourselves a fighting chance. This solution is off the table." She shot a scowl in Aroska's direction and snapped her fingers impatiently. "Come on, next idea. Or is there any other damn thing I should know about?"

Based on the way he heaved a sigh and swallowed, there was indeed something. She crossed her arms and stared him down, daring him to continue.

"One of the objectives of this mission was to find something to pin on Matia Moryi so we'd be justified in bringing her in," he said. "The Royal House may have wanted her...*you* alive, but nobody knew who Moryi was or why she was working for Ibarra. Since she hadn't committed a direct offense against Haphez or any of its citizens, the higher-ups had no real grounds for arrest or prosecution."

'Had' was the key word there, and Ziva saw where this was going. "Until she assaulted an HSP agent," she said, cursing under her breath.

He nodded. "The agency is aware of the shooting, and because there's no physical evidence against Moryi, all the Royal House has to go on is my testimony. I imagine they're expecting it immediately."

She swore again and sat back down in the chair, resting her elbows on her knees and massaging her temples. This had all been a disaster already, from the team's arrival to her blown cover to Manes's escape, but it seemed things were growing more complicated by the second. Keeping

Tobias happy enough to not kill her while simultaneously keeping her team from getting downgraded would be a delicate balancing act. Her self-preservation instincts were now in active conflict with her protective instincts.

The door opened again before she could put any more thought into a solution. She looked up and found Serenity standing a couple of meters away, hands on her hips, regarding her with a look of disapproval. But then that same look shifted toward Skeet and Zinni.

"Are you putting undue stress on my patients?"

The question likely wasn't meant to be an all-out demand, but the woman's harsh accent made it sound like one by default. Still, Ziva couldn't help but notice the way she'd used the plural 'patients.'

Zinni slid off the edge of the bed and stood bolt upright. "Who are you?"

Serenity sighed and offered a look that seemed almost apologetic before checking something on the small screen she carried and moving up to stand at the foot of Aroska's bunk.

"Serenity Best," she replied gently to Zinni, her tone a far cry from anything Ziva had heard from her before. "Tobias's chief medical officer."

"And his wife," Ziva added, though she instantly regretted it. It may have been an objective fact, but she'd meant it as a sort of jab, and she'd *said* it as a sort of jab. The hasty sharing of personal information was petty payback for the fact that the woman had clearly ratted her out to Tobias after their little spat outside the docking bay. The fact that such behavior had become so unconscious and mundane after dealing with Kimbra for two years left her cringing.

She looked up at Serenity long enough to ascertain that the former doctor was displeased before lowering her elbows back to her knees and staring down at the floor. The woman made no move to snap back, a relief considering Kimbra had always been glad to keep the bickering going strong. It was just one more reminder—albeit an unorthodox one—that she was done being Matia.

"It's a long story, and perhaps one Payvan will tell you in its entirety later," Serenity answered, an accusatory bite in her voice. "But yes, Tobias originally married me so he could invoke spousal privilege when I was in trouble with the law."

Something deep within Ziva's mind—so small it felt like a single spark against the black void of space—clicked just then, but before she had time to allow the thought to develop into anything more, she heard Zinni draw in a sharp breath.

"What if you two did that?"

Ziva looked up and found the intelligence officer glancing between her and Aroska, then looked over to find Aroska already fixated on her, wide-eyed. To her chagrin, she felt her face flush, and she quickly returned her attention to Zinni.

"If nothing else, it would buy everyone some time, and you'd both benefit from it. Think about it—Aroska can't be compelled to testify, and you can, you know, not get arrested."

Ziva found herself groaning and resuming her temple massage before Zinni had even finished speaking. *At least until we can figure something else out* went without saying; there was no possible way this would turn out to be a reasonable plan. But maybe that was merely the reluctant part of her brain talking. As much as she didn't even want to entertain the thought, the more she considered it, the more it objectively seemed like their best shot. Nobody had come up with any better ideas yet.

"Worked for us," Serenity said.

Glad her face was still obscured, Ziva sat in silence until the renewed heat in her cheeks dissipated. She looked up at Aroska and once again found him already looking her way. He offered a small shrug. "It's worth a try."

She muttered another curse and slumped back in the chair, at a loss. "I admit I have heard worse ideas in my lifetime," she said, rubbing her eyes and unable to believe the words coming out of her mouth. "But would that even work? I mean legally, would Haphez even allow it?"

"You're the police and you don't know your world's own laws?" Serenity said, lifting a brow.

"Frankly, this particular team's job has never been to enforce the law."

"I can reach out to someone who would know," Aroska offered, "or someone who can find out."

Skeet shook his head. "We still haven't reported to the director."

Tarbic looked up at him. "And I almost wonder if we should bring him into the loop. If all of this goes sideways, the galaxy knows we're going to want someone in a position of power who can advocate for us."

"You think he would?" Zinni asked.

"I think he might, and if he doesn't, the world will know Ziva's alive, we'll be downgraded, and nobody will be any worse off than they'd be if we didn't try at all."

Ziva had to appreciate the analytical approach he was taking to all of this. She was certain he still allowed his feelings to control his actions more often than the rest of them—that much was evident in the way he'd chased after her on the beach, leaving her with no choice but to shoot him—but four years in spec ops seemed to have been good for him.

"Well, let's get on with it, then," she muttered.

"Not so fast," Serenity said, catching her by the shoulder to keep her from standing up. "You aren't going anywhere yet." This was directed at Aroska. "And you—" she turned her attention back to Ziva "—have a full medical workup and mesh treatment waiting for you. Tobias's orders. He wants you back in top condition and requests that you report to the bridge for a debrief when you're done here."

As tempting as it was to tell Tobias to go to hell, and as disconcerting as it was to know he must still have plans for her, a little rehabilitation didn't sound half bad right now. Her thorough shower had gotten most of the dirt and grime off her skin, but it had also been a reminder of—and had revealed—numerous small injuries and irritants aside from the one Ken treated.

"Fine." She rose from her seat, with no resistance this time, and looked down at Aroska. "See what you can find out about the legal aspects of this lovely little venture we're embarking on."

"As a recognized authority from an independent world, Tobias can facilitate the union," Serenity offered.

"We'll reconvene on the bridge after your treatment and debrief," Skeet said.

The older woman turned toward him and Zinni. "I can give the two of you a medical workup as well if you need it. Otherwise, there's food and supplies available in the crew quarters. The ship is at capacity so unfortunately we don't have any extra bunk space, but feel free to utilize the lavatory facilities and make yourselves at home in the common areas."

Skeet dipped his head in thanks and gave Ziva a shrug before ushering Zinni toward the door. The medbay remained silent until the two of them had departed, then Serenity moved off to the far side of the room to begin prepping some sort of treatment capsule. Ziva crossed her arms and looked down at Aroska, pleasantly surprised to find that he appeared nearly as unsure about all of this as she felt. The situation could be worse on so many levels, but with her botched mission and Blain's death still fresh on her mind, and with the potential consequences of this endeavor hanging over her head, she found it impossible to be optimistic.

Aroska held out a hand to her, a simple offering of affirmation, and she unfolded her arms long enough to reach down and squeeze it. "Good luck," he said.

She snorted. "You, too."

Chapter 5
Niiosian Cruiser - Deep Space

The medbay was warm and silent as Aroska lay there contemplating how best to articulate the questions he needed answered. The few other patients who'd occupied the room when he'd first awakened had been discharged even before Ziva's visit, their injuries minor. With an airborne battle like the one over Tabaco, fighter pilots and soldiers either made it out relatively unscathed or didn't make it out at all. He detested the fact that he—a stranger, an outsider—had ended up being the most severely injured party aboard, but objectively, he had to be thankful he was alive and that the damage wasn't any worse.

He looked down at his injured leg and studied the sleek bio boot that encased his foot and extended almost to his knee. From what he recalled of his experience in the tunnels, the break had been severe. Not only had the boot set the shattered bones, but he could feel a variety of contact points inside the shell adhering to his skin at intervals and injecting meds directly into the most damaged areas. The outside of the casing was equipped with servos and hydraulics that would soon allow him to walk freely while the boot bore all his body weight and continued the healing process.

His gaze drifted across the room toward the woman who was responsible for the fact that he was still breathing. Ziva stood motionless inside a cylindrical pod, her head, neck, and shoulders visible through a small observation window. Her eyes were closed, and Serenity had ordered that her entire body be wrapped in a layer of the same sticky blue mesh he wore on his face. A fine mist swirled around her inside the chamber, no doubt some form of additional healing agent. He found it interesting that Tobias was still so concerned with making sure she was in top condition after the debacle on Panuco. He was glad she was receiving proper medical treatment, especially considering the way she seemed to have neglected her own well-being as of late. But he couldn't help but wonder what else Tobias would ask of her once she was back on her feet.

A fresh pang of guilt hit him as he recalled the look on her face after he'd shot the young man—Blain, she'd said—in her apartment. He'd firmly believed he was neutralizing a threat. Protecting her. The extent of her reaction had completely shocked him in the moment and still left him baffled; the raw emotion she'd shown went far beyond anger over her foiled escape plan, demonstrating just how much she'd come to care about the kid throughout her time on Panuco. She herself had said that nobody out here was innocent, and the boy *had* betrayed her earlier in the day, but those thoughts failed to bring Aroska much comfort at this point. The part that stung the most was that by hurting the young man, he'd also hurt her. It was just one more detail creating a wedge between them and leaving this whole reunion far less ideal than what he'd always envisioned.

His eyes lingered on the treatment tank for another moment before he shifted his attention down to the communicator he'd been idly turning over in his hand as he reflected on his situation. He still didn't know exactly what he was going to say, and the thought sent a nervous ache creeping through his stomach. But there was no sense in delaying the inevitable. He hit the transmit command, sending a request to the comm code he'd already entered several minutes earlier.

It took a moment for the transmission to connect, and when the hologram of Adin Woro's face rendered above the device, it took another moment for the Alpha field ops lieutenant to realize who he was talking to.

"*Sheyss*, what happened to you?" It was early morning Haphezian local time, but concern wiped the bleariness from the man's eyes in an instant.

"Nice to see you, too," Aroska said.

"You're only a few days into your independent service term and you've already *frouched* up your face again? I'm beginning to recognize a trend."

"This is only the second time, smartass, and last time it was one little cut." Aroska swallowed. "Listen, I need a favor."

Adin sobered. "I'd say 'anything,' but you know I can't get involved in independent spec ops matters."

"And I'm not necessarily asking you to. But I *am* asking you not to tell Emeri you spoke to me."

The man gaped. "Wait, you're laid up in a medbay somewhere and you haven't reported to him yet? Are the three of you okay?"

"Believe me, I got the worst of it. We'll check in with him in due time, but I need some information first."

Adin's sigh wasn't audible, but Aroska recognized the subtle rise and fall in his old friend's shoulders just before the man rubbed his eyes. "How can I help?"

"I need a rundown of Haphezian spousal immunity laws."

"What the hell for?"

"Adin."

"I mean, as far as I know, we don't have anything like that, at least not the way a lot of the Federation worlds do. When you run your judicial system on a guilty-until-proven-innocent principle, you tend to not allow for any provisions that would enable people to circumvent that."

Aroska sighed. "That's what I thought. Are there *any* concessions? What kind of verbiage are we dealing with here?"

Adin shot him a less than thrilled look, then his face disappeared from the projection for a moment as he relocated to his home workstation. For a couple of minutes, the only sounds that could be heard were the purr of the medbay's machinery and a faint tapping in the background of the transmission.

Finally, the field ops lieutenant hummed to himself, and a blinking light on the comm unit indicated that an attachment had been sent. Aroska brought the file up in a separate projection and began to read even as Adin spoke.

"Haphezian law does recognize marriages performed on other worlds, as a sort of 'diplomatic courtesy' to other races. But if any non-Haphezian were ever to be arrested and tried here, chances are the individual's homeworld government would also get involved and you'd end up with a whole new mess of extradition requests, bureaucratic red tape, and other *sheyss* to wade through before you could even consider whether a spouse might need to testify."

Aroska only half-heard him, fixated as he was on the text in front of him. As he pored over it and considered the language, he felt a twinge of hope. "What if two Haphezians were married on another world, or by a recognized governing figure from another world?"

"Why would any self-respecting Haphezians do that?"

"Humor me, Adin."

The man sighed again and adjusted his position at the terminal. For a moment, he appeared ready to argue further, but as he read over the text again, all he could do was shake his head. "I just don't.... Hm." He was quiet for another few seconds. "Technically—" he drew out each syllable for dramatic effect "—there's nothing in here that allows for such a thing. But—"

It would be enough to buy some time, Aroska thought.

"—neither is there anything that explicitly *disallows* it. Granted, I can't imagine a marriage like that would hold up long in a Haphezian court setting, and I would by no means consider myself HSP's premier legal expert, but if you're just looking for my professional opinion, I'd say that's enough of a loophole to at least ruffle some feathers."

Well, it was the best shot they had. "Thanks, Adin. I appreciate it."

"I don't suppose you could tell me why the hell you're asking about all of this."

Aroska smirked. "I might tell you someday. In the meantime, do yourself a favor and erase your search logs."

The man opened his mouth to protest but Aroska ended the transmission before he could get a word in. The text file remained suspended above the comm, and he read over it one last time before turning his attention to Ziva again.

The thought was almost preposterous, but now the woman who had just saved his life was about to become his wife.

Chapter 6
Niiosian Cruiser - Deep Space

While Skeet appreciated Serenity's offer of hospitality, particularly after the *less* than hospitable encounter immediately after boarding the ship, the *Saber* afforded he and Zinni their needs better than crew quarters on a human vessel could. After returning to their ship to change clothes, apply caura treatment to some minor cuts and scrapes, grab something to eat, and discuss what the best use of their time might be, they found themselves on the way back to the bridge to find Tobias himself.

Entering the command center sans the stares and hostile reactions they'd witnessed earlier was a relief. A few people spared them curious glances as they passed, no doubt unaccustomed to seeing Haphezians out on this side of the galaxy, but nobody yelled or drew their weapons, and the two of them made their way up to the mezzanine unhindered.

The mobster briefly acknowledged their presence but then returned to his conversation with Ken and several of the ship's officers. Skeet turned to admire the sight through the front viewports while he waited for the man to finish. He'd felt the vessel drop out of FTL shortly before they'd gone to visit Aroska in the medbay but wasn't sure where they'd stopped, and now he had his answer. Clouds of gas and cosmic dust floated by outside, ranging from vivid red to dark brown. The nebula had an official name few people could pronounce, but for centuries it had been known colloquially as the Blood Water. He imagined this was due in large part to its color, though he'd heard stories from traders on Aubin about ancient battles that had taken place within it and countless ships that had unsuccessfully attempted to cross this sea of red to avoid using established FTL lanes, so the name likely had a more gruesome meaning as well. All the moving particles in nebulae tended to interfere with ships' scanners and make it difficult to detect obstacles—asteroids, planetoids, other vessels—hence the reason FTL lanes almost always cut around them. Ergo, he imagined the Niiosian fleet was currently well-hidden from any Ibarra ships that might have chased after them. But the Blood Water was less than halfway between Panuco and Niio, and he wondered why they had stopped so soon. Maybe Tobias had something planned.

"Breathtaking, isn't it?"

Skeet turned and found the man approaching, a gentle smile gracing his lips, the red hues from outside reflected in his spectacles.

"It's certainly something," he answered, abandoning the view in favor of devoting all his attention to the mobster. Despite several relatively cordial encounters in the past, he'd never felt comfortable turning his back to the man.

Zinni silently appeared on Tobias's opposite flank, no doubt thinking the same thing. Out of the corner of his eye, Skeet saw Ken move up to stand just behind his boss. He couldn't help but smirk at this subtle dance they were all performing, the signs of unease barely masked by a thin veil of amicability.

Tobias moved forward to the viewport, taking a moment to watch the rest of his fleet drift about. None of the other ships—Skeet estimated there were around fifty—came anywhere close to being as large as the one in which they stood, but they all remained in a disciplined formation, and trios of fighters patrolled the perimeter in the distance. The Niiosians may not have been military, but they seemed to know what they were doing. Funny to think that many of these same ships had probably been present in the fight against the Resistance forces four years ago.

"Agent Duvo, isn't it?" Tobias turned to face him, then shifted toward Zinni. "And Agent Vax. I'm pleased to see you in good health after all of that unpleasantness with Ronan."

He stepped back between them and moved past Ken to look out over the CIC. "I'm afraid we got off to a somewhat rocky start, so let me extend an official welcome aboard my flagship, the *Revenant*. A fitting name for a resurrected Federation vessel, no? She was salvaged as a derelict after the Feds' initial war with the Resistance and has been extensively refurbished, with everything from advanced weaponry to modern comforts and luxuries." He ran his hand along a well-polished console. "Also a fitting name for the location of a reunion with an old friend thought dead, I'd say."

"We knew she was alive," Skeet said. It felt strange to admit such a thing after spending most of the past four years doubting all the clues Aroska presented, but after everything that had transpired over the last couple of days, it would have felt even stranger to respond any other way. "What we didn't know was that she was Matia Moryi, and I think it's time to set the record straight about a few things."

Tobias shot him a quizzical look over the rim of his spectacles, then nodded and motioned for them to move closer to the viewport. Ken followed and lingered on the periphery, but otherwise they had some relative privacy.

Skeet folded his arms. "Look, I realize our presence on Panuco essentially blew your little operation. Believe me when I say that was not our intention. News of a rogue Haphezian operative reached HSP, and we were charged with retrieving and transporting her home for questioning."

The mobster's eyes narrowed. "What was the source of that information?"

"A report from Pahl Starcer, one of your contracted developers based on Delatori. He allegedly has a set of schematics that might aid you in your conflict with Ibarra, and he needed Moryi neutralized so he could safely reclaim them. Now, I don't particularly like the idea of taking sides in this fight of yours, but Officer Vax and I talked things over, and as a show of good faith, we're willing to travel to Delatori and recover your specs."

He watched Tobias's face as he spoke and was surprised to see that smug look transform into genuine confusion. "I'm familiar with some of Starcer's work," the man replied, "but I haven't dealt with him or anyone else on Delatori in months. There came a point where the planet became a lost cause—once Ibarra gained a sufficient foothold there, their expansion into our territory slowed, giving us time to regroup and come up with new defensive plans." He shook his head. "I don't know anything about any specs."

Zinni muttered a curse. "Starcer must have taken all of this upon himself. It's understandable that he wouldn't have known Moryi was an undercover Niiosian asset, but we assumed you were the one who'd commissioned the retrieval of those schematics."

Skeet barely heard her, preoccupied by the idea that this man had been willing to use an entire planet as a pawn if it meant gaining an advantage over his rival. This was nothing if not characteristic for someone like Tobias. Delatori may not have had official ties to the Mob, but considering the circumstances—particularly the actions of that certain Niiosian asset—it was disconcerting to think about.

"You realize Ziva was on Delatori," he said. "Your own 'asset' was responsible for killing dozens of project managers who had pledged their loyalty to you."

Tobias's face went cold. "I may have heard something along those lines."

"And you allowed it to happen."

On the other side of the mobster, he saw Zinni shoot him a warning glance, and he was aware of Ken tensing up behind her. This was neither the time nor the place for a confrontation, especially after he'd just been celebrating the lack of hostility. Truth be told, a militaristic world like Haphez might make a similar sacrifice for the sake of the big picture, so he wasn't bothered as much by that concept as he was merely about Ziva's involvement...both the fact that Tobias had allowed it and that she'd been willing to go through with it.

Tobias also seemed to recognize tensions were mounting, and, to Skeet's surprise, initiated the deescalation. "I believe I owe you all another apology," he said, shaking his head. "It's true that I did blame you for Agent Payvan's folly when I learned you'd been present on Panuco, but you would not have even been there if Pahl Starcer had brought his concerns to me rather than taking matters into his own hands. It seems he is the true catalyst of these mishaps."

Skeet was torn then between being relieved by the mobster's new-found understanding of the situation and wondering what the implications were for Starcer. Tobias often cited himself as a man of principle, but in this case that could just as easily mean sparing Starcer as it could mean eliminating him as an apology to Ziva. It was tempting to recommend HSP keep the man in protective custody for a while longer.

Tobias drew a breath to continue but hesitated when he noticed something behind them, and they all turned to find Ziva standing at the base of the mezzanine, watching them as though she didn't approve of the fact that they were all conversing without her. She wore a plain black top and dark gray tactical pants identical to what most of the *Revenant's* crew wore, but she still carried her own weapons. Whatever treatment she'd undergone appeared to have reduced some of her newer scars to muted versions of what they'd been. The gash on her forehead was hardly more than a pink line now, and all the swelling around the bridge of her nose had gone down, with just the faintest hint of one black eye remaining. She'd done nothing more to fix her hair, leaving it in a tiny, ratty ponytail that was essentially a shorter version of Matia's hair, but Skeet was pleased to see her looking more and more like herself.

She approached when she realized she had become the subject of their attention. "What am I missing?"

"Agent Duvo and Agent Vax have kindly offered to travel to Delatori and fetch a set of schematics one of our developers believes could give us an edge in our fight with Manes," Tobias replied.

"Delatori," she said, glancing at Skeet. "Starcer?"

He nodded.

"I'll come with you."

He shook his head. "I think you know that's not a good idea."

He'd expected her to launch into a full-blown debate, but instead she merely stepped toward him, jaw set, brows drawn together. He couldn't help but tense in response, certain she had grown accustomed to using intimidation and threats of physical violence—or *actual* physical violence—to get her way during her time as Matia. But then she blinked and halted her advance, as though she suddenly recognized she'd set him on edge.

Her expression remained stony. "I know Delatori. I could help."

It took considerable effort for him to not blurt something about how she only knew Delatori because of all the carnage she'd been responsible for there. "No," he said, the discomfort of saying that word to her softening his tone more than he'd planned.

Something verging on pain flashed through her eyes, perhaps in response to being spoken to like that, perhaps because she knew he was right. The truth was she *could* be a huge help thanks to her familiarity with the resource-rich world, but taking the assassin who'd destroyed Starcer's family to retrieve his schematics likely wouldn't bode well. Skeet wondered if her offer to help was a subconscious—or even purposeful—attempt to atone for all the things she'd done.

"If I may," Ken said, stepping forward into the midst of the conversation, "having reviewed much of the intel Agent Payvan was able to transmit to us regarding Ibarra operations, I've become relatively familiar with the situation on Delatori myself and would be willing to accompany you." He turned to face Ziva. "And perhaps I can learn more during our debrief."

Unless it was Skeet's imagination, she appeared almost crestfallen, like a young child who'd been told she wasn't allowed to participate in an activity with her older siblings. The most concerning part was that she made no move to fight the decision. If she was demoralized enough that she'd lost her will to argue, then he truly felt sorry for her, despite still wanting to loathe so many of her actions.

She finally offered a nod of concession in response to Ken's offer, and Tobias clapped his hands enthusiastically. "Splendid," the man said. "I think the three of you will make quite the team. Inside Niiosian knowledge combined with Haphezian brute strength? That's a potent mix. Delatori is about a twelve-hour FTL journey from this location. There's no sense in traveling all the way back to Niio—we'll hold our position here in the Blood Water until you return, and then a decision will be made regarding our next course of action once we've determined how to best put those schematics to use."

"We can contact Starcer once we're planetside," Zinni chimed in. She cast a glance in Ziva's direction, as though reinforcing the fact that this was why it would be a bad idea for her to come. "He should be able to point us to where we need to go even while in agency custody."

The emphasis she put on that second part was undoubtedly directed at Tobias, and while Skeet had no particular fondness for Starcer, he was glad he and Zinni were on the same page regarding the man's safety in relation to the mobster.

"Add that to the list of things to brief the director about." He turned back to Ziva. "Did you learn anything from Tarbic before you left the medbay?"

The way the disappointment melted away from her face and transformed into the same old unimpressed stoicism he'd always known brought him a sliver of comfort. For a moment he wasn't sure if she was even going to answer, but then she managed a nod.

"He contacted Adin while I was undergoing treatment," she muttered. "He says it'll work, but he reiterated that it's a very temporary solution."

"Well, we were counting on that." Skeet turned and found Tobias watching them curiously. "There's one more thing," he said to the man. "We need you to marry Ziva and Sergeant Tarbic."

A sly smile spread across Tobias's face as he directed his attention to Ziva. "How very interesting."

"Don't make this more complicated than it needs to be," she snapped. "We're in the same boat as you and Serenity."

"Ah," he said. "Having experienced this situation firsthand, I can see how your predicament might be causing undue stress. I would be happy to oblige."

Man of principle, Skeet thought, though it was impossible to tell whether the mobster was legitimately offering to ease Ziva's burden or merely doing what he could to ensure she was in a better mental position to take part in his designs.

"Why don't we get this debrief out of the way," Tobias continued. "That will give your friend time to complete his treatment and your team time to prepare for their journey to Delatori."

Now Ziva simply looked mad, but while Skeet dreaded the thought of her being forced to dredge up memories of being Matia when she was already struggling to return to her old self, the more she could tell them about the industrial planet, the better.

"We'll be around," he said, motioning for Zinni to follow him as he began to depart the mezzanine.

The two groups parted ways, and when Skeet looked back just before exiting the bridge, he caught one last glimpse of Ziva disappearing into a room on the far side of the CIC with Ken and Tobias hot on her heels.

CHAPTER 7
NIIOSIAN CRUISER *REVENANT* - BLOOD WATER NEBULA

The door of the small conference room slid shut behind them, blocking out the noise from the CIC and the main corridor. Tobias and Ken filed around to the other side of the table, leaving Ziva standing with her back to the entrance. Certain that had been intentional, she slid down to the head of the table before choosing a seat, forcing the two men to turn sideways to address her. Tobias appeared less than thrilled but made no comment.

"We have all of the reports you were able to transmit over the past couple of years," Ken said, consulting a data pad, "but there are a few events I'd like to go over in more detail. I'm confident this information will give us the upper hand, if not put Manes and Ibarra at a direct disadvantage."

Reliving all her experiences from her time with the Cartel wasn't the least bit appealing, but she'd fully anticipated a session like this once she was reunited with the Niiosians. She nodded, inviting Ken to begin.

"Let's start from the top," he said. "You first gained access to the Ibarra Cartel when you killed Jerrick Taan, Manes's previous assassin. Tell me more about that encounter."

The words hadn't been said in any particular way, but the fact that he'd opted to start by asking about Taan all but confirmed what Ziva had already deduced: the two men had been brothers. "It was a long process tracking him down," she answered, searching his face as she spoke. "I finally managed to locate a Niiosian informant he was hunting and turned my sights on Taan under the pretense that I was keeping him from killing my target. It wouldn't be the first time I've gone after someone to keep them from taking my bounty."

Ken frowned; the man had to realize his brother was a traitor, if an unwilling one who had succumbed to Manes's manipulation, but it couldn't have been easy for him to be the 'expert' responsible for tracking Taan in the days prior to her arrival on Niio. And after spending so long with the Cartel and seeing how Manes had affected her own mind, she couldn't help but feel a twinge of sympathy for Taan as well, at least as a lost Niiosian asset and a brother. As a Cartel assassin, he was just one more obstacle to be dealt with in her quest to get to Manes, and deal with him she had.

"May I ask, Agent Payvan...was his death painless?"

Ziva remained silent for a moment as images of the destruction the indoctrinated Taan had wrought among Niiosian ranks flashed through her mind. The day she'd finally caught up to him, she had hoped to reach him before he slayed several of Niio's soldiers, but she'd been too late. The amount of blood at the site had been uncharacteristic considering the precision cuts the man typically used, and as near as she could tell, he'd deliberately spread it around to create a more gruesome scene for whoever happened to stumble upon it first.

"No," she replied, blinking away the lingering shades of red, "it wasn't."

Her gaze flicked to Tobias, who observed with cold indifference.

Ken hesitated for several seconds, then offered a single nod. "I appreciate the honest answer. May I ask, then, how he died?"

In response, she reached to her thigh and unsheathed the combat knife. She had come to think of it as her own over the years and had put it back on immediately after finishing up her treatment in the medbay, but maybe now it was time to turn it over to someone who might find more meaning in it.

She laid the weapon out on the table, allowing him to catch a glimpse of the delicate engravings in the metal before pushing it toward him hilt-first. He stared at it in silence for a moment before sighing as though he understood perfectly what she was alluding to. Out of the corner of her eye, she saw a smirk spread across Tobias's lips as the same realization dawned on him. The eye-for-an-eye approach to taking Taan out of play had seemed appropriate at the time, but sitting there now in front of Ken while Tobias looked on approvingly negated any satisfaction she might have previously felt.

Ken finally pried his attention away from the blade and lifted his gaze to meet hers. "Thank you for doing what I couldn't, Agent Payvan. I think...I believe you put my brother out of his misery."

It seemed like a morbid way to think about it, but it was probably accurate. And surely it was better than knowing the exact details of what had occurred, such as the way she'd injured and cornered Taan like a frightened animal after a grueling chase, the way she'd drawn his own blade across his throat as slowly as possible and then left him to drown in his own blood as retribution for taking so many lives. People she didn't even know. People who weren't even her allies. She'd lashed out in the moment, had repaid brutality with brutality because she knew she was capable of it. She'd let rage take control—

The noise in her head dialed back several notches when Tobias cleared his throat. He placed a hand on Ken's shoulder, maybe—just maybe—in a commiserating fashion. "As enlightening as this has been, the more prudent use of our time would be to discuss the specifics surrounding our friend Alastair Manes."

The man nodded and looked down at the data pad again, swiping through several reports on the display. "Six weeks elapsed between Taan's elimination and Manes's invitation to join Ibarra, correct?"

It took Ziva a moment to muster up a response, preoccupied as she was with a sudden mental image of Manes leering at her through the cell bars in the detention block, his face slightly distorted by the shimmering energy shield. "Ibarra forces apprehended me after I killed Taan, as planned. They transported me to Panuco, though I remember nothing of the journey, and I was held prisoner while Manes had me...vetted." She saw herself struggling briefly with one of the countless men she'd killed during that process. A pop in the bulkhead just then sounded eerily similar to the sound of his neck breaking. "For roughly six weeks, yes."

"And that was enough to build a decent rapport with him?"

"Relatively speaking. I don't believe he ever fully trusted me, but the nature of our relationship afforded me access to some information I may have never obtained using my own resources alone. That is, until my team arrived and disrupted my operation." This she said while looking Tobias in the eye.

Something bordering on regret flashed through the man's eyes, similar to what Ziva had seen the day he shot Cole. "I feel I must apologize to you again, Agent Payvan," he said. "As I was telling Agent Duvo, had I been aware of Pahl Starcer's plot to enlist your team's help in taking out your alias, I may have been more understanding of the circumstances. It would seem this scheme to recover his specs from Delatori is what ultimately brought us to where we are now."

"Indeed," she muttered.

"Speaking of Delatori," Ken said, "what else can you tell us that might aid us in our mission to retrieve those specs?"

"I can tell you Delatori has been Manes's obsession for the better part of a year, and the fact that Ibarra managed to take control of it might actually be buying you people time to act. I've done what I can to sabotage Cartel projects over the past few months, but Manes has been getting closer and closer to being fully equipped for an incursion into the heart of Niiosian territory. One of the primary reasons that hasn't happened yet is because his crew is busy strip-mining Delatori for all it's worth in order to reinforce their fleet and armament."

"And the same resources they're after would benefit our forces in return," Tobias mused, staring vacantly at the opposite wall. "I would wager a bet that if we were to regain control of Delatori, it would be an even more devastating blow to Ibarra than what we dealt on Panuco."

"You've been on Delatori recently," Ken said to Ziva. "What's the Ibarra presence like?"

"They're there in force," she replied. "Granted, once all the major settlements were evacuated, they scaled back and most of the remaining presence consists of mercenaries, workers, and scientists overseeing the recovery of materials. Firepower isn't as strong as it once was, but overall numbers are...not insignificant."

"Our scouts have reported that the Ibarra vessels that escaped from Panuco fled toward the Errol sector, away from Delatori," Tobias said.

Ken nodded. "Regrouping at the Naris outpost, you think?"

"I do. And with the majority of their firepower located there, that leaves Delatori ripe for the taking."

"Do *we* have enough firepower to deal with the force on Delatori?" Ziva asked. The word 'we' left a sour taste in her mouth; the sooner she was free of all this, the better. But for the time being, it would be pointless to ignore her role here.

"Perhaps not to completely overwhelm them and ensure an unconditional surrender, but we would if we pooled our resources just as Manes seems to be doing. If we act quickly while he is still licking his wounds, we can gather the remainder of our ships and move to reclaim Delatori without compromising Niio's defenses."

The plan was borderline ludicrous, but the only reason Ziva even remotely cared was because if the Niiosians decided to bite off more than they could chew, she and her team would be stuck dealing with the consequences as well. If Skeet and Zinni hadn't already volunteered to go find Starcer's specs, she would have made sure they got the hell out of here the moment Aroska was back on his feet. This wasn't their fight.

Tobias stood and began pacing back and forth along the far wall, hands clasped behind his back. "Ken, the Delatori mission parameters have changed. Once you and the Haphezian agents have recovered the schematics, you will act as an advance team and perform reconnaissance of the area. If the three of you are noticed, no one should suspect the Haphezians of being involved with us. Meanwhile, we will remain hidden here in the nebula while the remainder of our forces gather—a couple of days, at least. Then we'll bring the full fleet to Delatori en masse." He turned to Ziva. "Is there a particular asset that, if lost, would cripple Manes most severely?"

She heard the question, but it was little more than an echo in the recesses of her brain as she stared at the wall and gnawed on the inside of her lip. In her mind's eye, she stood in the doorway of a dark sitting room in an abandoned house, looking straight at the cabinet where she knew good and well Pahl Starcer's son had just gone to hide. She'd meant it when she told him he shouldn't have run; if he had escaped the planet with his father instead of trying to be a hero, he would have prevented more killing. Would have allowed her a respite—even a short one—from this charade for Manes. *Wouldn't* have ended up paralyzed on the floor and shot in the head soon thereafter.

The sharp intake of air as Tobias drew a breath to address her again was enough to bring her back to the present. No way would she allow him that satisfaction.

"Zocrum," she murmured, albeit not removing her gaze from the distant, unknown point she'd affixed it to. "If there's one resource he wants more than anything else on Delatori, it's zocrum."

She was vaguely aware of Ken swiping through the data pad again. "The primary zocrum repository is under Ibarra control," he confirmed as he came to a stop on the corresponding report. "The facility sustained damage in the initial Ibarra occupation..." His voice trailed off as he paused to consider what he was reading. "If Manes is able to recover even a portion of the materials there, he could amplify his fleet's weaponry tenfold."

"Then we'd best claim them before he does," Tobias said with a brief chuckle. "Agent Payvan, is there anything more you can tell us about the—"

This time, the images flashing through her mind were of fire. Blood. Bodies. All the 'accidents' she'd taken great pains to arrange in such a manner that both Ibarra's progress and chain of command would be disrupted without Manes ever realizing she was responsible. It seemed she'd escaped that violence only to be thrown into more.

Another explosion tore through her memory and she stood abruptly before he had even finished his sentence. "Everything 'I can tell you' is right there," she muttered, jabbing a finger toward Ken's data pad. "You figure your *sheyss* out and then just tell me where to go and who to kill next."

Both men watched her in stunned silence for several seconds until she spun on her heel and angled for the door, but Tobias's voice stopped her just as she reached the hatch.

"Don't wander too far, Agent Payvan. I believe I've got a wedding to conduct here shortly."

She ground her teeth behind clamped lips, but no adequate response came to mind. With that, she hit the door controls and saw herself out.

CHAPTER 8
NIIOSIAN CRUISER *REVENANT* · BLOOD WATER NEBULA

She did wander, torn between wanting to get all of this over with for the team's sake and a petty desire to never give Tobias exactly what he wanted. She'd been perfectly serious when she reminded him that he had to let her do things her way if he wanted to see any results, but she feared he was also correct in his assessment of her current value. Now that her cover within the Ibarra Cartel was blown, she wasn't as crucial to his operation, and she imagined he wouldn't have nearly as much trouble finding a reason to get rid of her if he felt the time had come. Part of her didn't really care anymore.

The other part found it strangely poetic that she was now in the same boat with Tobias as she'd been in with Manes. Being expendable certainly added an element of thrill to one's life.

The *Revenant* was a massive vessel and reminded her a great deal of the *Marauder*, the Resistance battlecruiser aboard which she'd faced Tav Ronan and had sealed her fate regarding her Nostia. As such, she liked to think that by taking some time to wander aimlessly, she was also familiarizing herself with her environment, something she preferred to do regardless of the hostility of said environment. By observation alone, she could tell how much money had gone into this ship, no doubt long before the Mob's struggles with Ibarra had begun. Despite being battle-ready, there was a certain elegance about the interior. There were lounges and comfortably furnished observation decks in addition to the armories, heavy batteries, and cutting-edge technology. Even the communal lavatory where she'd cleaned up was halfway luxurious, and of course Serenity's medbay was state of the art. It was all a far cry from the places where she'd spent most of her time on Panuco, and as she roamed, she couldn't help but revel in the fact that she was somewhere other than that wretched world, even if this wasn't an ideal locale, either. At least she had relatively comfortable accommodations here. The situation could always be worse.

That very thought, however, reminded her of just how bad the situation truly was, though for reasons that went far beyond mere discomfort. She stopped in an alcove with some plush furniture and settled on the edge of a cushy chair, bringing her head to rest in her hands. First and foremost was the fact that not only had her Matia Moryi cover been blown, but Manes also knew her real identity. Who knew what the implications might be and when they'd come to bear? Then of course there was the idea that her team was supposed to be hunting her. Failure to bring her in alive would almost certainly result in negative consequences for them, but following through on their mission would almost certainly result in death for her. Neither of those things could be allowed to happen—or at the very least, needed to be avoided to the best of everyone's abilities and for as long as possible— so here she was about to engage in a sham marriage in what would hopefully be a semi-successful attempt to keep everything from deteriorating any worse than it already had.

This 'marriage,' she decided, was the least of her problems, and that was saying something. Aroska was a good man, a damn fine agent, and—who was she kidding—she could certainly do worse in terms of physical appearance. There was no point in denying the deep connection she shared with him, but after four years of forcing herself to forget that connection existed, it was hard to remember what it felt like. Hard to remember how to trust. Hard to remember to allow herself to relax and fall back on him when needed. Things were...complicated, to say the very least. In the past day alone, she'd shot the man, they'd gotten into a brawl, backed each other up, complimented each other on their marksmanship, he'd killed Blain, and then she'd risked her own skin to save his life. If that wild hyperspace trip wasn't indicative of how their entire relationship had gone thus far, she didn't know what was. And now here they were about to be wed by the head of the Niiosian Mob. You couldn't make this stuff up.

Ziva checked the time, noting that it had been nearly an hour since she'd stormed out of her debrief. It was probably time to get things moving along. Even if the team could get Emeri on board, she didn't see a way out of this for herself. If she had to spend the rest of her life running, then so be it; that was what she'd counted on when she'd left Haphez, after all. But maybe—just maybe—if Aroska could avoid testifying for a while, some arrangement could be reached for him and the rest of the team.

She stood and resumed her tour, still moving at a leisurely pace and taking stock of her surroundings but this time headed for the bridge. When she reached the CIC, she found Tobias and Ken standing on a comm pad beside the large conference table on the mezzanine, patched into a conversation with life-size holograms of several people whom she assumed to be the captains of the other Niiosian ships hovering along-side the *Revenant*. Skeet and Zinni hung back against the wall, listening as Tobias delivered what sounded like a fleet-wide briefing on the plan to recapture Delatori. The rest of the bridge crew remained hard at work performing their respective duties and paid her no mind as she approached the mezzanine and found a vacant spot at the table.

No sooner had she settled into a comfortable position than movement caught her eye across the room, and she looked over to see Aroska strolling onto the bridge. He was dressed identical to her in a crew-issue black short-sleeved shirt and gray tac pants, his own clothes having gotten trashed in the tunnels. The mesh had been removed from his face, leaving behind only a thin scar and some discoloration to show what he'd been through. His gait was slightly unsteady, and she shifted her attention down to his leg. His injured ankle remained encased in the bio brace as it continued its work mending the broken bones. Based on the slight grimace on his face, he was still in some pain, but a glimmer appeared in his eyes upon spotting her.

She moved aside to give him space at the table and sent him a questioning glance that she hoped did a decent job of asking how he was doing. He responded with a single nod that she imagined meant 'as well as I can be.'

Satisfied, she returned her attention to the charts and projections suspended above the table and listened as Tobias wrapped up his briefing. The situation was ridiculous on so many levels, and yet she felt...nervous. Of all the things to be apprehensive about...

The mobster finished addressing his men; those physically present began to disperse, and the holograms flickered away one by one. Skeet and Zinni circled around to flank Ziva and Aroska in an almost protective fashion as Tobias set his sights on them and approached.

"Agent Tarbic, I don't believe we've had the pleasure," he said, looking Aroska up and down approvingly. "I trust you've been well taken care of since arriving aboard the *Revenant*."

Ziva had to appreciate the fact that Aroska appeared to be putting conscious effort into maintaining a stony countenance in the man's presence. "Fairly," he replied.

Tobias stepped back and took a long look at both of them over the rim of his spectacles. "Are you two ready?" he asked, far too amused for Ziva's taste.

"Let's just get this over with." She turned and looked to Aroska before leading him around to the control station on the far side of the table. "This is not how I imagined this going," she muttered.

"I'm surprised you ever imagined it happening at all," he replied, eyebrows raised.

"I didn't. That's the point."

Tobias met them at the control terminal and assessed them silently for several more seconds, smirking for the duration. "You know, we can do a full ceremony if you want. Wouldn't be the first one I've performed."

"No," they said simultaneously.

The man's smirk widened into a full smile as he went to work pulling up the correct files on the console. "Just checking. You're sure you want to go through with this?"

"Worked for you and Serenity, didn't it?" Ziva said, crossing her arms.

Tobias's smile faded, and he spared her a glance from the corner of his eye. "Ah, here we are," he said, selecting a file and waving it up into the table's projection. "If you could please enter your names here."

Aroska stepped forward and went first, then input Matia Moryi's name. Ziva had almost forgotten *that* was who the man was supposed to be testifying against. Supposed to be protecting.

"Marrying an alias, are we?" Tobias said.

"Hence the reason this is a very temporary solution," Aroska replied.

The mobster accepted the stylus from him and set about filling out the rest of the form. "To have and to hold..." he murmured to himself. "'Til death do you part, which, considering your line of work, might not be too long from now..." He finished by scrawling a large, flourishing signature across the input pad. "By the power vested in me by...me, I now pronounce you husband and wife, as recognized by the sovereign colony of Niio and the league of independent worlds."

"We'll be needing a copy of this," Skeet said, peering over their shoulders to get a look at the projection.

"You have one...now," Tobias said, entering a command on the console. The holographic interface shifted to show that the file had been added to the ship's database, accessible to anyone with a means of connecting.

"Okay. We'll go set up a transmission with the director. Meet you two aboard the *Saber* in a minute."

His tone—and the urgent look he shot over his shoulder as he and Zinni departed—gave Ziva the impression it had hardly been a suggestion. She knew he was eager to check in with Emeri, and while she had no intention of dawdling in that regard, she couldn't help but feel apprehensive about bringing the director on board. It would either solve all their problems or multiply them tenfold, and there was no way to predict which outcome they'd see.

She beckoned for Aroska to follow as she began to walk briskly in the direction Skeet and Zinni had gone, though she slowed her pace once she'd made it off the bridge and out from under Tobias's scrutiny. As much as she wanted to move on to the next task without a discussion, she doubted Aroska would let that fly. Nevertheless, it was all she could do to keep from cringing when she heard him draw a breath to speak.

"That was...an experience," he said, slowing to a stop.

She could have just kept walking, and he might not have been able to keep up with her while wearing the bio brace, so she hated herself when she came to a stop as well. "Yes, it was," she replied, turning back to face him with her hands on her hips.

"I'd say it was a shock and I can't believe this is happening, but with this team, it's hardly surprising." He chuckled and moved closer to her. "And hey, at least this isn't a total sham."

It honestly wasn't, thanks to what remained of this connection they'd once shared. But his tone made it sound more like a question than a statement, and as much as she wanted to respond, she realized she had no idea what she could or should say. She simply swallowed and shrugged. "Sure."

The twinkle in his eyes faded instantly. "Okay…? I thought…with the way things left off right before you left—"

She shook her head. "We can't just pick up where we left off."

"Why not?"

She advanced toward him and lowered her voice as a couple of the *Revenant's* crew passed by. "You mean aside from everything that's happening right now?" she snapped. "Everything that's happened or changed in the past four years? We can't pick up where we left off because I don't *know* where we left off." She huffed a sigh. "And I don't think you truly do, either."

It was almost maddening how patient he could stay. "Can you explain what you mean by that?"

"Aroska, think about this," she said, raking a hand back through her hair and doing her best not to grow more exasperated. "You really don't even know me." *Especially after who I've had to be these past couple of years.*

The disappointment in his face transformed into amusement. "There's a solution for that, you know. Your mind forms coherent thoughts that are then conveyed out loud through your mouth. It's this fascinating process called 'talking'."

"Don't be a smartass."

"Fine. But what do you mean? I've known you for over four years now. Longer, if you want to get technical, but I tend to not count anything that happened before Dakiti."

"You realize we only spent a total of like three weeks in each other's presence before I left."

"Sure, but you have to admit we experienced more in those weeks than a lot of people have in a lifetime. The situation is unique. I mean, I've seen you at your worst."

"Have you?"

The uncertainty returned to his eyes, and she wondered what precisely he'd been referring to. Honestly, there were a number of options, and while they might not have truly been her worst, they were certainly things nobody else had ever had the opportunity to see. Still, the idea that he might be wrong about her had clearly caught him off guard.

He recovered more quickly than she'd expected. "Well, you've seen me at my worst."

In this case, she assumed he was referring to the state she'd found him in upon seeking his help after Ikaro Tachi's assassination, but she couldn't help but ask anyway. "Have I?"

Aroska scoffed and forced a disgusted smile. "Damn it, woman, what do you want from me?"

"What's my favorite color? Favorite food? Favorite childhood memory?" None of these were things she'd ever had any desire to be asked about or share with anyone, but she could think of no other way to get her point across. When she considered it, she wasn't sure how easily she could even come up with answers.

"Those are all facts. Would it kill you to go with your gut and not be so logical all the time?"

Her face remained deadpan. "It might."

He didn't appear angry. Maybe just weary. They both were. *All* were. And this was hardly the time or place for this discussion, though part of Ziva—the part that had never quite managed to block out the memories of everything she'd left behind on Haphez—recognized that it probably needed to take place at some point.

Rather than badger her further, Aroska merely closed the gap between them, placed a gentle hand on the back of her shoulder, and urged her to continue in the direction they'd been headed. "Come on. Let's go see if we can find out exactly how much trouble we've just gotten ourselves into."

CHAPTER 9
NIIOSIAN CRUISER *REVENANT* - BLOOD WATER NEBULA

By the time they made it down to the docking bay and boarded the *Saber*, Skeet was already standing before a life-size rendering of Emeri Arion. The lieutenant spared them a look over his shoulder before resuming his conversation with the director, most of which was drowned out by a sudden ringing in Ziva's ears. The sight of Emeri there on the comm pad reminded her that he was just one more person she had deceived, one more person who had meant more to her than she'd ever realized. They'd had their differences, but there'd been a mutual respect there that, if she was honest with herself, had often caused her to think of him in an almost paternal capacity. He looked older now—more weathered, tired— whereas she didn't remember ever noticing much change in appearance in the ten years she'd known him before leaving Haphez.

Aroska cast her a reassuring glance as they came to a stop beside Zinni against the comm room's back wall and waited for Skeet to finish his rather unorthodox debrief. An odd sensation coursed through her stomach; it hadn't even been this uncomfortable to reveal herself to her teammates, now or back in Argall after staging her death on the river-bank outside Haphor. Of course, in both of those cases, someone some- where had known she was still alive. In this current situation, not only had it been four years since she'd disappeared, but like the rest of the galaxy, Emeri had thought her dead. More than dead. Obliterated. Vaporized. Gone without a trace.

She snapped back to attention when she sensed Aroska shift beside her and she looked up to find Skeet stepping down from the projection pad. He shrugged and gave them each a look that seemed to silently wish them luck.

"You're up," he said quietly, clapping Tarbic on the shoulder as the two of them passed.

Ziva straightened and crossed her arms as Aroska took his place on the comm pad and Skeet settled in beside her. The stony look on Emeri's face was as clear as it would have been if he were standing there in the room with them. It was a look she was very familiar with, having been on the receiving end of it numerous times after doing something foolhardy.

"Sergeant," the director began, his voice quiet but firm, "Lieutenant Duvo just presented me with a very interesting document, and I find that in this situation, I'm more confused than anything else. I'm hoping you can give me a reasonable explanation for *what the hell* you're doing over there."

Aroska didn't even flinch. "Sir, the situation isn't what it seems."

"It seems fairly basic to me," Emeri growled. "Shall we review the facts? I sent you after Matia Moryi. She *shot* you, leaving no physical evidence. The Royal House has been awaiting your testimony, which would have been the one and only thing that could give us cause to arrest and prosecute her. That is until you—and I'm still having trouble believing this—*married* her, under the authorization of Tobias Niio of all people. You're telling me this isn't what it looks like? Explain to me what exactly I'm missing here."

The room was silent for several long seconds. Ziva, Skeet, and Zinni kept their eyes locked on Aroska, who stood motionless in front of the hologram with his gaze directed toward the floor.

"Are you alone, sir?" he finally said. "Is this a secure channel?"

Ziva swallowed and took a single step forward, despite the heaviness in her stomach. Revealing herself to the director may have been part of the plan, but that didn't make it any easier, and nobody had discussed exactly *how* or *when* it would happen. As much as she wanted to keep her presence and involvement in all this a secret, letting Emeri into the loop might facilitate that task. He could stall the Royal House, throw them off her trail. It seemed he'd been stuck with that role more often than not throughout her career at HSP.

The graveness of Aroska's tone seemed to have captured the older man's attention. His hologram hesitated and reached out of the projection for a moment, perhaps to lock the door or otherwise secure the room. "Yes," he answered, "my eyes and ears only."

Aroska sent Ziva a questioning glance. She drew a deep breath and nodded, able to feel Skeet and Zinni's gazes boring into her back as she made her way toward the communications console.

"I married her to protect her," Aroska explained. "I realize she has done some terrible things, but there's more to the story. I can't—won't—testify against her."

"And just why not?"

Ziva stepped up and joined Aroska on the comm pad without a second thought. Her appearance triggered another silence, this one weightier, more substantial. For a while, the director's hologram stood so still that she wondered if there'd been a short in the transmission. But then he blinked, breaking eye contact with her for the briefest of moments, and that seemed to be enough to snap him out of his trance. He finally managed to clear his throat, but when he opened his mouth to speak, no sound emerged.

"Nice to see you too, Director," she said.

"I, ah..." Emeri cleared his throat again and shifted on the comm pad. "I suppose after nearly fifteen years, I should have learned to stop being surprised by anything you do." He paused to take a breath, and the faint flickering of the hologram made it difficult to tell if there'd been a slight tremor in that breath. "I can't begin to understand how this is possible, but it *is* good to see you."

"Aroska is right. I've done some things I'm not proud of while I've been...away. But he's also right in that the situation is more complicated than you realize."

"That is an understatement."

"And, obviously, there's still a lot of explaining to do, but that should be left for later."

"Just to be clear, you're Matia Moryi?"

She hesitated a moment before nodding grimly.

"How...I...where the hell are you all right now?"

"Aboard the Niiosian Mob's flagship, if you can believe it," Aroska answered.

"But Matia Moryi is supposed to be—"

"A Niiosian asset *undercover* within the Ibarra Cartel," Ziva cut in. "I know how that sounds, considering her...my...reputation, but this is an operation that has spanned months—*years*—and was truthfully on the verge of success until the team came after me." She shrugged. "And if it makes you feel any better, Ibarra has been developing weapons using stolen niobi crystal tech, which they no doubt acquired on the black market during Diago Dasaro's operation in Argall. You could say we had a stake in this, too."

Emeri wasn't impressed. He glanced behind him as though searching for somewhere to sit and appeared disappointed there was no chair in the vicinity. Instead, he dragged a hand over his face and stood massaging his chin for a moment as if trying to suppress barely contained rage.

"I warned the three of you about getting involved with the Niiosians, did I not?" he said, looking Aroska in the eye as he spoke.

"You did say something to that effect, yes," Tarbic answered.

"You can't get much more involved with them than being aboard their flagship."

"Respectfully, sir, we're here for Ziva. The Niiosians happened to be able to provide us with the resources we needed in the moment. They were a means to an end, nothing more."

"Well, I can't very well tell the Royal House this assassin they've been waiting for is in actuality a former HSP agent whom everyone—including the *Federation*, might I remind you—has presumed dead for the last four years." Emeri paused, the muscles in his jaw flexing as he ground his teeth. "How are you even expecting this to work? This 'marriage,' however legitimate it may be thanks to Tobias Niio, might be enough to postpone any testimony and stall this investigation. I'll grant you that. But if the Royal House finds out who Matia Moryi truly is, it will be the end for all of you."

"We were hoping you'd be able to help with that," Ziva said.

The director's mouth twitched. It had been a long time since she'd seen him this agitated, her absence from the agency notwithstanding, and without his usual calm poise and composure, it was more difficult to predict the outcome of this encounter. Yes, they were springing an abundance of shocking information on him all at once, so his reactions were justified in that sense. Still, she couldn't help but bristle the longer this went on. Be ready to run. Ready to fight.

When Emeri made no immediate move to respond, Aroska cleared his throat. "And if you are unwilling or completely unable to help, I think we would all appreciate it if you'd explicitly say so right now and not waste our time."

Ziva lifted a brow and shot him a glance. It was all she could do to keep from smiling as Emeri's eyes narrowed in response to Aroska's steely gaze. The man had a pair, that was for sure.

"Sergeant Tarbic, we will discuss proper decorum while addressing superior officers another time."

Some of the tension in Ziva's shoulders released. Emeri may have been pissed, but if his first reaction wasn't to threaten them or otherwise thwart their plan, then maybe they were on the right track.

"And Lieutenant Duvo! Officer Vax! I have no doubt you're still there."

Skeet and Zinni appeared at her side and crowded onto the comm pad.

"I seem to recall you all spinning a wonderful story about how none of you knew who Moryi was. Upon completion of this mission, the three of you should be prepared for a formal reprimand for blatantly lying during an official reporting session."

"It was my call, sir," Skeet said, stepping forward as best he could in the confined space. "While much of what we told you was true, I instructed Sergeant Tarbic and Officer Vax to alter their accounts of the events near the beach and omit Ziva's involvement until we had a better grasp of the situation."

Ziva was honestly shocked to hear they had chosen to protect her, even if it was in their own self-interest, especially since whatever debrief they were talking about seemed to have occurred *after* she'd shot Aroska and led them to believe she was a hostile Ibarra agent. But she was glad they had, because if the Royal House had gotten wind of her presence before they'd had a chance to come up with this shoddy plan, they'd all be screwed.

"While I don't particularly believe you, Lieutenant," Emeri said, "I can appreciate the idea of taking responsibility for your team. In that case, *you* should be prepared for a formal reprimand for blatantly lying in an official report."

Ziva felt Skeet stiffen beside her. "Sir," he said quietly, dipping his head in concession.

The director watched them all with grave features for several more seconds before sighing and rubbing his eyes. When he spoke again, his tone had softened significantly. "Dare I ask what your plans are from here?"

"As a token of good faith to Tobias for his...hospitality, we've offered to retrieve Pahl Starcer's specs from Delatori," Skeet explained. "Zinni and I will be departing with a Niiosian agent within a couple of hours."

Emeri drew a breath, no doubt to admonish them again for working with the Mob, but then he clamped his mouth shut and offered a reluctant nod, waiting for more.

"We hoped Starcer would be willing to provide the specs' location and walk us through how to access them," Zinni said.

"I imagine something could be arranged." The director shook his head, and Ziva watched as the creases in his aging face once again deepened along with the scowl he'd been wearing for the duration of the conversation. "If nothing else, fulfilling his end goal may help divert his attention away from the fact that the rest of this mission has completely gone to hell."

Skeet nodded. "We'll be in touch, then. You can reach us here aboard the *Saber*."

It felt like an awkward way to end the conversation, but there was really nothing more to say without going into meticulous detail about the politics of Ibarra and Niio and what she'd been up to for the last four years, and as she'd already told the director, there would be time for that later. That was, *if* he really wanted to know. It might be better if he didn't.

Zinni stepped down from the comm pad, followed by Aroska, with Ziva falling in behind them. But when Emeri cleared his throat, she turned back and found Skeet still standing there.

"Something further, Lieutenant?"

Based on the man's tone, he had no desire to be subject to any more of the team's demands, but Skeet held fast. "What can the agency do about protecting Ziva's identity at this point?" he began, his tone imploring rather than challenging. "Alastair Manes knows who she is, who she *really* is, thanks to the bulletin that circulated following Ikaro Tachi's assassination. I know there's probably nothing we can do about the information that has been copied or saved on local systems around the galaxy, but we can still cut it off at the source. Stop it from spreading."

They all fell silent as they waited for Emeri to respond. Ziva took a step back toward Skeet but refrained from moving onto the comm pad. After some of their interactions over the past day, it was perplexing that he was currently attempting to defend her. While she appreciated the effort, the fact that he was choosing to do this despite the anger he still harbored toward her only worsened her guilt.

"She is 'dead,' after all," Skeet added.

"I'll look into it," the director finally said. "In the meantime, I would like all of you—including you, Ziva—to please try your very hardest to not make this predicament any worse than it already is."

The hologram flickered and disappeared before they could say anything else that did just that.

Chapter 10
HSP HEADQUARTERS · Noro, Haphez

Emeri wasted no time in going to his desk, yanking a glass and an antique bottle of dark liquor from the drawer, knocking back a couple of fingers, then collapsing into his chair with a second glassful in hand. He'd been doing this job for years. He knew how to handle stress. He knew how to tactfully deal with difficult situations. But after everything he'd just learned, the realization that he was currently considering doing exactly what his agents had asked of him made him wonder if he'd in fact been at this too long.

He couldn't shake the image of Ziva standing there alive and well out of his head. It was the last outcome of this damn mission he'd ever expected, and it certainly wasn't what he'd expected when he'd received the official declaration telling him Sergeant Tarbic married Matia Moryi and was refusing to testify. She looked good—perhaps a little haggard, perhaps a little angrier than she always had, which was saying something. Aside from her hair looking rather unkempt, she didn't appear nearly as barbaric as the image he'd formed in his head after listening to Starcer's initial description of Moryi, so either people had merely feared her imposing stature and fierce nature, or he was missing something. The latter seemed more likely, though he wasn't sure if he wanted to know what that 'something' might be.

He downed his glass in two large gulps, hoping the burning liquid would dissolve the heavy lump that had formed rather suddenly in his throat. There, that was exactly the problem. When you supervised the same agents for too many years, and when those agents were damn good at their jobs, you couldn't help but develop a certain level of fondness for them. And when one of those agents appeared out of thin air four years after the brutal explosion that had supposedly killed her, well.... He lifted a hand and held it level in front of him, mercifully unable to perceive the slight tremor he was certain he could feel.

Not only was Ziva *not* dead, but the rest of the team now seemed to be neck deep in this whole mess between the Niiosian Mob and the Ibarra Cartel, the very thing he'd warned them not to do before they'd left. Granted, they truly hadn't known what they were getting into, so he couldn't fault them completely. Maybe the more accurate description was that Ziva was fully involved in the conflict—both sides, somehow—and they'd followed right after her. Now *that* was an all-too-familiar scenario. As tempting as it was to order them home before the situation could deteriorate any further, he recognized that wasn't an option, at least not yet. The fact was the Royal House was itching to hear Tarbic's testimony and take custody of Matia Moryi. Truth be told, he wasn't nearly as concerned about Ziva returning to Haphez as he was about what might happen if the Federation ever found out she was alive, so that alone was enough to rule out the idea of handing her over for any sort of high-profile trial in the capital. And if he wasn't going to do that, then Tarbic's statement was pointless. He could only imagine what sort of unpleasantness the Royal Officer and the other higher-ups in Haphor would bring to bear when they got neither of the things they wanted.

Emeri sighed and examined his empty glass, trying to decide if he wanted another shot before he got down to business. He could start by simply stalling the Royal House, though he'd have to come up with a plausible explanation for the lack of testimony and lack of ruthless assassin relatively quickly. For now, there was another step he could take that would give him time to come up with some ideas.

He put the glass and liquor bottle back in his drawer then reached for the intercom button on his desk. "Have Pahl Starcer brought in, please."

A solid half hour passed before the buzzer sounded at the office door and he granted the caller entry. Starcer strode in sporting dark circles around his eyes but otherwise looking no worse for wear than he had since his arrival in Noro. He and the two bodyguards accompanying him had been put up in a nearby agency safehouse, and so far, any mission updates had been delivered via secure comm. Emeri hoped a face-to-face meeting would give Starcer a sense of optimism, especially considering there was nothing particularly optimistic about the news he needed to deliver.

He stood and motioned for Starcer to come join him in the plush chairs by the large picture window on the far side of the office. "I hope your stay has been comfortable thus far, Mr. Starcer."

The man settled into a chair, watching Emeri warily as he did so. "You have good news?"

As much as he wanted to say yes, he couldn't bring himself to do such a thing at this point. "I have...an update," he replied instead, noting the way Starcer bristled at the lack of immediate positive response. "I've just been briefed by the team. Circumstances are such that they will be traveling to Delatori and would like to recover the schematics on your behalf if you'd be willing to provide their location."

Starcer stiffened further. "Where is the team now?"

"I'm not at liberty to say." The phrase left Emeri's mouth with practiced ease, but when he stopped and thought about it, he realized he couldn't answer honestly even if he wanted to. His agents had been on Panuco during their last couple of check-ins, the heart of the Ibarra Cartel's territory, but if they'd somehow fallen in with the Niiosians in the past several hours, they could be anywhere right now.

"You have to understand, Director—those schematics detail a project that has been highly classified, and I'm not exactly comfortable with the idea of them being in the hands of a third party."

Emeri had plenty of experience remaining diplomatic when it was the last thing he wanted to do, so he had no trouble recognizing that was exactly what Starcer was doing right now. He'd also run out of patience about halfway through his conversation with the team and had no desire to suffer nonsense from anyone else.

"And *you* have to understand just how skilled my agents are," he said, leaning forward, "and how trustworthy. You recruited them for a reason, and that reason is the same reason they are in fact the best suited for this task." He hesitated, unsure how far to elaborate. "I can tell you Matia Moryi is not out of the picture yet. At this point, we believe it would still be too dangerous for you to return to Delatori. In the interest of saving time, this is the best course of action."

That seemed to capture Starcer's attention. The truth was Emeri didn't believe Ziva posed any real threat to the man; she'd been hunting him while undercover, and her undercover time seemed to have come to a close. But if a small lie was what it took to ensure his cooperation, then so be it.

Starcer muttered a curse and leaned back in his chair, looking out at the Noro skyline as he massaged his forehead. "This isn't exactly going as planned, is it."

You have no idea, Emeri thought. "I realize this isn't what you initially wanted, but will you provide the team with a walkthrough when they reach Delatori?"

The office fell silent for what felt like several minutes. If they couldn't get Starcer to agree, Emeri had half a mind to send the team after the schematics anyway. But none of them knew for sure where the specs were, and when it came down to it, the only thing that even made this their problem was Starcer's commission. The man's options were to either comply or risk recovering the plans on his own.

"I'll tell them the location on one condition," the developer finally answered.

Emeri forced a soft smile to conceal gritted teeth. "Go on."

"I want them to find my son first. Or...whatever might be left of him. It's been long enough since I've heard from him that I'm convinced Moryi got to him before he made it off Delatori. I don't know where he might have ended up, but I can tell you the general area where he last was."

As tempting as it was to tell Starcer to stop wasting their time, the thought occurred to Emeri that if Ziva had indeed killed the man's son, she'd be able to tell them exactly where the body was. The fact that he considered this a silver lining felt preposterous.

He made a point of remaining silent for several more seconds to create the illusion of deliberation. "I'll see what we can do," he finally replied, though he doubted it would take much coercion to get the team to agree.

Starcer nodded and stood. "Then I await their communication." He turned to leave, then paused and spared Emeri one last glance. "I sincerely wish this whole situation would have turned out differently."

Again, he had no idea. Emeri stood as well and saw him out, then returned to the window to gaze at the cityscape. It was tempting to go pour another drink, but a moment of consideration led him to the conclusion that maintaining a clear head would be more prudent than numbing himself to the chaos, no matter how appealing the latter sounded. As Prime Director of Haphez's finest police force, he liked to think he'd become adept at not bowing to anyone's wishes, yet he'd just done so twice in the span of an hour. He didn't mind acquiescing to the team's request as much as he did Starcer's, and it struck him that this mode of thinking meant he'd subconsciously made up his mind to help Ziva. Or, more accurately, he'd made up his mind to not alert anyone to the situation yet, if ever. Sending the team to Delatori to recover the specs would buy some time and keep the Royal House from badgering him about Tarbic's testimony for at least a little while longer, and thus agreeing to Starcer's demand was simply a means to an end.

The thought also occurred to him that, despite the threat of reprimand he'd just brought down on Lieutenant Duvo, there was little chance he would be able to make good on that threat. Punishing him for lying or withholding information would lead to questions regarding what he'd withheld information about, which in turn would increase the risk of exposing Ziva's presence. They'd need to forego the reprimand altogether, or else concoct a different story. Though Emeri detested the thought of allowing the team to get away with their transgression, he would just have to see how things played out.

With a sigh, he wandered back over and took a seat at his desk. He let his hand hover over his workstation controls for a moment before bringing up one of the old alert bulletins that had gone out after Ziva escaped police custody in the wake of Tachi's murder. It was almost startling to look into her striking red eyes for the first time in at least a couple of years; out of necessity, he'd moved on as well as he could following her death—he still couldn't help but think of her departure in that way—and had shut her out of his mind in favor of the hundreds of functional agents still under his command. He'd gotten to where he looked back on those days and truly regretted the way he and the rest of the agency treated her following the assassination. The rock-solid evidence may have pointed to her, but he should have known. Should have trusted her. Of course, it was easy to dwell in hindsight now.

Before he could second guess himself any longer, Emeri hit the command to delete the bulletin from HSP's system. Lieutenant Duvo was right; erasing this information wouldn't stop anyone with hard copies from seeing it. But it would stop it from circulating any further, and he had to admit it made him feel better.

Her arrest record had been expunged years ago after the truth about Dasaro's plot had been brought to light, but he found himself double checking anyway. Before he knew it, he was staring at her old personnel file. Due to the nature of her role within the agency, there wasn't much to see, but reading through the few mission reports that weren't completely redacted brought back memories of what had been quite the era at HSP. The agency was by no means suffering, and the operations divisions in particular were thriving, but he simply hadn't realized how much he missed having an agent like Ziva in his ranks until she was back within his reach.

Sheyss, he really needed to not go down that road.

His eyes lingered on the display for another couple of minutes, though he found he wasn't retaining any of the information as the wheels inside his head spun. Then, one by one, the files began to disappear, prompted by the seemingly unconscious press of a button on the console. He was almost glad the action didn't feel like it was his own, as it took the edge off the roiling in his stomach. Then, before he could stop himself, he hit the command again, deleting the personnel profile itself. The action wasn't illegal, per se, but it was certainly unprecedented. According to HSP records, Ziva Payvan no longer existed.

But, just as Skeet had said, Ziva Payvan was also dead, so what harm could he really do?

Chapter 11
Niiosian Cruiser *Revenant* · Blood Water Nebula

Zinni slowed to a stop as she approached yet another comfortable alcove in front of yet another wide viewport at the end of yet another long corridor. She wasn't sure if she'd ever get used to seeing these kinds of luxuries aboard a military craft, but then again, the Niiosians were no ordinary military force. The Haphezians emphasized utility and efficiency above all else and wouldn't be caught dead wasting workable space on furniture, minibars, and the dozen other types of amenities she'd seen as she'd searched the vessel for Ziva. By providing his people with these things, Tobias ensured their comfort and happiness. She scoffed. Which ensured their loyalty.

She leaned against the bulkhead and took a moment to watch her old friend in silence. They'd all taken some time to eat and rest, as well as reconvene with Emeri to review Starcer's terms. Now it was nearly time to depart for Delatori with Ken, and she'd been surprised when Skeet of all people had brought up the fact that none of them had seen Ziva since the director called back. After admitting that she had indeed killed the developer's son, she'd vanished at some point during the ensuing discussion on how to proceed.

It was reasonable for her to want to escape that conversation, but the woman seemed to have a general penchant for wandering off somewhere in the ship; the galaxy only knew where she'd disappeared to in the time leading up to the awkward wedding—if it could be called that—on the bridge, and they'd determined she wasn't carrying a comm. Zinni had no doubt that the circumstances surrounding her return to relative normality were making it more difficult than anticipated. Hell, coming out of a multi-year undercover operation would be hard for anybody, even if the proper steps were taken for extraction and rehabilitation. The desire for some quiet time to reflect on everything was understandable. But with all those same circumstances in mind, the whole team had agreed that leaving Ziva alone was the worst possible option.

So here Zinni stood, having traversed what felt like the entire *Revenant* before finding her former lieutenant's latest hiding place. She'd taken it upon herself to get the job done; Skeet was still too hot—her personal opinion—and given what Aroska had just shared with them about the fate of the young techie on Panuco, she wasn't sure if Ziva would be as receptive to him as usual. Besides, she'd hardly had a chance to speak to her old friend in the couple of months leading up to her disappearance four years ago, so this was both an intervention of sorts and an opportunity to get some closure. She reached down and muted her comm, determined nothing would interrupt this encounter.

Ziva sat in the viewport's cushioned window seat, staring out at the other Niiosian vessels with one leg drawn up against her, the other dangling toward the floor. She no doubt knew she was under observation—Zinni could see her own reflection in the viewport from here—but she made no move to acknowledge anyone else's presence.

Zinni approached quietly, hands folded at her waist, and came to a stop a couple of meters from the window. The silence lasted just long enough to become uncomfortable before she spoke. "Mind if I sit?"

Ziva met her gaze in the reflection and gestured half-heartedly toward the spacious bench beside her, all without turning away from the view outside.

She stepped forward and took a seat on the cushion, folding one leg under her but remaining bolt upright. This wasn't the time to relax. She took a moment to watch the other vessels outside as well, but when it became apparent that Ziva would make no move to initiate the conversation, she turned her attention to her and her alone.

"You owe me an apology."

The truth was she still owed *all* of them apologies, but at least Skeet and Aroska had gotten something already.

When Ziva once again made no move to respond, Zinni leaned forward. "You hear me?"

"Yes, Zinni, I heard you," the woman said, her tone sharp. She finally pried her gaze away from the window and lowered it for a moment before making eye contact. "Words aren't going to fix anything."

No, they weren't, but they were at least an acknowledgement that she cared about the things she'd done. Or hadn't done, as the case may be. Zinni forced her features to remain impassive-verging-on-cold in hopes of proving she was serious, and given her displeasure for the whole situation, it was easier than expected.

"I'm sorry you all got dragged into this mess," Ziva murmured, turning back toward the viewport and resting her head against the glass. "I'm sorry for everything I put you all through in those months after the Dakiti mission. And...I'm sorry you and I never had the chance to talk. *Pazska*, we barely got to say goodbye."

There. That was all Zinni had wanted. Once upon a time, Ziva might not have apologized to anyone for anything, and she might have even spat something like 'for what?' when asked for an apology. But she was also smart enough to realize such a response would have simply been a filler to delay the inevitable. They were supposed to be teammates. Sworn to protect each other. The fact that the woman still seemed to recognize the significance of their relationship was reassuring.

But the unfamiliar word she'd just used was no doubt something common on Panuco, which meant she hadn't completely dropped all aspects of the Matia act yet. As much as Zinni wanted such a thing to happen, she knew it was unrealistic to expect it to happen this fast. Even if you weren't undercover, when you lived in a place for two years and had been working to familiarize yourself with it for even longer, you picked up new habits. Body language. Ways of speaking. But when you were undercover, particularly when you had to maintain a role like your life depended on it, those habits became deep-rooted. Ziva may have had enough control of her faculties to know who her friends were and who she was really working for, but Matia Moryi was not something that would go away overnight.

The pained, defeated look on her face was quite foreign after knowing her as a relentless soldier for so many years. She may not have been Moryi anymore, but she certainly wasn't her old self, either. Hoping to keep her engaged in the present, Zinni opted for a change of subject. "I'm sorry about your friend. Blain? Aroska told us what happened." She winced when Ziva shut her eyes; this wasn't helping the situation. "Sounds like he made a tough call in a nasty situation."

"Yeah." The response was little more than a whisper. "I can't fault him completely, but—" Ziva muttered a curse and looked away for several long seconds, lips clamped together. Then she swallowed, cleared her throat, and straightened a bit. "The kid may have been an idiot, but that was no place for him." The faintest hint of a smile appeared, as though a thought had come to mind. "He was headstrong. Inventive. Reminded me a lot of Jada."

A resemblance to her younger sister would certainly explain why she'd grown so close to the boy. "I think we were all surprised you'd found someone during this whole operation who meant so much to you," Zinni said.

"I shouldn't have. I knew I'd eventually need his help with some of the more technical aspects of my departure from Panuco, so I kept him close. But I never should have let it go any further."

"You needed an ally in enemy territory." Zinni hesitated. "How did you end up there? Working for Manes, I mean."

"Tobias sent me after a former Niiosian operative turned Ibarra assassin. He was Ken's half-brother, actually. I inserted myself into the midst of a Cartel mission, killed him, and allowed myself to be captured by their forces. The expectation was that Manes would recognize my skill set and bring me on as a replacement, which, fortunately, is what happened. But not before I spent six weeks as a Cartel prisoner while he vetted me and I purported to deliberate his offer."

Zinni couldn't help but notice the way she'd said 'my' skill set rather than Matia's. It felt wrong to be analyzing every aspect of her speech and behavior like this, but after everything that had transpired on Panuco, she found she was still on edge. "And what would you have done if he hadn't offered?"

Ziva watched her quizzically for a moment, no doubt picking up on the dubious element she'd been careless with in her tone. "The plan was that I would approach him instead and offer my services. I'm glad it didn't come to that—letting him feel he was in control of the situation was key."

"He could have killed you."

"But he didn't."

"And you were willing to risk that just so you could fulfill a promise you made to someone—" she gestured off toward the *Revenant's* bridge "—who's no better?"

"But he *didn't*," Ziva repeated, "because I did my job well."

"Maybe that's what's bothering me." Zinni caught herself when heat began to flood her cheeks; there was no sense in getting just as angry as Skeet, especially when she'd come here in hopes of avoiding a full-blown confrontation. She sighed. "Look, I don't want to argue. I just...want to understand."

"I get it. I do. But I don't think there's any more I can say that will make you understand. Honestly, I never imagined having to justify myself to anyone."

"So there were no rules, is that it?"

"Frankly," Ziva answered, her brows dropping into a scowl, "no, there weren't."

The implications of that were...potentially concerning, to say the least. After thriving in such a lawless environment, it would be all too easy to allow one's behavior to carry over upon returning to a relatively normal setting where you were expected to operate in a civilized fashion. The Niiosian Mob didn't necessarily deserve the utmost respect and cooperation, but letting Moryi loose aboard this ship wouldn't be a smart move on Ziva's part. Perhaps that was the reason for her persistent melancholy—she was tired, at a loss as to how to move forward, and was doing her best to keep herself reined in.

In that sense, Zinni was glad Aroska would still be here while she and Skeet accompanied Ken to Delatori. Even though he and Ziva were somewhat at odds at the moment, he was always so good with her— hopefully even after being apart for four years—and would be best suited to keep her from retreating too far into her own head.

Ziva leaned back over and brought her forehead to rest against the viewport again. "Being Matia, being on Panuco...it wasn't all bad."

Again, Zinni found herself bristling without meaning to. In spec ops, they'd had to do some things she wasn't proud of for the sake of the bigger picture, sure, and much of what Ziva had accomplished for Manes was no different. But from the sound of it, she had done things that went far beyond that in the process of simply establishing herself as Matia, then had continued to cross lines while she played the part. She'd always had principles, a sense of honor, and if she had become jaded enough to lose those principles, that was a problem.

"You want to explain what you mean by that?"

"I mean living there, okay? I'm not trying to make excuses for anything I did." Ziva drew a breath and released it slowly, apparently struggling to remain civil herself. "Tabaco may have been a *sheyss* hole, but looking past that, there were parts of the environment I enjoyed. Great seafood, if I'm being completely honest. Lots of ways to keep in shape—coves to swim in, rocks to climb, beaches to run. If you get to where you can keep up a decent running pace in loose sand, you can run anywhere. It reminded me of when they used to make us run in the sand along the Tranyi during basic training." She turned and gazed wistfully out the viewport. "Made me wish I'd spent more time at the coast back home."

Zinni looked out as well, marveling for a moment at the sight of the Niiosian fleet drifting about against the impressive backdrop of the Blood Water nebula. It was easy to look back now and wish a lot of things. As much as she hated to admit it, their careers, their relationships with Ziva, their very lives...none of those things would ever be the same after this. She supposed every mission was like that to an extent; she returned from nearly every assignment changed—affected—in some manner, some certainly more drastic and noticeable than others. But nothing had ever affected her as deeply or as long as Ziva and her actions had, and those sour memories left her pining for the good old days more fervently than normal.

"What about you?" the woman asked after a prolonged silence. "What have I missed at home? How are you doing?"

Zinni turned and found herself under scrutiny. She genuinely wasn't sure if she'd ever heard such a phrase out of Ziva's mouth, but the fact that she was hearing it now of all times was encouraging. "I, ah...we've all been better. Aside from all the competition in the ops divisions, the job itself has been going fine. But there are still times when thinking about the fact that, you know, my blood samples helped the Resistance create lethal forms of nostium that killed dozens of Haphezians kind of gets me down."

She added a soft chuckle for levity in hopes of masking the discomfort wrought from admitting this. It was strange having to explain an issue that had plagued her for four years to someone for the first time, particularly when it was old news to everyone else she'd been close to. Once, her old lieutenant would have been the first to be made privy to such information.

Ziva drew a breath to respond but simply offered a grim nod of understanding.

Zinni sighed. "Four years later and it still becomes the topic of conversation at the quarterly psych evals."

"Ah, I remember those well."

"I think we've all been struggling with slightly different things. There's me with my survivor's guilt, I guess you'd call it. It's no secret that Skeet's had some anger issues, and then there's Aroska with everything he's been through. We're a little bit of a mess. A lot of people were after the Resistance attack. Things were different for us because we had such a personal stake in that whole thing—nobody else even came close to what we experienced, and none of our experiences were quite identical, either." She paused. "But you've certainly been a common factor for all three of us."

The perceptive glimmer in Ziva's eyes vanished instantly. "I didn't mean to hurt anyone."

"I know," Zinni replied, though as soon as the words left her mouth, she wasn't sure if she *did* know. If Ziva had cared about not hurting people, she might have made some different decisions in the months leading up to her departure. "But you did, and we can't change that now. I don't know that I can speak for Aroska, but I know Skeet and I are having a hard time dealing with the fact that we spent four years simultaneously missing you and being angry with you. When you add all this Matia Moryi business onto that, it's quite the recipe for confusion, to say the least."

"If it makes you feel any better, this isn't the reunion I was expecting, either. Of course, there wasn't supposed to be a reunion at all, but here we are."

"Here we are," Zinni echoed with another sigh. She drew a breath to continue but hesitated, unsure how to adequately convey the mess of feelings about being face to face with the woman again. "It really is good to see you."

"Are you still speaking for the whole team, or just yourself?"

"Myself and Aroska, I'd say. Give Skeet time—part of the reason he's so bitter is because he wants to be relieved but knows he shouldn't be. Can't blame him."

Ziva opened her mouth as if to comment but turned and glanced down the corridor at an approaching figure just as Zinni noticed the person in the viewport's reflection. She looked as well, just in time to witness Aroska slow upon realizing he was the center of attention. He paused a moment as though unsure whether he should interrupt, then took another couple of quick steps toward the two of them.

"Skids up in ten," he said. The words were directed at Zinni, though she couldn't help but notice the way his gaze shifted subtly toward Ziva as well.

"Be there in a minute," she replied, adding a slow, deliberate nod.

He seemed to take the hint and respectfully withdrew, striding away in the direction from which he'd come, his bio-boot-assisted gait already much smoother than it had been even an hour ago. Zinni turned back and found Ziva still watching him depart, uncertainty glistening in those crimson eyes that had always been so full of confidence. Tarbic had a peculiar effect on the woman, that was for sure, and if Zinni didn't know what to make of it, then surely Ziva didn't, either. And four years was a long time to be separated from someone you weren't sure how you felt about.

"Friends?" Zinni said, drawing Ziva back to the present. She extended a hand.

Ziva watched her for a moment, searching for sincerity in her face. Then, draping an arm over her drawn-up knee, she reached out and grasped Zinni's hand, giving it a solid squeeze. "Friends," she answered.

Zinni slid from the window seat, working to keep her mind off Delatori mission prep for just a couple more minutes. She looked down the hall in the direction Aroska had gone then turned back to Ziva, unable to conceal the sly grin spreading across her lips. "I suppose I should congratulate you on your wedding," she chuckled.

"*Sheyss*, don't remind me," Ziva groaned, burying her face in her hands before running them back through her hair. When she looked up again, red had flooded her cheeks. The fact that she was embarrassed and not merely pissed made Zinni smile all over again.

"You could do a lot worse, you know."

"Believe it or not, I have considered that."

It was tempting to tell her about all the effort Aroska had put into tracking her down over the past few years, but she decided it wasn't her place. Besides, maybe it was best not to portray him in that noble light when he was currently just as uncertain as she and Skeet were after the events of the past couple of days.

Instead, she reached out and took Ziva's hand again, dragging her from her seat. "Now come on, walk with me. I haven't gotten to tell you about our decidedly epic escape from Panuco."

"Not a clean getaway, I presume?"

The two of them set off for the docking bay where the *Saber* waited. "Well, it was after a certain point..."

"But?"

"But there may or may not have been a grenade launcher and some gravity-defying acrobatics involved before that."

Ziva smirked. "This I have to hear."

Even with keen Haphezian hearing, it took Skeet a moment to realize the faint sounds he was hearing were approaching footsteps, and even then, it took him another second to ascertain the location of whoever they belonged to. Someone had been approaching the *Saber's* armory but had stopped suddenly, and with the number of Niiosian crew members who'd been coming and going from the vessel to help with mission prep, it was impossible to pick out one specific person's scent. All humans smelled the same anyway.

He turned and found Ken Oda standing just inside the armory doorway, admiring the impressive array of weaponry around him. The man was good; it was nearly impossible to truly sneak up on a Haphezian, but the attempt he'd just made warranted merit. Then again, it was mildly disconcerting that he'd chosen to do such a thing. His intentions seemed sincere enough, and ordinarily Skeet would have been delighted to partner with someone—a human, at that—who possessed a skill set so similar to his own. But the fact that that 'someone' was employed and held in high esteem by an organization like the Niiosian Mob justified maintaining a fair degree of caution throughout this endeavor.

"This truly is a spectacular vessel," Ken said upon realizing his presence was known. It may have been Skeet's imagination, but he almost looked disappointed his stealthy approach hadn't been completely successful. "Fast, efficiently designed, powerful. It will serve us well on this mission."

Skeet returned his attention to the weapon components he'd been working with on the armory's workbench. "And if we execute this mission correctly, we shouldn't require any of those features."

"Just the same. Better to have them and not need them than to be found wanting."

He had a point. Skeet finished up his task and the two of them made their way out into the *Saber's* main corridor, where they found Aroska entering through the boarding hatch. Tarbic approached, sparing Ken a glance as the man moved away to allow them to converse.

"You trust him?" Aroska asked in Haphezian, voice low.

"Not particularly," Skeet replied in Standard, loud enough that Ken could no doubt ascertain he was the topic of conversation. He crossed his arms and sighed, then lowered his own voice. "But for now, this arrangement is the best way for everyone to get what they want out of this situation."

"Well, this goes without saying, but watch your back, huh?"

Skeet grunted an affirmative and watched the hatch Ken had disappeared through. Given the man's role within the Mob, he was in an excellent position to assist with this mission...or to ensure a different outcome should the parameters change behind the scenes. It would not be out of character for Tobias to somehow double-cross them, but seeing as how the mobster would almost certainly lose Ziva's cooperation if any harm came to her team, Skeet doubted he'd risk it. Besides, they were a means to an end for him right now, too. Chances were slim that he'd compromise that, but again, it seemed prudent to err on the side of caution.

"You find Zinni?" he asked, shaking these thoughts from his mind for the time being.

Aroska nodded. "Her comm was muted, but I traced her location and found her with Ziva in an observation port a couple of decks up. She seemed to want some privacy, but I told her you were ready to go."

It was phenomenal how Zinni could always be counted on to be the voice of reason, and considering reason seemed to be what Ziva currently needed most, she'd been the perfect candidate to hunt the woman down. Skeet may have been the one who'd first pointed out the fact that she'd gone missing, but he wasn't ready to take initiative with her again just yet. He was still having a hard enough time processing why he'd chosen to stand up for her and ask Emeri to help erase some of her records. The only explanation he'd managed to conjure up so far was that it had been the right thing to do. But doing the right thing for someone who had wronged him so many times wasn't easy.

"How about you?" he said, walking alongside Aroska into the cargo bay. "You all set here?"

"As set as we can be. Serenity's people just finished restocking the medbay, so you're well-equipped on that front. I need to grab a couple of personal effects, and then I'll be out of your hair."

"Listen, you two keep your eyes open on this end, too. Things seem to be changing on a whim around here." He cleared his throat. "And take care of her. She needs you, even if she doesn't realize it. Or act like it."

Aroska's steely features reflected the sincerity in his tone. "You know I will."

Skeet reached out to shake his hand, then drew him in close for a quick embrace and clap on the shoulder. They parted ways, with Aroska heading toward the comm room and Skeet making his way to the boarding hatch and down into the *Revenant's* enormous docking bay. He found Ken at the bottom of the ramp conversing with Tobias and Serenity, and when he looked across the bay and saw Zinni approaching, he was surprised to see Ziva with her. Given all that had occurred between them, he'd convinced himself she probably wouldn't be there to see them off, but maybe he was simply projecting his own lingering sour feelings onto her. The fact that she'd come after all was reassuring, and he kicked himself for having jumped to the worst-case scenario.

Still, despite the fact that their conversation in the locker room seemed to have been mutually beneficial, he recognized that it might be a while before they were back to a good place. He didn't particularly like the idea of splitting up, but perhaps spending a little time apart after they'd managed to clear the air would serve them well. She needed help and support, and he was still upset enough that he didn't trust himself to provide either of those things, at least not to the extent he once had as her second-in-command.

Zinni was animated, waving her hands around as she rattled on about something humorous, based on the smirk on Ziva's face. For just a moment, the sight of his two oldest friends enjoying each other's company brought Skeet an immeasurable amount of comfort.

The two women sobered as they drew nearer and realized they were the subject of attention. Zinni moved through the group to stand between him and Ken while Ziva came to a stop on the periphery, looking around as though she didn't particularly want to stand with anyone in attendance. Aroska appeared in the boarding hatch just then donning a backpack, and, prompted by a subtle jerk of Skeet's head, made his way down to stand by her.

"Let's review the plan, shall we?" Tobias said, appraising everyone with his hands clasped behind his back.

Skeet stepped forward. "Pahl Starcer has agreed to provide us with the location of his schematics on the condition that we first locate the body of his son, who was killed by Matia Moryi." His gaze shifted toward Ziva, who looked on somberly. "Upon entering Delatori airspace, we will make our way to the vicinity of Starcer's development center." He held out his comm, projecting a topographical rendering of Delatori's surface, and magnified it until they had a clear view of the area in question.

"Most of the development centers and residential sectors are occupied by Ibarra forces," Ziva said, moving toward the projection. She indicated what appeared to be an isolated cluster of buildings on the edge of a settlement about three kilometers from Starcer's office. "The...body...is here, but you'll risk being spotted if you bring the ship into this area. If you set down somewhere out here—" she waved her hand through a heavily forested region in the center of the hologram "—you should be able to avoid being seen. I can tell you where you need to go from there."

"We'll make contact when we arrive, then. Once Starcer's terms are satisfied, we will move on to his office." He panned the projection toward the development center. "We will deal with any Ibarra presence at the facility, then locate and procure the specs."

"Which you will then transmit here for analysis forthwith," Tobias said. "The rest of our forces from Niio should be underway by then. We have designated a rendezvous point on the edge of the Sterro system—we will coordinate our arrival with theirs, and then we will complete the journey to Delatori together and retake what is ours."

Ken gave him a firm nod. "And we will continue to scout the area in the meantime, particularly around the zocrum repository."

It wasn't entirely concrete as far as plans went, but if there was one thing consistent about most spec ops missions, it was adapting on the fly. There wasn't much more they could do to prepare anyway without knowing the exact situation on the ground on Delatori, and it sounded as though that situation remained fluid.

Skeet looked to Ziva, who glanced around and then beckoned for him, Zinni, and Aroska to join her in a more secluded spot a few meters away. She crossed her arms and looked each of them in the eye. The subtle sag of her shoulders made her appear smaller than usual.

"Look, I'm sorry I got you all mixed up in this. Be smart, okay?"

The thought occurred to Skeet that this exact predicament was due more to Starcer's original assignment than anything else, but if she wanted to blame herself for it, he wouldn't argue. He reached out and shook her hand; it felt like a ridiculous thing to do to someone he'd once been—and, admittedly, still was—so close to, but for now it was the most reasonable neutral response.

"See you in a couple of days," he said, addressing both her and Aroska. He spared Tarbic one last lingering look that he hoped did a decent job of silently reiterating their discussion aboard the *Saber*, then he and Zinni headed for the ship.

Ziva stood in silence beside Aroska as the *Saber's* boarding ramp retracted and the hatch closed behind Skeet, Zinni, and Ken. The roar of the ship's engines echoed through the landing bay, followed by the groan of the mag clamps opening. The vessel lifted from its dock, and the two of them turned and watched until it passed through the bay's force field and disappeared. Part of her wished desperately to be accompanying them on this trip, if for no other reason than to escape Tobias's expectations, even temporarily. She felt better about where she stood with her old friends after the conversation with Zinni, but relations were still shaky enough that going with them might well have been nearly as stressful as staying aboard the *Revenant*. Thus, she was looking forward to finding a new hiding spot she could retreat to, somewhere she didn't have to speak to anybody and was free of all obligations.

She became aware of another presence and turned to find Serenity standing beside them, looking them both over with her hands on her hips. "When's the last time either of you got any real sleep?" the woman asked. Her intense gaze shifted to Aroska. "And being unconscious in the medbay doesn't count."

It had been a while. Ziva thought back to how drowsy she'd been while visiting Aroska, but aside from the brief respite afforded by the treatment capsule, events hadn't slowed down much since arriving aboard the battlecruiser. She found that she once again hadn't realized how tired she was until someone brought it up, and she mentally added 'nap' to her list of things to do in her new hiding place, wherever that might be.

Tobias sidled up beside his wife, his lips curled upward in that same amused smirk they'd seen just before the ridiculous marriage. "With Ken gone, I can offer you his quarters, the XO's cabin. Think of it as the honeymoon suite."

If he was trying to goad her into stabbing him, he was nearing success. "I'll sleep aboard the *Talon*, thanks," Ziva muttered, eyes narrowed.

"Not if you want a dozen technicians coming and going for—" he checked the time "—another few hours, at least. They're scouring every centimeter of your ship for the intel you've gathered and anything that will give us additional insights about Manes." The glimmer in his eye transformed from pleasant to chilling so quickly it was almost frightening. "I for one refuse to allow any detail to slip through the cracks."

"Take the damn cabin, Payvan." Serenity's accent gave the command a harsh bite, but there was a surprising amount of patience in her face. "You'll be more comfortable."

Ziva clenched her jaw, unsure why these orders—mere instructions, when it came down to it—were on the verge of causing her to lose composure. She drew a breath in through her nose, ready to spit out some threat or argument she was well aware would do nothing to help the situation, but the feeling of Aroska's hand coming to rest on her shoulder drew her back to the present. She blinked rapidly several times, then turned and met his gaze.

"Hey," he said gently, nodding toward Serenity. "Come on. She's right."

Before she knew it, the two of them were standing just inside the cabin, listening as Serenity departed and the door hissed shut behind them. They'd stopped at the *Talon* just long enough for Ziva to grab a few things—nothing pertinent to the Niiosian analysts' investigation, galaxy forbid. She'd followed Aroska's example and now carried a backpack of her own. They both stood quietly for a moment, taking in the scene. Immediately to the right lay a short countertop, sink, and small cooler. A half-wall separated this kitchenette area from an office space that included a sofa. On the far side of the kitchen, a full wall obscured what must be the bunk space. Another narrow door stood open, revealing a small private lavatory.

She ventured forward toward the couch while Aroska moved over to investigate the sleeping quarters. Based on the overall immaculate condition of the cabin, she guessed Ken didn't spend much time here even when he was aboard the ship. With a sigh, she set her pack in his desk chair. She unfastened her gun belt, as well as the empty knife sheath she'd continued wearing out of habit, then peeled her shirt off, content to sleep in the fitted tank she wore underneath. She was in the process of folding up all three items and laying them out on the desk when Aroska emerged from the other room and let out a low whistle.

"If these are the XO's quarters, I'd love to know what the captain's cabin looks like," he said with an incredulous wag of his head. "That's a double bunk in there, you know. Plenty of room for two."

She studied him for a moment, concluding it had been a distasteful joke before kicking off her boots and flopping down on the couch.

"What are you doing?"

"Going to try to get some sleep," she replied matter-of-factly, trying not to wince upon realizing how stiff the furniture was. "Doctor's orders, right?"

"Okay, but you should at least take the bed."

Well, this conversation was all too familiar. Ziva rolled over to face the back of the sofa and drew her legs up. "Leave me alone, Aroska."

He merely sighed. She considered the situation and decided it was nothing personal against him; she had just run out of patience due to a combination of factors the day had brought on, and it wouldn't be fair to subject him to the resulting frustration. Not when he was her only real ally aboard this ship.

"Are you sure you don't—"

"Good*night*, Aroska."

She remained motionless until she heard his footsteps retreating toward the bedroom. He was only trying to help, and she had no doubt that Skeet and Zinni had instructed him to keep a watchful eye on her. But for now, her desire to have him at her side throughout all of this was trumped by her desire to be left in peace.

The cabin fell silent, and she lay there studying the patterns in the sofa's upholstery as she waited for sheer exhaustion to consume her.

CHAPTER 13
NARIS BASE - ERROL SECTOR, FRINGE SPACE

In many ways, the world of Naris reminded Manes a great deal of Panuco. It was primarily arid, with rolling golden-brown rock formations in lieu of an ocean, at least in the immediate area around the Ibarra base. The rocks and hills helped fortify the area from ground assaults—no aerial force fields here—though there weren't any local combatants stupid enough to attack from the ground. The base had originally been built on the outskirts of a small settlement with a simple spaceport, but over the years Ibarra had slowly encroached until the town had essentially been absorbed by the base.

In terms of physical space, this stronghold here was larger than the one in Tabaco, though that compound had employed more personnel, stronger fortifications, and higher tech. But today, the extra space was what mattered most, as it could accommodate their current ships plus all the other Ibarra vessels they were to rendezvous with.

Manes watched out the viewport of the *Oblivion's* landing craft as rocks and cacti were replaced by concrete and steel. The little ship glided along above beige stone rooftops for a moment before veering off toward the larger, more sophisticated Cartel structures. They swooped into the docking area, touching down near a vacant loading platform where a woman waited with a complement of soldiers.

Kimbra accompanied him down the boarding ramp along with several of his own men. He drew a breath of fresh air; the absence of sea salt in the light breeze was a stark reminder of all they'd lost and all that remained at stake, but he couldn't help but revel in the familiar smells of the desert.

The woman on the platform approached, offering him a quick

salute before standing at rest. "Glad to see you alive, sir," she said.

Despite having been dishonorably discharged by the Federation navy over two decades prior, Karol Zysk had never lost her military edge. It had made her an excellent candidate to assume command of Naris Base after Manes left to take his father's place on Panuco. A strong understanding of both the Feds' and the Resistance's inner workings—however outdated—made her a valuable asset when it came to protecting Cartel interests throughout Fringe Space.

"You received our messages?" he asked.

She nodded a sharp affirmative, not a single strand of her graying hair out of place from where she wore it slicked back. "We have twenty-three ships on site with five hundred guns between them. I've put out a call to all our patrols in the sector—we're tracking them now and they should all arrive within the next day. That'll be an additional fifty vessels, a solid combination of gunships and frigates with a light cruiser thrown in."

Manes turned and surveyed the area as the remainder of the atmocapable ships he'd arrived with touched down for repairs and resupply. Even as they did so, smaller shuttles lifted off, transporting fuel and necessities up to where his larger ships waited in orbit. He had to commend Zysk for being quick on her feet.

"Good," he replied, taking a moment to mull over what he was about to say. "You'll be commanding those ships once we're underway."

Zysk faltered for a split second before schooling her expression. She knew better than to question what was essentially a direct order, but if he knew her, she was also working hard to conceal outright giddiness at the thought of having a space-worthy command again. It was a gamble leaving his secondary base of operations without its leadership and without its fleet, but if they could move quickly enough, secure the materials at Delatori, and use them to bring an end to Tobias Niio once and for all, he would no longer need to worry about leaving his strongholds vulnerable.

"We will travel to Delatori as a unit," he continued. "I want all of our manpower there focused on material recovery." He turned to Kimbra. "*All* of it. Foot patrols, whatever enforcers are still in the city, even the team we've had sitting on Pahl Starcer's office—they all get sent to the repositories. Double the shift size at the zocrum facility. I want that place functional by the time we get there. And make sure the transport fleet is still holding position. We'll be needing their payloads."

She nodded and stepped away, pulling out her comm. "I'll make the call."

Zysk watched her leave and then fell into stride beside Manes as he began to stroll down the length of the docks. "Any indication of where Tobias went since you first contacted me?"

He shook his head. "Our scouts tracked them as far as the Achiuq sector and lost them in the Blood Water nebula."

She scoffed. "The great Tobias Niio, hiding like a coward."

"Mmm." As much as he wanted to agree, he knew Tobias was anything but a coward. The man may have taken his ships into the nebula to hide, but there was no way it was anything but a temporary maneuver. If he was anything like Manes—and evidence suggested he was—then he'd surely be high-tailing it back to Niio to rally his forces for another strike. That, or prepare for a full defense of Mob territory against an Ibarra incursion. Either way, with Delatori's resources at their disposal, the Cartel would be ready.

"I can divert a couple of vessels," Zysk offered. "Send them to Niio to scope out the situation."

It was tempting, but Manes shook his head. "No. We'll need them here. I will organize a proper reconnaissance mission once Delatori is secure."

His comm buzzed before he had time to think any further on the matter, and he dismissed the woman with a wave of his hand. "Yes."

"It's Tal, sir. I've found something interesting while looking into the defense grid security breach. You'll want to see this."

Manes was back aboard his shuttle in seconds and docking with the *Oblivion* in minutes. The trek up to the command level was a blur as his mind focused solely on getting some answers. He found Brady Tal in the same place at the command center, the three-dimensional rendering of Panuco once again projected above him.

"The Niiosians were broadcasting as Ibarra ships," Tal began without fanfare.

Manes nearly stopped dead in his tracks. The man's original theory was that Tobias had somehow managed to change the parameters in the defense grid's core code so the system would accept his vessels. It would have taken a skilled hacker—a whole team of them, probably—to get the job done, but it was plausible. Manes had found himself hoping that was the case; it wasn't an acceptable scenario by any means, but at least the blame could be placed elsewhere.

This, though.... If Tobias's fleet had been able to present itself as Ibarra, it meant all his ships had clearance codes. There'd been no incidents reported recently that might have involved codes being stolen or even missing.

Which meant someone had given them to him.

"Show me," he growled.

Tal's countenance hardened as he tapped at a data pad, manipulating the projection. The planet rotated within a translucent blue bubble that portrayed the defense grid, moving through what seemed to be a time lapse. One by one, red dots began to appear on the edge of the projection, representing the Niiosian ships. With each appearance, a clearance code was added to a scrolling list.

"These are the codes that came through. I can tell you right now that nobody in my department would have thought twice about them if the ships they were attached to hadn't, you know, launched a full-scale attack against our base. As near as I can tell, they weren't stolen, and they weren't cloned from any of our existing ships. They were brand new codes."

All the pent-up rage Manes had been trying to contain since leaving Panuco was in grave danger of manifesting itself. He clasped his hands behind his back, clenching them so tightly the rings on his fingers began to cut into his skin. "Who had access to these systems in the hours leading up to the attack?"

"That's the other thing, sir. These codes were generated nearly a year ago."

"Tell me I just heard you correctly."

"You did."

He began to demand to know how that was possible, how any

party involved could have known that far ahead of time how many ships would be coming. But it struck him that information might not have been pertinent at all. As long as the larger vessels were broadcasting— the battlecruisers, heavy frigates, and what have you—they could carry as many smaller ships into Panucan airspace as they could manage. The number of codes used might only represent a quarter of the fleet size.

"So," Manes mused, stroking his chin as he began to pace back and forth in front of the console. It almost made him sick to speak the words. "We have a traitor in our midst."

"It would seem that way," Tal replied. His features were still hard, the embodiment of cold professionalism, but Manes imagined the man must be relieved to know the defense grid he oversaw hadn't been hacked, something he would have been blamed for whether it was truly his fault or not.

"The question now is whether the guilty party was lost on Panuco, or whether they're right here with us." This was where it got tricky. Most of the evacuees who'd accompanied him to Naris were higher-ranking Ibarra members, personnel whom the parameters of Operation Recovery deemed key to maintaining organizational structure. In other words, they were some of his most trusted people. But that same elevated status would have given many of them the privilege of generating fresh clearance codes, free of scrutiny.

"I can see what I can do about checking personal logs," Tal said, voice low.

Manes nodded his approval even as his mind drifted to alternate possibilities, and he commed back down to the planet below. "Kimbra. Did you ever receive a status update on that young hacker? Blain Reed?"

"No," came her reply. "The team I sent to Payvan's apartment to take him out never did check in. But assuming he somehow survived that, there's no way he would have survived the bombardment. The structures above the Tunnel were slated for demolition as part of Operation Recovery anyway."

He ended the transmission and stood in silence for a moment, the comm receiver pressed to his lips. Someone like Reed would have had the skills to generate codes even without proper clearance. Why, though, would he have had any reason to be in league with the Niiosians?

Unless it hadn't been him at all. Perhaps it had been someone he was close to. Someone whose dwelling he spent a considerable amount of time at. Someone who might have coerced him into generating the codes without him realizing what he was doing, or who might have used his tech without his knowledge to generate the codes herself.

Technically, he could ask the same question about Matia: why would *she* have any reason to be in league with the Niiosians? How did the Haphezians connect to Niio at all? They didn't in any way he could immediately see, so it was tempting to dismiss this theory before he devoted too much energy to it. All he knew was that Moryi—Payvan— seemed to be at the forefront of any problems he'd been having in the couple of days prior to leaving Panuco. Come to think of it, she had certainly been in a position to ruin him from within. His thoughts drifted to all the disturbances he'd written off as coincidence over the past several months, the ones that had done a marvelous job of ensuring he was never quite ready to bring all of Ibarra's strength to bear against Niio. The mysterious deaths, the lab accidents, the warehouse explosions— none of these things were outside the scope of her capabilities.

Part of him still needed to know *why* before he jumped to any definitive conclusions, and part of him was ready to grab and run with this first idea that made sense after two years of dealing with so many things that made no sense at all. If Payvan was working for Tobias, it didn't really matter why or how; the fact was she'd spent months playing him for reasons that went much deeper than the Haphezians investigating their stolen niobi crystal tech.

"Well done, Niio," he murmured.

Even if she wasn't working for the Mob, and even if she hadn't survived the Niiosians' assault, she and the agents who'd come after her had still divided his focus. If not for them, maybe he would have noticed the security breach. Would have been better prepared to defend Tabaco. Could have even beaten Tobias.

Or maybe not. But he liked having someone to blame.

He was vaguely aware of Tal asking him a question, but he strode away without answering, ready to return planetside and get things moving along. Up until now, he'd insisted on treating the Niiosians and Payvan's betrayal as two separate issues, but maybe that was no longer necessary. The few hours he'd have to wait before his fleet was at full strength—before he could exact his revenge on everyone who'd wronged him—would be some of the longest hours of his life.

CHAPTER 14
NIIOSIAN CRUISER *REVENANT* - BLOOD WATER NEBULA

A change in the air brought Aroska out of a rather fitful sleep. His eyelids fluttered open and he held perfectly still, staring across at the bulkhead as he smelled and listened, trying to determine what was different about the room. Bare feet moved quietly across the thin carpet. His ears picked up a subtle creak in the floor just before the mattress shifted and he sensed the heat of another body behind him. A feeling of contentment preceded realization that morphed into confusion and finally concern. He lifted his head and listened again for a moment before propping himself up on his elbows and turning over.

Ziva lay on the far edge of the bed with her back to him, legs curled slightly, arm folded up under the bunk's other pillow; it was nearly identical to what he'd seen when he'd left her on the couch—he checked the time—a mere hour ago. He was surprised he'd even fallen asleep so quickly.

"You okay?" he asked.

She didn't move. "That sofa is even more uncomfortable than your old one."

"I saw your bed on Panuco. If you can sleep on that, you can sleep on anything." He smirked as realization dawned on him: she had made the choice to come in here, whether she admitted it or not. It certainly seemed like a step in the right direction.

"I, ah...never got much sleep there."

The smirk melted away as he considered what she meant by that. It didn't require any particular observational skills to tell the woman had been exhausted for some time now; the dark circles around her eyes seemed like a permanent new facial feature. Perhaps it had been a matter of sleeping with one eye open for fear of an Ibarra attack, or perhaps she had been plagued with terrible dreams. Neither scenario would have surprised him, given her penchant for hyper-vigilance and the things she'd endured. And the things she'd done.

Regardless, he decided not to press her on the matter right now. "Well, *sheyss*. Here. Make yourself more comfortable." He reached over and snatched up his data pad from where he'd left it lying on the bed-spread before drifting off. Ziva seemed to sense the newly empty space and scooted a bit farther toward the center of the bunk, but she still didn't turn around.

Aroska watched her for another few seconds before settling down on his back and staring up at the ceiling, one arm behind his head. He ran his other hand along the edges of the data pad for a moment. The device contained copies of all the files from his memory stick, files that showcased his ongoing battle to find her over the past four years. He had every intention of showing them to her, but it would have to be at the right moment, and so far, this wasn't it.

He'd spent a while thinking about what she'd said, that nonsense about him not knowing her...except he'd finally decided it wasn't non-sense. She was right. She'd told him the same thing back in the days leading up to the showdown with Ronan and the Resistance, and while the two of them had shared some enlightening moments following that accusation, the four intervening years were more than adequate for things to change. Goals, desires, relationships. Skeet had been totally right in his assessment that neither Ziva nor Aroska were the same per-son they'd been before.

And so, he would be patient. She'd been through so much—the physical, mental, and emotional toll this whole operation had taken on her was unimaginable yet understandable. The best thing he could do right now was give her enough space to figure things out while remaining close enough to offer her the support she needed and hopefully wanted. He was encouraged by what she'd said in the medbay about there not being anyone she'd rather have backing her up; in that sense, it was like nothing had changed. But when it came down to it, it would essentially be a matter of getting reacquainted, then, preferably, getting *more* acquainted.

She'd also been right in that despite everything they'd experienced, they truly hadn't known each other that long. The problem was just that now was kind of a terrible time to be trying to spend quality time together, what with preparing for battle against an arms cartel and dealing with the potential consequences of their efforts to keep her presence under wraps.

Aroska rolled his head across his pillow and studied what he could see of her back in the room's dim light. The muscle definition was outstanding, and the better part of her elaborate tattoo was visible between the straps of her tank. The pattern appeared to be perfectly symmetrical, and though the design was rather severe, it was still somehow...pretty. Elegant. It stretched from shoulder to shoulder and, he knew, curved forward and nearly reached her collarbones. The overall shape was triangular, and based on the angle of the taper, it appeared to stretch about two thirds of the way down her back. He had to restrain himself from reaching over and tracing the swirling design with his finger.

"Have you ever been out to Mairo?"

Her voice startled him. She hadn't moved since getting settled in, and he'd started to wonder if she'd already fallen asleep.

"What?" he said, more confused about where the question had come from than what she'd asked.

"Mairo. Sea of Haphez. In the nearly thirty years I lived on Haphez, I never actually went there. Flew over it dozens of times, but never took the time to stop. Didn't realize that until after I left."

Aroska blinked and looked back up at the ceiling for a moment. "Sure, I've been out there for work a couple of times." He shrugged. "I was actually born there."

"Really?"

The mattress shifted again, and he turned to see Ziva roll over onto her back and shoot him a quizzical look.

"Yeah," he answered. "We moved to Noro before I was even a year old, so I don't have any real memories of it. Going out there for work hasn't given me much time to enjoy the sights, but from what I've seen, it's a beautiful area." It occurred to him that it might be fun to go visit

Mairo together, though it was a terrible time to be thinking about that, too. "What about you? You were born in Noro, right?" He realized he actually had no idea.

She hummed an affirmative. "I was born in that house by the river, for that matter. Lived there until shortly after my father died. I bought it back after I started working for HSP."

Unless it was Aroska's imagination, her voice trembled the slightest bit at the mention of the agency. He was sure it was difficult for her to speak to anyone about her past in general after spending so long keeping it locked away, but the knowledge that nothing would ever be the same was likely eating at her as well. He felt an uneasy knot forming in his own stomach. So much time had passed; the night she'd come to his apartment following the Resistance attack in Noro, she'd grieved for that house and for Marshay and Ryon. Now she could add her role at HSP to the list of things that were no more.

"I'm sorry," he murmured, unsure what else to say. The idea of her losing this thing that had been such a constant in her life broke his heart. "So, you mentioned your father dying...what's the deal with your family?"

She snorted, and he glanced over just in time to catch a glimpse of a disgusted smile before it faded from her lips. He'd asked her the same question after the wild process they'd gone through to stage her death in Haphor while running from Dasaro. "My father was Grand Army, second lieutenant in the marines' ninth platoon. He was killed by Sardons in the Fringe War when I was six. His sacrifice saved the Royal General's life." She paused. "Er...Njo's. I don't even know who the new General is."

"Is that how Njo and your mother met?"

"Yeah. He moved us to Haphor and sort of took us under his wing when the War was over, saying he owed my father a great debt. Before I knew it, he and my mother announced their engagement—when you're that young, you don't really recognize the signs. Then when the twins were born, I ran away back to Noro."

It wasn't much of an explanation, considering he had no idea about anything that had happened between then and when she'd killed

Jak Gamon, garnering HSP's attention. She'd obviously been training and getting some form of an education, and many of the details were probably pretty dull. Based on her tone, however, she didn't want to share anything more with him right now, and he was so accustomed to her remaining distant and reserved that he almost felt guilty about pressing her for information. Quite frankly, he was surprised by how much she'd shared already, but at least they were talking. This was a good sign.

"I guess both of our families are a little messed up, aren't they?" he said.

"Yours is only messed up because of me."

Aroska's first instinct was to deny it, but it struck him that she wasn't entirely wrong. The Tarbics had had their share of typical family problems over the years, sure, but Soren's death and the subsequent turmoil had certainly cultivated further pain and bitterness. As much as he hated the way Ziva always tried to blame herself for everything, that blame might be justified this time.

"Tell me a little about your dad," he said, opting to steer away from that murky topic.

She sighed and remained silent for a moment. "Truth be told, I don't remember a lot at this point. He was away pretty often, especially during the early stages of the War. I do know he was kind. Patient. Selfless. I guess I ended up taking more after my mother on that front."

He couldn't tell if she was making a self-deprecating joke, taking a jab at Namani, or some combination of the two. "The symbol on your tree," he said, recalling the *ETERNAL* carving he'd asked about when he'd found her outside after dealing with Jayden Saiffe and the Tantalis. "He made it, didn't he."

The pillow shifted a bit as she nodded. "We spent a lot of time under that tree in the days leading up to his death—I think he knew there was a high chance he would never come home, and that's why he carved that symbol." She paused, appearing almost amused by whatever thought had just come to mind. "One of my last memories of him was when he was home on liberty just a few days before he died. He took me out and taught me how to shoot."

Aroska chuckled. "At six years old?"

"My mother was furious," Ziva replied. "But you know plasma pistols. Low recoil. Pretty lightweight, even for a kid that small. I loved the feeling of it. The rest is history."

As humorous as it was, the thought sent a sudden chill creeping across Aroska's skin. The image of the innocent little girl squeezing the trigger with all of her might was replaced by one of the ruthless operative she had become. He by no means blamed her father's shooting lessons for that—he'd done plenty of shooting with his brothers as a boy—but she was right: the rest was history. Something inside of her had changed at some point, and whether it was due to her upbringing, her Nosti training, or some other factor, he wasn't sure. There remained a part of her that was unforgivably dark. In the time he'd known her before, she'd been able to keep it relatively under control. But now she'd spent over two years unleashing that darkness as Matia, and he didn't know what the implications of that might be.

At the same time, he'd experienced her particular brand of compassion firsthand. He'd seen what kind of person she could be when she wanted to. She'd even admitted once that she cared, but he knew how she was. It wasn't a normal type of 'caring'—he wasn't sure if it could even accurately be called compassion. Maybe just...principle.

"Well, speaking of shooting, I think we can finally consider us even in terms of shooting each other."

While that was true, it had been harder than expected to deliver the words enthusiastically. This inside joke they'd shared during their previous time being acquainted had lost some of its charm given the circumstances.

"Agreed," Ziva said.

He cleared his throat. "When I went into the Ibarra compound to find Skeet and Zinni, I knew the chances were high that I'd run into you in the process. I still wasn't convinced of whose side you were on, and I found myself contemplating how easily I could shoot you."

"So you could."

She'd said it as a statement rather than a question, and he found he wasn't sure what she meant. He turned and looked at her; she still lay flat on her back, staring up at the ceiling, hands folded across her stomach, legs crossed at the ankles. She seemed to be aware of his con-fusion but made no move to elaborate unprompted.

"What?"

"You'd made the decision that you *could* shoot me, and it would just be a matter of ease."

Once again, it was a statement. He hadn't thought of it in those terms, but he supposed she was right. He'd been in defensive mode at the time, prioritizing his own well-being, followed by Skeet and Zinni's. It was a concept she was no stranger to.

"I don't blame you," she continued matter-of-factly. "You were all operating based on the information you had. I'd portrayed myself as a threat and you reacted accordingly."

"It wasn't just *you* giving us that impression, Ziva. Adler—the informant you killed at the shipping yard—told us about some of the things Matia had done over the last couple of years. *Sheyss*, shooting to wound and then baiting your target? That's not you. That's not how we do things."

She didn't raise her voice, but her retort was no less authoritative. "I couldn't exactly be 'me' now, could I."

"Granted. But to deviate that severely from everything you've known—"

"Who says it was a severe deviation?"

Aroska sighed. Previous experience said so, for one, but if she was going to be difficult about this, he had no desire to argue further. He'd known her to be brutal, but always in an efficient sense. No unnecessary killing, no waste, no missed opportunities. Nevertheless, it took a cer-tain disposition to make someone as good an operator as she'd always been. He still didn't possess that disposition to the extent that most other spec ops agents did; Skeet and Zinni led in that department while he lent the team a more analytical eye. But Ziva had them all beat.

"How old were you when you first killed someone?" The question spilled out of his mouth before he could stop it. All along, he'd had a hunch she'd killed before beginning her career at HSP, even before Jak Gamon. If that was true, it was no wonder the agency had singled her out as a prime spec ops candidate. And if she was as special to him as he thought she was, knowing her—and any of the horrible, unspeakable things that might entail—was essential.

She was quiet for so long he half-expected her to get up and walk out. "Thirteen," she finally said.

Something deep inside him insisted he shouldn't be surprised—what had he expected her to say, if not this? But another part of him was paralyzed by some combination of fear, regret, and general discomfort. It was empathy for Ziva, remorse for broaching the topic. But it was also on an internal level. Lying there so close to her, but knowing what she'd had to do, what she was capable of...regardless of how long ago it had been, it was disconcerting.

Judging by her tone of voice, she felt just as uncomfortable telling him as he did listening to her. "I was getting ready to forge my kytara blades. Got careless while looking for scrap metal in an alley. This old homeless man witnessed me use my Nostia to lift a piece, and...." She turned her head to look at him. "You probably don't want to hear the rest."

No, he didn't. For one, he didn't need to hear her confess to a murder, one that could very well still be a cold case buried deep in HSP's archives. Secondly, the mental image was slowly wrenching his stomach into a fresh knot. He'd had to kill a number of people over the years—almost all of them, he realized, during his stint in spec ops—and she obviously had, too. But this was different. It was something she'd probably tried hard to forget, and something he was sorry for bringing up.

At the same time, her tale had sparked a thought. "How did you get me out of those tunnels in Tabaco? The last thing I remember is getting completely buried by rubble."

"If you're asking in this context, I assume you have a pretty good idea."

Just as he'd suspected, then—she'd once again conjured her Nostia in order to save his life. "I wouldn't have thought you could do that after all this time."

"I wasn't sure if I could, either. But it was the only option."

Her gaze drifted to the data pad that still rested on his chest. After a few seconds of silence, he felt a faint vibration ripple through his shirt and across his skin, followed by some resistance as the pad tried to slide out from beneath his hand. He released it and watched as Ziva used her mind to lift it up, allowing it to teeter on one corner against his sternum. A nervous tingle shot through his body at the thought of her seeing its contents before he was ready, but when he realized she was trembling and turned to see the tendons in her neck straining, his concern shifted to her and her alone.

"Hmm," she said suddenly, yanking her hand up to her nose. The data pad fell harmlessly onto his stomach. She lay still for a moment, and when she pulled her hand away, her fingers were bloody.

"There you have it," she muttered, rising from the bed and disappearing into the lavatory.

Aroska waited in complete silence until she returned, stricken by what a sacrifice she'd made to rescue him, even after he'd shot Blain. It was a prime example of the way she never stopped fighting, of the way she clawed and scraped her way through the most desperate situations. How she could continue functioning like that was beyond him. He tossed the data pad into his backpack on the floor and listened as she lay back down, sniffling a couple of times and heaving a sigh before settling.

Once upon a time, he'd had his fair share of baggage, but he'd never known anyone who had as many mental and emotional scars as she did. At this point, the metaphorical scar tissue had grown so thick and calloused—scars upon scars upon scars—that he couldn't say whether it would ever heal completely.

The thought drew his attention to her physical scars. The treatment Serenity subjected her to had helped clear up some of the newer ones he'd first noticed during their confrontation in the Tabaco alley, but he knew she had no shortage of others. His gaze drifted down to her stomach, where a bit of bare skin was visible above her waistband and below the hem of her tank. Somehow it was just as shocking to see the scarring there as it had been when he'd caught his first glimpse of it in Kat's garage on Chaiavis. Without even meaning to, he reached out to touch her. The instant his fingertips contacted her flesh, her hand shot out, taking hold of his wrist with a vice-like grip. Startled, he shifted his attention up to meet her steely gaze.

She didn't release him, but he did feel her relax, albeit slowly. Her features softened a bit, and unless it was his imagination, she genuinely hadn't meant to react in such a way. It was merely a reflex, a conditioned response to physical contact that was a byproduct of her violent lifestyle.

"Will you let me see your scars?" he asked, lowering his voice by way of apology.

For several seconds, she only stared at him. Then she flung his hand away with a quiet huff, tugged the tank hem down, and returned her focus to the ceiling. "You've seen them, if I recall," she muttered.

He started to argue but clamped his mouth shut before he could say anything that made matters worse. *I just want to know you*, he thought, though he had to admit he was surprised by how much new information he'd learned about her already. "I don't care what they look like."

She rolled over, turning her back to him. "I don't care what they look like, either. Appearance is beside the point." Her tone told him the conversation was on the verge of collapse.

Aroska sighed and turned to face her, fixating once more on the swirling design of her tattoo as he worked to curb his frustration. "They're part of who you are. They may be a harsh reminder of where you've been and what you've endured, but they also show how strong you are. What you're capable of."

"*Sheyss*, Aroska. Enough with the therapy session."

"I'm just saying."

Ziva propped herself up on one elbow far enough to turn and send him an unimpressed look. "No, you're doing that *thing* again where you try to paint me in some sort of heroic light. I've told you before, I'm—"

"—not a hero, just a problem solver," he finished for her, "and you don't classify yourself as good or evil because right and wrong are often relative to the work you're doing. I know." He propped himself up as well and met her gaze in hopes of assuring her he wasn't being sarcastic. "I really do."

Her eyes narrowed.

"I'm saying you've somehow managed to take all these horrible things that have happened to you, and you've turned them into some sort of armor. You don't let them become shackles...the way I used to."

He shook his head. "I've always envied that about you, and I'm finally understanding everything you once tried to explain to me. All along—even as Matia, maybe *especially* as Matia—you've been using your tragedies to your advantage. You've figured out how to survive."

It was hard to tell if she was taking any comfort in his words or if she just thought he was insane. But then one corner of her mouth curled upward, a good sign. "Problem solver," she said, tapping a finger against her temple before turning away from him again.

He breathed a quiet sigh of relief and settled back down as well, glad the situation had been somewhat salvaged. Here he'd been contemplating all the reasons he needed to be patient with her, and now he was on the verge of getting defensive when she didn't respond the way he hoped. Baby steps.

His eyes were once again drawn to that gorgeous tat, and without even thinking about it, he reached out and brushed a knuckle along one of the curving lines. He started to yank his hand away when he felt her bristle in response to the touch, but then she relaxed just as quickly, and he cautiously resumed his tracing.

"When did you get this?" he asked.

She rolled over onto her back, prompting him to withdraw, and hummed in thought for a moment. "Just a few weeks after graduating from the spec ops track. All three of us got one. They'd suggested some basic bonding exercises for all the new teams, but this was Skeet's idea. I ran with it."

Aroska visualized the designs on Skeet's shoulder and forearm. Over the years, he'd also caught glimpses of a large tat on Zinni's right side that stretched from her ribs down to her hip. All the designs bore similarities to Ziva's now that he thought about it. "I suddenly feel left out," he chuckled.

"I never imagined getting matching ink with anyone, but I figured it couldn't hurt to have a little fun together to get us started."

He snorted, drawing another irritated glance from her. "I'm not sure if I've ever heard the word 'fun' out of your mouth."

That elicited a full scowl. "You think I'm not capable of having fun?"

To be fair, her definition of fun probably differed from his. She was the type of person who considered painting faces on melons and shooting them from progressively farther distances a leisure activity. It wasn't that he didn't enjoy that sort of thing too, but a squad of green HSP ops recruits getting matching tattoos was a different matter entirely.

"Well, you haven't done much to convince me otherwise."

"Try me."

He couldn't help but crack a smile as he stretched out and folded his hands behind his head. "We'll see."

The fact that she seemed to be taking offense at his comment when she herself had once chastised him for joking around on the job was legitimately humorous. Surely she had to realize how cold and dry her outward persona was. The thought occurred to him that, whether intentionally or not, she was simply reinforcing the fact that he didn't really know her, not completely. Maybe she did have a sense of humor.

He lay there just long enough to allow the silence to become awkward. "Oh hey, did you hear anything about that weird sinkhole that suddenly appeared in the middle of the HSP campus about three years ago?"

She flipped over and sat halfway up as though ready to leap out of bed and investigate. "No," she answered, her features twisted with concern. "Did it have to do with the wreck of the *Vigilance*? How big?"

"Wasn't anywhere near the crash site," Aroska answered. "And it wasn't large. Just a deep, perfectly round hole. Agents were looking into it."

He smirked and tried not to look at her as he waited for a reaction. It took a second, but the shift in her expression from earnestness to annoyance was so obvious he could see it even in his peripheral vision. He wondered briefly if she might hit him, but she merely flopped back down, folded her arms across her chest, and sighed.

"Damn you."

He stifled a chuckle. Even after the discussion just moments before, it was as if she'd been ready to fly to Noro, purge the area of any potential danger, and solve the mystery herself. Her past experiences had taught her to always expect the worst, apparently even in as casual an environment as this. "So far you're not making a very good case for yourself."

"Yeah, well, you can do better than that."

"Okay, fine. Here's something that actually happened. Back in my field ops days, we crossed our fair share of interesting characters. Whenever something exceptionally outrageous happened, Jole always managed to make some terrible play on it." He couldn't help but laugh a bit at the mere memory of the scene. "We were working this one case where we'd sent an informant into a bar to meet with a contact. Our guy was just supposed to be friendly, do a little schmoozing, get the contact to give him some information we could use for our case. We had him bugged, so we could hear every word.

"Anyway, they went on and on and were doing more drinking and bantering than anything else. They ended up getting totally wasted, and a full-blown fight broke out over—I kid you not—which one of them was going to pay for the drinks. By the time we got inside to intervene, the contact was gone, and our guy had been thrown over the counter into the display cases. Found him lying there covered in broken glass and soaked in spilled liquor. As Jole observed, drinks were on him."

This time he risked a glance at Ziva and was pleased to find a hint of a smile on her face. *There we go.*

She nodded her approval. "We've pulled a stunt or two in spec ops, but I'll bet you've got some crazy field ops stories."

"Oh, five moons, I do. In spec ops, you reminisce about insane missions on quiet nights because you're happy to be alive. Field ops missions tend to be the ones you joke about while consuming alcohol—" he paused and considered it for a moment "—also some-times because you're happy to be alive."

"Sounds like you've got something specific in mind."

"We were doing a joint operation with one of the field ops chem control teams, working to bust a drug ring developing this crazy experi-mental upper that had been frying people's brains. The chem agents found the lab but encountered what they called 'heavy resistance,' so my team got called in. When we arrived on the scene, the lab was empty, but two of the drug runners were still there. These guys were totally out of their minds. Frenzied. Delirious. They were incoherent, unarmed but ready to bite and claw us apart. Correspondence we recovered later revealed that they'd volunteered to stay behind, shoot themselves up, and run interference for any law enforcement that showed up while the rest of the crew escaped."

"You have to take them out?"

He nodded. "It was a disturbing scene for sure. I fired a concussive round at one of them, center of mass. Tore him open and knocked him on his ass. That *huhren shouka souhn* was so jacked that he got right back up and came at us again. I'm sure he would have bled out in just a few minutes, but a clean headshot took care of that." He grimaced and forced a disgusted snort. "I mean, the guy reached into the hole I'd blown through his torso and started throwing his own intestines at us. All of that just to make sure the rest of their people got away."

"That took guts."

It took him a split second to process what she'd said, and when he glanced over at her, she was already looking his way, one eyebrow raised, a totally foreign glimmer in her crimson eyes. Despite the unsettling nature of the topic, when he realized what she'd just done, he couldn't help but burst out laughing.

"*Sheyss*, that was terrible," she muttered, shaking her head. A soft but undoubtedly genuine chuckle escaped her own throat, unlike anything he'd ever heard from her.

Some combination of the simplicity and morbidity of the line—as well as the fact that it had come out of Ziva Payvan's mouth, of all things—had made the statement particularly comical. "It was pretty bad," he sputtered, trying in vain to quell a fresh bout of laughter.

For the next several seconds, the only sounds in the room were her amused chuckles and his heavy breathing as he tried to calm himself. If only for a short time, everything else had melted away. Soren's death, Ziva's revelation of her Nostia, her disappearance, the hunt for Matia Moryi, the conflict between Niio and Ibarra. All forgotten. Despite everything they'd both endured, all that remained was this moment, where two...special friends...shared a laugh over something stupid. Aroska couldn't help but wonder when—if ever—the last time was that Ziva had been relaxed enough to laugh like this about anything, with anyone. Frankly, with as high as the stakes still were everywhere outside this room, he was surprised she was even comfortable enough right now.

She cleared her throat, and when she spoke, her voice was as dry and humorless as ever. "I should clarify that I by no means find the throwing of entrails funny."

He looked over and found her face completely deadpan, as if she were actually concerned he would think such a thing of her. The thought elicited another fit of laughter.

She scowled and shook her head again, though that smirk returned as she did so. "Stop it," she said, socking him in the shoulder.

Part of him didn't want to, and part of him legitimately couldn't. Even the good-natured hit was somewhat painful, but it only made him laugh harder. Her terrible pun replayed in his head and got him started all over again.

"Shut up!" she ordered. She was still smiling, but the elbow she drove into his chest immediately had him clutching his still-fragile ribs as they shuddered under the impact. He tried to relax, hoping his reaction hadn't been as severe as it had felt, but based on the way Ziva immediately sobered in concern, the recovery hadn't been fast enough. The pain was minimal compared to what it had been before—the blow was more startling than anything—but damn, the woman packed a punch even when playing.

"Sorry," she murmured, averting her gaze. "Sorry." She lay still for a moment, staring up at the ceiling in silence before rolling away from him once more. "Goodnight, Aroska."

Despite the ache in his torso and the awkward, anticlimactic end to the conversation, a deep calm settled over him as he contemplated everything that had just occurred. As much as he wanted to keep the positive interaction going, they did both truly need to rest; it was why they'd been sent up here, after all. But this had been a good start to what was bound to be a lengthy journey for the two of them.

"Goodnight," he answered. He rolled over with his back to her, content to merely be occupying the same space, confident the healing had begun.

CHAPTER 15
SABER - STERRO SYSTEM, FRINGE SPACE

Zinni caught a whiff of human body odor seconds before she spotted Ken's reflection in the *Saber's* front viewport, but if not for these things, she wouldn't have known he was there. The man didn't make a sound. It was certainly a testament to his skill as an operative, and while she was glad to have him on the team when they were short a body—two bodies, she supposed, if Ziva counted—the fact that he continued to act this way even after they'd been traveling together for nearly twelve hours was a bit unsettling. Whether he had a legitimate reason to be sneaking, was merely trying to keep them on edge by showcasing his prowess, or was so accustomed to moving that way that he didn't even realize he was doing it, she didn't know. Regardless, the behavior was doing nothing to nurture the working relationship the three of them were supposed to be forming.

She lounged in the pilot's seat, feet kicked up on the control board, twisting a gel-like toy ball in one hand. "You catch some sleep?" she said without turning around, not about to allow him the satisfaction of thinking he'd snuck up on her.

"I did," Ken replied, his voice as smooth and calm as ever. He lingered against the cockpit's back wall for another couple of seconds before moving up and leaning against the co-pilot's chair, staring out at the swirling silver FTL tunnel as the ship surged forward. "Are you ready to go? There might be time for another few minutes of shut-eye while we make our approach. I can bring us in if you'd like—I know you're probably exhausted."

"I'm good," Zinni said, making a conscious effort to not stop and clench the gel ball in her fist. She truthfully was still feeling drained, both due to the excitement they'd been through on Panuco and the emotional turmoil that followed, but approximately thirty seconds after departing the *Revenant*, she and Skeet had unanimously decided one or the other of them would stay up with Ken at all times. The simple fact that he worked for Tobias Niio was adequate to make them both leery. She'd hit the bunks first, grabbing about five hours of fairly rejuvenating sleep before trading off with Skeet. He was still resting but would no doubt be up to the cockpit shortly. Ken had disappeared in the direction of the dormitory a couple of hours ago; Zinni was glad to know he seemed to be feeling refreshed as well, though she wagered a guess he'd been better rested than the two of them from the start.

Rather than press her further, he swiveled the co-pilot's chair around and took a seat, crossing one leg over the other as he turned in a slow circle and admired his surroundings. "I was telling Agent Duvo what an extraordinary vessel this is. Well-suited for this mission. Your team stumbled onto the scene at an opportune time—I consider us lucky you're here."

By 'us,' Zinni assumed he was referring to the Mob. "At least someone does," she muttered. After Ziva had continually berated them for coming to Panuco and after the less than cordial welcome aboard the *Revenant*, it was hard to believe anyone was glad to have them around.

Ken remained silent for a moment. "It's true that your arrival complicated matters," he said with a sigh, "but what I said before still goes: there's nothing we can do to change what happened and we simply must play this hand we've been dealt. But you, your ship, your resources, your intel—these things all represent a new card we weren't expecting to play, and I believe it could be a game-winning factor."

Leave it to a Niiosian Mob enforcer to talk about this whole situation in terms of gambling. It was tempting to tell him this wasn't their fight and that they had no intention whatsoever of assisting the Mob any further in their struggle against Ibarra after this, but Zinni had a strong suspicion they'd end up involved for the long haul. If they walked out after recovering Starcer's specs, Ziva would be left fending for herself, caught in a battle between two power-hungry galactic criminals who'd both tried to use her as a piece in their respective games. Normally Zinni would have every confidence she could handle herself, but after seeing firsthand how damaged the woman was after her ordeal with the Cartel—*and* the Mob, for that matter—the last thing she wanted to do was abandon her out here. She was certain Aroska felt the same, and at this point Skeet might, too.

"So you were Ziva's handler during her time undercover."

"I was," Ken answered. "It began with me feeding her intel about—" he hesitated "—an...assassin...whom Manes was using to perform surgical strikes against Niio."

Ah, that must have been the brother Ziva mentioned.

"Then, since the aim was to have her assume that position once she was accepted into Ibarra ranks, I ended up taking on the role of handler, drawing on all my previous knowledge of the Cartel to help her acclimate as seamlessly as possible...and keep her from damaging Niiosian assets to the extent that the whole operation became counterproductive."

"But you'd never officially met before the *Revenant.*"

"Not face-to-face, no. For the most part, communications were encrypted and relayed to the *Talon* through deep space comm buoys while she was out on missions for Manes, which, fortunately, were frequent. If she was planetside in Ibarra territory, comms were even riskier and often consisted of short, coded bursts that would have looked like noise to anyone unfamiliar with our methods. Sometimes a message would only consist of a single character or digit."

"Clever."

"Agent Payvan is an impressive individual. She is admittedly not what I was expecting, and simultaneously exactly what I was expecting. The way she conducted herself throughout this endeavor required a level of cunning, intelligence, and, frankly, ferocity many operators never live up to. It has been fascinating to get a look inside her mind for the past few years, and then finally be able to put a face to that mind, so to speak."

The way he talked about Ziva reminded Zinni a great deal of the way Ziva had often spoken about targets and assets back in the day. It was exactly what had happened with Aroska, after all. The very nature of her work required a degree of thoroughness and diligence that often resulted in the formation of deep connections with those whom that work brought her closest to, even if those connections were soon severed as she eliminated a target. With Aroska, that bond had only strengthened the longer the two of them were involved with one another. Now it seemed Ken was experiencing a similar phenomenon, having formed some level of connection with this person he'd looked out for—though from a great distance—during an assuredly trying time.

She allowed some of the tension in her shoulders to release and returned her attention to the front viewport, twisting the ball between her fingers. "It's damn good to see her, especially considering we weren't one hundred percent convinced she was alive." She hesitated a moment, not sure it would be proper to place any of the blame for Ziva's current mental state on the Niiosian Mob during this conversation, regardless of how much she wanted to. "She's always been reclusive and aloof—it's part of what made her such a great agent. But the way she's been since we found her…"

This time, she allowed herself to trail off completely, unwilling to divulge her true thoughts to this stranger. The past couple of years couldn't have been easy for Ziva, but in some ways, it was like she wasn't quite Ziva anymore. At least not the Ziva Zinni remembered.

"People change, Agent Vax, especially in high-pressure situations," he said, telling her he got the gist of her thought process. "Agent Payvan has had to adapt in many ways to fulfill her mission. To survive. I've seen that better than anyone. Consider that you might have missed out."

Zinni's eyes narrowed. She looked toward him and found him already pointedly meeting her gaze. Yes, it *was* possible that Ziva had changed, and she'd certainly needed to go to some extreme lengths to maintain her cover, but she'd also clearly drawn on her past skills in order to create that cover, and she still cared about her teammates. Her friends. She was still herself, maybe just trapped behind a wall constructed by her false identity.

"Don't you dare pretend you know her better than we do," Zinni said, pulling her feet down from the control board and swiveling to face him. "You didn't spend ten years by her side, watching her back while she watched yours, pulling her ass out of the fire while she did the same for you. Yes, she's an enigma, but the relationship required to even remotely begin to understand her takes years to cultivate. Don't think you've reached that level." *Or ever will.*

Ken watched her, unblinking and unfazed. Something about his demeanor felt colder than it had a moment ago. "Well, perhaps we can agree that we simply know different versions of the same person."

Two could play that game. Zinni matched his stare with her own icy blue eyes. "Perhaps," she muttered.

She turned away from him when she heard footsteps coming up the corridor; no need to get Skeet involved in a conversation that was guaranteed to set everyone on edge for the remainder of this mission. They had almost reached Delatori airspace anyway, and it was time to focus on the approach.

He strode into the cockpit. "ETA?"

She glanced at the nav computer. "Six minutes."

Against the silvery backdrop of the FTL tunnel, she could see his reflection studying her for a moment. He'd known her long enough that he could detect even the slightest hint of agitation in her voice, regardless of whether she herself realized it was there.

He turned his attention to Ken. "We anticipating any airborne resistance?"

"According to the most recent intel provided by Agent Payvan, Ibarra has employed a limited number of surface-to-air installations and utilizes a few airborne drone patrols in higher-traffic areas planetside. The only space-faring presence we need to look out for is their transport fleet that's been responsible for moving resources between Delatori and Panuco. Their schedule is sporadic, as they've been having difficulty recovering some of the most prized materials, so there's no way to predict where the fleet will be. But with luck, it's somewhere between here and Panuco right now."

Skeet grunted in apparent agreement and tapped the back of Zinni's seat. "Bring us out of FTL early. Let's be sure we get a good look around before making our final approach."

"You got it," she replied, returning her focus to the nav computer and adjusting the parameters. The location they'd originally chosen as their drop point was already a reasonable distance from Delatori. First and foremost, it was a stealth measure; even though the *Saber* had a nearly nonexistent emissions signature, jumping out of FTL too close to the planet would create a ripple that might show up on a scanner somewhere. Secondly, Delatori was surrounded by a pair of narrow rings composed of large rocks, some bigger than the ship. The last thing they needed was to come all this way and get pulverized upon leaving FTL in the middle of what was virtually an asteroid field.

"Cutting in sub-light engines," Zinni announced, easing a lever on the control board back. "In three, two, one..."

The swirling silver outside the viewport faded as the *Saber* exited the travel lane and the space around them solidified. All three of them sat in silence as the ship drifted forward, scouring the black expanse as they might if they were carrying out a mission on the ground. Delatori lay far ahead, the outermost of four rugged terrestrial planets in the Sterro system. Through the glare of the distant sun, the planetary rings were barely discernible.

"Confirming stealth drive is engaged," Zinni said, guiding them forward. "Scans are clear. Approach is green." *For now.*

"Based on the proposed landing coordinates, we're on the wrong side," Ken pointed out.

"Complete our approach and bring us into low orbit," Skeet suggested. "We'll do some aerial recon as we go."

They once again fell silent, eyes peeled as if they might somehow spot any signs of danger before the ship's scanners did. Delatori loomed progressively larger in the viewport, its surface a mesh of dark green and brown, all enveloped by cold white clouds. It reminded Zinni a great deal of the upper latitudes on Haphez, away from all the cities and the Tranyi River, where the forests were so thick they looked like carpet covering the planet. If Delatori was so rich on the surface, it didn't surprise her at all that so many valuable resources lay beneath its soil.

Another ten minutes brought them to the edge of the largest ring. She took hold of the controls, marveling at just how big some of the rocks were as she prepared to maneuver the ship underneath, but a blip on the scanner caught her attention.

"What do we have?" she asked, not prepared to take her eyes off the precarious flight path in front of her.

"Contact at thirty degrees starboard," Ken replied.

Zinni brought the *Saber* down to glide along just beneath the ring and pointed the ship in the direction he had indicated. She could see nothing, but that was unsurprising given the quite literal billions of rocks in her field of vision.

The scanner beeped twice more, then several more times in such quick succession it was difficult to tell how many signatures it had picked up. "*Multiple* contacts," Ken corrected. "I count ten...twelve... thirteen. Same vector."

Another moment of drifting and Zinni thought she caught a glimpse of one of the unidentified ships in the distance. She set the *Saber* on a stable course and slowed a bit, then took a look at the scanner herself. "Is this our transport fleet?"

"Could very well be."

Skeet scoffed. "And they're on the orbital path we want. Headed this way?"

A couple of seconds of studying the screen confirmed that was the case. "Mmhmm."

He cursed under his breath. "Let it play. Stay on course."

She shook her head but didn't deviate. The *Saber* may have been hidden from these ships' instruments, but that wouldn't stop anyone from seeing it with their naked eye. If they broke away from the cover of the planetary ring, there was a high chance of being spotted. This was a fast vessel, and they shouldn't have any trouble outrunning these unfamiliar ships if needed, but that would in turn require disengaging the stealth drive and burning on full power, which virtually guaranteed they'd be seen. Even if they turned and fled in the opposite direction around the planet, these ships—whoever they were—would surely know they'd been there.

Zinni eased the *Saber* up closer to the underside of the ring, grateful the ship's matte gray exterior was similar in color to many of the larger chunks of rock. The unidentified vessels continued forward on their same trajectory, neither hurrying nor slowing down. In fact, if they were following an orbital path as Skeet had suggested, it meant they weren't going anywhere in particular.

"Cut power," Ken exclaimed suddenly.

'Exclaimed' was merely relative to his normal speaking tone; he'd barely raised his voice, but he spoke with the same authority he'd used while addressing Tobias on the *Revenant's* bridge. Zinni complied without question, bristling in response to whatever unknown danger had prompted his reaction.

The cockpit was pitched into darkness, and the hum of the ship's engines winding down faded until it was so deathly silent she could hear her own heartbeat. No sooner had all of that occurred than a pair of fighter craft came ripping by on the far side of the ring, heading straight toward the small fleet. If Ken hadn't spotted them when he had, they no doubt would have seen the residual light emitted from the *Saber's* thrusters. There was truthfully no guarantee they *hadn't*, and the three of them watched with bated breath as the two fighters continued by, separated from them by a mere couple kilometers of rocks and dust particles. They must have been stealthed as well, or the scanner would have picked them up.

For a while, Zinni couldn't tell for sure whether the little craft posed a threat to the fleet or were joining up with it, but when the larger ships showed no reaction to their presence, she concluded it was the latter. They took a couple of laps around the group before falling into place within it, and the whole procession continued forward toward the *Saber's* hiding place.

As they drew nearer, she reached up and entered a command on the control board, leaving the engines shut down but allowing enough auxiliary power to boot up the ship's targeting systems. Taking a shot at any of these vessels was out of the question, and floating there as though they were simply part of the ring, there wasn't a clear shot to take anyway. But the HUD would allow them to take a closer look at the other ships without moving from their current position, and regardless of whether this was the transport fleet, its presence here was significant. The more data they could gather, the better.

With reconnaissance mode engaged, the holographic targeting reticle slid across the viewport, directing the *Saber's* array of front cams toward the ships. On a separate display projected from the control panel, a series of magnified snapshots flashed by as the computer worked to create composite images of each vessel, cobbled together from glimpses between rocks. None of the ships bore any distinctive features or corporate logos; this fleet of thirteen—fifteen, counting the fighters—consisted of ten mid-sized freighters and three small gun-ships, no doubt a security escort.

Ken studied the images with furrowed brows. "They're definitely Ibarra," he said quietly, as though even the slightest sound would somehow be heard through the vacuum of space. "But this looks to be a holding pattern. They're not going anywhere."

Skeet's voice was just as soft as he responded. "If they've got security, they must be hauling. Even if their Panuco base was destroyed, you'd think they'd want to be taking their payload *somewhere*."

"Agreed. Something isn't right."

"Tag all of these ships, including the fighters, if possible," Skeet instructed, touching Zinni on the shoulder. "We'll continue tracking them while we're planetside, and we'll report their locations once we've reached the LZ and established comms with the *Revenant*."

"Done," Zinni said, flagging the signatures for all the vessels visible on the scanner. The two fighters were nowhere to be seen on the screen, but that hardly mattered; they'd be a moot point once the full force of the Niiosian armada arrived here.

All there was to do now was wait. The *Saber* floated in a lazy circle, bumping into nearby rocks and invisible to anyone who wasn't looking closely. Or so she hoped. Her eyes darted back and forth, searching what felt like every square centimeter outside the viewport for any movement akin to the fighters that had nearly managed to sneak up on them. Judging by the silence and tension within the cockpit, Skeet and Ken were doing the same. With each painfully slow rotation of the ship, the little fleet made painfully slow progress forward until it was finally out of visual range. Still, they sat and watched until all but a couple of the thirteen visible signatures had disappeared from the scanner.

Then, to the untrained eye, it would have looked like one of the larger rocks from Delatori's innermost ring suddenly detached itself from the gravity field and began traversing around the planet. But rocks didn't have thrusters or stealth drives. A faint blue light glowed from its tail end as it descended, descended, descended, eventually disappearing amid the wispy clouds over one of the dense green forests below.

Chapter 16
Niiosian Cruiser *Revenant* - Blood Water Nebula

The creak of the floor and scrape of a door opening manually both sounded so real they couldn't possibly be part of her dream. Her mind managed to form two words in response: *He's coming.* She couldn't pinpoint exactly what that meant. She was lying in her cell in the Ibarra prison block, listening to these sounds that always preceded the arrival of someone important. Someone she was expecting. Someone dangerous. But her surroundings smelled fresh, familiar, and thus *un*familiar. This was wrong. She wasn't supposed to be here.

He's coming. The silent approach of her visitor was also different. Wrong. She heard no squeal of hinges and no clang of metal. *Danger, danger!*

A certain buried instinct allowed her to awaken, but she kept her eyes closed and remained motionless. The soft sounds hadn't stopped, and she could sense movement somewhere behind her. She was lying on a bed, much cleaner and more comfortable than the one from her apartment, and a far cry from the rough stone floor of her cell. The fresh smell of the room was the same as it had been in her dream, but she didn't understand how it was possible. She couldn't remember how she had gotten there.

He's coming, her foggy brain reminded her again. She lay on her side in a semi-fetal position, and all she could tell was that the intruder was still somewhere behind her. Her eyelids parted slightly. The room was dim—the light source was behind her as well—and she saw a shadow rising up on the wall on the other side of the bed.

The feeling of a knee coming to rest on the mattress jarred her fully awake. She flipped onto her back and grabbed the arm that was reaching for her, yanking it downward. Kicking her legs up, she pinned the man's chest between her calves and threw him face-down onto the bed, using his forward momentum to haul herself into an upright position the same way she'd done with all the other soldiers who came to torment her. In one fluid motion that was so ingrained in her mind it hardly felt like her own, she wrenched his arm behind his back and reached for his holster with her free hand, drawing the gun she'd subconsciously made note of when she'd first seen the shadow. So much more efficient than the stun baton. *Thanks for making my job easier.* She pressed the barrel to the back of his head. Her finger settled against the trigger.

Only then did she notice the way he wasn't struggling, and only *then* did she notice the amber stripe running through his black hair. Her eyes widened and she drew in a sharp breath.

"Ziva, it's me," he said, the words partially muffled by the bed-spread into which his head was mashed. Even with most of his face obscured, she could tell his features were contorted with worry.

She rolled off him and came to rest on the opposite edge of the bunk, lowering her head into her hands as she listened to her own pulse hammering in her ears. *What is wrong with you?* she wanted to scream. She gritted her teeth and squeezed her eyes shut, fighting the tremor in her breathing. *You're aboard Tobias's ship. You're aboard Tobias's ship.*

Aroska was moving around somewhere behind her, and she felt the mattress shift just before one of his hands came to rest on her shoulder. With the other, he reached around and took his sidearm back from her; she hadn't even realized she was still holding it, resting her forehead against the cool metal casing.

Once the weapon was secure, he began to massage her shoulders and the back of her neck. She was sure he was just trying to comfort her, but his touch stung. Burned. Cut deep.

"Who did you think it was?" he asked quietly. His fingers trembled ever so slightly as he encountered the remains of one of her newer scars.

I don't know, Ziva thought, unable to force the words from her throat.

"What did you think was going to happen?"

She was almost certain she knew what he was thinking, and she doubted he'd believe her answer even if she spoke it aloud. *I don't know.*

The ferocity of his massaging increased for a moment. He was angry, maybe at her for refusing to answer, maybe at whatever imaginary figure could be making her feel so afraid she was unable to explain herself to him. Or maybe because she'd almost blown his head off.

"Talk to me," he said, leaning closer. "Please."

You're aboard the Revenant. *You were resting in Ken Oda's cabin.* Even with confirmation that she was safe, her brain was still in full self-preservation mode, insisting she either fight or flee. Fighting was out of the question, though her muscles were wound so tight she feared they would act of their own accord if she didn't remove herself from the situation fast. She didn't particularly want to run from Aroska, which left only one option.

"Get out," she muttered, her hands still obscuring her face.

The massaging came to an immediate halt, and he sat in silence for a moment before sliding off the bed and kneeling in front of her. "Ziva, listen to me," he said, taking her hands in his and leaving her with no choice but to look at him. "You—"

She stood abruptly, forcing him to rise with her, and yanked her hands from his grasp. "Get. Out," she repeated through clenched teeth. Despite the fact that their faces were mere centimeters apart, she could barely see him past the wall of hot tears welling up in her eyes.

When he made no move to comply, she brushed past him and skirted around the end of the bed, shying away when she sensed him reach for her arm. *Escape. Remove yourself.*

"Ziva—"

She sprinted the last couple of strides to the lavatory and shut and locked the door before he could catch up. She heard him pound a fist against the wall outside, but he said nothing more.

The relative peace and stillness in the tiny lav rendered her own thoughts extra loud inside her head. Realistically, that was no better than staying outside, but at least in here she couldn't *accidentally kill anybody* who got too close to her. The tears broke free from her eyes, clearing her vision a bit, and she looked down at her trembling hands. *What the hell is wrong with you?*

Feeling as though her legs were about to collapse beneath her, she staggered into the shower stall, turned on a lukewarm stream of water, and sagged to the floor with her head in her hands, not caring that her clothes and hair were soaked in seconds. The scene replayed in her mind, faster and more intense each time, and with each repetition, her body shook more violently. She couldn't understand how she'd managed to get through the entire routine she'd always used to bring down her prison attackers before realizing who Aroska was. Was her mind simply *that* fractured? Did she truly have that much trouble differentiating between imagination and reality? As she stared down at the shower floor, it felt as though cracks were crisscrossing through her vision, just like what she'd seen while looking at her reflection in the shards of the mirror she'd shot in her Tabaco apartment. Yet another example of lashing out against an imaginary enemy.

Over and over, she saw herself press the barrel of the gun to the back of Aroska's head, positive she could smell the gore and brain matter that would've resulted had she followed through. She couldn't identify what precisely had caused her to hesitate, but whatever it was, it was all that had saved him. She'd been so poised to act that she might have pulled the trigger if someone had merely bumped her. The thought made her want to chop off her own hands. Douse them in acid. Cripple them somehow before they could cause any more damage. She pulled them away from her face as the tears began to flow freely.

She was not a person who cried. It took a certain mental and emotional constitution to do the work she'd always done, for HSP and otherwise. A few tears had been shed over the past few years, but the last time she could remember legitimately crying was the night she'd gone to Aroska's apartment following the Resistance's attack on Noro and the two of them had mourned everything they'd each lost throughout the day.

That had been weeping at best. Whatever was starting to happen now went far beyond that. She couldn't breathe, couldn't stop shaking. The feeling of the deep sobs wracking her body was so foreign it was terrifying, which only made them worse.

But the *most* terrifying part was that things had been fine—relatively speaking—since coming aboard the *Revenant*. Things had been 'fine' on Panuco for the last several days as well. She'd made conscious decisions about deceiving Manes and saving her team, and she'd even tried to defend herself when they accused her of dissociating. She'd thought she was doing okay. And after all of that, they'd been right. How were they supposed to trust her when she couldn't predict her own actions? It was one thing to shoot a mirror and storm around her apartment because she thought someone was there, but it was a different matter entirely to come within a hair's breadth of murdering a man she'd grown so close to. Once upon a time, she'd pushed him away to protect him from the misery and hardship that constituted much of her life. That was all futile now that he was a full-fledged member of her old team. Now, it seemed *she* represented the most direct threat to him.

She was out of control.

"I almost killed you," she cried in the general direction of the lavatory door, not sure and not caring whether he was even within earshot anymore.

She slid further to the floor, letting the sobs overtake her and wishing the hot tears and shower water would simply drown her.

Chapter 17
NIIOSIAN CRUISER *REVENANT* · BLOOD WATER NEBULA

Aroska stood motionless outside the lavatory, fist resting against the wall, forehead resting against the locked door. He closed his eyes; just on the other side of this slab of metal, he could hear Ziva's labored breathing as she tried not to cry. He couldn't understand why she didn't just let herself do it—he was fighting to keep tears from making an appearance himself.

But part of him was angry, and part of him was afraid. His heart had yet to stop racing after what had just happened. It had taken a moment to fully process how close she'd come to killing him, how long it had taken her to even recognize him. Her reaction to his presence had felt learned, practiced, as though she had repeated that same disarming routine over and over during her time on Panuco. That meant something had happened to her over and over that required her to defend herself. The thought made him seethe.

He turned around and leaned against the door, listening as Ziva crossed the little room and turned on the shower. In the moment, the thought hadn't occurred to him to defend himself because he'd never expected her to go so far, and now he kicked himself for it. It was just as he'd been contemplating while preparing for his excursion back into the Ibarra compound to find Skeet and Zinni—he didn't want to hurt her, didn't want to fight her, but he also didn't want to let her hurt him.

Whether she meant to or not.

His heart shattered into a thousand pieces when a new sound reached his ears: a violent sob, unlike any noise he'd ever heard her make. It was all he could do to keep from somehow breaking down the door and rushing to her side. But she'd wanted to get away from him, and even if he thought that was a terrible choice, trying to go against her wishes right now would undoubtedly make things worse.

One thing was for sure, though. Ziva was not okay, regardless of how sound her mind and reasoning had been throughout the past couple of days. *Ziva Payvan* may have been herself, but *Matia Moryi* was responsible for what had just occurred in the bedroom, and there was no way Matia and her experiences were going to magically vanish. While the two personalities did indeed share many traits, the former was in some ways being held hostage by the latter.

The sobs from within the lavatory intensified, and then Aroska heard her voice. The words were choked and shaky, but there was no mistaking them: "I almost killed you."

He shuddered as events replayed in his mind, recalling the brief feeling of terror and defenselessness when it dawned on him that it was too late to fight back. He caught himself wanting to withdraw from her in return, simply from a self-preservation standpoint, and the guilt hit him like a punch to the gut. As shaken as he was, surely Ziva was more so, and there was no way she was going to get the help she needed from anyone else on this ship. So, despite the discomfort, it would have to be his duty to offer her support when she wanted it. And even when she didn't.

It struck him that he had wanted to see her scars, and now he was getting a firsthand look at them, just not in the way he'd expected. Not all scars were physical; what he was seeing now was a direct result of everything she'd been through, evidence of hidden wounds that had never had the chance to heal. Wounds that had been exacerbated— perhaps even purposely—by Alastair Manes and, ultimately, Tobias Niio.

Aroska ground his teeth and checked the time. The mobster had summoned Ziva to the bridge for a quick briefing as Skeet, Zinni, and Ken touched down on Delatori, the reason he'd gone to awaken her in the first place. She'd surely be expected by now, but there was no way he'd be able to secure her cooperation in the next couple of minutes. He had no desire to let Tobias or the other Niiosians see her in her current condition anyway.

He stood and listened to her cries for a few more seconds before peeling himself away from the wall and striding out of the cabin, feeling almost sick to his stomach at the thought of leaving her behind. If she wanted to be alone, then so be it, but there had to be a happy medium between what she wanted and what she needed.

His legs carried him down the corridor toward the elevator bank on autopilot as his mind continued to process everything. The previous night—if it could be called that, considering day and night tended to lose meaning while traversing deep space—had given him so much hope, and he'd gained some unexpected insights into Ziva and her life. The fact that she had even come into the bedroom—to talk, just as he'd suggested they should do—was such a massive step forward, and he'd drifted off perfectly content with the state of things.

Upon awakening, he'd spent a while simply watching her sleep, ever fascinated that she could look so peaceful. Glad she *did* look peaceful. He'd found himself wondering when she'd last slept so soundly, especially given what she'd said about not sleeping well on Panuco. She hadn't even stirred when he got up. He liked to think it was because she felt safe, whether because he was with her or merely because she was out of Ibarra's clutches. Now it seemed any semblance of safety had been obliterated by the tricks her own mind was playing on her. After all the progress they'd made, it felt as though they were back to square one. Maybe worse.

The elevator dropped him on the command level, and he angled toward the bridge. He made a point of dragging his feet a bit, partially to allow himself more time to think, partially to give Ziva time for...something, anything, and partially just to not give Tobias the satisfaction of being cooperated with. The man may have saved their skins, but he was also responsible for Ziva's current state—indirectly, maybe—and Aroska was feeling less than gracious.

He squared his shoulders as he strode into the CIC. The mobster glanced his way as he approached, then did a double take upon noticing Ziva's absence. His eyes narrowed behind his spectacles.

"Where, pray tell, is Agent Payvan?" he asked as Aroska came to a stop at the control center.

As much as he wanted to say 'she's not coming,' antagonizing the man would get him nowhere. "She'll be here on her own time," he replied instead, offering no further explanation.

The displeasure on Tobias's face took on a more ominous tone. "I sincerely hope her schedule accounts for the fact that the ground team has arrived at Delatori and is already awaiting her instruction. The sooner we fulfill Pahl Starcer's request, the sooner we can acquire his schematics, and the sooner we do that, the sooner we'll be prepared to take back what's ours."

"She'll be here," Aroska repeated, hoping that was true.

Tobias gazed at him dubiously for a moment before turning and pulling up a holographic rendering of the terrain on Delatori, identical to what they'd looked at with Skeet before the *Saber's* departure. "The coordinates we've just received put the landing zone here." He jabbed a finger into the interface, and a pulsing yellow reticle appeared where he had indicated. "A suitable middle ground between Starcer's office and the neighborhood where his son's body is allegedly located. I have no doubt that Agent Oda and your comrades will be able to cover that distance quickly."

The man's eyes did all the talking: Ziva had approximately ten minutes to get her ass up here and cooperate. Aroska wished desperately for the luxury of some spare time, both to allow her to recover and to string Tobias along a little. But given that those *were* his comrades out there trekking through enemy territory with no backup, he was more inclined to listen. For now.

The mobster drew closer, seemingly unfazed by the fact that the top of his head barely surpassed Aroska's shoulders. "Agent Tarbic, I'd be much obliged if you would help expedite this situation," he said, voice low and vaguely menacing. "I regret that I do not know you very well, but you seem to have quite a profound effect on Agent Payvan, something I can honestly say I never imagined was possible." A glimmer briefly appeared in his cold eyes, as though the mere thought was somehow entertaining, but it faded nearly as quickly. "A man of your skill and constitution—surely you recognize the gravity of what we're doing here. I would have expected Ziva to as well, but considering she has been less than cooperative since her arrival...." He drew a breath to continue, then paused pensively. "I hope you will use your rapport with her to help ensure her compliance from here on out."

Aroska got the distinct feeling the man had been planning on making a more explicit threat against Ziva—perhaps to punish her for her behavior somehow—but had thought better of it, and rightfully so. Nevertheless, she was in trouble for not cooperating, but the galaxy only knew what Tobias had in store for her, so she could very well end up in just as much trouble if she did comply. Aroska had no intentions whatsoever of forcing her to participate in the mobster's schemes, but his thoughts once again drifted to Skeet and Zinni waiting somewhere in the Delatori woods, and he muttered an affirmative before pivoting and striding away from the command center.

No sooner had he reached the corridor outside the bridge than Ziva appeared from the direction of the nearest elevator bank. She slowed upon spotting him, as though trying to decide whether to bolt, but then she continued forward with the same resigned look on her face that she'd exhibited as they crossed the beach outside Tabaco.

It took him a moment to realize he'd slowed upon seeing her as well, and another moment to realize it had been a defensive response. Regardless of who she was, the trained operative in him insisted this person approaching might somehow cause him harm, purposefully or not. But the friend and confidant was relieved to already see her up and about; he may have taken his time getting up to the bridge in the first place, but he hadn't been gone that long. It was a shock to see her here so soon, especially considering the state he'd left her in.

As he drew nearer, however, he saw that she had hardly emerged from that state. Her eyes were swollen and bloodshot, now from crying in addition to exhaustion, and the dark circles surrounding them appeared twice as deep as they had before. Her hair—still ragged from whatever she'd done to haphazardly cut it—was stringy and wet, but at least she sported dry pants from her pack and once again donned her crew-issue black shirt. Her rugged boots and gun belt completed the sorry ensemble.

Aroska opened his mouth to address her as she came within

earshot, but she held up a hand to halt him, her steely expression warning him against making another attempt. "Just don't," she muttered, averting her gaze as she strode past him.

"Ziva, we need to ta—" He didn't bother finishing the sentence as he swiveled and watched her go by; she clearly wasn't in a listening mood. "The ground team is waiting for you."

"I figured as much."

He stood and watched until she rounded the corner and disappeared into the CIC, wanting desperately to follow but not wanting to make things worse. She needed to focus right now, and then needed time to cool off and process what had happened. Hell, he did, too.

With a sigh, he turned and continued on, content to do things her way for now. He would gather himself, consider all that needed to be said, and allow her to make contact with Skeet and Zinni. Then it would be time to get to work. It wasn't like they had anything better to do than twiddle their thumbs as they waited for the rest of the Niiosian forces to mobilize, and it wasn't like they had any shortage of experience hashing out difficult interpersonal issues. The biggest question for the moment was whether Ziva would accept his assistance, and so far, her behavior wasn't giving him much hope. But he would try.

Driven by a renewed sense of determination, Aroska strode forward and ducked into the nearest open elevator, hitting the controls to return to the cabin.

To wait.

Chapter 18
Landing Zone - Delatori Forest

At first glance, the forest seemed absolutely silent. But if one really stopped and listened, it wasn't silent at all. A slight breeze whistled through the coniferous growth, and a soft creaking could be heard occasionally as the trees' upper trunks swayed in the stronger winds higher up. In the distance, birds—large ones, based on the timbre and volume of their shrieks—called to one another, perhaps coordinating an attack on prey in the underbrush. And even farther away, in the brief lulls between the sounds of nature, the rumble of vehicles and machinery broke the calm of the forest.

To anyone passing by—in the event there was actually someone around—Skeet would have been nearly invisible, just another boulder perched on the edge of the rocky plateau atop which the *Saber* was docked. Passersby were precisely what he was searching for. Any signs of movement at all, for that matter, human or otherwise. His eyes roved over the landscape, peering into the trees, fixating on the odd rock or shadow for a moment before moving on. He'd seen nothing of consequence since they'd landed, but they were close enough to Ibarra-controlled areas that he thought it best to stay vigilant. His rifle lay across one knee, held loose but always ready.

Elevated above the forest floor, he had a nearly unobstructed view of the surrounding area from the top of the plateau, yet anyone at ground level wouldn't have an immediate view of the *Saber*. And if someone happened to be traveling on foot between the development center and the outskirts of the nearby settlement, he could only assume they would choose the path of least resistance, which likely wouldn't constitute clambering up a rock face. The ship was safe enough; the only way someone might spot it was from the air.

By his best estimation, it was currently late autumn in this hemisphere of the planet—cold enough that a glittering, early-morning frost still blanketed the ground but warm enough that the light precipitation hadn't quite turned to snow. A thin cloud of steam billowed in front of his face with each breath. There was something calming about the chill, the stillness, despite the fact that the forest hid untold dangers. He could easily say he felt more at peace here than he had anywhere else in the past few days.

Upon landing, he'd sent out a brief transmission informing Tobias they were ready to proceed under Ziva's instruction, then he, Zinni, and Ken had chosen their loadouts and donned stealth suits in preparation. Ken was stuck with Aroska's suit, but the garments were semi-adaptive, capable of shifting in color to resemble the surrounding landscape, so the ill fit was worth it if they were all able to move about undetected. The bigger problem was that they'd already been waiting for—he checked the time—too long considering the timetable they were working with. Part of him was beginning to fear it had been a bad idea for the team to split up; the Niiosians may have appeared to be the lesser of two evils for now, but there was no denying how dangerous Tobias was. If he happened to decide that two Haphezians would be easier to deal with than four, then the simple truth was that Ziva and Aroska likely wouldn't fare well aboard the *Revenant*.

Another concern was Ziva's mindset. She'd seemed engaged enough during the short mission brief just before the *Saber* departed, and Zinni had told him about her enlightening conversation in the observation alcove, but that engagement didn't seem to be consistent. Despite the anger and disappointment he still felt toward his old friend, he'd meant it with all his heart when he told Aroska to take care of her. Her mind was broken, and as much as he wanted to give her time to heal, they all needed her to perform right now.

Satisfied that there was no one in the immediate vicinity, Skeet stood, heaved a sigh, and adjusted his suit's fitted hood to block the draft that had begun to chill his ears. The camouflage pattern in the material shifted to a lighter shade of gray as he moved out of the shadows. To anyone observing, it might have appeared that the boulder suddenly sprouted legs and grew two meters. He made his way back up to the *Saber*, taking care with his footing on the frosty rocks, and found Zinni waiting at the top of the ship's boarding ramp. She gave him a subtle shake of her head as he approached, indicating that there'd still been no contact from Ziva.

Ken appeared in the cargo bay as the two of them moved into the ship. "It's not a transmission problem," he said. "We're patched into the *Revenant*. They're still waiting for her on their end, too."

Skeet couldn't help but feel some measure of relief that the lack of communication wasn't specifically due to Tobias. And yet, if the mobster was stuck in the same stalemate as they were, then he imagined the man's patience was running as thin as his own.

He checked the time again. "Then we move without her. We have a general idea of where we're going—we'll leave now and hope she checks in by the time we get there."

A dubious look flashed briefly through Zinni's eyes. But she stood tall and resolute, pulled her hood up over her hair, and nodded her apparent agreement with the plan.

They took a couple of minutes for final equipment checks then moved out, leaving the *Saber* secured on top of the plateau just as they'd left it on the beach outside Tabaco. Skeet pulled up the topographical projection they'd reviewed with Ziva, made note of their current position, and pointed them in the direction of the neighborhood where they would find the remains of Starcer's son. He took the lead, keeping himself a stride in front of Ken, and sensed Zinni fall back to cover their rear without being asked. He got the feeling it was to keep an eye on the Niiosian agent just as much as it was to keep an eye on their surroundings.

None of them said a word as they moved, their footsteps equally silent on the half-frozen ground. Skeet's ears were once again at work, listening for unusual sounds farther away while his attention remained fixed on his footing and the forest around him. In the edges of his vision, he was aware of the body of his suit shifting between greenish-gray hues while the lower legs adopted a silvery shimmer to match the frosty earth. The earpiece nestled inside his hood remained silent as well, and the apprehension about Ziva's status settled back in like a rain cloud over his head. If she wasn't in any danger—at least that they knew of—then why the hell was she leaving them hanging like this?

Behind him, Zinni shuffled forward, turning in a slow circle and backpedaling every few strides as she swept both her gaze and her weapon over the environment. Their eyes met for the briefest of moments when he cast a glance back at her, and he saw his own unease reflected in her face. Always on the same page.

"Ground team."

Skeet stopped in his tracks and held up a fist to halt their procession before dropping into a crouch. Ken and Zinni followed his example, their suits once again allowing them to become one with their surroundings. "Ziva," he said, almost a question to ensure he'd correctly heard the voice that had just come through the earpiece. Finally.

"I'm here."

As much as he wanted to demand an explanation for what had taken her so long, now was not the time. "What do you have for us?"

"I'm tracking your position. Continue on your current trajectory for another half klick."

Taking one last look around, Skeet rose to his feet and resumed his journey, as did Zinni and Ken. At least Ziva was acknowledging that they had started moving without her. But it was fascinating what kind of instincts were coming alive right now, even after being separated from his old lieutenant for four years. When you worked so closely with someone for so long, you learned things about them, learned how to read them. It was the reason he and Zinni had grown so adept at knowing what the other was thinking, and it was the reason he could now hear a certain quality in Ziva's voice, even through a transmission from light years away. It was something he hadn't heard often, but it told him something wasn't right.

"Is Tarbic with you?" he asked, self-conscious about how loud even the soft murmur sounded against the quiet of the forest.

"No."

It wasn't like this was an opportune time to reach out to Aroska and ask what was amiss, but the abruptness of the response combined with the sergeant's absence was telling enough. Something was most certainly wrong, perhaps between the two of them.

They continued walking for another couple of minutes. Just as Skeet caught his first glimpse of a structure through the trees, his earpiece crackled again. "You're coming up on one of the outermost houses. Move in and let me get a look around."

He reached into the pocket on the front of his stealth suit as he moved, pulling out the delicate pair of cam goggles within. He fitted the lenses over his eyes and patched the goggles' feed into the transmission; a tiny cam built into their frame would now stream anything he saw to whatever display Ziva was looking at aboard the *Revenant*.

"Good image," she confirmed.

The three of them gave the house a wide berth as they moved around in front of it, treading more carefully than ever now that they had entered a once-populated area where someone might still be lurking. It was warmer here closer to civilization than it had been farther out in the woods, and the melted frost left the ground sticky and muddy. No way were they going to be able to move around without leaving evidence of their presence. With luck, the steadier rain that had begun to fall would help wash away their footprints.

Skeet brought them to a stop just inside the tree line and crouched down again, sweeping his head around to give both himself and Ziva a better look at the scene. Their immediate surroundings consisted of three large houses situated in a semicircle around a wide clearing, probably a private drive. Similar clusters of three homes could be seen beyond. These properties no doubt belonged to individuals made wealthy by Delatori's trove of natural resources who still longed for the seclusion of the forest.

"That one," Ziva said, her voice distant in more than just a physical sense.

He paused the rotation of his head and fixated on the house on the far side of the nearest cluster. "You're sure?" he asked, not thrilled with the idea of having to traverse the entire clearing.

"Yeah."

They sat motionless for another several seconds before moving again, certain there were no obvious threats awaiting them. The dreariness of the weather felt strangely appropriate given the task they were here to perform. Skeet could picture Starcer's son rushing across this very clearing in a panic and sprinting for that last house, maybe after trying unsuccessfully to enter one of the nearer ones. He could almost feel Ziva coming up behind him, emerging from the trees as the team had just done, terrifying in her Matia Moryi getup. They'd hunted people like that on missions back in the day, but never had it been an innocent person at the behest of a power-hungry cartel leader.

Having an acute Haphezian sense of smell meant he picked up the putrid scent of rotting flesh while they were still a good distance from the house, but it didn't take long for Ken to also grunt in disgust. The stench intensified as they neared the front of the residence, and when he opened the door—already unlocked thanks to what appeared to be some jury-rigged wires in the control panel—the reek of decay exploded outward.

He stepped inside, grateful none of the three of them were strangers to death. That never made situations like this pleasant, though. Ken and Zinni filed in behind him, shutting the door and then fanning out to surround the corpse lying just strides from the entrance.

"Found him," he announced grimly, though with the cam goggles streaming, surely Ziva already knew that. He turned to Zinni. "Let's bring Emeri and Starcer on."

As she worked to patch in the transmission to Noro that had already been set up aboard the *Saber*, Skeet and Ken made a quick sweep of the house before returning to the foyer. He hadn't expected to find anything of interest, and it was doubtful anyone would want to hide out in here with the stink, but being ambushed was the last thing they needed.

Zinni tapped her earpiece and nodded his way as he stooped down to take a closer look at the body. "Radio silence, Z," he said. "We're going on with the director and Starcer."

"Copy," Ziva answered.

There was a soft click as the new transmission transferred to his own earpiece. "Lieutenant?" came Emeri's voice. "What do you have?"

"We've discovered a corpse approximately three kilometers from the development center. We have reason to believe it's Starcer's son."

It felt strange to say such a thing, considering they already knew the man's identity. Emeri could be heard conversing in the background for a moment, then he sighed. "Starcer would like to identify the body."

Unsure if giving the man a visual was the wisest idea, Skeet adjusted the cam goggles and pulled back a bit to provide a wider angle. Zinni stepped forward with a light source.

The silence that followed seemed to stretch into eternity, and it felt even more eerie indoors—there in the presence of death—than it had outside. Finally, someone on the other end of the transmission drew a shaky breath, and then Starcer spoke.

"That's him," the man said, voice hoarse. He hesitated for several more seconds. "Can you tell me how he died?"

The single projectile entry point in the son's forehead seemed obvious enough, but Skeet indicated the wound anyway, guided by Zinni's light. "Single gunshot to the frontal lobe. He didn't suffer."

Even as he said the words, however, he found himself taking a closer look at the amount of blood on the rest of the man's body. A fair bit had soaked into his clothes around his stomach, though there didn't appear to be any sort of injury there. A puddle had formed under his midsection, black and rancid after drying out, and separate, Skeet realized, from the similarly dry but smaller puddle beneath his head.

Drawing a deep breath through his mouth in hopes of momentarily escaping the stench, he moved to roll the corpse over. The exterior of the man's body was in surprisingly good shape considering how long he'd been lying here, no doubt preserved somewhat by the chilly weather. Despite the lack of severe bloating and putrefaction, however, his form was already soft, and his abdomen caved under the gentlest touch.

"Got a secondary injury here," he announced, walking himself through what he was seeing just as much as he was describing it to Emeri and Starcer. "Appears to be another gunshot to the lower spine."

"The amount of blood would indicate his heart was still beating when he was shot here," Ken said. "This happened first."

"It would seem that way." In his mind, Skeet ran through what must have happened to leave the man in this condition. Ziva had never divulged exactly how she'd killed him, just that she'd done the deed. But if the wound was on his back and he had blood on his stomach and sides, that suggested he'd been lying face-down for even a brief time before either rolling over or being rolled over by someone else. Most likely the latter, as a shot to the spine like that would have almost certainly paralyzed him.

Ken's voice was little more than a distant echo as the man relayed Skeet's exact thought process out loud to Tobias. If Starcer's son had been shot in the back, that obviously meant the shooter—Ziva—had been behind him at the time. He glanced around the dark room, identifying a wall that might have concealed her. His stomach twisted itself into a knot as the realization dawned on him, and as Ken spoke the words aloud:

"...ambushed him, shot him in the back as he tried to flee, turned him over to face her, then executed him."

Skeet stood, angling his head away from the corpse so Starcer wouldn't be forced to look at it any longer than necessary. Again, it wasn't the murder itself that bothered him so much as it was the fact that Ziva had committed it on the order of someone like Manes, and against an indirect ally of the man she was truly working for, to boot. Plus, shooting a fleeing person—an *innocent* fleeing person—in the back was a foul move regardless of who you were or who you worked for. Ziva had always been a killer, but her sense of honor should never have allowed for this.

"Advise," Zinni said when the silence began to drag.

Rather than Emeri's even voice, the response was a string of expletives so loud Skeet could hear it through Zinni and Ken's earpieces, too. Starcer.

"Agents, I..." A fierce combination of anguish and fury turned the words into almost a wail. "I realize the parameters of this mission have changed and that if you're able to recover my schematics for me, it renders my original commission to take Moryi out of play trivial. But this—"

Skeet could picture the words being spoken through clenched teeth as the man leaned ever closer to Emeri's comm receiver.

"—is the work of a being so vile that hell itself spat her back out. Matia Moryi is a plague, infecting and destroying wherever she goes. And like a plague, she must be eradicated. Do you understand me? Wipe her out in the same way she has wiped out everything I've ever loved, everything I've worked—"

The garbled noise that followed sounded like Emeri trying to calm the man, then having him either removed from the office or at least moved away from the comm. It took the director another few seconds to rejoin the conversation.

"I'll talk with him, get him to tell us where those specs are stored. What can you do with the body?"

Skeet looked to Zinni, who nodded and pulled a handheld device from the utility pouch strapped to her thigh. "We have a beacon we can mark this location with if Starcer has people he can send to recover it. But I wouldn't recommend sending anyone for at least a couple more days—this region is still hot with Ibarra forces."

"Might I remind you, Lieutenant, of what I said about involving yourselves in this conflict."

"Message received, sir. We're here to recover those specs and do a little scouting. Nothing more."

"I'll hold you to that. Contact me when you've reached the development center and we'll be ready with the specs' location."

There was a soft click as the connection cut out, and the entire house once more fell eerily silent without Emeri's voice and Starcer's wailing in the background. Skeet took one more moment to process everything before drawing a deep breath and tapping his earpiece to revert to the previous transmission. "Ziva?"

"Yeah."

Her tone was one of confirmation, both that she was still there and that she'd heard every word Starcer had just said. *Sheyss.* "Any news for us from your end?"

She sighed and could be heard conversing briefly with Tobias before answering. "The fleet is starting to mobilize through the nebula, traveling sub-light for now. Word is the rest of the Niiosian forces will be underway in a couple of hours, and then we'll be headed for the rendezvous point."

"Copy that," he replied. He drew a breath to continue then paused, unsure what he wanted to say. Secondhand regret about the things Starcer had said combined with disgust about what she'd done to the man's son created an odd dissonance in his head.

"Keep us apprised, okay?" Zinni said, looking him in the eye as she did so.

Ziva's only response was another half-hearted 'yeah' before ending the transmission. It took Zinni another several seconds to break eye contact, her features tight with concern as she stooped down and positioned the little beacon beside the body on the floor. A small red light began to flash, piercing the darkness of the room at intervals.

Unsure what more there was to do or say—at least here, at least now—Skeet jerked his head toward the door. "Move out."

The three of them set out, their footfalls just as silent as before as they began the trek back to the *Saber*. The precipitation had solidified into a light snow by the time they made it to the tree line, and they became one with the forest once more.

Chapter 19
Niiosian Cruiser Revenant · Deep Space

Seven hours.

Aroska checked again just to be sure. Yes, it had been almost exactly seven hours since he'd passed her in the corridor on her way to the bridge to contact Skeet and Zinni. He should have known better than to think she'd actually return to Ken's cabin when she was done, especially when he hadn't explicitly asked her to come and she hadn't explicitly said she would. He'd waited there for a little over an hour before realizing his error; it couldn't even fairly be considered an error on his part. He cursed himself yet again for not just loitering on the bridge until she was done with her comms. Or better yet, joining the conversation with the ground team whether she wanted him around or not.

Now here they were, having confirmed the rest of the fleet's departure from Niio, completing the trip to Delatori at FTL speeds—another ten-hour journey or so from their current position. And he couldn't shake the feeling that he wasn't ready. For anything.

He sighed as the elevator door opened, and he stepped out into the corridor and headed for the cabin. He'd checked there two other times throughout the day, to no avail. A few searches of the *Talon* had yielded similar results; both locations were the most accessible, the most comfortable, and thus the two places he'd finally concluded she was least likely to be. But that hadn't stopped him from checking again out of sheer desperation, and *desperate* was certainly how he found himself after methodically scouring the entire battlecruiser three separate times and coming up empty. Even the cushy alcove where Zinni had found her before was deserted.

He let himself into the cabin and stood motionless, eyes closed as he wracked his brain trying to come up with more ideas for how to find her. She still wasn't carrying any sort of personal comm, or if she was, he had no way of contacting it. He'd ruled out alerting Tobias to the situation, as it seemed the man was already losing patience with her and wouldn't take kindly to knowing she was hiding somewhere aboard the ship, likely engaged in the galaxy only knew what self-destructive behavior. Even paging her or asking a security officer for assistance in locating her would alert everyone to the fact that she was missing. Serenity might be someone he could confide in if it came down to it, but he wanted to make sure he'd done absolutely everything in his power to resolve the situation himself first.

For a few seconds, he thought it was just due to his thoughts about the doctor, but after another beat, he realized the cabin did indeed smell vaguely of medical supplies. Upon opening his eyes, the first thing he saw was Ziva's backpack in the desk chair across the room, undisturbed. Then his attention was drawn to the little kitchenette counter on his right. Some discarded packaging lay there, and when he approached, he found three empty autoinjectors in the sink. The corners of his mouth curled downward as he picked up the package and read the label. The injectors were for stimulants, the kind used by fighter pilots to stay alert during long patrols or missions. While not inherently harmful, their involvement was alarming given everything else he knew about Ziva's current state of mind.

Regardless, this meant she had been here, which he chose to take as a good sign despite the presence of what was quite the stim cocktail. She must have been on the move throughout the day, never staying in one place long enough for him to find her. Then he recalled what she'd said the night before about not sleeping much on Panuco. At the time, he'd assumed she meant because Manes kept her so busy, or because she was too paranoid, or even because that poor excuse for a bed was too uncomfortable. But the simpler explanation was currently staring him in the face: she didn't sleep because she'd been shooting up. Perhaps it *was* due to the paranoia and she felt a need to keep herself awake and vigilant as often as possible. Maybe it was even a way to avoid nightmares like the one that had almost gotten him killed.

He gathered up the wrappers and spent autoinjectors and discarded them in the trash, wanting to be angry with her but simultaneously stricken by how much she was clearly struggling right now. Hadn't he just been praising her for the way she typically handled all her burdens and issues? That armor she'd fashioned out of all her tragedies seemed to be deteriorating in real time, and he felt a great need to stop it before it got any worse.

"You don't let them become shackles...the way I used to."

It was a long shot, but the thought spawned one more idea for a place to look before involving Serenity. He hadn't checked it previously because he didn't think it made any sense, and if he was being honest, he wasn't entirely comfortable going there himself. But perhaps those two things made it the perfect hiding place.

He brought his hand to rest against the cargo pocket of his pants, feeling the outline of the data pad he'd been carrying around most of the day. Then, mustering his resolve, he headed back out to the elevator and took it down one level. As he'd already discovered today, the corridor here was longer and wider than the one he'd just come from and was lined with rooms, some offices, and some ranked crew members' cabins. Nestled between two doors halfway down was a narrow hallway that claimed to lead to an officers' canteen, and based on the limited space available, it couldn't have been more than a hidden alcove with a small wet bar.

He made his way down the hallway, which felt barely wide enough to accommodate his stout frame, and couldn't help but notice the lack of Niiosian personnel coming and going from this lounge even though no one had anything better to be doing right now. He rounded the corner; as he'd hoped, it was because someone had intruded upon their space.

"What the hell are you doing?" he asked, sheer relief and weariness softening his tone despite the nature of the question.

For a moment, Ziva didn't acknowledge him. She sat at the little room's single table, shoulders hunched, head drooping, silent. In her left hand, she spun an empty glass in a slow circle. Her right hand was curled around the base of a dark brown bottle of something he had no doubt was old and expensive. The open cabinet behind her revealed a selection of similar bottles, with an empty slot for the one she held. Aroska wondered how much Tobias might have spent on such a fine collection for his men.

Finally, she lifted the bottle and twirled it by the neck, watching the remaining liquid slosh back and forth in the bottom. "I am having a drink," she proclaimed, nonchalant. Her unfocused gaze shifted his direction. "Why don't you join me?"

His hands curled abruptly into fists in response to her invitation. He could have—and probably should have—merely shrugged it off as drunken belligerence, but she wasn't completely drunk, at least not yet. There was something far too purposeful about the way she'd spoken, about the way she'd looked at him. She knew better than to offer him alcohol; he'd been sober for over four years, in no small part thanks to her. He knew exactly what she was doing here. The thought whisked him back to the days when they'd first been forced to team up, when she'd spent every waking moment antagonizing, manipulating, and trying to get a rise out of him in order to keep him at arm's length. Keep him mad enough that he wanted to stay away from her.

In that case, the worst possible thing he could do right now was let her goad him into getting angry. It would admittedly be more of a challenge than expected given the sensitive subject matter, and she knew that good and well, which irritated him even more. But he was determined that her passive-aggressive attacks would be met only with patience and firmness. He drew a deep breath and released it slowly through his nose, allowing his hands to relax.

"I think you know that's not going to happen," he said.

Ziva watched him through narrowed eyes for a moment before shrugging. "Suit yourself," she muttered, taking a swig directly from the bottle.

"How much of that have you had?"

"Not nearly enough."

She wasn't going to make this easy, was she. "Come on, why are you being like this? This isn't how Ziva Payvan handles her problems."

"I'm not 'being like' anything. This is who I am, but you wouldn't know that."

Another jab about him not truly knowing her. "This *isn't* who you are, because I know you're capable of carrying on a serious conversation. I also know you don't drink. You're the one who told me even the smell of alcohol makes you sick. What do you think you're accomplishing here?"

She once again held up the bottle and examined the remaining liquid. "I am doing my best to drown out the fact that I am a plague. Hadn't ever thought of it that way, and haven't ever been one to care what people say about me, but that's what Starcer called me, and it's true. Everything I touch dies." She forced a disgusted, abrasive chuckle, though the first signs of tears glistened in her eyes. "And you know, you'd think as a trained killer I'd be used to it. But you take a moron like Blain...I never intended to hurt him, but he was done for the moment I met him. So were Marshay and Ryon. Now it seems even *you* can't escape from me unscathed. Who's next? Skeet? Zinni?"

"Okay," Aroska sighed, exaggerating both syllables of the word. He stepped toward the table and reached out to take the bottle from her, but she yanked it away. He held his hands up in surrender and retreated a bit. "You have to remember what a disaster I was when you came to find me after Tachi's murder. Take it from me, Ziva. Drowning your sorrows doesn't work."

"Might as well give it my best shot. You may have been a disaster, but at least it helped you forget all the *sheyss* you were going through." She looked up at him. "Didn't it."

She wasn't asking a question. The truth was it *had* helped him forget, but only because between the drinking and the govino smoking, his brain had been reduced to the consistency of mud and he'd managed to keep himself locked in a numb, unfeeling stasis. Come to think of it, it wasn't all that different from Ziva's default apathetic state. Maybe the silver lining in all of this was that she was currently behaving this way to keep herself from feeling. Which meant she *was* feeling something.

"But at what cost?" he replied. "Trust me, you don't want to go this route." He peered closer at her neck, able to discern a series of red marks from the autoinjectors. "And you're fooling yourself if you think you can get wasted after shooting up stims. You'll metabolize every-thing too fast and the combination of upper and downer will just wind up making you miserable."

She scrunched up her nose and shook her head as she began to pour some of the remaining liquor into her glass. "Well, that's no different than how I've felt for the past four years, so here's to being miserable."

She was halfway through the motion of bringing the glass up to her lips when Aroska reached out and snatched it out of her hand, flinging it against the canteen wall. Shattered glass and amber liquid exploded everywhere. Ziva merely stared at him, brows furrowed, mouth slightly agape.

"You have to stop this," he said, leaning down over the table and looking her in the eye. "You've been avoiding me all day, and we need to talk about what happened. I was encouraged after last night. I thought you were doing okay. I thought *we* were doing okay."

"We were," she replied nonchalantly, studying the bottle in her hand as though she were considering using it as a weapon, "but then I almost killed you. That can't happen."

Obviously. "And your solution is to destroy yourself?"

"Guess so," she said with a shrug, turning the bottle up and taking another generous gulp.

Aroska whirled away from her and planted his hands on his hips before he could reach across the table and shake her. Damn but she was being ridiculous. Never in his life had he imagined her going to such lengths to drive him away that she debased herself so. That was some-thing he might have done—and *had* done—once upon a time, but not the stoic Ziva Payvan. And they may have just had downtime for the remainder of the trip to Delatori, but it still seemed odd for her to be doing anything that might compromise her mental faculties when there was any semblance of an important mission looming on the horizon. The fact that she was choosing to behave this way and was choosing now to do it told him how desperate she was to prove her point, what-ever it was supposed to be.

He stood in silence for a moment, commanding himself to keep it together. This felt all too similar to when they'd first met; at the time, he'd simply wanted to be the bigger person and not stoop to her level when she was being such a heartless *shouka*. Then, as he'd gotten to know her and grown closer to her, she had legitimately inspired him to better himself. Part of that was due to her nagging and abrasiveness, which was nothing if not characteristic, but he'd also recognized the need for self-improvement as a means of helping her, in her battles both internal and external. And after all of that, it now felt like they were back to where they'd started, this time with a significant amount of shared history that couldn't be erased. That made it even worse.

"Ziva," he said quietly, refraining from turning around for a couple more seconds. "I need you to listen to me. This isn't you. This isn't even the same woman I was talking to last night. I realize you've been through a lot—hell, I'd be concerned if you *weren't* struggling right now. But you absolutely cannot go down this road, do you hear me? You are letting Alastair Manes and Tobias Niio break you."

He paused and studied her for a moment: her flushed face, furrowed brows, mussed hair, tear-filled eyes. She was a sorry sight to be sure, and the thought of all the burdens she was carrying—both from the past four years and long before—turned his stomach. He wanted...*needed* her to be strong, to take control the way she always had, because that was the caliber of person this upcoming battle would require.

"But I think you know that," he continued quietly, drawing a fresh scowl from her. "You know you're broken, and you think you have to push me away because you're afraid of what you might do before your mind heals. Believe me, what happened this morning scared the hell out of me, too, but I want to help you. And you can be damn sure that no matter how much of an asshole you are to me, I'm not going anywhere."

She watched him silently for several seconds before averting her gaze and turning the liquor bottle in a slow circle just as she'd been doing with the glass. He wanted nothing more than to just embrace her, hold her, comfort her, but she wasn't someone who typically responded to gestures like that anyway, and they almost certainly wouldn't be welcome now. There was a fine line between giving her the space she desired and remaining close enough to support and protect her, whether from herself or from those who had done this to her.

His fingers once again came to rest against the pocket where his data pad sat. After four years of examining how he felt, he'd been so ready to pick up where they'd left off. Even after the revelation that she was Matia Moryi, he'd hoped to reconcile and work things out if she was willing to try as well. Nothing had changed until the close call that morning, but as unnerved as he still was, he couldn't let himself stop fighting now. He couldn't let her, either.

He slid the data pad from his pocket. "Let me show you something," he said, studying the device for a moment. This wasn't quite what he'd envisioned in terms of the right time to bring it out, but he feared she would keep slipping away if he didn't do something to prove how serious he was.

She scoffed and massaged her forehead, eyes closed, lips curled upward in a vaguely disgusted smirk. "I remember what happened last time you said that."

Aroska ground his teeth. 'What happened last time' was that she had bared her soul to him, confessed the truth about Soren's death, and allowed them to really connect for the first time. She made it sound like a bad thing, when in reality it was exactly what needed to happen again.

He slapped the pad down on the table, harder than he'd meant to, and shoved it toward her with enough force that it bumped into her arm. She glanced down at it in annoyance, then looked up and met his gaze from behind knit brows as he moved to loom over her.

"I want you to look at that," he said, voice firm. "I want you to think about what it means, and then when you're ready, I want you to come find me, because we need to talk about it." He stared into her eyes, hoping he wasn't simply imagining that he'd finally captured her full attention, then pushed off the table and turned to leave. "I'll be in the cabin."

Chapter 20
MEANWHILE—INDUSTRIAL PARK · Delatori

The development center Starcer worked out of was part of a large industrial park about the same distance from the *Saber's* hiding place as the neighborhood had been, just as Ziva demonstrated aboard the *Revenant*. The road from the settlement to this particular park had been relatively devoid of traffic—whatever raw materials Starcer worked with must not have currently been the target of Ibarra's operations. From what they'd observed so far, any resources the Cartel was accumulating were being transported straight off-world. Or, considering their tracking data indicated the shipping fleet was still maintaining its holding pattern, being stockpiled at the nearest spaceport.

That left the development centers—or at least this one—virtually untouched for the time being, a welcome discovery considering Ziva's intel about the local Ibarra presence. As with any evacuated area ravaged by war, a handful of looters and scavengers had shown up to pick through the abandoned buildings, though Zinni wasn't nearly as concerned about running into any of those sorts as she was about running into an active Cartel patrol.

Their footsteps barely made a sound as they darted toward their destination, moving briskly without outright running. Pressing close against the structure's exterior wall, they progressed as a unit toward the entrance to the offices, with Zinni sweeping around to cover the area behind them just as she'd done on approach to the neighborhood. They reached the stairs and hurried up to the door, crowding in under the entryway.

"*Sheyss*," Skeet muttered after what seemed like only a split second of studying the door controls. "Zinni."

She looked to Ken, who nodded and shuffled down to cover their backs while she stepped up to see what the problem was. She'd expected to find some form of high-tech control panel that would require her tools to breach; that may well have still been the case, if there was a panel left at all. Fused metal and wires jutted haphazardly from a darkened area on the wall beside the door, probably the result of some sort of high-powered plasma blast. Whatever it was, it had been done intentionally, and it had been done out here. Not only could the three of them no longer enter here, but anyone still inside the building at the time had been either locked in or forced to seek an alternate exit, perhaps one of the attacker's choosing.

The corners of her mouth curled downward as she recalled what Starcer had originally told them about Manes putting out hits on all the development managers, and about the way Matia Moryi had methodically cut them all down. Had Ziva been responsible for this? Realistically, there was no way to know for sure short of asking the woman, which was something Zinni had no desire to do.

Content to assume this had been done by a whole squad of Ibarra soldiers, even if under Moryi's guidance, she stepped back and shook her head. "We're not getting in this way—simple as that."

"Bound to be more than one entrance," Skeet said.

Ken turned to face them. "I suggest we split up. Cover more ground."

He took off before either of them could respond, his wiry frame low to the ground, his stealth suit shifting from drab gray to frosty silver as he transitioned from the concrete stairs to the snow-dusted ground. He turned right, circling around the building in the direction from which they'd come, and was out of sight.

Zinni and Skeet exchanged a glance before proceeding down the steps and to the left. Initial long-range scouting of the property had revealed some damaged areas around the face of the building; maybe one of those would yield an entry point.

"Not sure it was a good idea to let him go off like that," Zinni said quietly, certain Skeet was already thinking the same thing.

"Wasn't going to waste time arguing," he muttered. "Splitting up could be beneficial anyway." He was quiet for several strides, his gaze still directed ahead. "You think Ziva did that to the lock?"

It was always like he could read her mind. She'd already decided to quash the thought though, as this was hardly the time or place to be wandering around with knots in her stomach, angry about something that may or may not have happened.

"I'm trying not to," she answered, adding enough of a jab to her words to signal that he should do the same. He sighed and cast a glance back at her but said nothing more.

They rounded the corner and found themselves in some sort of courtyard, its snow-covered foliage and masonry the last vestiges of over-indulgent decor separating the office building from the strictly utilitarian development center. On the other side of this open space, three mismatched groundcars sat parked. None were running, but neither were they covered in snow; they'd arrived in the relatively short time since the last precipitation.

Both Zinni and Skeet were on the move, their legs carrying them into cover behind the courtyard's low wall almost of their own accord. They remained motionless for a moment, their suits adapting to blend with the wall, but several seconds of observation revealed no movement or activity around the cars.

Skeet continued forward first, stepping out and leveling his weapon before freezing for another split second. With a wave of two fingers, Zinni emerged as well, and the two of them split off, moving in tandem up opposite sides of the courtyard. As they neared the vehicles, it became clear that all three were empty. Zinni reached out and placed a hand against the engine compartment of the closest one. Cold. They may have arrived since the last snowfall, but they'd been parked for a while.

She placed a finger on her earpiece. "Oda, be advised we may have company here."

No response. Somehow she wasn't surprised.

Skeet was already on the move again, so she performed one last sweep over the cars before falling into stride behind him. They stuck to the building's outer wall just as they had on initial approach. As they drew nearer to the development center—a very industrial structure with its exterior exhaust ports, catwalks, and metal staircases—the muffled sound of rushing water reached her ears.

A few more seconds of walking brought them to the entrance to a maintenance tunnel...or what used to be the entrance. The door and its entire facade had been blown away in what looked like a clumsy breach attempt, leaving a mess of scorched metal and concrete surrounding a hole that was probably three times bigger than intended. The scent of smoke and explosives lingered in the air. This had been done recently.

The blast had also blown open some pipes running up the side of the building, leaving several to gush and spray water all over the immediate area. The ground in front of the entrance had been transformed into a giant mud puddle, and more water streamed inside, flowing freely down the steep staircase and disappearing in the darkness within.

Zinni shrugged. "Not exactly an ideal entrance, but—"

"It'll do. Ken, we have an entry point."

"Likewise," the man's quiet voice crackled in their earpieces. "Meet you inside."

Of course he would. She sighed. "At least it's not a sewer."

Skeet might have huffed a chuckle just before turning and pressing on; she couldn't quite tell over the noise of the water. At least that noise might help conceal their arrival from whoever had made this mess.

They descended into the dark one after the other, pausing on what felt like every other step to ensure their footing was sound on the slippery stairs. Upon reaching the bottom, they found themselves in ankle-deep standing water, the flow and subsequent rushing sound both diminishing the farther inside they moved. This tunnel seemed to extend under the development center's main floor and, judging by the thick conduits running along the ceiling, appeared to be leading them to the power mains for all the labs and assembly lines in the facility above.

Several meters ahead, the solid ceiling was replaced by a metal grate, the underside of some sort of walkway on the next floor up. Ambient light shone through from the hallway above, though it was dimmer than expected. Basic emergency lighting, probably.

A shadow passed across it just then, pitching the tunnel into momentary darkness. Zinni and Skeet raised their weapons, otherwise motionless as they fixed their gazes on the space beyond the grate. A form drifted by, accompanied by the barely audible hum of repulsors. The red hues of the emergency lighting glinted off something metallic.

The two of them exchanged a glance and continued forward, keeping close to the tunnel walls and watching for further movement as they angled for the short staircase now visible on the far side of the power junctions. They proceeded upward, leaving the darkness and the sound of running water behind, and found themselves on the ground level of the main factory. No signs of life in the direction the bot—or whatever it was—had gone. Whether it was part of the facility's security system or belonged to whoever had breached the tunnel, Zinni wasn't sure; the latter seemed more likely, considering the rest of the building appeared to be completely shut down. Abandoned.

She marveled for a moment at what little she could see of the factory from where they stood. Heavy-duty conveyors spanned the length of the massive floor, some sporting clamps, some sporting molds, all flanked by an array of mechanical appendages that lay dormant under the emergency lights. She could only imagine what this place must be like when it was up and running—the sight of the sparks flying, the scent of soldering irons, the sound of metal clanging against metal as the resources harvested from Delatori's rich crust were refined then formed into workable materials. At least two more levels of suspended walkways hung above them, running alongside yet more conveyors whose function she couldn't make out from down here on the floor.

"Surprised this place isn't crawling with Ibarra," she whispered.

"I imagine they've long since come through and taken anything of value," Skeet said just as quietly, continuing to scan the floor even as he spoke.

If Ibarra wasn't actively on site, it meant the vehicles outside—and the bot, for that matter—probably belonged to scavengers. This was good in that those types of people were typically amateurs, but bad in that they were entirely unpredictable for that very reason. Also bad in that it meant Zinni, Skeet, and Ken were outnumbered and might have some competition when it came to searching the facility's labs and offices.

She was on the move before her brain could fully process the fact that she could hear the bot's repulsors again. Ducking into kneeling positions below the plane of the nearest conveyor, she and Skeet watched as the little machine floated into view. It was spherical in shape, roughly the size of her head, with a large sensor-eye on one side and a small antenna array sprouting from the other. Aside from that soft hum of its repulsion system, it was completely silent.

The hairs on the back of her neck stood on end as the bot paused and faced the stairwell leading up from the access tunnel. By the time it swiveled toward them, its sensor-eye glowing the same red as the emergency lights, she was already reaching for her supply pouch.

Skeet followed suit as she sank farther down below the assembly line and readied her muscles for action, listening as the hum drew nearer. The moment the glow of the sensor spilled over the plane of the conveyor, she leaped up, flinging a thumbnail-sized electromagnetic charge toward the bot. The charge adhered to the machine, enveloping it in a ball of blue electrical current. It convulsed and spat smoke and sparks for a moment before crashing to the floor, emitting an ear-piercing squeal as it went.

"*Sheyss*," Skeet muttered. "How much do you want to bet whoever that thing belongs to knows we're here?"

She was sure he was right. "We need to find those specs."

He nodded and took off toward a wide entryway that appeared to lead back into the office building. "Hustle."

"What about Ken?"

"He'll find his way."

If she knew Skeet, what he really meant was he didn't currently give a damn where Ken was or what he was doing. Besides, if they commed Starcer for directions, the Niiosian operative would be able to follow those directions as well.

Lack of power eliminated the elevators as a transportation method. She opened a transmission to Emeri's office as the two of them angled for the stairs, moving upward as quietly as speed would allow. "Sir, we're inside the development center. Entered the fabrication area through an access tunnel, and we're not alone in the building."

"Where exactly are you now?" the director asked.

"Moving west from the factory back into the admin area," Skeet answered. "Heading upward."

Starcer chimed in. "Continue in the direction you're going. Go past the labs and get to the top floor. My office is in the far southwest corner—you'll see signs."

Manager with a corner office. Made sense. "Acknowledged," Zinni said, picking up her pace. If they could stick to the stairs and avoid the floors where scavvers might be picking through valuables, they'd be in the clear.

No sooner had the thought crossed her mind than they came to a landing where part of the wall and the flight of steps above had collapsed into their path. The concrete was scorched and still smelled vaguely of plasma. Who had set off a grenade in here and when, she didn't know, but they weren't getting through this way.

"Stairwell is blocked between the third and fourth floors," Skeet said, turning back to the level below.

Starcer cursed. "Okay, you'll have to cut through the third-floor labs. It's a straight shot all the way to the other end of the building, and you'll find another stairwell in the opposite corner."

Zinni switched back to their internal comms as she fell into stride behind Skeet. "Oda, acknowledge."

Again, no response. *Damn it.* Where was he?

The two of them burst through the door onto the third floor and found that Starcer's description had been quite literal. A long, wide corridor stretched ahead, lined on either side by floor-to-ceiling windows looking into what must be the labs. There wasn't so much as an alcove or storage container that could be used for cover, leaving them completely exposed for the duration of the trek across the floor.

"Well, *sheyss*," Zinni muttered.

"You can say that again."

They both took off without another word, moving up opposite sides of the corridor, not quite running, their steps in sync. Zinni kept her eyes locked on what lay ahead, using her peripherals to take stock of the labs and watch for any movement therein. Glass partitions. Heavy hammers and drills. The scent of flamer fuel. This was no doubt where the materials that were manufactured downstairs got put through their paces to ensure whatever vehicles and weapons they created would serve their purpose. Her cursory glances into the rooms didn't reveal any signs of said materials, but the plethora of expensive lab equipment here would be like candy for scavengers and mercenaries.

The end of the hall still seemed hopelessly distant when her ears picked up the sounds of rummaging and hushed voices somewhere ahead. In the glow of the emergency lights—a soft yellow here rather than the red of the factory floor—she could make out a smattering of broken glass in front of one of the observation windows. All the laboratory doors had key readers mounted outside, impossible to hack with the power out. That left the windows as the only real entry option if someone wanted to get inside, but even they had security wire running through them, rendering them difficult if not dangerous to break.

Unless you had another bot that could blast its way through. Right on cue, the machine—identical to the one they'd encountered in the factory—floated out into the hall, immediately swiveling and fixing its sinister red sensor-eye on them. With a blaring metallic scream, it charged.

There hadn't been time to get a good look at what kind of weapons systems the bot downstairs had been packing, and there certainly wasn't time now. The drone got a single shot off before exploding in a cloud of sparks, the result of several direct hits from both Skeet and Zinni's weapons. By the time the cloud of fire and smoke dissipated, two shadowy figures were stumbling out of the room, abandoning their armloads of loot in favor of saving their own skins.

"Don't let them go upstairs," Skeet said as they closed the distance.

Ahead, the corridor opened into a wider, foyer-like area that seemed to be somewhere above the building's front entrance with the fried control panel. The two men angled for the far-left corner where Starcer had indicated the other stairwell would be, shouting as they went. More footsteps echoed on the stairs, and from what Zinni could tell in the short amount of time she had to process everything, they were coming up from the floor below.

The events that transpired over the next few seconds seemed to happen in slow motion. The two men who'd fled the lab hesitated at the stairwell, frozen with panic. One began descending. The other whirled around, newly revealed pistol in hand. Zinni dropped him before he even managed to raise the weapon. His friend had no choice but to turn and come back up, unable to move against the current of the four comrades responding to the bot's alarm and the calls for help. Yet another drone accompanied them. Skeet put it down at the exact moment an additional shadow joined the fray, dropping in like liquid from the stairs above. It landed atop one scavenger's shoulders, throwing him to the ground with a *crunch* of vertebrae and somersaulting away to drive the blade of a hefty combat knife into the spine of another.

Admittedly somewhat pleased to know Ken was even still in the building, Zinni closed in on the remaining three scavvers with Skeet moving in tandem beside her. The men began to scatter, but with a sweep of his foot and a fluid hooking motion with his leg, Ken had one of them down on the floor. Disarmed him. Looked up. Seemed to register Skeet and Zinni's proximity. Took aim for them.

Pure reflex had Zinni ready to return the favor, but she was halfway through the motion of bringing her rifle up when the hum of yet more repulsors reached her ears. She whirled, sighting up the bot Ken was truly aiming for, and squeezed off a shot just as he did the same. The machine crashed to the floor with a squeal like the others. Then everything fell silent.

She pivoted back around to find that Skeet had come within a hair's breadth of shooting the Niiosian and had yet to pry his finger from the trigger. He cast her only a brief glance before they closed the remaining distance between themselves and the scavvers, who appeared to have given up the fight entirely. They weren't pros, just as Zinni had suspected; they carried only small arms, and with their drones neutralized, they were helpless.

"Don't even," Skeet growled in Standard, motioning with the barrel of his rifle as one of them took a single step toward the stairs. "Hands."

Zinni nudged the casing of the bot that had accompanied them with her foot. "Any more of you people or your toys we should know about?"

They lifted their arms and shook their heads, moving closer to where Ken still had their comrade pinned to the floor, combat knife pressed to his neck. "Who are you and why are you here?" Oda asked, his smooth voice especially frigid given the context.

"We're...nobody," the man replied, his throat working beneath the blade. "Just looking for salvage, that's it."

"This whole industrial park has been a mess since the Ibarra occupation," one of the others chimed in. "A lot of the other buildings have been picked clean by other enterprising individuals such as ourselves, but nobody wanted to touch this one while the Cartel was watching."

Skeet finally lowered his weapon. "Ibarra was here?"

"They came through and took everything they wanted a couple of weeks ago, just like they did with all the other development centers. But then they left a small team here, almost like they were staking out the place."

Zinni suppressed a shiver. In the time since they'd arrived planetside, they'd seen no sign of Ibarra activity in the immediate area. The idea that they might have missed something—

"And then they pulled out real quick," said the man on the floor, alleviating her fears.

Ken removed the knife from his throat but made no move to get up. "When?"

"Early yesterday?" one of the others replied, looking to his friend for affirmation. "It was like they either got what they were waiting for or gave up on it. I don't know. We didn't bother trying to get in here until this morning, just to be safe."

Now Ken did pull away, drawing his knee back to kneel beside the scavenger in close enough proximity to still make the man think twice about moving. "So Ibarra was staking out *this* particular building, though it offers nothing more of value to them," he said, the blade of the knife reflecting the yellow lighting as he twirled it. "Why?"

"Waiting for Starcer to come back, maybe," Zinni offered.

"And suddenly they're not? This combined with the transport fleet's movements...we should inform Tobias immediately."

The mention of the mobster's name sent all three scavvers squirming. "Whoa," one said, raising his hands in surrender despite no one ordering him to. "You guys are with Niio?"

"Look, we didn't mean nothin'," said the one on the floor. "We haven't even taken anything. Well, okay, we took a few things, but you can have 'em back, I swear. Just tell Tobias we—"

Ken cut him off. "I suggest you leave now."

The man hesitated as though shocked they were being allowed to go, then nodded vigorously. "Yeah, yeah, sure."

They watched as he scrambled to his feet, running headlong into one of his comrades in his haste to escape. With whispered exclamations, they clambered down the stairs, leaving the packs they'd been carrying behind along with the destroyed bots.

Ken slid the knife back into the sheath on his hip and adjusted his rifle strap, bringing the weapon back around front. "We should continue," he said, extending an inviting hand toward the stairs.

Skeet and Zinni exchanged a look before proceeding upward, following the same old formation with Skeet in the lead, the Niiosian in the middle, and Zinni bringing up the rear. As they walked, Ken opened team comms to the *Revenant*.

"There's no longer an Ibarra presence at the development center?" Tobias asked after the enforcer had explained the situation.

"Affirmative. As of yet, we don't know where they went or why."

"After your prior report about the transport fleet, this intrigues me."

"I was thinking the same thing."

"What's Ziva's take?" Skeet asked.

"I've neither seen nor heard from Agent Payvan since she assisted you earlier." The mobster grew silent for several seconds, and if Zinni wasn't mistaken, there'd been more than a slight note of agitation in his voice. "Give us a moment to consider the situation. Let me know when you have the schematics."

"Yes, sir," Ken said, muting the channel.

They reached the uppermost floor momentarily and angled for the southwest corner Starcer had specified. This level of the building appeared to be exclusively administrative, with spacious offices, conference rooms, and neatly arranged communal workspaces. There was nothing of real value up here, at least not like there was in the labs and in the factory, but the area appeared to have been ransacked anyway.

Starcer's office—marked with a name placard like he had said—had floor-to-ceiling windows like the corridor downstairs; even with the glass partially tinted, it was clear the room was a bigger mess than anywhere else on the floor. Ibarra had likely tossed it. It was impossible to tell whether they'd been actively seeking the schematics or were simply looking for signs of where Starcer had gone. Regardless, Zinni hoped they hadn't succeeded in their quest.

The three of them advanced into the room, and Skeet opened comms back up with the director. "Ground team here. Apologies for the delay—resistance neutralized. We're at the office and awaiting instruction."

"Stand by," Emeri replied.

In the several seconds of silence that followed, Zinni took a moment to survey the mess. Starcer had originally told them the specs were in physical form, and most of the debris on the floor consisted of discarded data pads and broken furniture. She chose to take that as a good sign, but she couldn't help but wonder where in this minimalistic space a physical file might be stored.

Starcer himself chimed in after a moment, preceded by a sigh that gave her the distinct impression he sincerely wished he wasn't having to share his precious hiding place with anyone. "Behind my desk, there's a metal sculpture on the wall."

The sculpture was an arrangement of bronze cylinders of varying widths and lengths, all lined up parallel to each other to create an asymmetrical wave-like shape. It had been pulled from the wall and currently sat lopsided on the floor, but it appeared undamaged.

"The third pipe from the right is hollow. Twist the right-most one ninety degrees left to release the compartment."

Running a hand briefly over the cylinders in question, Skeet hefted the whole sculpture up onto the desk. With a twist of the right-most cylinder, something popped from the base of the other, and he removed a protective tube from inside. He tipped it toward the desk, and a roll of transparent films slid out. Zinni released a sigh of relief.

"Got them," he announced.

"Let me see," Ken said, moving over to the desk and shining a spotlight on it.

"Hopefully they're something Niio can use," Starcer said.

Skeet slid around to the front of the desk to give Ken space. "We'll keep you posted. Ground team out."

They watched as the Niiosian unrolled the films and laid them out side by side. There were several sheets, some with blueprints, some with instructions and data. What exactly they portrayed, Zinni couldn't tell from where she stood. Ken's brow furrowed in consternation as he studied them, and for a moment she worried he was finding them to be useless and they'd gone through all of this for nothing. But then he nodded to himself and tapped the films approvingly.

"These schematics could play a crucial role in this fight," he said absentmindedly. He rolled the sheets back up and returned them to their tube. "Orders?"

Zinni's gaze had begun drifting around the office again, but it snapped back to Ken in response to the question, as did Skeet's. He stood rigid, staring straight ahead at the two of them, but his eyes were out of focus, as though he were listening intently. Something inside her came alive, and she zeroed in on his hand when she saw that it had come to rest on his holster. He hadn't been asking them for orders or talking to them at all as he studied the specs. He was communicating with someone else.

Her mind began running through a series of microsecond calculations—her angle and distance to the door, her remaining ammo, his potential exit trajectory given his proximity to the desk—but he relaxed suddenly, startling her, and removed his hand from his weapon.

"Understood," he said, his voice still characteristically cold but lacking the sheer ice it had contained a moment before.

Then Tobias's voice crackled in all their ears, back on the team channel, and Zinni was convinced that's who the man had been talking to. "In light of what we've discovered about Ibarra's movements, I'm ordering the three of you to remain where you are. Carry on with your reconnaissance of the area and await further instruction. We will continue our journey toward you, but I'm deploying scouts to see if we can ascertain Manes's plan and whereabouts. I suspect our timetable has just moved up."

It was the last thing Zinni wanted to hear. They would have ended up staying here until the Niiosian fleet arrived anyway, but there was something more disheartening about doing it under these circumstances...and feeling like they'd just been sucked deeper into this mess.

"Copy," Ken replied. "Standing by for orders." The transmission cut out, and he turned to Skeet and Zinni, holding up the tube containing the specs. "I propose we get these back to the *Saber* forthwith and store them somewhere safe, as well as see about creating a digital copy."

As tempting as it was to look up at Skeet, Zinni found herself unable to pry her attention away from the Niiosian. The *assassin*. Assuming he'd been on a private channel with his boss, what had he meant by asking for orders? Had he been prepared to kill them? If so, why, and why did it seem Tobias had stopped him? She and Skeet didn't give a damn about these specs. They were only here because of Starcer's commission, so it wasn't like Niio had any reason to view them as competition for the blueprints' use. But perhaps tying up loose ends was tying up loose ends.

Skeet stood fast. "After you."

Now she did look up at him, and he at her. There was understanding in Ken's eyes as he turned and strode toward the door, his back to them. They filed out behind him, reaching a silent agreement to not let him out of their sight again.

Chapter 21
NIIOSIAN CRUISER *REVENANT* · Deep Space

Aroska had barely settled onto the little sofa in Ken's cabin when he heard the heavy footfalls coming up the hallway outside. Giving Ziva the data pad and then leaving her to her own devices had been a bit of a gamble, so part of him was overcome with relief that she was choosing to seek him out, especially so quickly. But at the same time, he felt compelled to brace himself for whatever attitude might accompany those stomping feet.

He'd opted to leave the door open to allow her easy entry. She burst into the room, face contorted by the same scowl she'd worn in the officers' lounge, and pounded a fist against the control panel behind her. Technically, this door and others like it couldn't slam—mechanisms within the wall forced them to shut at a uniform rate every time—but based on her demeanor, slamming had been the intention, whether the speed of the closure changed or not.

"The hell is this?" she demanded, bringing one hand to rest on her hip. In her other, she clutched the data pad with white knuckles.

"That," he began, rising to his feet and moving over to stand in front of her with his arms folded, "is a little project I've been working on for the past four years."

Her scowl didn't abate, but something about the way she hesitated ever so slightly gave him the impression he'd caught her off guard. "You knew I would be on Panuco."

So she'd at least taken the time to read some of the pad's contents. Still, it was a statement rather than a question, and there'd been something oddly accusatory in her tone. "I wasn't positive," he answered, "but it was the best lead we had."

"You *lied* to me," she said, voice low. Her jaw trembled and tears glistened in her wide eyes once more.

"We didn't lie, Ziva," Aroska replied softly, shaking his head. "What Zinni said was true—we came to Panuco looking for Matia Moryi per Starcer's request and had no idea the two of you were one and the same." He gestured at the data pad in her hand. "But yes, we knew there was a chance you might be there, and we hoped that if we managed to make contact, we could recruit you to help us bring Moryi down. In a sense, that's exactly what happened, but things are obviously more complicated than we'd envisioned."

Those tears—hot and angry—broke free and spilled down her face. "But you..." she began, thrusting a finger toward him and grinding her teeth as though struggling to articulate what she wanted to say. When she spoke again, she was nearly shouting. "You *knew*. You did all of *this*." She hurled the pad at him. "I told you not to look for me!"

He allowed the device to bounce off his chest and clatter to the floor without flinching. "No, you told me not to stop you or come after you when you were surrendering to the Feds. Once the *Intrepid* blew, I figured that didn't apply anymore. Did you seriously expect me to sit idly by once you let me know you were alive?"

She swore and whirled away, moving to lean over the little kitchenette counter with her back to him.

"I had no intention of compromising your safety," he continued. "But the point is, I never once gave up on you in the past four years, so it's killing me to see you giving up on yourself right now."

Her shoulders quivered as a quiet sob wracked her body. It was still such a foreign sight that he was almost afraid to approach; he wouldn't be surprised if she had shown more emotion today than in the rest of her life put together. At the very least, it had been many years, and as enlightening as it was to see her like this, he found himself desperately craving the stoic, confident Ziva Payvan he'd known before.

"You don't know what I've been through!" she wailed, turning back to face him with her hands on her head as though ready to pull her own hair out. Her eyes were like crimson fire, crazed and burning, and when she locked gazes with him, he could almost feel the heat of her rage physically consuming him. "You have no *frouchten* idea!"

"I have absolutely no doubt that's true," Aroska said, holding his hands out in surrender and venturing a couple of steps closer to her. "I can't even begin to imagine some of the things you've had to endure as Matia, and even before we met. But you've never stopped fighting before. You told me once that surviving is all you know how to do, and I want to help you survive. If you want to talk, or even to just not be alone, I'm here. And if you're not ready, I'll be here until you are."

She sucked in a ragged breath and wiped hopelessly at some of her tears, then shook her head in disgust. "*Sheyss*. You never could just leave me alone, could you."

The words struck him like a punch to the gut, leaving a wave of what could only be fear coursing through his stomach. Fear that the past four years had changed her irreparably after all. Fear that he'd gotten too caught up in his own feelings and desires to realize what she'd felt and desired even before she left Haphez. Fear that she'd been purposely leading him on for some morbid reason and he'd been stupid enough to fall for it. The more rational part of his mind assured him none of that was likely true, but he swallowed and steeled himself anyway in preparation for a question he knew he needed to ask, one he almost dreaded the answer to.

"Is that what you want?"

She looked up immediately, as if taken aback by the abruptness of the inquiry. The reaction surprised him—if that was truly what she wanted, then surely she would have been the first to suggest cutting to the chase and not wasting time dancing around the issue. But the fact that she didn't answer immediately told him all he needed to know. In fact, she didn't answer at all. Some of his apprehension dissipated.

"Ziva, come on," he said softly, venturing closer to her once more. "I realize these past few years have been rough, and that's putting it lightly. And I know your mission didn't end the way it was supposed to. What I don't understand is why it's affecting you the way it is. Even if everything had gone according to plan, you would have come back here to Tobias and things would basically be playing out the same way. Why are you acting like this?"

"Because *you're* here!"

The words were spat out with so much force she trembled as she said them. For several long seconds, all Aroska could do was stand there in shock, caught in her fiery gaze. Her jaw twitched and a vein in her forehead bulged as though she were about to explode.

"*Sheyss*, you just don't get it, do you," she sneered, beginning to pace back and forth without removing her eyes from him. "I spent four years—" her voice faltered "—convincing myself I was never going to see any of you again and subsequently trying my damnedest to forget you. I have *explained* this to you."

It struck him that she had, when she'd first come into the medbay and he'd been pretending to be asleep. But the emotion with which the words were said now painted them in a whole new light.

"And then you all had the audacity to come quite literally barging back into my life, reminding me of everything I can no longer have. And *you...you're* the worst—" She shook her head, unable to even complete the thought, and flung her hand toward the discarded data pad. "After all of that, I find out you've been busting your ass trying to find me for the past four years instead of just forgetting me and moving on with your life like you should have!"

"Well, I'm sorry for caring."

She advanced toward him, teeth clenched. "So you cared and I didn't, is that it?"

"I don't know. You seem to think forgetting and moving on was some casual, simple matter."

"You think I wanted to forget?" she snapped. "You think it was easy? That it didn't hurt like hell every single day? Meanwhile, you were on the other side of the galaxy, playing hero, living out some fantasy like I was fine and—"

He'd begun to walk away, recognizing that he was becoming too hot-headed for his own good, but that was a step too far. How *dare* she accuse him of not suffering, too.

He whirled on her abruptly. "You think *that* didn't hurt?" he shouted, flinging a hand up as heat flooded his face. "You think I want-ed to spend what felt like every waking moment hoping, searching, all while knowing I'd probably never see you again?"

"Then why'd you do it?" she demanded. Her eyes burned with angry defiance, and she slammed the heels of her hands into his shoulders. "Hmm? Why!"

"Because I love you, damn it!"

The words spilled out without warning, startling him just as much as they did her. He hadn't planned on that sentence being part of this conversation, but it had simply been a gut response to her question, so maybe it was good that it was now out in the open. It wasn't like it was a big secret at this point anyway.

For a second, Ziva remained completely frozen, her mouth hanging slightly open as though her next argument had evaporated completely. But the change in her face was both immediate and obvious; her brows turned upward, and the tears flowed anew, now out of genuine sadness and maybe even fear rather than anger. "Why?" she repeated, voice wavering.

He allowed some of the tension in his shoulders to release and raised an eyebrow. "You know, that's not exactly the conventional response when someone tells you they love you."

And just like that, some of the rage returned. "Damn it, Aroska!"

Bad move. "Okay," he said, shrinking back a bit. He raked a hand back over his head, taking a moment to gather himself. "It took me a long time to reach that conclusion. You played a big role in destroying my life and my family, and sometimes I remember all of that and I still want to hate you. But despite everything you took from me, you've given me so much in return. You've saved my life countless times. You've taught me lessons I can't really explain, whether you meant to or not. This connection you and I had...*have*...it's some combination of compassion, empathy, affection, intimacy. I still don't fully understand it, but I know it's special, and I know all of those things are included in the definition of love."

She stood motionless as he spoke, face stony, eyes swollen. It was easy to look back on their time together before her disappearance and be sure she felt something in return. But after so long pretending to be someone else, someone who felt nothing for no one, perhaps she needed to be reminded what she was capable of. That fire—their connection—was still there; he could feel it in the way she'd saved him in the tunnels, the things she'd said to him in the medbay, their interactions the night before. But right now, it had been reduced to a dwindling ember in desperate need of rekindling. He only hoped it wasn't growing colder.

"So, there's your 'why'...along with a hundred other reasons I can't put into words," he said with a shrug, searching her face for any sign of understanding. "And I will say it again: I am here for you. I want to help you, but you have to talk to me. Help me help you."

Ziva's eyes narrowed even as the tears continued flowing, and she shook her head. "You have no idea what you're talking about."

It felt more like he had no idea what *she* was talking about. "What?"

"No, you think you've got all of this figured out, but I see exactly what's happening here." She forced a shaky, disgusted smile as she resumed her pacing. "You're intrigued by me. Whatever's drawing you to me? It's just curiosity. When it comes down to it, I'm just a puzzle you think you can solve."

Five moons, where was all of this coming from? "Ziva, that's not—" His argument fizzled then and there when he realized he'd once thought of her in those exact terms. But it wasn't the bad thing she was making it out to be. Surely she had to understand that.

"I just want to know you," he said, finally able to articulate aloud his train of thought from the night before.

Her scowl remained. With her tear-streaked face, the dark circles around her eyes, and a sheen of greasy perspiration that had appeared on her forehead not long ago, she was a sorry sight indeed. But she made no move to push him away or retreat. Instead, she swore under her breath and spun away with her hands on her hips. "You are ruining my life. I hope you know that."

If by 'ruining,' she meant disrupting the callous, distant, apathetic structure upon which she based her day-to-day function, then he chose to interpret that as a good thing, even if she refused to acknowledge it. Based on her reactions, however, he was beginning to wonder if some of this anger stemmed from—dare he say it—*guilt*. Guilt that he'd put forth all this effort to demonstrate his devotion to her and she hadn't done the same. The idea brought him a measure of relief, as it meant she cared enough to even feel that regret. At the same time, it ate away at him. When it came down to it, he'd been free to do as much searching and pining as he pleased, while she'd needed to forget everything and everyone from her past life in order to protect herself. He'd never considered how their disparate approaches to being split apart might sting, mostly because he truthfully hadn't expected to ever find her. He'd certainly never intended to hurt her.

"Ziva, I'm not trying to guilt you, not by any means."

"Damn it, I didn't *want* to forget," she said, drawing in a shaky breath. She turned back to face him, her skin pale, her forehead glistening more and more by the second. "But I thought I *needed* to!"

"Are you okay?"

She slowly released another breath, placing a hand over her eyes. "It's just really hot in here..." She cleared her throat and stood with her fist clenched in front of her mouth for a moment, then turned without another word and strode toward the lavatory, breaking into a sprint for the final couple of steps into the tiny room. The sound of retching emanated from the darkness within, followed by a grotesque splattering as she vomited.

Aroska sighed and followed her, turning on the light to find her collapsed against the toilet and clutching the rim of the bowl as she gagged into it. He moved around and stooped down behind her, running a hand over the top of her head. "Here," he murmured, doing his best to gather up the hair that had come loose from her ragged little ponytail and keep it out of her face.

It was difficult to tell whether the sound that followed was a grunt of gratitude or a cough. "Gaghhh—it—" she sputtered just before heaving again "—b-burn-s."

She said that as though it was somehow a surprise. He bit the inside of his lip and turned away, partially to keep himself from saying 'I told you so' and partially because the gloriously putrid smell of regurgitated alcohol stirred up such a jumble of unpleasant memories his own stomach threatened to protest. At least she was getting this out of her system early; a Haphezian trying to purge something—solid *or* liquid—that had made it into their secondary stomach wasn't a pretty sight.

"Yeah," he whispered, "it does."

An image of a situation not unlike this one crept into his mind, but their roles were reversed. He'd been the one spewing his guts all over his kitchen table while Ziva looked on, unimpressed. The memory of her cold, unfeeling features elicited a brief smile, for the whole setup had been nothing if not indicative of their two personalities. But it also prompted another thought. When he'd told Ziva she'd seen him at his worst, he'd been referring to that whole mess of addiction and misery she'd found him wallowing in. When he'd suggested that he'd also seen her at her worst, he'd been referring to the times when she had seemed out of control, killing remorselessly, refusing to listen to reason. But looking back on it, there'd still been a measure of calculation and focus about her actions—they were traits that had allowed her to thrive as Matia, and it made him reevaluate what he'd previously thought. He considered what he had seen in the past day, even in the past hour: this raw, disturbed state where she felt compelled to push away any help and try to destroy herself to escape the despair. Her 'worst' wasn't while she was being brutal and merciless. This was.

And in that sense, their 'worsts' weren't all that dissimilar.

She finally managed to stop heaving, and he knelt in silence stroking her hair while she remained slumped against the toilet bowl. After a few moments, she brushed his hand away—not so much a gesture of frustration as merely a signal she needed some space—and began to haphazardly haul herself to her feet. Aroska reached out and flushed the toilet and all its vile contents, then retreated to the tiny lav's far wall and watched as she moved to the sink to splash some water over her face and rinse her mouth out several times. Then, for what felt like a long time, she simply stood there with her head bowed, her muscular arms braced against the sides of the sink. It was difficult to tell whether she was staring into the running water or whether her eyes were closed.

Finally, she shut the water off, patted her face dry with a towel, and swiveled to lean against the sink with her arms crossed and her gaze directed toward the floor. The dark circles around her eyes had taken on a greenish tint, and though her skin was still deathly pale, her cheeks and ears had reddened with shame.

"Are you ready to talk to me like a reasonable person?" Aroska asked, mimicking her posture as he moved to hover beside her.

She snorted in disgust. "*Sheyss*, I'm making an ass of myself," she muttered, running the heel of her hand across her eyes.

"You sure are."

"I, ah..." She straightened a bit and lifted her head, though she still hesitated another couple of seconds before meeting his gaze. "I... apologize...for every single thing I've said to you in the past...well, all day, I suppose."

He stared silently into her eyes for a moment, equal parts marveling of his own accord and reeled in by their intensity, just as he had been the first time he'd seen her all those years ago. They weren't unlike the Blood Water nebula, numerous shades of crimson with flecks of dark burgundy around the edges of the irises. He drank in the sight, aware of just how much he'd forgotten after four years apart.

"Every single thing?" he said, allowing a soft smirk to grace his lips.

She tilted her head.

The smirk widened and he narrowed his eyes, feigning thoughtfulness. "I wasn't sure what to make of it when you said I was 'the worst,' but I'm starting to think I should take it as a compliment."

The red in her face and ears deepened. She managed a weak smile and her gaze drifted to the floor. But when she looked up at him again, fresh tears glittered in her eyes, and he saw the muscles in her jaw twitch as she worked to keep her chin from trembling. "I don't know what's wrong with me," she said, barely more than a whisper.

Without further fanfare, he reached out and took her by the shoulders, pulling her to him and wrapping his arms around her. She did likewise and buried her face against his shoulder, and it took only a moment to feel the tears soaking through his shirt. Her muscles were tense, and she quivered slightly as though she was making every attempt to keep herself from physically falling apart. Seeing her like this, it was easy to forget who he was dealing with. It felt like he was trying to console a lost, suffering girl, not the cunning warrior he'd come to love. His own chest tightened as his heart wrenched itself into a knot.

Instinct insisted he tell her there was nothing wrong with her, but that was so far from the truth he doubted it would help the situation. "You know what I think?" he said, pulling back and taking her face in his hands. He passed his thumbs under her eyes, clearing away the tears that streamed anew down her cheeks. "I think this is a reasonable response to everything you've done, everything you've *had* to do. I think you reached a breaking point, and whether you ever realized it or not, you always had a support system back home. Then you got out here, and suddenly you were alone."

She reached up and took hold of one of his wrists, giving it a quick squeeze. Her crimson eyes bored into his, imploring him, pleading with him, though he wasn't positive what she was asking for. Help?

Her voice was still hardly more than a whisper. "I am so tired."

It was a simple phrase, but her tone combined with the look in her eyes combined with the whole context of the encounter gave it so much more power. This was a confession. She was physically exhausted—there was no doubt about that. But it was also a mental exhaustion. She was tired of fighting an uphill battle on multiple fronts, she was tired of doing it on her own, and she was tired of being uncertain. On top of all that, she was afraid. Afraid of hurting him again. Afraid of losing control.

"I know you are. But you are not alone. Not anymore."

She shut her eyes and leaned into his hand for a moment before turning away from him and hovering over the sink again. Then, before he could fully grasp what she was doing, she reached down and tugged her shirt off, exposing her back to him. Save for the thin straps of the compression bra she wore, he had a nearly unobstructed view of her tattoo, of her unfailingly impressive build.

And of the scars.

They were no more or less horrifying than he'd imagined them based on the brief glimpses he'd gotten in the past, but the sight of them left him paralyzed nonetheless. These markings were...*grotesque* seemed like a strong word, but it was also appropriate. The highest concentration of damage lay in the more sensitive area at the small of her back, though several of the longer scars extended upward to cut into the lower part of her tattoo. They were jagged, raised stripes carved into her skin, probably made with some sort of serrated blade.

He reached out to touch one, startled by the texture beneath his fingertips. If proper caura treatment was administered within an adequate time frame, you never saw scarring on this scale anymore. The idea that she'd been trapped in that Cobian bunker for days while the pirates sliced her open and then left her for dead made him fume. He placed his hand flat against her back and closed his eyes to keep his own tears at bay.

The thought suddenly occurred to him that this was the first time he could ever recall where he'd initiated contact and she didn't flinch, pull away, or bristle at the very least. He dragged a finger over one of the scars, following it until it intersected with the tattoo, which he then traced all the way up to the back of her neck. "I'm sorry about this," he murmured, certain there was no other condolence he could offer that would adequately reflect both the anger and heartache he felt.

She scoffed, lifting her head just far enough to meet his gaze in the mirror. "Why? It's not your fault."

Leave it to her to concoct such a response. "*Sheyss*, Ziva," he sighed, massaging her neck between his thumb and forefinger, "you know what I mean."

They were both quiet for a moment before she looked down again. "I'm kind of a mess, aren't I?"

Her tone gave him the sense she wasn't just talking about her physical body. She was talking about her entire persona.

"Not going to lie—you really are. But you're also a survivor, and this is the evidence." His fingers shifted around to trace the scar running from her earlobe down her neck, one of several that had thinned significantly but hadn't completely faded even after Serenity's treatment. "What happened here?"

She reached up and placed her own hand over the mark, almost as though realizing for the first time it was still there. She turned to face him, propping herself against the sink once more. "That one's from a freelance job before the Cartel days. Caught a piece of shrapnel when an IED detonated. That's probably been my closest call over the past four years."

An image formed in his mind of her dragging herself aboard her ship, stranded on some distant world with neither Niio nor Ibarra's support, using up her meager resources in a desperate bid to keep herself from bleeding out. *Never again.*

His eyes dipped to her powerful abdominal muscles, where several more long scars crisscrossed over her flesh. These were hardly more than discolorations in her skin—his fingers barely registered a difference in texture when he touched them—but they were there nonetheless. "And here?" he asked, shifting his attention to some dark spots on her hip just above her waistband.

"The *Intrepid*," she murmured, swallowing hard as her eyes flicked back and forth over his face. For just a moment, it looked like fresh tears were preparing to make an appearance, but then the corners of her mouth twitched upward. She brought her palm up to his face and ran her thumb over his left eyebrow, pausing on the short scar cutting through it. "What's this from?"

The thought elicited an audible chuckle. "It's, ah...not as exciting as you might think. I walked into a door frame out on Xater Prime on the first day of last year's independent service term. You know how short the Rama are. Adin won't let me live it down."

Ziva arched a brow. "You didn't treat it?"

"I cleaned it up, but if I'm being totally honest, I kind of wanted the scar."

"And I kind of like it." A mischievous twinkle appeared in her eyes, and maybe it was just because it was a hopeful glimpse of her old self, but it sent his stomach aflutter. He suddenly wanted nothing more than to pull her close, hold her, kiss her, feel her strength, be strong for her.

She turned her attention to his left arm, pushing his shirt sleeve up a bit and probing the area around his bicep. Like the scars on her stomach, the place where she'd shot him in the Salex warehouse had been reduced to a mere discolored spot, but she found it without much trouble.

"You know, I never did get an apology for that," he said.

The playful glimmer vanished instantly. "You're the one who got in the way of my shot. If anyone needs to apologize, it's you."

The realization that she was serious made him laugh out loud. Her reaction reminded him all too much of the night before when she'd responded to his joke in just as grave a fashion. She did have a point, though; he'd made the idiotic decision to run into the line of fire. He was lucky his arm was all she'd hit.

"Okay, here's a good one." He lifted his shirt and pointed out a misshapen patch of tissue on his left oblique just below his ribcage. "Knife fight with a Durutian bounty hunter a couple years back—she landed a good hit before I sent her packing with a couple of nasty injuries of her own. We were out of caura so treatment was delayed. But where's the fun in trying to erase every sign of battle? A good scar means you experienced something and lived to talk about it."

She reached out and traced the edges of that patch of skin, then slid her hand over to touch a dark spot farther around his side. "And what's this one?"

She had a good eye; he'd almost forgotten about that one. "Took a plasma hit. Same mission, actually. Different day."

Brows drawn, she laid her palm flat against the old injuries as if she could somehow will them to heal completely. Then, with hesitant but ever-fluid movements, she reached over and took his shirt hem from him, tugging it upward, upward. He lifted his arms and allowed her to peel it off over his head, and he was vaguely aware of it being cast to the floor somewhere behind him. She placed a hand against his bare chest, softly probing the new, pink flesh at the place where her plasma bolts had impacted on the Panucan beach. Her touch didn't hurt in a physical sense, especially considering it wasn't her elbow like it had been the night before, but seeing the pain in her eyes as she assessed her handiwork sent an abstract ache creeping through his own body.

He closed his eyes and drew a breath in through his nose when her hand began to slide down over his stomach. *Let her.* He drew closer, relishing her touch as her fingers traced his abdominal muscles. It was fascinating that hands which could cause so much destruction—hands that could kill a man if she desired it—could also be so gentle. But maybe the more accurate term would be precise. Thorough. Analytical. Calculating. This woman sharing this space with him was one hundred percent lethal. They both were. The concept thrilled him and sent a sharp tingle up his spine. Her mere presence made him feel invincible, unstoppable. He could only hope he had the same effect on her.

Her left hand slid around the small of his back while her right snaked up his arm, over his shoulder, and wound around the back of his neck. It was all he could do to keep from taking over, moving forward. *Let her. Let her.* He leaned in without hesitation when she pulled him closer, but rather than the expected sensation of her lips meeting his, she merely brought his forehead to rest against her own. It was an incredibly simple gesture, but considering the source, it felt more powerful than the deepest kiss or strongest embrace. He placed his hands on her waist, reveling in the raw strength beneath his fingertips.

For several long moments, it felt like time itself had stopped as the two of them stood there drinking each other in. Aroska felt her warm breath on his face as she brought her mouth within a centimeter of his, but then she released a sharp sigh and dipped her head.

"I can't do this," she whispered.

"What can't you do?" he asked, immensely curious what her definition of 'this' was.

She lowered her hands and pulled back, and he had to put conscious effort into not fighting her as she retreated to lean against the sink again. "Give you what you want."

He folded his arms and tilted his head. "And what, exactly, do you think it is that I want?"

Her gaze flicked up to meet his. "Normal."

All he could do was scoff. "Ziva, I've known from the beginning that you're not normal, and I've never expected anything different." He took a step closer to her, pleased to see her features soften. "You know what I want? I want to be with you. I want to be by your side. I want to know you. I want to protect you. I want to back you up." He paused. "I want to solve problems with you."

That prompted the slightest hint of a smirk. She straightened a bit, her eyes glinting with a familiar intensity.

"I want to be your partner in every sense of the word." He reached out and tipped her chin upward, ensuring he had her undivided attention. "Now, you're Ziva Payvan. You don't need anyone, right? But what do you *want*?"

Based on her dilated pupils and the pulse he could feel racing in her neck, he had a decent idea of what she wanted. But when she swallowed—hard—he knew he wasn't going to get a straight answer.

"Let's try a different question. When was the last time you did something just because you wanted to? Not because you were ordered to, not because you had to, not because you needed to in order to survive. Just because it was what you wanted."

He sensed her stiffen. Her eyes darted to and fro, threatening to break away from his face. She drew a short breath in through her nose and tilted her head, parting her lips as if to speak but clamping them shut again before she could.

Everything that came next happened so fast it took Aroska a split second to process it. She snatched her shirt up from the edge of the sink, ducked around him, and strode out of the lavatory, pulling her top back on as she made a beeline for the cabin door.

"Ziva."

She didn't look back. The door hissed open and shut, and she was gone.

CHAPTER 22
NIIOSIAN CRUISER *REVENANT* - DEEP SPACE

She made it exactly nine and a half strides down the corridor before coming to an abrupt halt; she knew this because her mind had subconsciously started counting her echoing footfalls the moment the door had shut, a desperate attempt to focus on anything other than what had just transpired in the cabin.

What are you doing?

I'm running.

She wasn't even sure why she'd stopped—she certainly hadn't meant to, at least not the part of her that still seemed to be thinking coherently and hadn't gone completely off the rails. This was a disaster. *She* was a disaster, standing there with her heart hammering, her brain clambering, grasping for a shred of logic or reason to snatch and run with as she stared straight ahead at nothing in particular. *Sheyss*, a complete disaster.

Where are you going?

...I don't know.

Her hands had curled into fists at some point during the short walk, and she slowly pried her fingers open, flexing them and curling them back up again. Flexing. Curling. Flexing. She shook her hands out and let out a similarly shaky breath, releasing a jaw that had been clenched tighter than she'd realized.

Why are you running?

...I don't know.

But she did know, her mind insisted. She simply couldn't bring herself to accept it.

Why are you running?

...Because I am afraid.

Then came a thousand questions about what the great Ziva Payvan could possibly be so afraid of. First and foremost, and perhaps what had started this whole mess, she was afraid of losing control. The lengths she'd gone to in order to adopt and maintain a new identity had resulted in a measure of emotional damage she hadn't fully acknowledged until being reintroduced to a civilized environment, and that emotional damage had in turn nearly resulted in the death of the man she'd just run away from.

Secondly, that man said he loved her for the galaxy only knew what reason, not only after what she'd almost done to him that morning but after everything she'd done to him years prior. She didn't know what to do with that information. Thinking back on it, maybe it was something she'd already known, particularly after everything they'd been through together while facing Ronan and the Resistance. But it was another matter entirely to hear the words spoken aloud, especially after she'd spent four years trying to forget any feelings either of them might have had. How could he have kept trying so hard to find her when he knew they were never supposed to meet again?

It wasn't fair.

On top of all that, she hated—*hated*—the fact that she could bare her soul to him with such little effort. Blurting things. Telling him things she couldn't tell Skeet and Zinni. Or, as she'd once put it, telling him things she couldn't even tell herself. It had been this way practically since they'd met, even back when they'd still been at odds, and it was all because of this damn connection they shared. What was it about him?

She was good at a lot of things, but this was not one of them, and that was what scared her most. This all defied the logic she was so desperately grasping for, which meant there were no rules. No clear path to follow. No manual to tell her what she needed to do next. What she *had* to do next.

So, Ziva Payvan, what do you want?

Without even realizing it, she had pivoted around to look back down the hall at the cabin door, still and silent. She'd continually pushed him away because it was the easy route. *That* was something she knew how to do. Feelings were not her forte. Neither was admitting something she didn't want to admit. But maybe it wasn't even a matter of not wanting to admit it; it was merely a matter of not knowing how.

Her feet were carrying her back toward the cabin of their own accord, the edges of the corridor blurring in her vision. The man inside that room was right about her in so many ways it was maddening. She *had* always had a support system at home, whether in terms of physical backup or emotional bonds, and that system had been absent for the last four years. It was a form of intimacy she'd never fully recognized until she no longer had access to it. And now it was back on the table, offered by someone who was not only willing to help her but also seemed to want nothing *but* to help her. At the very least, help was what she both wanted and needed right now, and if there was a single person in the entire galaxy she could choose to receive that help from, it was Aroska Tarbic.

"There's no one I'd rather have backing me up."

It hardly felt like her movements were her own as she came to a stop in front of the cabin door. She stood and drew one last deep breath as she stared at the brushed metal texture. The red light on the control panel indicated she'd locked herself out. All too appropriate. She reached out to press the buzzer, but a split second before she hit the button, the door hissed open. Aroska stood there, his hand lingering on the interior controls a second longer. He remained completely relaxed, not at all like he'd been about to burst into the hall and chase her down. No, he'd simply known she would return, and he was waiting for her. Damn him. And damn her for coming.

He reached out to her, palm upward, inviting her in. He said nothing, but in his eyes, she saw wisdom. Understanding. Unrelenting kindness. But also a spark, a familiar, intriguing glimmer of intensity. It wasn't an I-told-you-so look, even though he had every right. Instead, it was an offer. For refuge. Safe haven.

Love.

She only hesitated a moment longer before she took his hand and stepped back inside.

The door slid shut behind her.

Chapter 23
Ibarra Vessel *Oblivion* - Deep Space

The soft hum of the FTL drive. The cool sheets beneath his skin. The lingering scent of bitter liquor wafting from the open bottle on the bedside table. The sensation of Kimbra's fingernails grazing his arm. Alastair Manes was objectively aware of each of these things, but they resided so far in the back of his mind that they might as well not be happening. He lay flat on his back, one arm folded behind his pillow, his other hand curling tighter and tighter around a fistful of the sheet as the turbulence inside his head intensified. Staring aimlessly at the ceiling of his cabin was ultimately unhelpful. He needed to do *something*, needed to act on all these thoughts plaguing him. But the fact was there was nothing more he could accomplish until they reached Delatori, and it was killing him. Every distraction he'd managed to conjure up—including his second-in-command's company—had been temporary at best, leaving him with only his obsessions. Rinse and repeat.

"What are you thinking about?" Kimbra asked. She withdrew her hand and folded both arms up under her own pillow, her blonde hair falling over her shoulders as she settled onto her stomach.

Manes lay in silence for several more seconds before rising from the bed without answering. Assuming he wanted to respond, he didn't know where to even start explaining what was going through his mind. He poured himself another drink and wandered over to the viewport, placing one palm flat against the window as he sipped at the potent liquor. The sight of the rippling FTL tunnel had helped calm him before; it wasn't quite having the same effect now, but he found that after a couple of minutes, he was at least able to sort all his swirling thoughts into a linear order.

The first thing that struck him was the idea that the rest of his fleet was somewhere out there, zooming forward right along with him. The exact same realization had been discouraging on the journey away from Panuco, but now that they'd absorbed all of Naris Base's space worthy forces *and* were due to make another pit stop to rendezvous with a few more of their gunships, the thought was downright invigorating. On top of that, he once again had Karol Zysk under his direct command. Once they reached Delatori, recovered the necessary materials, and completed all the retrofits he'd been working toward for months, she would make the fleet dance.

It all made him feel unstoppable.

The problem was that, while he was certainly looking forward to that whole process, he couldn't help but jump ahead and think about the result: putting a permanent end to Tobias Niio. In fact, he'd gladly sacrifice whatever pleasure this feeling of invincibility evoked if it meant he could skip straight to the part where he put a bullet through the old mobster's head. Or maybe a blade through his heart. There were so many options, and it was impossible to decide from where he stood right now.

The Niiosians were like an itch he couldn't scratch. Sometimes that itch was at the forefront of his mind, and sometimes it wasn't, but it was always there, tormenting him. Now here he was, *so close* to subduing it for good. This had been his goal for the past four years. Longer, he supposed, considering the countless arguments he'd gotten into over his father's unwillingness to expand into Niiosian territory. Oron Manes had simply grown too old—too old-*fashioned*—to be an effective leader when and where it counted, and it had cost him his life. Soon Tobias would suffer the same fate. Survival of the fittest.

The thought of finally putting an end to this struggle should have brought Manes a sense of relief, and he almost wished it would. Instead, it ate away at him, dominated his focus, consumed his every waking moment. He couldn't rest, couldn't relax, not until this was over. He'd allowed himself to grow complacent in the past; that was the only logical explanation for why this hadn't all ended months ago. He'd begrudgingly accepted the idea of starting over when things went wrong, and he'd wasted too much time trying to ensure Ibarra was *ready*. The Niiosian attack on Panuco had forced him to acknowledge an unpleasant truth: maybe they would never be ready. There came a time when you simply needed to act, because even going in unprepared was better than the consequences of not acting at all. He only wished he'd had the guts to make that first move. The idea that Tobias had beaten him to the punch only agitated him further.

Add to all of that the fact that Niio had only caught him off guard because he'd been so preoccupied by Matia Moryi and the Haphezian agents. He should have killed her and her comrades from the outset, instead of wasting time toying with them. Instead of asking himself 'what if?' Instead of wanting to 'wait and see.'

He tilted his head back and finished his glass, wincing as the burning liquid slid down his throat. No more hesitation. No more uncertainty.

In the viewport's reflection, he saw Kimbra roll over and prop herself up on her elbows. "Hey," she said softly, "come back to bed."

That sultry voice made it tempting, but like everything else, the thought faded to the back of his mind, strangled by the images of his ships laying waste to Niio Spaceport, of Tobias begging for mercy at his feet.

Unless he'd completely lost track of time—and he liked to think he'd kept track just fine, considering his obsessive mind was incapable of doing much else right now—they had just bypassed the Blood Water nebula. At Karol Zysk's suggestion, he'd reluctantly agreed to take the extra time necessary to give it a wide berth; as much as the idea of another delay—even just a few extra hours—killed him, he could admit it was the smartest move. He sincerely doubted the Niiosians were still in there, but the nebula interfered with instruments to the point that he'd never be able to tell without going in to check for himself, and the last thing he wanted was to be taken by surprise again. Best to take steps to avoid an ambush altogether.

That was the thing about all of this. Manes considered himself a reasonably intelligent man, so he recognized that the objectively wise thing to do if he wanted to win this war was employ patience. But damn it, he was so tired of being patient. His time had come to shine, and he was fully prepared to charge full speed ahead. He made up his mind then and there that he would continue taking Zysk's tactical guidance under advisement if it was in the best interest of maintaining his power and control over the situation, but the moment she suggested anything that directly hampered his progress, she'd be finished.

"Come on," Kimbra said again, stretching out and sweeping her arm over the empty space beside her. "Come back and keep me company."

Manes sighed. He had half a mind to comply—

"There's nothing else you can do right now anyway."

—the hand he'd kept pressed against the viewport curled abruptly into a fist, which he then slammed against the glass. "Do not tell me that."

"You know it's true."

She was right, after all. He'd been acknowledging this very issue mere minutes ago. But there was a big difference between admitting it to himself within the privacy of his own head and hearing someone articulate it out loud. Worse, having someone *tell* him. The woman's nerve was often an admirable trait, but right now it made his blood boil.

"Do not tell me what I can and cannot do," he growled, turning to face her. "I have waited over four years for this."

She sat up. "I want this too, you know."

The scent of her perfume and the way she wore her hair loose made her seem so much softer now than she ever did while she was at his side overseeing Cartel operations. But even there in the quiet of his cabin, there remained a steely focus in her eyes. This combined with her muscular build reminded him that she would always be his weapon. Both his sword and his shield. Ready to fight at his behest just as much as she was prepared to defend him against his enemies. Unfailingly loyal.

Despite that, there was no way she really wanted this, not in the same way he did. She might simply want to exact revenge on Niio after the attack on Panuco. She might simply want to acquire Niio's resources on principle, anything to benefit Ibarra. She might simply want these things because he did—that's how priorities worked when you were as devoted as she was. But at this point, those reasons all felt almost superficial. The roots of his desire ran deep, deeper than he could articulate with words, deeper than she could ever understand. Hearing her say these things was almost insulting.

He whirled, letting out a growl of rage, and hurled his empty glass across the room. It shattered against the far wall, leaving shards to rain down over his comm terminal and workstation. He advanced toward the bunk, ready to deliver a fresh tirade about the full depth of the situation, but the buzzer at his cabin door cut him off. He glared in that direction, ready to berate the caller for merely daring to exist, but the thought occurred to him that this might be something that could serve as a new distraction, even for just a few minutes.

"No, you don't," he muttered, snatching up a wrap and tying it around his waist as he strode for the door. She merely flopped back down in exasperation.

He left it at that and hit the controls, bracing one arm against the bulkhead. "*What?*" he demanded before he'd even processed the identity of the person standing outside.

Brady Tal flinched ever so slightly and held up the data pad he carried. "Got a minute?"

Manes stepped aside and extended an arm, inviting him in.

"I've been looking into individual user history searching for any evidence as to who might have generated the clearance codes the Niiosians used." Tal paused abruptly upon noticing Kimbra still sprawled in the bunk and turned, eyes wide, his gaze flitting momentarily to Manes's bare chest. "Am I...interrupting...?"

"No," Manes answered without hesitation.

"I, ah..." The man swallowed and looked over his data pad again as though trying to remember what he was talking about. "I started by checking logs for everyone who accompanied us from Panuco, or at least those who would have had the privileges necessary to create new codes. Granted, this sort of security analysis isn't really my specialty, but as near as I can tell, nobody I looked at was responsible for the breach."

Manes stroked his chin, allowing this topic to break through the haze in his head and become the center of his focus. The sense of relief was immediate. "So. If there is a traitor—" no, it wasn't even a question of *if* "—they're not in our midst."

Tal shrugged. "That's one man's opinion."

It was a comforting thought. The last thing they needed when going up against Tobias was to have the person who'd aided him before still working from within. "And there's no way to tell whether someone created those codes directly or if they hacked their way in."

"Not with the resources I currently have available, no."

Realistically, some Niiosian hacker could have accessed the system remotely, but they still would have needed some understanding of how the codes worked—what different sections of the strings signified and whatnot—in order to do it successfully. He thought back to Jerrick Taan, the former Niiosian agent who'd been ousted while undercover on Naris and converted into an Ibarra asset. It was possible he could have forwarded instructions to Tobias before getting caught, but he'd been dead for two years now, killed and replaced by Matia months before the codes had been generated if Tal's previous analysis was accurate.

The silence dragged on for several more moments as Manes considered all of this, then Tal cleared his throat. "I simply wanted to give you another update, sir. The fact is I'm not sure if we'll ever know who was responsible."

Once again, it was probably true, but it still wasn't something he wanted to hear out of someone else's mouth. He supposed, however, that knowing nobody in his immediate vicinity had actively betrayed him was a plus. "Thank you for your service," he muttered, still somewhat lost in thought. He turned and gazed pensively toward the viewport, signifying that the discussion was over for now.

Tal excused himself after a few seconds, the sound of the door sliding shut bringing a heavy silence over the room. Maybe the interruption had been a good thing; having something else to devote his attention to had reduced that insatiable itch in his mind to an agitated tickle. But if he thought too hard about it, he recognized how the traitor he sought was essentially responsible for his current predicament, and that idea threatened to send him over the edge again.

He went and sat on the bed, his back to Kimbra, elbows resting on his knees, chin resting on his fisted hands. The train of thought about Jerrick Taan and Matia had rekindled the theory he'd previously entertained about Moryi being involved with the breach. She was smart; he wouldn't put it past her to be able to generate those codes herself *and* cover her tracks, but if she'd had assistance from someone like Blain Reed, that surely would've sealed the deal. He simply didn't know *why* she would have done such a thing, especially given everything he'd learned about her true past just before fleeing Tabaco. He decided to write off his suspicion about her hiding out on Panuco because she was a Nosti; surely her Haphezian cohorts wouldn't have been so friendly toward her if that were the case. The most logical explanation was that she'd been part of a long-term undercover operation surrounding the use of the Haphezian niobi crystals in Ibarra weapons development, and the arrival of the others—her handlers, her partners, whoever they were—had unfortunately coincided perfectly with the arrival of the Niiosians. After all, what reason would she or any other Haphezian have to be working for Tobias?

But then again, what reason would any of his people have?

He felt the mattress shift as Kimbra crawled up behind him. Her hands slid over his shoulders and down his chest and he felt her warm breath against his skin just before her lips skimmed his neck. "You're not convinced by a word he just said, are you," she whispered.

It was tempting to shrug her off, but he felt as though he'd managed to reach a point of...not acceptance, but perhaps neutrality. There *was* nothing more he could do right now, and thus if she wanted to provide him with a new diversion, she was free to do so. In fact, she should be rewarded for her service, both here in the cabin and on the front lines. He knew of one thing in particular she would enjoy.

He turned his head, closing his eyes and breathing in her scent. "When this is finished," he began, "when we've *won*, you have my full authorization to use whatever resources are necessary to make sure Ziva Payvan is dead."

CHAPTER 24
NIIOSIAN CRUISER *REVENANT* - DEEP SPACE

The lavatory door hissed open, releasing hot steam out into the cabin where it could be more efficiently whisked away by the *Revenant's* air filtration system. Ziva reached up and wiped some of the condensation from the mirror, staring at the glass as the blurry silhouette she saw in the reflection slowly sharpened into her own face. Somehow that gradual, foggy transformation felt appropriate. Her hair was still a shaggy mess, and damp wisps stuck out in all directions, but she could objectively say she looked better. Or at least better than she had when she'd first come aboard the ship. The reddish tint from her face paint had nearly disappeared, and the swelling around her nose had vanished completely thanks to Serenity's treatment, each replaced only by some residual redness and puffiness from all the tears she had shed over the past day. *Sheyss*, how pathetic. Pathetic, pathetic, pathetic.

And yet, after all of that, she could honestly say she also *felt* better. Nowhere near normal yet, but...liberated, maybe. It was like a bomb had gone off in her mind, devastating and chaotic in its destruction, but once the fire died down and the dust cleared, she was left with a sense of clarity. A mess still remained, one that could not be remedied in any short order, but sometimes tearing something down was the first step toward building it back up.

A mild headache crept through her skull, no doubt a consequence of the drinking, the stims and awful purging notwithstanding. But she'd changed into some clean clothes—the tank and tac pants that had gotten a good rinse during her breakdown in the lav the day before—and was otherwise feeling refreshed after a proper shower, some half-decent sleep, and....

She sensed Aroska outside the lavatory doorway just before she saw him appear in the mirror. He stood and watched her for a moment, frozen halfway through the process of fastening his gun belt. His eyes were intense but wary, and when she finally met his gaze, he blinked and finished securing his holster before stepping forward into the tiny room.

"How are you feeling?" he asked quietly, dragging his fingers across the small of her back as he stepped past her and recovered his shirt from where it still lay on the floor.

It was hard to tell whether his hand itself was warm or whether it was his touch that sent a more abstract warmth curling up her spine. The truth was she felt rather numb. Maybe a little confused. Definitely processing. It was without doubt an improvement over the sheer brokenness and despair she'd felt over the past day, but she could think of no accurate way to articulate what she was feeling now, if anything at all.

Aroska tugged his shirt on and moved up behind her, wrapping his arms around her waist before leaning down and resting his chin on her shoulder. "Better?" he prompted, meeting her gaze in their reflection.

She reached up and placed a hand against his arm. Even being touched and held like this was unfamiliar, contributing further to the confusion. But 'better' was the description she'd already settled on, so she nodded.

He lingered there a while longer and studied her in silence. For a moment, she feared he was waiting for some elaboration she was incapable of giving, but she concluded he was simply trying to decide whether her meager response had been a truthful one. Finally, he straightened, leaned in and kissed her gently on the side of the head, then pulled away to leave.

She spun and snatched his wrist, merely hoping to catch him before he escaped her reach but fearful she'd moved too fast and startled him. Based on the way he whirled and stared at her hand with wide eyes, that was exactly the case.

"Listen," she said, releasing her grip on him and sliding her palm down over his. She swallowed and took a moment to examine his hand, running her thumb over the calluses just as she had in the Ibarra cell block. The vast majority of Haphezians had rough, calloused hands after a career with either HSP or the military, but it seemed his had become more so during the time they'd been apart. Her own calluses, wrought from years of hand-to-hand combat and handling heavy weaponry, had worsened as well. The thought occurred to her that the moment their two paths had crossed, Aroska had turned and followed her down the turbulent road she'd always walked. Slowly at first, yes, but the damage had been done. There was no turning back for him now.

He'd stopped in the narrow lavatory doorway, so she stepped around and leaned up against the opposite side of the door frame, placing her hands on his shoulders in hopes of reassuring him. With him slouching slightly, they were at exactly eye level, but she found it was harder than she'd expected to maintain eye contact. She drew in a short breath and willed herself calm.

"Listen," she said again, still aware of her own pulse hammering in her ears. "I don't know how else to say this—I don't have a clue what I'm doing right now."

Something soft flashed through Aroska's eyes. Concern, maybe.

"This is completely new territory for me," she continued, "and you know as well as anyone that when I'm in unfamiliar territory, I'm immediately set on edge. I apologize for that, but I can't just switch off years of instinct."

She felt the muscles in his shoulders relax. He reached across what little space remained between them and slid his arms around her back, albeit holding them loose and leaving her a little breathing room. Always so perceptive. The crazy thought occurred to her that there was no way in hell she deserved him.

"Then let me help you," he said.

Several long seconds passed before she managed to shake her head, and as she did, she felt some of the tension return to his body. "There's clearly something not right with me. My mind is playing tricks on me, as you...experienced yesterday."

He snorted. "Oh, I remember."

At least he was keeping a lighthearted attitude about all of this. She stared into his amber eyes, searching for some shred of the discomfort she was convinced he should be feeling, and slid her hands down to rest on his arms where they were wrapped around her. "I don't want something like that to happen again."

"I don't, either, if you can believe it."

"Aroska. Be serious."

"I am gravely serious."

"You're infuriating, do you know that?"

"Are you done making excuses?"

She scowled, though it was admittedly half-hearted. "No, I'm not. I meant what I said before. Whatever *this* is—" she gestured between the two of them "—can never be normal, the most obvious reason being I'm supposed to be dead. But...that and the fact that I can't control my own mind aside, I don't know if I'm wired for this sort of thing, and...I don't want you to be disappointed. I don't want to waste your time."

"And *I* meant what *I* said before. Nothing about my life has been normal since the day we met, and I'm fully prepared for it to continue being that way." He reached up and attempted to smooth down some flyaway hair that had refused to cooperate since she'd gotten it wet. "Look. I'm not under any illusion that I can fix you, or that I can single-handedly heal your mind. I may be good with people, but I think that's outside the scope of my capabilities. You are undeniably broken, but I'm prepared to do whatever I can to help you pick up the pieces."

She looked down and sighed. "When I'm around you, I'm...I'm...." The word refused to form on her tongue.

He smirked. "Charmed? Delighted?" Then he sobered and ran a hand up and down her back. "Vulnerable?"

She grimaced at the mere concept and nodded.

"And you don't like feeling vulnerable." It wasn't a question.

"I do not."

"Do you trust me?"

She glanced up and found his warm gaze fixed intently on her. "More than anything."

"Then what do you have to worry about?"

He had a point. "Nothing, I guess," she replied. "This is just..."

"New. I know." He pulled a hand away and reached down to grasp one of hers. "Can I ask you something? When was the last time you were truly happy?"

Ziva blinked, taken aback by the nature of the question, and let her gaze drift back down to the floor as she contemplated a response. It depended, she supposed, on the definition of 'happy,' which was an objectively *subjective* term. There were times when she'd been content, certainly, but did that count? After what felt like hours of consideration, she found she couldn't deliver a specific response.

Aroska seemed to recognize this as well. "At the very least, you were neutral throughout all the time I knew you before, and right now you're miserable. I'd certainly like for you to be happy, but I'd settle for helping you get back to a non-miserable state." He reached out and tipped her chin upward, prompting her to meet his gaze. "Got it? I'm not asking you to settle down or even to give up this crazy life you lead. I'm only asking that whatever you choose to do, whatever path you decide to follow, you leave some room for me. You think you can handle that?"

How he could remain so patient and optimistic was beyond her. Unsure what to say, she looked up and gave his arm a quick squeeze by way of a response, then let out a soft snort. "Miserable, huh?"

"You said so yourself."

Ah yes, during her idiotic display in the officers' canteen. "I suppose I did."

"Can I ask you something else?" he said, one corner of his mouth quirking upward.

She allowed a partial smirk of her own. "Depends on what it is."

"Did you really think making a fool of yourself like that would be enough to scare me away?"

Heat flooded her face, much to her chagrin. "I don't know. I guess so." She shrugged and forced a stiff chuckle. "I didn't know what else to do."

"I'm sorry you thought you needed to do it at all. Promise me one thing, okay? Promise it won't take you getting half-drunk to tell me how you feel again."

His eyes were kind, but there was a certain severity in his features that told her he was only partially joking. "Deal," she said, having no desire to reduce herself to such a state ever again.

For several long seconds, he just stood in silence and watched her. It was difficult to tell whether he was waiting for her to say more, trying to think of something more to say himself, or merely studying her. He made this all sound so easy, when part of her was still convinced it would've been simpler if they'd never crossed paths again. But at the same time, his confidence was reassuring.

"We'll figure this out," he finally said. Then he winked. "We'll solve this problem together."

They parted and continued through the doorway, with Ziva moving over to recover her own gun belt and Aroska perching on the edge of the bunk as he worked his foot into the single boot he'd worn since being fitted with the bio brace. The thing barely hampered his movements anymore, and it certainly didn't seem to have any negative effect on his spirit.

"Can I ask *you* something?" Ziva said, checking her pistol before sliding it back into its holster.

"Anything."

She hesitated a moment longer, unsure how to articulate a question she'd never anticipated asking. "When did you first know? That you felt something."

"About you?"

She nodded. "I haven't given you much of a basis. You have every right to still hate me."

"That is both true and false," he said. His eyes narrowed in thought for a moment. "It's not something I was able to put into words until a while after you left—you never know what you've got until it's gone, right? And you and I objectively have a very complicated history. But when I looked back and thought about it, if there was a single defining moment, it was when I saw you lying in a pool of blood on that landing pad in Argall. The way I reacted when I didn't know whether you were even still alive...for several seconds, there was this crushing, almost debilitating feeling I can't even describe, followed by a flood of relief when I discovered you were still conscious. I realized later that those things had to mean something, even if I hadn't figured out what it was at the time."

The memory sent a chill through Ziva's body, and her fingers unconsciously came to rest against her abdomen at the place where the pressure of Aroska's hand had been the only thing that kept her from bleeding out that day. He looked over and seemed to note the movement but didn't comment.

"What about you?" he said instead. "When did you know?"

She should have known he would ask and silently kicked herself for even broaching the subject. "I'm not sure."

"Come on. First instinct."

Satisfied with the state of her belt and holster, she picked up her boots and went to sit on the edge of the bunk beside him. "I don't think it's any secret that you've been an issue for me from the beginning. For a long time, I was so angry because I didn't know how to handle you."

Sheyss, here she was again spilling her guts to him. Part of her was developing a morbid fascination with the phenomenon. She set about strapping on her footwear, taking another few seconds to search her mind for some sort of 'defining moment,' as he had put it. Things were rarely so black and white. "Maybe when I told you the truth about Soren. Maybe *why* I told you the truth about Soren." She cast him a brief glance. "Or when I was trying to catch up to you aboard the *Marauder*. I could smell blood, *cha'sen*...I wasn't sure what I was going to find."

It occurred to her that both examples they'd just given had to do with fear they'd each felt about the other's unknown fate, as well as an almost primal drive to protect one another. The idea brought her a welcome measure of comfort.

She turned to face him with every intention of asking how the hell he expected any of this to work given all the problems they were facing, but a klaxon blared over the ship's comm system, cutting her off. That single alarm narrowly preceded a sudden jolt that threw each of them from their positions. Ziva staggered forward, managing to catch herself against the edge of Ken's wardrobe just before her face collided with the bulkhead, and she turned to find Aroska in the process of picking himself up from the floor. The residual hum of the FTL drive decrescendoed into silence, and the stars outside the room's narrow viewports came into sharp focus.

"Why are we stopping?" she asked no one in particular.

In response, the comm system crackled again. "Would Agents Payvan and Tarbic please report to the bridge."

They were already on their way out the door.

CHAPTER 25
NIIOSIAN CRUISER *REVENANT* - DEEP SPACE

The scene on the bridge wasn't what Ziva had expected given the abrupt departure from the FTL tunnel. There was a certain urgency in the movements and behavior of the crew, but not the chaotic frenzy she'd braced herself for. A glance out the viewport confirmed they had stopped altogether; the rest of the Niiosian vessels floated about outside, nothing but distant stars beyond them. Unless she had completely lost track of time in the cabin, they had to still be at least an hour's journey from the Sterro system.

She spotted Tobias in his customary place up on the mezzanine, but instead of his usual clean-cut, sophisticated look, he was dressed like the rest of his crew in tac pants, a plain short-sleeved shirt, and utility vest. Save for his spectacles, he looked like an entirely different person.

"What's going on?" she demanded as she and Aroska jogged up to where he stood at the conference table.

For the briefest of moments, he appeared annoyed at being interrupted, but that annoyance morphed instantly into relief. "Ah, good," he said, passing a data pad off to the man beside him, thus putting an abrupt end to whatever conversation they'd been having. "Join me down here at the strategy center."

All three of them began to move at once, with Ziva bumping squarely into Aroska in her haste to comply. They each mumbled a quick apology, and as he placed a steadying hand on her arm and guided her forward, she couldn't help but notice the subtle glance Tobias threw over his shoulder.

The corners of the mobster's mouth curled upward as they all came to a stop at a bank of terminals on the main floor. "I must say the two of you are in much better spirits than you were when I last saw you." He studied them both over the rim of his spectacles for a moment, eyes glinting with that same old faux omniscience that hinted at the possibility he knew some grave secret about whoever he was talking to.

He could speculate and allude to things all he wanted. Ziva folded her arms and directed her attention to the consoles before she could respond in an adverse way she'd regret later. "We're not at Delatori," she said, prompting him to cut to the chase. "What's the situation?"

Tobias sobered and turned his attention to the nearest terminal. "No, we're not at Delatori. We've received confirmation from our scouts that Alastair Manes and his fleet are headed this way, on a direct course for the planet if their FTL routes are any indication. The plan has changed."

He gestured at the display in front of them, pointing out two clusters of small transports. "Our approach to retaking Delatori has become a two-pronged one. I'm sending a contingent of ships—smaller gunships, freighters, and what have you—ahead of the fleet. Upon reaching the planet, half of these ships will descend to establish a presence on the ground, while the other half will work to neutralize Ibarra's transport fleet, which we've received intelligence about from Agent Oda and your friends." He tapped the screen and brought up a series of visuals taken through what appeared to be the rocky debris that made up Delatori's rings.

"Are those ships carrying?" Ziva asked, leaning in for a closer look.

"We have reason to believe they are and that they've been stuck in a holding pattern following the destruction of the Panuco base. As such, they represent a valuable target. I will take a squadron to eliminate the security escort and capture the freighters and their cargo, after which we will wait on the far side of the planet out of Ibarra's reach." Tobias turned his attention to the two of them. "We have a limited number of ships with stealth capabilities, yours among them. The *Talon* will lead the squadron transporting soldiers to the ground—it is already recognized as an Ibarra vessel, reducing the chances of anyone catching wind of our presence planetside. There you will rendezvous with Agents Duvo, Vax, and Oda and devote all resources to retaking the zocrum repository." He looked them over approvingly. "I want you leading the assault."

A tingle of excitement crept up Ziva's spine at the prospect. It took her a moment to pinpoint exactly what had prompted it; the idea of getting to take charge, to have control—and to do it with her team—made her feel more alive than she'd felt in weeks. She found herself fighting to appear indifferent and not allow the smirk tugging at her lips to manifest itself.

Aroska sounded less sure. "Leading?"

Tobias smiled. "While I take pride in Niio's forces, Agent Tarbic, and while many of my people do come from a variety of military backgrounds, I'm under no illusion that we are what you would consider an organized military force. I recognize that you and your team aren't, either, not exactly, but given Ziva's intimate knowledge of Delatori and Ibarra operations, for the purposes of this mission, I feel you and your people are best suited to take charge." He indicated the console again. "In addition to providing intelligence about the transport fleet, the ground team has been and will continue to be performing reconnaissance of the area surrounding the zocrum facility. They will establish a connection with you so you can prepare during your journey."

Ziva checked the time. If the sector map projected from the control table up on the mezzanine was correct, that journey would only take a couple of hours, tops. That wasn't much time to prepare for a full-scale ground assault against an enemy post. But she'd worked with worse, and if she knew her team, the intel they were gathering would be both thorough and reliable, which could only help the situation.

As eager as she was to have a new task to focus on after being cooped up aboard the ship and allowing herself to be so raw with Aroska—no matter how beneficial that might have been—she got the sense Tobias had yet to paint the full picture for them. "And what of the fleet?" she said, waving toward the other vessels visible through the viewport across the room.

Some of the animation in the mobster's face vanished, almost as if he'd hoped she would never ask. "The fleet," he began, motioning for them to follow as he began to stroll back toward the mezzanine, "will continue traveling ahead as well, though Delatori is not its destination, not immediately."

They came to a stop in front of the conference table, where the hologram of a ringed planet a meter wide hovered over its surface. Several dots floated on the outer edge of the projection, the largest of which Ziva guessed represented the ship in which they now stood. Those dots periodically changed position within the hologram as the Niiosian soldiers at the control panel cycled through several approach scenarios.

"The original rendezvous point we set with the remainder of Niio's forces is here," Tobias continued, inviting one of his men to demonstrate. The hologram of Delatori shrunk to reveal the Sterro system where the planet was located; a yellow beacon pulsed on the outer edge. Then the planetary system shrunk to reveal the local star cluster, and the beacon slid outward. "This is the new spot. Here our forces will wait until the Ibarra fleet arrives, suitably distant so as not to appear on their scanners. Once their ships are in position, we can close the distance with a seconds-long FTL jump, enveloping the planet and effectively trapping them against Delatori's rings or on the ground."

Ziva's eyebrows dropped lower and lower into a scowl as she studied the way the man's face changed as he spoke. There was something indescribably cold present, not unlike what she'd seen as he shot Cole, or when she'd first offered him her services in exchange for his help tracking down Skeet and Aroska. It was something devious, something remorseless, and it made the hairs on the back of her neck stand on end. She unfolded her arms and brought her hands to rest on her hips; it would be suicide to draw her weapon here on the bridge, but having it within closer reach brought her a modicum of comfort.

"And then?" Tobias clasped his hands behind his back and stepped away, leaving the two of them at the table as he moved over to stare solemnly out the viewport. "The systematic eradication of the Ibarra Cartel will commence."

Something odd coursed through her stomach just then, equal parts elation that Manes would soon meet his end, a repulsive yet intrinsic desire to defend the man after two years of being paid handsomely to do just that, and general confusion as to what exactly Tobias meant. "What?" she said, voice low, taking a single step toward him.

"Make no mistake," he continued as though she hadn't even asked a question. "It will take time to root out all of Ibarra's forces. Their network throughout the Fringe extends just as far as Niio's. But you must admit the opportunity to cut the head off the snake and simultaneously reclaim a trove of valuable resources is too good to pass up, and there's something almost poetic about stripping those very resources away from Alastair Manes before his eyes."

"This isn't what we agreed to."

"What's wrong?" Aroska asked quietly behind her, his voice sounding impossibly distant as her focus zeroed in on Tobias alone.

The mobster turned away from the window, hands still clasped behind his back, and began to stroll toward her. "And what, precisely, did we agree to?"

Everything ground to a halt as Ziva's mind spun, working feverishly to recall every word of the conversation four long years ago when Tobias had first briefed her on his plan to infiltrate Ibarra. Technically, she supposed, they'd never agreed to anything, not in exact terms. But she'd been led to believe there was a plan, one that never involved the complete annihilation of the Cartel.

"You wanted to cripple Ibarra," she answered in response to both Tobias and Aroska's questions. "Stop them from encroaching on your territory. Maintain balance. The idea was to undermine operations on Panuco and send Manes running, not wipe them out entirely."

"Agent Payvan, it almost sounds as though you have a problem with wiping them out entirely."

She sensed Aroska draw up beside her as he too began to detect the threatening element in the mobster's tone, and she took another small step forward, keeping herself in front of him. "I don't," she said, though even as the words left her mouth, she wasn't sure how true they were. She found herself once again mulling over the same pros and cons as she had four years earlier when Tobias first proposed this venture. Neither this man nor Alastair Manes were upstanding citizens, and though their respective organizations were responsible for a myriad of illicit activities, they each represented a crucial structural element of Fringe Space. In many ways, they were the very *essence* of Fringe Space, independent bodies operating outside the control of the Federation. If one or the other grew too large or too powerful, that structure would surely be disrupted. The original goal may have been to curb Manes's expansion, but now what would the consequences be if Tobias was allowed to gain too much power?

The man's deadpan features told Ziva he wasn't particularly convinced. "I'll have to take your word for it," he muttered, moving back past the two of them and angling for the conference table. Those gathered around it—including Serenity—had been warily watching the scene unfold, and they all made a feeble attempt to appear occupied as their boss approached.

"Tell me this hasn't been your plan from the beginning," Ziva called, drawing the attention of additional Niiosian crew members. "Tell me you gave me all the pertinent information four years ago."

"What do you want me to say?" Tobias spat, voice rough and guttural and unlike anything she'd ever heard from him. "That I lied and used you as a pawn in my quest to take complete control of these sectors of the Fringe?"

She shrugged indignantly and shook her head. "Deny it."

He merely stared at her in silence for a beat before turning and resuming his journey back to the table. Maybe he had withheld information from the start. Maybe he had changed his mind about his goals somewhere along the line while she'd been on Panuco. Or maybe the mere prospect of retaking Delatori had altered his mode of thinking within the past couple of days. Regardless, she didn't like the situation, but she was now stuck dealing with it; it was no different than countless scenarios she'd worked her way through under Manes.

And therein lay the issue. Dealing with situations and solving problems may have been her strong suit, but these problems she'd spent the last four years solving—however voluntarily—were ultimately not *her* problems. After the pep talk from Aroska, the idea of taking matters back into her own hands was more appealing than ever. Something had ignited inside her, a spark that had once burned bright but had been lying dormant for far too long. She was done being used, done being manipulated. It was easy to view Manes as the greater threat, but even while she'd been under his control, Tobias had been the one pulling the strings behind the scenes. And now here he was acting no different than the Ibarra leader.

She drew a breath to speak her mind, but the first voice to ring out was Aroska's. "Do you have any idea what you've done to her?" he growled in Tobias's direction, stepping in front of her.

"Aroska, don't."

He spared her the briefest of glances, his golden eyes like fire. "Do you have any idea what she's been through? What sacrifices she's made in the name of this *frouchten* mission you've concocted?"

"Easy, big guy," Serenity warned, moving up beside Tobias. Two of the Niiosian soldiers followed suit, and Ziva's hand crept closer to her holster.

Aroska didn't bat an eye. "Let me get this straight. Not only did she destroy herself for you, but now you have the audacity to change the rules mid-game."

"Considering I invented this game, that's my prerogative," the mobster said. "And Ziva knew exactly whose game she was playing when she began."

"Huhren shouka souhn!"

The next few seconds were a blur. Aroska charged forward, drawing cries of alarm and prompting every Niiosian crew member within a ten-meter radius to swarm toward the mezzanine. Ziva leaped after him, catching his arm just as he wound up to take a swing at one of the men who'd stepped in front of Tobias. Someone drew a weapon; she released Aroska just long enough to knock it away. Threats and shouts bombarded her from all sides, somehow still audible over the thundering pulse in her ears. She was aware of noise coming out of her own mouth, but she was fairly certain that's all it was: noise. Something to shift the attention from Aroska to her.

"Hey, hey, hey, that's enough!" she hollered, heat flooding her face as she managed to slide around and wedge herself in between Tarbic and the Niiosians. She shot a scowl in Tobias's direction, daring him to try anything, before turning and placing both palms flat against Aroska's chest.

"I said that's enough," she snarled, fighting his forward resistance. She brought her face within centimeters of his and spread her arms to keep him from getting around her. "Walk away," she ordered. "Walk away!"

It seemed to take him a split second to even process the fact that she was the one addressing him. He glared past her for a moment longer before briefly locking gazes with her, turning on his heel, and storming off under the wary eyes of all the nearby crewmen.

Ziva brought her hands to rest on her hips and watched him long enough to ensure he was really leaving, ensure nothing happened to him, and process what should come next. The truth was they'd been walking on thin ice since coming aboard, regardless of how hospitable Tobias and the Niiosians had seemed, but if what just occurred hadn't already broken that ice, then it had at least set the process in motion.

But that was primarily Tobias's fault. She turned back to face him and found both of the soldiers flanking him holding their weapons at the ready, though they refrained from leveling them at her. Even Serenity had brought her hand to rest on her own holster.

Tobias studied her grimly for a few more seconds before waving his fingers, prompting those around him to stand down. "I'm entrusting you with an important task, Agent Payvan. Keep your pet on his leash or we're going to have a problem."

She wasn't sure whether to be relieved or disturbed that he spoke of a 'problem' in the future sense; if the current situation wasn't a problem, she dreaded to know what was. "Do me the decency of telling me whether this was your plan all along."

The man's cold gaze didn't waver. "What would that change?"

"Nothing. But if you lied before, the least you can do is tell me the truth now."

That classic, vaguely amused smirk appeared on his face, and she wasn't sure what bothered her more: the expression itself, or the fact that a demand for the truth had prompted it. But then it disappeared entirely, as though whatever thought had brought him that brief moment of entertainment had been smothered like a weak flame. He drew closer to her, appraising her like an antique whose value he was no longer sure of.

"This is what's best, Ziva."

She should have expected such a non-answer, but it was infuriating all the same. "For who?" she muttered, searching his face in vain for a better response.

Her gaze flitted over to Serenity. "Did you know about this?"

The woman said nothing, but a shadow passed over her face and she looked away.

The gesture could have conceivably meant either yes or no. Maybe it didn't really matter. Even if they had deliberately betrayed her, no one could change what had already happened. She turned her attention back to Tobias. "The *Talon* better be fueled and the rest of your ground crew transports better be ready to go by the time I get down to the docking bay."

She pivoted and strode away, grinding her teeth as she worked to shift her focus toward events to come. She'd allowed herself to become a Niiosian puppet and had spent two years suffering under Manes as a result—no question about it. But to find out she'd been used to an even greater extent than planned? The notion threatened to send her into another nervous breakdown, but sheer anger drove her forward. As liberating as it had felt to reconnect with Aroska and put her role as Matia behind her, perhaps drawing on some of that same old apathy and callousness now was a good thing.

She found Tarbic pacing back and forth just outside the blast doors leading onto the bridge. "That was *not* helpful," she growled as he fell into stride beside her.

"You know, I don't get you," he said, tone just as rough. He matched her pace for several strides before placing a firm hand on her shoulder to stop her in her tracks. "After everything you've been through, how can you be willing to continue letting him use you like this?"

"I am not 'letting' him do anything," she snapped, wrenching his hand away. But maybe that had been a poor choice of words; when it came down to it, she *was* allowing Tobias to use her as a piece in this game he'd concocted. It wasn't like she was too blind to see it—she'd volunteered her services initially, after all. There was still a measure of self-awareness about the whole situation, similar to what she'd held on to throughout her whole charade for Manes. Somehow that was different than being an unwitting pawn.

She took a step back and sighed, closing her eyes for a moment. This was also not the time to be arguing with Aroska, but when she opened her eyes again, she found him watching her with a tilted head and an arched brow, clearly not buying what she'd just said.

"Okay, look," she said quietly. "Skeet was right—I made the decision to go to Niio in the first place. I got myself into this mess, and the fact is I'm in too deep to back out now."

"Ziva, listen to yourself. After all you've been through, after all the ways you've been hurt…. Here you are finally on the verge of getting back to some semblance of…of *normalcy*, and now you're willing to jump right back into the situation that broke you in the first place?"

"Manes broke me!" she hissed. "I may have only been on Panuco because of Tobias, but if the emotional damage is what you're concerned about, then your focus should be on Ibarra. At this point I want to see Manes burn just as much as Tobias does, if not more."

"But if Ibarra is eradicated and the Niiosian Mob seizes control of all their territory and operations, how is that any better than what Manes has been striving for?"

"It's not, you're right. And if it makes you feel any better, I truly don't think total eradication was on Tobias's agenda back when this all started."

"You're sure you weren't just being too trusting?"

Now it was Ziva's turn to raise a brow. "I've been accused of being a lot of things, but 'too trusting' was never one of them."

"Okay, that wasn't fair of me." He dragged a hand down his face and glanced up and down the corridor before lowering his voice. "You know I'm with you no matter what, but I don't think this is the smartest move. You can leave—*we* can leave—before things get any worse."

She swallowed and looked him in the eye. "And desert Skeet and Zinni on Delatori with the Niiosian Mob's top assassin who will follow any and every order Tobias might give him if I don't cooperate?"

Aroska looked down and said nothing in response. She doubted he'd been implying they should leave Skeet and Zinni behind, but he also clearly hadn't considered the possibility that Tobias would use them as leverage. Chances were high that at least one of them would survive an adverse encounter with Ken, but the hitman was a wildcard, and it wasn't a risk she was willing to take.

"Think about this," she continued quietly. "We're in charge of the ground assault, which means we'll have more control over something than we have at any point thus far. We can use that to our advantage. Level the playing field a little. I would like very much to settle the score with Tobias, too, but there's an order of operations here. Right now, he's still the lesser of two evils, and I don't know about you, but I'd rather not be fighting this battle on two fronts."

"Focus on what we have control of first."

She nodded.

He sighed and studied her a moment longer. "I still don't like it, but...okay." They resumed their journey down the hall. "Let's get to work."

Chapter 26
Zocrum Repository - Delatori

A thick, chilly fog crept through the clearing below Skeet's observation post, reducing the few Ibarra soldiers who populated the area to blurry, bipedal shapes. Large spotlights mounted on tall poles lit up the expanse before him as if it were daylight, but behind him, the forest was dark and silent, the fog rendering it more so. His stealth suit had turned almost completely black to match.

On the other side of the clearing lay the zocrum repository. Operations continued overnight; he wasn't sure if that was the norm or not, and the graveyard crew was almost always smaller than the daytime one, but it seemed significant nonetheless. If the team's previous observations were any indication, heavy vehicles would roll in right around dawn to deliver new shift workers from wherever they'd bunked and whisk the night workers away, then return to transport materials from the repository to the spaceport.

The facility itself consisted of a two-story structure that butted up against a steep rise on the far side of the clearing, almost like a bunker. According to Ken—or more accurately, according to Ziva's reports—the bulk of the repository extended multiple levels underground, which made sense as the zocrum was mined from Delatori's crust. Intelligence suggested the facility functioned almost like a well, with machinery, catwalks, and the like situated around the edges of a massive pit. The issue was allegedly that parts of the internal infrastructure had been damaged during the conflict when Ibarra first wrested control of it from the Niiosian allies who managed it, impeding or even halting the Cartel's recovery process. The outside of the building had seen better days, too; every so often, he caught a glimpse through the fog of all the plasma scoring on the walls, of the small craters dotting the clearing, of the outbuildings where it appeared a fire had raged not long ago.

Upon receiving word that Manes was also on his way to Delatori and the plan was now to focus solely on retaking this zocrum repository, Skeet and Zinni had taken turns teaming up with Ken to perform recon of the facility at different times of day, compiling each of their individual observations into a single report that could be used to draw up a plan of approach. According to Tobias, Ziva and Aroska were on their way with a ground team and—he checked the time—should be arriving shortly. This final recon trip in the wee hours of the morning was rather superfluous at this point, but if they were going to be launching a full assault on this facility with an advance notice of mere hours, then it couldn't hurt to get one more look.

The thought also occurred to him that now that Manes was on his way here, it rendered the recovery of Starcer's schematics moot. The Niiosians would still be able to make use of them down the road, certainly, but there wasn't time for them to serve their original purpose in giving Niio an edge over Ibarra. Skeet had a feeling the deciding battle between the two warring organizations was going to take place right here and in a matter of hours.

He reached up and touched his earpiece, his lips barely moving as he spoke. "How's it going?"

It felt like an ironic question for him—the solo operative out in the dark in the middle of enemy territory—to be asking, but Zinni was the one stuck at the ship keeping an eye on Ken, which could easily be just as perilous of a situation.

"All quiet," she replied.

The innocuous exchange could feasibly be both a general status report and an update regarding the Niiosian agent, though Skeet couldn't help but treat it more as the latter.

"Same here. Nothing new going on. Heading back now."

As satisfied with what he was seeing as he thought he'd ever be, he ran his gaze across the foggy scene one last time for good measure, then slipped backward into the trees and was absorbed by the darkness.

TALON - Sterro System, Fringe Space

Aroska made his way out of the *Talon's* cockpit and down the corridor toward the ship's little armory, skirting around the Niiosian soldiers who'd made themselves comfortable on the floor along the walls rather than hole up in the much colder cargo hold. They all appeared battle-ready, cradling their weapons in scarred or tattooed arms as they rested up in preparation for whatever awaited them on Delatori. There were ten of them here, and another dozen or so in each of the three other ships that would accompany the *Talon* planet-side. They'd been gracious guests for the duration of the journey, which mostly meant they'd been quiet and kept to themselves. Despite their grizzled appearances, their continual wary glances gave Aroska the sense they were intimidated by their Haphezian escorts. He certainly didn't mind if that happened to be true.

He found Ziva in the armory just as he'd expected, methodically checking inventory after—as she'd put it—'Tobias's analyst scum had put their filthy hands all over her stuff.' She'd already laid a selection of weaponry out on the workbench, no doubt to take down to the planet.

"This ship," he said, letting one arm hang from the rim around the doorframe as he studied the shape of the room. "It's been extensively modified, but I know Haphezian design when I see it. This is the *Zenith*, isn't it?"

She sighed and paused her examination of the weapons long enough to spare him a glance over her shoulder. "One of Tobias's many 'investments' in this mission when I first came to him," she muttered. "I was leery about using a familiar vessel while undercover, but as he put it, this ship had too many desirable attributes to pass up. I'm glad to have had it these last couple of years."

Aroska drew closer to the workbench as she launched into more detail about some of the larger modifications that had effectively transformed the *Zenith* into the *Talon*, eyeballing some of the unfamiliar ordnance before him. He knew the Ibarra Cartel was into weapons dev but hadn't considered the fact that Ziva might have gained access to some of their goods. He ran his fingers over a hefty plasma pistol, glad it wasn't the one she'd shot him with. Beside that lay what appeared to be a compact shotgun, similar in design to a classic slugthrower but with three barrels.

At the end of the table lay one of the most magnificent long guns he'd ever seen. This rifle was not an Ibarra creation. Like the ship, it bore a distinctly Haphezian design to someone who knew what to look for. Though it was currently fitted with a bulky, unfamiliar receiver, a standard projectile receiver lay on the bench nearby; a unique set of grooves along the chassis led him to believe the two could be swapped for one another. The thought occurred to him that he had seen this gun before, or at least parts of it, as Ziva had cleaned it in the safe house on Aubin. This must be the rifle Skeet had told him about, the one that could be configured to fire her signature bariine rounds. The one she had once used to save them from the Durutians in the desert and again at the Tabaco shipping yard just days ago.

He hefted it up and pressed the stock to his shoulder, sighting up the far wall of the room. It was lighter than expected, but there was a certain sturdiness about it that gave it a more abstract weight. This was a weapon designed to inflict maximum damage across maximum distance, and if he knew one single person who could wield it to its full potential, it was Ziva.

Lost in thought, it took him a moment to realize she had stopped talking. He lowered the gun, cradling it in one arm while supporting the barrel with his other hand, and found her watching him in silence, her eyes twinkling in amusement.

"What?" he said, cracking a grin.

She blinked, as though just now realizing she'd been staring, and shook her head. "Nothing." The corners of her own mouth curled upward. "That's not a bad look for you."

He filed that away as the highest form of compliment. "Well, I concede that you're still undoubtedly the expert in the long-range sphere," he said, passing it over to her. "Thank you for allowing me the honor of touching your treasure."

An odd melancholy settled over her features as she accepted it and began to look it over, something he was sure she'd already done multiple times. "I've killed a lot of people with this gun," she said quietly.

Well, sure. He knew of several right off hand. But there'd been something intentional about the phrasing she'd used, about the way she looked him in the eye immediately after. The flutter of excitement that had begun to take root in his chest transformed into a knot that descended into the pit of his stomach as he realized what she was alluding to.

It was tempting to ask for confirmation, just in case he was getting worked up over nothing, but an image of the bullet striking Soren's head ripped through his memory and rendered him speechless. The way Ziva turned and set the rifle down before leaning over the workbench and hanging her head was a confirmation of sorts anyway.

The armory fell silent for several long seconds before she huffed a sigh and whipped back up to face him. "Damn it, Aroska," she said, her voice a harsh whisper. "How do you expect this to work?"

He studied her a moment—the sorrow in her eyes, the confused tilt of her head, the way she'd flung one arm up in an exasperated shrug when she'd spoken—and concluded that 'this' was whatever the relationship was that existed between them, this unique, delicate thing they were both finally acknowledging.

"How do I expect this to work?" he repeated.

"You say you don't care if things aren't normal, but that can't possibly include being okay with the fact that I killed your brother before your eyes."

Hearing the words spoken aloud made his skin crawl, but he quashed the discomfort and reached out to her, placing a hand on each of her shoulders. "Listen," he said quietly. "I don't know that I'll ever be okay with the fact that Soren is dead, but after everything you told me in Salex, I know I can't hold his death against you. I...I'm sorry."

Her eyes roved over his face for a moment as though searching his features for sincerity. Then she nodded and gestured lamely at the rifle. "I just thought you should know. Telling the truth and all."

While he was certain he would have been happier not knowing, he had to credit her for the effort. Leave it to her to accidentally strike a nerve while attempting to be forthright. It was almost adorable, if anything Ziva Payvan did could ever be considered cute.

"But seriously," she said, stepping back and resuming her examination of the weapons before her. "From an objective, logistical standpoint, how do you expect this to work? I'm supposed to be dead. Even if I wasn't, I'm a fugitive from the *Federation*." Her voice dropped into a low hiss as she practically spat the word out. "On top of that, you may have noticed that situations like the one we're currently in seem to follow me wherever I go. That can't possibly be what you want."

"And what if it is?"

She blinked.

"What if I like it? What if I enjoy the thrill, the faster pace, and I never want things to go back to the way they were before I joined this team? Field ops was my home for a long time, but those days are over, and this is where I belong now." He paused to consider whether he was getting ahead of himself. "I told you before that what I want most is to simply be by your side, to back you up, and if all of this insanity is what that entails, then so be it. I'm *fine* with it. In fact, I might even welcome it. I wish you would believe me."

Ziva turned and placed her hands on her hips, watching him with stony features for a moment before shaking her head. "Well, congratulations, then," she said with a tired scoff. "You're full-time spec ops."

He tilted his head. "I've been full-time spec ops for the past four years."

"Sure, but the mindset is what really counts."

"Meaning...?"

He'd expected her to somehow be joking, so he was surprised when her face remained devoid of any expression whatsoever. "Meaning you've accepted the fact that your life has devolved into complete chaos," she answered, "and you've realized you'd be bored otherwise."

It never ceased to amaze him how philosophical she could be at times. He smiled. "Kind of a morbid way of putting it, but you're not wrong."

She managed a hint of a smile before her face hardened again. There was still so much uncertainty there—so much *fear*, though he doubted she'd ever admit it—and he once again reminded himself to have patience. She was right; there was nothing normal about any of this.

An alarm from the ship's nav computer chimed over the comm system, alerting him that it was nearly time to break out of FTL. "Coming up on the drop point," he announced, checking the time. "Five minutes and counting."

He strode from the armory and angled back toward the cockpit with Ziva hot on his heels, drawing the attention of the Niiosians lining the corridor. "Look alive, gentlemen," she said behind him. "It's almost time."

The sounds of the soldiers rising to their feet and readying their weapons echoed through the ship as the two of them entered the cockpit and took their places at the controls. The space was silent for those remaining five minutes while Ziva studied the approach vector Skeet had provided them with and Aroska kept an eye on the nav readouts. He signaled to her when the countdown was up, and she eased back on a lever, redirecting power to the sub-light engines. The swirling silver FTL tunnel faded away, leaving them floating in empty space. Delatori loomed ahead, light from its sun creating a halo around the near side, which was currently shrouded in shadow.

Aroska checked the exterior cams, ensuring the other three ships traveling with them had dropped out of FTL as well, then checked the scope, ensuring they were also adequately cloaked. Ahead, another cluster of familiar ships materialized from the FTL tunnel, the squadron under Tobias's command that would be responsible for capturing the Ibarra transport fleet. They sped away toward the planet, employing speed and the element of surprise to complete their mission while the ground team focused on stealth.

"Dagger squadron, form up on me," Ziva called over the wide comm channel. She guided the *Talon* to the front of the group, light from the sun reflected in her eyes as she directed her full attention toward what lay ahead. It was an intensity he remembered from before. Not the quiet fury of Matia Moryi, but a confident focus that told him she was ready for whatever both Ibarra and Niio were about to throw at her. It made him feel ready in return, and he sat there wishing there were words that could adequately convey this feeling, the very reason he wanted to be right here in the thick of things with her.

Even without removing her gaze from the front viewport, she seemed to know she was under observation. "As much as I'd like to say something along the lines of, 'if you want out, just say the word,' it's a little late for that."

Aroska smiled. "I appreciate the sentiment," he said, returning his attention to what lay before them, "but there's nowhere I'd rather be."

CHAPTER 27
LANDING ZONE - DELATORI FOREST

Ziva pulled her jacket's zipper up the rest of the way as she descended the *Talon's* boarding ramp, unprepared for the chill despite the weather report they'd received from Skeet as they made their approach. The forest was still dark, and the rolling fog made all the shadows here on the ground seem even thicker. They could certainly use that to their advantage.

The *Saber* sat on the other side of the small clearing in which they'd touched down. The only illumination in the area came from the landing lights of the five ships now docked there, all tinted red to make the vessels harder to spot from the air. Behind her, the Niiosians who'd stowed aboard the *Talon* filed down the ramp as well. Some of the soldiers from the other three Mob ships were already busy hauling equipment into the center of the clearing, including a couple of hoverbikes and a small, all-terrain vehicle built for one or two passengers.

She tightened her rifle's strap across her chest and angled toward the tall, orange-haired figure she could make out in the shadows. Skeet stood with crossed arms overseeing developments; in the dark, it was impossible to tell if he held any particular opinion—positive or negative—about her arrival. Despite the rather sour way they'd left things, she for one was relieved to see another familiar face after a long couple of days aboard the *Revenant*.

The moment she opened her mouth to call out a greeting, however, another figure caught her eye. Ken was just making his way down the *Saber's* ramp, conversing with one of the soldiers on the ground as he moved. He cast a glance in her direction, and she abandoned her current route to veer toward him.

"We need to talk." She thrust a finger at him, both to single him out and direct him back up the ramp.

Behind her, she was vaguely aware of Aroska continuing toward Skeet and warning the lieutenant to leave her be. Ken held his ground on the ramp, neither approaching nor attempting to elude her.

"Did you know?" she demanded as she advanced toward him, not caring that everyone could hear.

The man stood rigid. "I'm sure I have no idea what you're talking about."

Rather than make further threats or demands, she caught his arm and dragged him up toward the boarding hatch; he didn't resist, but she felt his muscles tense in response to the potential threat.

"Did you know?" she repeated, throwing him against the bulkhead just inside the hatch and pinning him there.

Ken's features grew rock-hard. "Agent Payvan, kindly take your hands off of me."

She glared into his frigid eyes for another couple of seconds, weighing the consequences of ignoring him, then complied—slowly. Despite her height advantage, she had no doubt he could put up a ruthless fight. They were both killers, both capable of unspeakable brutality...and both smart enough to know this was neither the time nor the place for an all-out brawl.

"Was this his plan all along? You're his *frouchten* second-in-command. You had to have known."

In the better light, she could see his steely expression soften as realization began to dawn on him. Still, he remained cryptic when he spoke. "I'm afraid you'll have to be more specific."

"My job—my entire mission—was supposed to be maintaining the status quo and maybe, just maybe, giving you people enough of an advantage to kick Ibarra back out of your territory. Now *your boss* is up there talking about wiping the Cartel out completely, and it's like I'm listening to Manes all over again. So I ask again: was everything I've done over the past four years meant to further some hidden agenda, and did you know about it?"

Unless it was her imagination, Ken almost appeared disappointed.

He dragged a hand over his stubbled jaw and stepped away to pace back and forth across the corridor a couple of times, gaze fixed contemplatively on the floor.

"Let's put it this way," he said quietly. "I didn't know, but I was beginning to suspect."

She crossed her arms, silently demanding elaboration.

"I noticed things, sometimes even as subtle as changes in word choice when discussing the operation. It's as though he was becoming...I hesitate to say 'fixated' or 'obsessed,' but—"

"You hesitate to say?"

He looked her in the eye and swallowed, the closest she imagined he might ever come to losing composure. "And that is my own shortcoming," he said, voice just as authoritative as it had been on the *Revenant's* bridge. "If you'd lost your brother, if you wanted Ibarra to crumble just as badly as Tobias, then perhaps you would also be reluctant to acknowledge what you were seeing."

For the briefest of moments, she felt a pang of sympathy, though she didn't dare allow her face to betray her thoughts. She *did* want to see Ibarra burn, maybe more than anyone else here given that her experience with Manes and the Cartel had been so up close and personal. As she'd told Aroska, it was the whole reason she was still on board with this mission at all.

Ken's expression reverted to the familiar, cool indifference she recognized, though in his dark eyes there was a measure of repentant candor that hadn't existed previously. "But I swear to you, when this operation began, I was not aware Tobias had any plans to exploit the advantages you were giving us for a complete takeover."

It was tempting to give him the benefit of the doubt, though she hated the fact that she was even entertaining the idea. After all, he'd stood up for her and talked Tobias down when she'd first come aboard the flagship. If what he'd told her about the mobster's increasing obsession with Manes was accurate, it was no wonder the man had been so irate with her that day, and even so unforgiving toward Cole four years ago. As an operator himself, surely Ken could commiserate with her desire to be presented with all the details before embarking on a mission.

"Would you have told me if you were?"

"I don't know if I can honestly answer that question." The cool demeanor slipped away again for a moment to reveal something verging on genuine sincerity. "I like to think I would have. At the very least, you were an outsider who was brought into this situation with little choice, and you deserved to know the facts. But...I don't know that this was Tobias's intention all along. He started out merely wanting to protect the Niiosian people and our endeavors, which you must admit is an objectively noble cause. The changes, as I said, have been gradual and subtle, but also concerning."

He began to pace about the corridor again. "The Niiosian Mob is and always has been a powerful institution, and it's in our best interest to do everything we can to maintain that power. But Tobias and those who came before him have always had standards. Principles, as he so often says. There's a certain level of etiquette that comes with running an organization like this, and if we abandon that etiquette and those principles, we're no better than the people we're fighting against." He shook his head. "No better than Alastair Manes."

"Suffice it to say you don't approve of the approach he's begun taking, then."

It had been both a statement and a question, but Ken made no move to give an explicit answer. His face remained stony as he stared blankly at the bulkhead for a moment.

"For the time being, I believe it would be most prudent to focus on the task at hand, but your concerns are valid and...I'll have a word with him if the opportunity presents itself."

Ziva was almost positive it wouldn't, but at the moment, that sentiment was all she could ask for. She studied him for another few seconds, cursing the fact that he was just as much of a closed book as she was, then turned and strode back down the boarding ramp without another word.

In the dim light outside, she caught sight of Skeet and Aroska conversing on the edge of the clearing. The former passed a small object to Tarbic, though she couldn't make it out in the dark, and then the two men approached, standing rigid and alert as they glanced behind her.

"What was that about?" Skeet asked in Haphezian, voice low.

Her gaze flicked to Aroska as he slipped the mystery object into his pocket. "An issue that can't be fixed at this point," she replied, "but that also shouldn't have a negative impact on the remainder of this operation."

Both of them appeared unsure, with a hint of confusion in Skeet's expression and doubt in Aroska's. Launching into a full explanation now would only aggravate them; Aroska may have claimed to be on board, but she was certain bringing Tobias's duplicity to light would only weaken what little confidence Skeet seemed to have in her right now.

"Everything still quiet here?" she asked, opting for a quick change of topic.

He nodded. "Most of the traffic in the area consists solely of ground vehicles, so we haven't worried much about being seen from the air. Had a vessel pass pretty close a couple of hours ago, but there's been no indication we were spotted. The dark may be all that saved us, and I'd recommend moving before it gets too light."

"You said on comm you've already got some ideas for a plan of approach," Aroska said.

"We do." Skeet beckoned for the two of them to follow and led them over to where Zinni stood over a cluster of supply crates, fiddling with a holoprojector.

The intelligence officer moved to embrace each of them while Ken sauntered back onto the scene, warily appraising Aroska for an extra split second before merely offering a silent nod of greeting. It struck Ziva that the two men had never officially been introduced, but despite being relatively encouraged by the conversation she'd just had, she was feeling less than cordial and decided an introduction wasn't necessary. All Ken needed to know was that another Haphezian was present, and that the Haphezians were in charge.

Zinni gathered a couple more of the crates that had already been emptied and laid them on their sides to create a crude table, then activated the holoprojector on its surface. Ziva found herself looking at a simplified map of the immediate region, composed of terrain data she'd provided previously and reconnaissance data the team had collected over the past couple of days. The zocrum repository was represented by a series of basic three-dimensional shapes, but that was all the detail they needed to get started.

"The facility is two klicks directly south of this position," Skeet explained. "We've counted at least five sentries patrolling the exterior grounds at all times. Recon indicates there are between forty and sixty Ibarra personnel on-site during a given shift."

"Sounds like a relatively fair fight," Aroska said. "Armament?"

"All standard security ordnance," Ken answered. "We haven't seen anything particularly outstanding, though considering some of the toys Ibarra has developed, it would be unsurprising if they have more firepower than they let on."

Ziva crossed her arms. "Even numbers or not, this is their turf, which gives them an advantage by default."

"Which is why we want to get them off their turf," Skeet said. "We'll split up, strike from multiple sides. They won't know what hit them."

Even in the semi-darkness, it was impossible to miss the twinkle of anticipation in his eyes. It reminded her of the old days as they'd planned some foolhardy mission, full of confidence and gusto, and for just a moment, she forgot where they were, what they were doing, and any bitterness that remained between them.

She let out a sharp whistle to summon all the Niiosians, already perfectly aware none of them had removed their attention from her since she'd gone to confront Ken. Still, they all began to amble toward the little mobile command center. "Who here has military or formal combat experience?" she called, sweeping her gaze over the group.

She had a hunch most of them did, but anyone who had fallen into the service of the Niiosian Mob had most likely defected, been dishonorably discharged, or otherwise had an unfriendly severance from whatever organized force they'd belonged to. She therefore thought it safe to assume anyone who readily admitted to their experience had more *valuable* experience, perhaps even holding leadership roles, and she was pleased when several of them raised their hands and stepped forward in response to her question.

"Good," she said, beckoning for those few to come gather around the projection directly. "You'll help coordinate this attack. We'll be splitting into teams." She glanced at Skeet. "How many? Two? Three?"

"I'd say three, using a shared comm channel," he answered, panning out so the hologram displayed more of the surrounding forest. "We'll want to avoid any bloodshed at the zocrum repository itself, or else Manes will know we're here the moment he arrives."

"So we drive them outside and away from the facility," Aroska mused, arms folded.

Skeet nodded. "The key, however, is to get them to evacuate without causing more internal damage. Exterior cosmetic damage isn't as much of an issue because the place is already a mess, but structural damage from the initial takeover is why Ibarra has had trouble recovering much of the zocrum, so we'll want to avoid making it worse if the Niiosians want their precious resources." This he said with a pointed look at Ken and a glance around at the soldiers.

"The repository sits in a shallow basin," Zinni said, indicating a slight change in elevation around the edges of the facility property. "We were thinking if we can draw them outside, a team positioned here—" she gestured toward the ridge "—can drive them out into the forest where another team is waiting."

Ziva nodded. "And the third team?"

Ken stepped forward. "The third group will be the bait. Our job will be to get their attention, lure them out. Let them think they're chasing us. That's when the surrounding team will move in." He paused in response to Ziva's raised brow. "Yes, I've already volunteered to lead the strike team."

Skeet spun the map and indicated a spot in the forest, far enough from the facility that it would eliminate any obvious signs of battle but still near enough that it wouldn't take long to lead the Ibarra workers there. "There's a shallow ravine here, a narrow strip of low ground with higher banks on either side. We'll want to herd them in here where there's no room to maneuver. The final team will surround them."

"Then what?" Ziva asked, moving her hands to her hips.

She was met with silence. She had no real suggestions herself but merely wanted to get an idea of what Skeet was thinking. The truth was there were only a couple of options if they wanted to maintain whatever leverage they'd just gained: take the Ibarra soldiers prisoner, or slaughter them like livestock. And the former option wouldn't leave much—if any—manpower to capture the repository itself.

The look he gave her suggested he had taken these things into consideration as well, though she got the impression he had half a mind to just let the Niiosians loose upon their enemy and call it good. As tempting as that was, some petty part of her didn't want to grant Tobias any special advantage here. But when it came down to it, Delatori had been Mob territory to begin with, and Ibarra represented a more immediate threat when it came to the zocrum.

"They will be given the opportunity to surrender," Skeet finally answered, though based on the volume of his voice, she got the sense he was addressing everyone present.

"You think they will?" a voice called out from the crowd.

Another brief silence. "They will be given the chance," Skeet repeated. "If they don't comply, we will act accordingly."

It reminded Ziva a great deal of the attempts they'd made to get the Resistance crew to surrender after the *Vigilance* crashed in Noro. Most of the Haphezian agents present had been itching for an excuse to exact revenge for all the damage Ronan's forces had caused, and she had no doubt the Niiosians felt the same now. The simple truth was she and her team would be powerless to stop them if they decided to act of their own accord.

"You mentioned a shift change in your brief," she said, opting to get back to the topic at hand. "When do you want to hit them?"

"We considered launching the attack just before the change and capitalizing on the fact that they're more likely to be tired after working all night," Zinni said, "but we'd risk the new shift arriving in the middle of the strike, and we don't have enough manpower to take on both groups at once."

"Thus, we concluded the best time to hit them is a few minutes *after* the shift change," Skeet said. "It'll be a fresh group of soldiers, but a more manageable number. And it will significantly reduce the risk of reinforcements showing up."

"And, if we execute the attack correctly," Ken added, "they should still be adequately scrambled and relatively easy to control. We have the apparatus necessary to jam their communications as well, while leaving all of our own comm channels functional."

"Okay," Ziva breathed, running through the scenario in her mind. She looked up; the sky itself was invisible through the treetops and fog, but the dense mist was starting to take on a lighter gray tone with the approach of dawn. "When is the shift change?"

Skeet checked the time. "If they stick to the same schedule we've observed? Twenty minutes from now."

Of course it was. "Lovely," she said, raking a hand back over her head. "Fine, let's get moving. First, this right here will be designated Rendezvous Point One. If for any reason this all goes to hell, this is where we fall back and bug out.

"Ken, pick your squad. You will be designated Fire Team. Skeet and Zinni, you're most familiar with the facility and terrain—you'll head up the second team. Take the *Talon* around to the other side of the repository. If anyone sees the ship, it's a familiar enough sight around here that nobody should question its presence.

"Finally, Aroska and I will head up the third team, keeping our Dagger designation, and go to the ravine." She turned and surveyed the Niiosians in the immediate vicinity who had indicated their military history. "You, you, you, and you will accompany Talon Team and take secondary roles. The rest of you are with me. Divvy up the remainder of your people as you see fit. We move in five."

Some of the soldiers whispered among themselves and regarded her with wary skepticism, but the majority simply shook their heads and grinned, no complaints about jumping straight into the action. The men she had singled out began to disperse among the remaining soldiers and split the group into teams as she'd instructed.

"Just like old times, huh?" Skeet said, crossing his arms.

"Damn right," she replied with a sigh, not fully realizing how much she'd missed the chaotic improvisation that sometimes came with spec ops until he'd said something. She found herself more and more pleased Tobias had explicitly placed the Haphezians in charge of this assault; if she had to follow a ludicrous plan, she would much rather it be her team's than someone else's.

"I'm surprised Emeri didn't veto this little undertaking with all due speed," Aroska said.

"Yeah, well, he'd have to know about it first," Skeet muttered.

Ziva turned and found him already looking her way. There were countless reasons for him to not alert the director, but there'd been something deliberate in his voice that told her he was mainly holding off on her account. In his face, she saw something more akin to sympathy and reassurance than anything else he'd shown toward her since reuniting. Regardless of the animosity that remained between them, the mere thought of working with him and Zinni again—these two people who had once meant more to her than anyone else in the galaxy—was surreal. But it was her fault they were here, her fault they were undermining Emeri's orders and taking part in this fight that wasn't theirs.

"Better grab anything else you need from your ship," she said quietly. "The *Talon* is ready for you."

He dipped his head, looking around as Zinni moved up to stand beside him and Aroska took his place beside Ziva. "Good luck," he said, offering a hand.

It could very well be a blanket statement directed at all of them, but there was something about the firmness of his handshake and the unexpected kindness in his voice that made her sure it was aimed specifically at her. For just a moment, everything was back to normal.

She stepped back, allowing her lips to curl upward in a mischievous smirk. "Let's roll."

CHAPTER 28
ZOCRUM REPOSITORY · DELATORI

The only thing that looked any different about the clearing around the zocrum facility was that most of the illumination now came from the natural light of dawn rather than the tall floodlights around the property. It was still a muted, gray light, subdued by the fog and a low cloud cover that had rolled in and threatened to start spitting cold precipitation.

Within the trees, lingering shadows helped conceal Zinni, Skeet, and one of the Niiosians where they lay on the low ridge overlooking the facility. They'd once again donned the stealth suits, with the Mob soldier sporting the one Ken had worn. The three of them were virtually invisible, the only signs of life being the thin clouds of vapor that appeared whenever they exhaled.

Approximately two hundred meters behind them, the *Talon* sat hidden in the thicker foliage; Ziva had been right in that its presence here shouldn't be a shock to any of the Ibarra forces, though as far as they could tell, nobody had spotted them during the short flight as they'd moved the ship from Rendezvous Point One to its current location. The remainder of the Niiosians assigned to Talon Team remained there, waiting for the signal to move in closer. No sense in bringing everyone right to the tree line and risking being seen. Besides, the ship could then serve as an additional fallback point in the event something went horribly wrong. Zinni didn't foresee such a drastic outcome, but it was reassuring to have some shred of a backup plan on such a hastily constructed op.

She watched intently as the last of the night shift Ibarra workers filed onto the transports that had just deposited a fresh shift at the facility's front doors. "I count forty individuals leaving," she said, peering through her scope as the transport doors were sealed and the heavy vehicles began to rattle back toward the front gates.

"And I counted fifty new arrivals," Skeet said. "Tracks with what we've seen before."

Zinni hummed an affirmative. They'd unanimously elected to assume there were around ten more men inside that nobody had seen yet; better to plan for the worst-case scenario and be pleasantly surprised if it didn't come to pass.

"Fire Team, begin your countdown," Skeet said into his comm.

"Copy," came Ken's quiet voice after a couple of seconds.

The plan was to wait five minutes after the departure of the transports, giving them time to travel an adequate distance away and allowing the fresh crew to ease into any routine they might follow. Zinni watched as many of the newcomers disappeared into the facility, while several others settled into the same sentry positions the team had noted during their previous observations.

Those intervening five minutes seemed to last an eternity. The only reason she even spotted Ken was because she knew exactly what to look for and where to look. Even without one of the adaptive stealth suits, the man succeeded in becoming one with the surrounding environment; he was hardly more than a shadow, visible every few seconds as he emerged from the trees and began to move about amid the small outbuildings and pole pavilions surrounding the main repository structure.

"Initializing comm interference," she said over their channel, flipping a switch on the handheld jammer she carried. Three other voices—Aroska's, one from the *Talon*, and one from Ken's small team— acknowledged, and an additional three lights appeared on the device, indicating jamming had commenced from those locations as well. Between the four of them, they should be casting a net wide enough to keep the Ibarra soldiers from contacting anyone, provided none of them strayed too far from the facility.

Lifting the scope back to her eye, she caught sight of Ken just as he emerged from behind the loading platform nearest the facility, his utility belt now devoid of the small charges he'd been carrying moments before.

He sidestepped and ducked low enough behind a large container to avoid being seen by a passing sentry, then continued toward a power junction on the exterior wall of the repository without missing a beat.

"Talon Team, into position," Skeet murmured into his comm, watching through his own scope as Ken pried the cover off the power box and began to fiddle with the configuration within.

Zinni could envision the Niiosians who'd been waiting at the ship beginning to mobilize. The idea was that they would fan out and advance toward the repository as a unit, creating a wall to help ensure the Ibarra personnel evacuated into the forest in the opposite direction, the direction of the ravine and Ziva's team.

Of course, if all went according to plan, Ken's small squad should be more than adequate to get the enemy moving that way. She directed her full attention back to the man just as an alarm began blaring throughout the facility grounds, triggered by a handful of cables he'd yanked from the power box. He took a quick step away and vanished somewhere behind the loading platforms, leaving the Cartel men who patrolled the area to stand about in puzzlement. If the placement of the box was any indication, Zinni guessed this alarm was designed to signal a blockage or pressure buildup in the thick vacuum tubes that transported packages of raw zocrum out of the repository and deposited them on the loading platforms. There wasn't truly a blockage, of course, but based on the sudden speed and urgency with which the Ibarra soldiers reacted upon realizing the source of the alarm, she had a sneaking suspicion any form of pressure buildup involving unrefined zocrum was not a good thing.

"Good call, Ken," she murmured, mostly to herself but not caring whether he heard her over comm. She, Skeet, and their Niiosian ally remained motionless, watching as workers poured out of the facility and began shouting to one another. The short amount of time since their arrival likely hadn't been adequate for them to get too deep into the mine, increasing the chances that most if not all of them would evacuate. Once they looked more closely, it wouldn't take long at all for them to realize it had been a false alarm. They just needed a few more moments...

"Headcount," Skeet whispered.

Zinni's eyes went to work, counting each individual who emerged from the repository, doing her best to track them even as they began to spread out and intermingle. "I've got six fewer than on arrival," she replied. "I'd call that a solid threshold."

Skeet grunted in agreement. "Fire Team, your turn again."

The roar of an engine somewhere in the trees was audible even above the screech of the alarm, drawing the men's attention as they continued filing out of the building. With the extra noise and the odd echo caused by the slopes and foliage surrounding the facility, everyone was taken by surprise when the small all-terrain vehicle the Niiosians had brought burst out of the forest and came skidding into the clearing. The two men aboard it opened fire in the general direction of the Ibarra workers, taking care not to hit any of them, at least not yet.

The soft crack of underbrush prompted Zinni to glance behind her. There she found the Niiosians that constituted Talon Team, weapons held at the ready, spread out several meters apart to create a perimeter around the basin. They were still mostly invisible here in the trees, especially with all the Ibarra workers focused on what they believed to be more pressing issues.

The whine of a second engine filled the air as one of the hoverbikes swooped onto the scene. It took the soldiers a moment to notice, and by that time the bike's pilot was already firing in their direction in the same manner as the ATV driver. Ken materialized from the chaos, hurdling a shipping container and leaping from the loading dock onto the back of the bike as it sped past. A handful of the Ibarra men took off on foot after the two vehicles, rushing toward the forest of their own accord. Several others piled into a pair of groundcars parked outside the facility, slinging chunks of dirt and slush as they peeled out and gave chase.

Zinni kept Ken centered in her scope as the bike disappeared into the trees. In his hand, he held what could only be the detonator for the charges he'd placed.

"Talon Team, stand by," came his voice over comm.

"Ready," she replied.

The charges weren't large, but when paired with the small amount of unrefined zocrum that had already been packaged and sat waiting on the platform, the resulting explosion was more than enough to get everyone's attention. The Ibarra crew who remained in the vicinity scattered, most fleeing in the same direction as their comrades. The rest would be easy enough to round up.

"Talon Team, go!" Skeet commanded.

He, Zinni, and the Niiosian agent with them leaped into action, already running by the time they were upright. The rest of their team pressed forward, pouring out of the trees and descending into the clearing with shouts and cries that only contributed to the chaos. In their already panicked state, any remaining mercs turned tail and ran, fumbling for weapons but ultimately more focused on their escape. A couple of Niiosians broke off from the group to chase down some men who'd strayed in a different direction, but otherwise the plan seemed to be executing as well as it possibly could.

Zinni grinned as she lifted her rifle and fired several plasma rounds at the heels of the fleeing men, driving them forward. "Dagger Team, you're up."

DELATORI FOREST

Despite the relatively short amount of time they'd spent aboard the *Revenant*, Aroska couldn't help but revel in the feeling of solid earth beneath his boots, the rough texture of tree bark at his back, the bite of the chilly forest air as he inhaled, exhaled. Inhaled. Exhaled.

While technically daylight now, a gloom still hung over the forest, rendering everything grayscale. The monochrome crew garb he, Ziva, and the rest of the Niiosians wore blended in as well as it could without being true camouflage. Like him, the remainder of their team also lay in wait behind trees and underbrush, creating walls on either side of the shallow ravine where the Ibarra crew would be corralled. Said ravine lay off to his right; it was a safe bet they wouldn't be able to funnel all the workers into it, but with Talon Team closing in behind them, it shouldn't take much effort to keep them contained.

Directly across the ravine, Ziva mirrored his position against a tree of her own. She stood with closed eyes, cradling her rifle, the red streaks in her hair adding the slightest splash of color to the drab landscape. He found himself wishing he could speak with her, but silence was objectively more important now. Even if he buzzed her over comm, everyone else on the channel would be able to hear anything that was said. Besides, a quick glance at the time revealed the signal from Ken would be coming through any second.

The thought made him hyper-aware of the second comm device resting in his pocket, which Skeet had given him just after they'd arrived while Ziva went off to speak with Ken. All their ground forces may have been using a comm channel impervious to the jamming being employed against the Cartel workers, but the lieutenant had suggested it would be wise for the four Haphezians to maintain an entirely separate means of communication of their own. There were two devices, both relayed through the *Saber's* comm system; Skeet and Zinni would share one, while Aroska carried the other and could pass information along to Ziva.

Just in case.

He hoped they wouldn't have any reason to use it, but none of them had much confidence in how the Niiosians were going to handle things when it came down to it. The Haphezians may have been given Tobias's blessing to run the show, but in many ways, it felt like they were still on their own out here.

"Fire Team, your turn again," Skeet's voice said in his ear.

They would learn how the situation would play out soon enough. In the distance, the rumble of small vehicle engines broke the silence of the forest as Ken's team began executing the first stage of the operation. Around Aroska, the other visible members of Dagger Team perked up, some peering out from their hiding places, some double-checking their weapons. If all went according to plan from here, they only had to wait about three more minutes.

Another ten seconds passed before the engine noise was joined by the roar of an explosion. He could picture the sheer chaos on the

facility grounds and only hoped everyone could get out of the immediate vicinity before exchanging gunfire. People were going to die this
morning, no doubt about it. *Who* and *where* remained to be seen, but it
needed to not be in the middle of the property where the sight of bodies
would immediately alert Manes that something was amiss.

Zinni's voice: "Dagger Team, you're up."

The forest came alive with invisible energy as the remainder of
the team made silent, final preparations and melted back into their
hiding places, ready to strike or otherwise adapt to a situation that was
no doubt evolving rapidly. Aroska watched as Ziva pressed a finger to
her earpiece and offered a brief acknowledgement before shrinking
back against the tree, rifle held close and ready. He shifted his own feet
back and forth in the semi-frozen soil, enjoying a couple more breaths
of the crisp air before readying his body for action.

"We've got at least two Ibarra vehicles in pursuit of Fire Team,"
Skeet announced. "Remainder of force is on foot."

Aroska listened as the engine sounds grew progressively closer,
now able to pick out the tones of multiple vehicles. Vibrations rumbled
through the ground as the ATV approached, accompanied by shouts
and gunfire. The vehicle itself was in visual range a moment later. It
tore up the little ravine, tossing rocks and dirt up in its wake. It was
followed closely by the hoverbike transporting Ken, which in turn was
followed by two groundcars from the repository.

The moment the former two vehicles blew past, Ziva stepped from
her hiding place and leveled her rifle at the lead Ibarra car, firing a round
directly into the engine block and sending the vehicle spinning out of
control. Aroska followed suit with the second car, sending it careening
into its counterpart. Both transports sank the short distance to the
ground and came skidding to a stop a couple dozen meters farther up the
ravine, their bodies dented, their engine compartments spitting smoke
and sparks.

As a unit, he, Ziva, and Ken's team closed in on the vehicles. "Out
of the cars!" Ziva hollered. "Weapons down! Hands up!"

She repeated the order in some dialect no doubt native to Panuco,
and the men slowly began to haul themselves out of the cars. Not that

they had much choice; Ken and the others moved in to help expedite the process, throwing them—bruised and bloodied from the crash—to the ground or forcing them to their knees.

More shouts echoed in the distance, and Aroska looked up the ravine to where all the Ibarra foot soldiers continued their approach. They charged forward, drawn toward the sound of gunfire and the sight of the smoke, but those in the lead began to slow upon realizing there was more at play. Unable to turn around as Talon Team came up behind them, they had no choice but to move closer. The remainder of Dagger Team emerged from their hiding places, lining up along the banks of the ravine and creating an impenetrable gauntlet.

Most of these Ibarra men were armed, but they kept their weapons lowered as they looked about and studied their predicament, no doubt weighing the consequences of making any sudden moves. Aroska couldn't see Skeet and Zinni from where he stood, but somewhere at the far end of the ravine, two voices—one male, one female, both with Haphezian accents—called for the soldiers to surrender completely.

"Tell them to drop their weapons," Skeet instructed over the open channel.

His words echoed from all the comms, but none of the Niiosians made any move to comply. Despite the murmurs rippling up and down the ravine, the forest felt strangely quiet, especially after all the commotion just moments before. The tension in the air was stifling, and in that instant Aroska understood the silence was merely the calm before the storm. He glanced at Ziva, then they both looked to Ken, who stood impassively watching the scene unfold.

Then the man gave a single nod.

The silence around them was shattered as all the Niiosians unleashed hell. A dozen Ibarra soldiers were struck down immediately, and the cacophony intensified as the survivors returned fire. Aroska hit the ground, vaguely aware of Ziva diving into cover behind one of the wrecked cars. Plasma bolts and bullets alike whizzed through the air from all directions. He could hear both Skeet and Zinni hollering for a ceasefire, but once again, no one heeded their words. A few Niiosians fell, their limp bodies sliding down the slope to join the corpses of their slain opponents. Others clambered down to better hem the Cartel thugs in.

By the time Aroska made it to his feet, most of the shooting had stopped. A few shots still echoed in the distance as soldiers engaged each other farther out in the woods. The fray—the slaughter—had lasted maybe ten seconds total, enough time to wipe out the entirety of the Ibarra crew. They'd been ripe for the picking, packed into an enclosed space without the advantage of high ground. But there was no shortage of Niiosians who'd been hit as well, and though the death toll appeared minimal after a cursory look, wounded soldiers would be useless in terms of holding down the repository.

His focus zeroed in on Ken. He stormed forward with the intention of demanding to know if the man had lost his mind, but Ziva came barreling into his peripheral vision, seizing Ken by the front of the shirt and forcing him to take a staggering step back.

"Are you insane?" she shouted. "We told you to give them the chance to surrender. Who's supposed to be calling the shots around here?"

"Agent Payvan, you know good and well we don't have the resources to take prisoners," he replied, his calm demeanor carrying a chilling undertone.

When it came down to it, he wasn't wrong, and under normal circumstances Aroska would have had no issue letting the Mob and the Cartel destroy each other. But as much as he wanted to say 'not my problem' and simply move on with the mission, it *was* his problem, because the Niiosians were supposed to be allies, and here they were getting themselves killed...and putting him in the crossfire in the process.

But what bothered him most at the moment was that by letting the soldiers open fire on their enemies, Ken had not only deviated from the plan but had circumvented Tobias's clear directive that the Haphezians were in charge. It wouldn't come as a complete shock, however, if this had been Tobias's plan all along. Given all Aroska knew about the man—and especially considering his newfound obsessive behavior—sacrificing a few of his own troops to wipe out an entire Ibarra force wasn't outside the realm of possibility.

Ken's gaze shifted out of focus even as Ziva held him. "Affirmative, sir. The threat has been neutralized."

Aroska realized he was speaking on comm, though he heard nothing in his own earpiece. Private channel. Why was that not surprising?

The man's placid expression slowly twisted into a scowl as he listened for another moment, then he returned his attention to Ziva. "The Ibarra cargo fleet has been captured, and Tobias is on his way down. We need to return to the repository immediately."

She watched him for several seconds as though trying to decide whether to comply, then she released her grip on him, looking up at the Niiosian soldiers who lined the ravine banks as she did so. Aroska couldn't help but notice several of the nearer men held their weapons ready, fixated on this woman who might be a threat to their leader. His concerns about the four of them being on their own out here intensified once more.

"Move out," Ziva called to those in the vicinity, repeating the order over the team comm channel. Skeet and Zinni acknowledged, and the whole troop turned and began the short walk back to the facility.

She fell into stride beside Aroska, shaking her head in disgust. It already felt good to be leaving this place behind, and even better to now be bringing up the rear in this little march where they could keep an eye on things. From this vantage point, he couldn't help but notice the Niiosian survivors were simply bypassing their fallen comrades, pausing occasionally to gather weapons and supplies from the dead ones but leaving the wounded behind as well. It seemed cold, but he supposed those soldiers would only slow the group down. If they could find the strength to make it back to the repository on their own and join the fight, more power to them.

If the two of them stuck close to the banks of the ravine, they could avoid most of the carnage, though Aroska noted that the Niiosians seemed to have no problem trampling directly over the Ibarra corpses. But one body in particular had fallen directly into his path, and as he moved to step over it, he saw an arm move. He paused; the man was so muddied and bloodied he certainly didn't look alive, but in one pale hand, he grasped a communicator, and he was pulling it progressively closer to his face.

Without a second thought, Aroska lifted his rifle and shot the man through the head. He wouldn't be able to transmit anyway with the jammers in range, but once they all returned to the facility, he might very well be out of that range. Besides, no sense in allowing him to suffer. There'd been plenty of bloodshed already, and the day had hardly begun. He lowered the weapon and rushed to catch up with Ziva as the whole group broke into a jog for the remainder of the journey.

They emerged from the trees and spilled out into the clearing. Smoke still curled up from the edge of the loading docks outside the repository, but aside from a couple of bodies sprawled in the dirt—one Niiosian and one Ibarra, it appeared—they'd succeeded in keeping the majority of the killing within the forest and out of sight.

A small shuttle emerged from the low clouds, breaking the relative calm that had settled over the area. The vessel touched down and Tobias appeared on the boarding ramp with Serenity and several more grizzled soldiers in tow.

"We have yet to sweep the facility," Ken announced as he approached, "but we've established a foothold here."

Tobias acknowledged him with a brief nod but continued forward into the midst of the group, his face contorted with urgency. "Ibarra forces have arrived in-system," he said. "Our fleets are still prepared to move in and surround theirs, but several ships including Manes's personal transport have already broken off from the group and are headed planetside. We have every reason to believe this is their destination, and they will be arriving in a matter of minutes." He turned in a slow circle, looking over the faces of his people as he let the information sink in. "Ladies and gentlemen, this is where we make a stand."

Aroska and Ziva exchanged a glance. She straightened a bit, adjusting her grip on her rifle as she focused on Tobias. This moment was pivotal enough for him as a mere player in this battle, but he could only imagine what might be going through her head right now. He hoped whatever happened brought her a sense of closure. At least her steeled expression told him she was ready to face whatever came next.

"What kind of numbers are they bringing?" Skeet called.

"Unknown. Scans showed two smaller personnel carriers in addition to Manes's ship." Tobias turned and approached Ziva and Aroska.

"Given what we know, tactical appraisal?"

'What we know' no doubt entailed all they'd just heard as well as intel about the zocrum facility Ziva had obtained during her previous exploits. Aroska turned and found her surveying the surrounding landscape, brows furrowed as her mind raced to find a solution in the limited time they had.

"We split up," she concluded, loud enough for everyone to hear. "Half inside, half in the surrounding forest. We draw them in, then hem them in, just like the fleet will do."

Tobias smirked. "I like the way you think, Agent Payvan." Then, to his men: "You heard the lady. You all here, inside. You and you, get these bodies out of sight. Serenity, take the shuttle and wait a distance away—be prepared for evacuation. The rest of you, conceal yourselves out here. Wait for my signal to move in. The element of surprise will be crucial."

There was a flurry of action as the mobster headed inside with his entourage and everyone else present scrambled to obey their latest orders. Aroska pivoted, already able to hear the rumble of ships approaching in the clouds. He began to suggest the four Haphezians join the group in the woods, but additional movement on the far end of the clearing caught his eye. A lone man loped along the tree line as fast as the limp he bore would allow, throwing a glance over his shoulder as he made a beeline for the property's front gate. Even from that distance, it was clear he was an Ibarra survivor. If he made it too far, he'd surely escape their jamming range and be able to warn Manes of their presence.

Ziva followed his gaze before he could articulate his thought, her rifle raised and leveled at the fleeing soldier even as she took several steps in that direction. Despite all the background noise, an eerie silence fell over the immediate area as she spared a couple of seconds to track the man in her scope. Then she pulled the trigger. The report of the rifle echoed all around them, rippling through the air and reverberating off the surrounding trees and repository structures. Another split second elapsed before the man's body jerked and he collapsed into the mud.

Ziva lowered the gun and began to step forward, but Aroska rushed up and caught her by the arm, his attention once again directed skyward. "No time," he said, able to make out the silhouette of a ship breaking through the clouds.

She glanced up and then met his gaze, something verging on fear in her eyes. He wasn't the only one wondering whether this whole operation had just been blown.

"*Sheyss*," she muttered. "Let's move."

They took off, making their way toward the tree line behind the loading docks where Skeet and Zinni already waited. The four of them slipped into the shadows of the forest once more, becoming invisible amid the trees as the roar of the descending ships grew deafening behind them.

CHAPTER 29
ZOCRUM REPOSITORY · Delatori

"Try it again," Manes instructed, determined the lump of dread in his stomach wouldn't be allowed to take root.

The comms officer seated in front of him did as he was told, but the only sound on the other end of the transmission was a soft crackling. "Still can't raise anyone," the man said, shaking his head. "I can transmit out, but the message bounces back on the other side." He frowned. "Scans show multiple life forms in and around the facility. Looks like a normal workday."

Manes ground his teeth within a clenched jaw. There were a number of reasonable explanations for the lack of response from the zocrum repository, but after all he'd seen—or more accurately, all he hadn't seen—upon arriving in Delatori airspace, he couldn't shake the feeling that something wasn't right. His transport fleet and all the precious materials it carried were nowhere to be found; again, there were several explanations for that, such as that the ships had relocated to stay out of Niio's reach, but when combined with all the mishaps Ibarra had already suffered over the last several months, he wondered if this was really a coincidence.

The personnel transport carrying him planetside from the *Oblivion* broke through the clouds, and the repository property materialized below. He peered out the viewport as his ship and the two other shuttles with him moved in for a landing. The massive clearing around the facility was completely devoid of activity, despite what the scanners had indicated just moments ago. A thin cloud of smoke lingered in the air, darker in color than the fog and cloud cover enveloping the forest. It appeared to have originated from a fire on the edge of the loading docks, though with the light rain that was falling, it was impossible to know how long that fire had been burning.

The vessels touched down in the center of the clearing. Even with the increases in shift size, this vast facility was only currently being manned by fifty or so crew who were all likely to be inside and hard at work. But combined with the unresponsive comms, the silence made Manes's stomach turn as he made his way down the boarding ramp.

The repository structure itself was scarred from battle, but aside from the active fire, it looked no worse for wear than he'd imagined it after reviewing damage reports following Ibarra's initial occupation. Most of the severe damage that had inhibited their zocrum recovery efforts had been internal anyway, so it was difficult to tell if anything was truly different now.

He took several steps forward, studying the series of footprints in the half-frozen mud. Several long furrows also cut across the ground, no doubt from the repulsors on the trucks that transported crew and materials back and forth to the little spaceport at the nearby settlement. He stooped down and touched the outline of one of the impressions. The mud gave a bit under his fingers but otherwise remained stable; these prints were fresh enough that the rain hadn't softened them completely yet. His men and his trucks had been here recently, but where were they now?

Manes turned to Kimbra as she emerged from one of the other ships. "Look around," he ordered. "Secure the perimeter."

She stood for a moment, taking in the scene for herself, then motioned for several men to accompany her as she turned and headed in the opposite direction toward the facility's front gates.

With a wave of his fingers, the remaining soldiers fell into stride with Manes as he made his way toward the repository itself. Aside from the low hiss of the rain and their footsteps squelching softly, the forest was much too quiet for his taste. Even as the head of a cartel that specialized in weapons development, he rarely had cause to use a firearm personally, but he found himself reaching for the sidearm he'd brought today. The men around him already had their weapons drawn, sweeping the landscape as they approached the repository's front doors.

The whole area had a damp, earthen smell thanks to the fog and precipitation, but he was almost positive he was picking up the lingering scent of plasma in the air as well. The exterior walls of the facility and all its outbuildings were riddled with black plasma scoring, and numerous shell casings from projectile weapons remained scattered in the mud. But again, it was impossible to know whether these were the result of the initial occupation of the area or a more recent event. Perhaps an event that had led to the virtual abandonment of the property.

Manes slid his weapon from its holster, watching as two of his men drew up to the door and began a thorough examination of it. They found it to be unlocked, and the rush of air as it slid open seemed to suck the air from his own lungs. The foyer inside was empty, a wide-open space with flickering lighting panels. A corridor off to the right remained caved in; this led to a handful of offices here on the ground floor, as well as upstairs to the final processing area where the raw zocrum was packaged and sent outside for transport. According to reports, only three of the seven available processing lines were functional, and further structural damage made it difficult for more than a few workers to get up there at a time, hence the holdup in recovery efforts. And, despite his orders, it didn't appear his men had made any progress toward getting the area cleared out and repaired before his arrival.

The wider access hall directly ahead, however, led into the heart of the facility and had been cleared as well as possible. Bowed metal jutted from the walls and debris still littered the floor, but as long as the corridor allowed his people direct access to the resources that lay beyond, that was all that mattered.

"Sir, look."

He glanced over to where one of the soldiers accompanying him had indicated. Across the foyer, off the beaten path toward the caved-in hallway, a pair of muddy boots protruded from behind a pile of debris. He approached, flanked by two of his men, weapon trained on the body. Upon closer inspection, it was two different boots. Two different bodies. Their limbs were entangled, their chests scorched by plasma. The mud on their footwear was still wet. They'd been placed here both hastily and recently. As his focus zeroed in on smaller cosmetic details, his heart rate spiked.

One of these dead men was Ibarra. The other had the signature Niiosian tattoos on his neck.

Manes had his comm out without hardly realizing it. "Zysk, send a squad down to my location immediately," he ordered, turning in a circle and sweeping his gaze back around the repository's foyer. The hairs on the back of his neck stood on end as his mind worked to conjure an explanation for the Niiosian's presence. The man may have been dead, but so was the Ibarra soldier; whether they killed each other or were killed by a third party, he didn't know, but someone had to have put them here, they had to have done it just minutes ago, and there was no sign of who that someone might have been. No sign of anyone at all.

It took him a moment to realize nobody had acknowledged his comm. "I repeat, send backup down here *now*," he said. He listened for another few seconds and was met only with silence, just as the shuttle had been during its descent. At the time, he'd assumed the silence was due to an issue with the facility's comms, but now he wondered if all comms in the area weren't actively being disrupted.

With all his senses amplified by the adrenaline rushing through his veins, the sound of the front doors bursting open was horrifyingly loud against the eerie stillness of the building. He and the men with him whirled, weapons leveled at the entering figures, but in his sights, he found only his own soldiers.

"I've been calling—why didn't you respond?" Kimbra demanded, shoving her way to the front of the group.

"Communications are blocked," he replied, convinced that was the only explanation for the situation. He paused, noting her wide eyes and heavy breathing. "What did you find?"

"There's a body near the property's front gate," she said. "Fresh plasma wound in the back...or so I thought. The wound registered that same bariine signature we saw in our men who were killed at the docks in Tabaco."

A chill coursed down Manes's spine. "Moryi," he growled. *Payvan.*

This all but confirmed she was alive and had escaped Panuco, and it was well on its way to confirming she was actively working against him. Had she killed this Niiosian man, too? Where was she now?

What the hell is going on?

"Go," he ordered, ushering Kimbra back toward the door and directing her men to join him instead. "Get as far away as you have to in order to get a message out. I want all available ground forces down here immediately."

She nodded and departed, and he motioned for all the soldiers to fall in behind him as he marched deeper into the facility. Matia may have had him fooled, whatever her motivations, whoever she was working for, and Tobias may have succeeded in driving him from Panuco, but there was no way in hell he was going to let this place be taken from him as well.

The big access corridor funneled them out onto a wide landing that led up to the edge of the cavernous mine. From there, metal staircases and catwalks stretched across and hugged the rounded walls of the massive, silo-style shaft. Hundreds of pulleys moved lifts up and down the space, carrying raw zocrum and depositing it on the few functional conveyors that would ferry it off to the packaging areas. Landings below led to control rooms, maintenance stations, storage spaces, and more, and beyond those, in the farthest depths of the mine, heavy machinery drilled into the earth, extracting the valuable materials that would eventually make his fleet unstoppable.

Or at least that was all what should have been happening. Manes brought his squad to a halt on the landing, only able to hear the sounds of the mining process echoing around him. The facility itself was pitch dark, and, aside from the racket of the machinery, completely quiet. No shouts, no orders relayed via intercom, not so much as a joke exchanged between workers. If his crew wasn't here, then what the hell were the life forms his landing craft's scanners had picked up?

The string of anomalies he'd seen since arriving planetside had led him to entertain the idea this might all be a trap, and he felt something come alive inside of him as he made up his mind that was exactly the case. If all the machinery was still functional, that meant the power hadn't been cut—the lights in the foyer had been dim but on, which meant someone had turned them off here. On purpose, no doubt.

Instinct told him to move. *Now.* "Someone get the power back on immediately," he growled.

His men began to fan out, some heading for a downward stairwell while he and the others made a beeline for another that led up, the metal railings barely visible in the ambient light from the corridor. They were well-trained, good soldiers with various combat backgrounds, but at the moment he couldn't help but feel a pang of dread, fearful they wouldn't be enough.

The moment his foot hit the landing at the top of the steps, an echoing hum—deeper than the noise of the mining equipment—reverberated throughout the massive shaft, narrowly preceding a muffled *boom* as the entire silo was illuminated. He flinched and held a hand up to shield his eyes, and past the spots dancing in his vision, he was able to discern several figures standing across the landing ahead of him. One stood out from the others; the bright lights around them shone against a bald head and reflected off a pair of old spectacles.

"Hello, Alastair."

It was funny, really—Manes had never met Tobias Niio in the flesh, but years of obsessing over the man almost made it feel like they were old acquaintances. He lowered his hand and straightened as his men trained their weapons on the old mobster. The Niiosian soldiers across the landing responded in kind, and the sound of more weapons being readied prompted Manes to look up to where two more sizable squads of Niiosians hovered on the catwalks above them.

Tobias took a small step forward. "I always anticipated greed would be your downfall, and it seems I was right. Coming here in person for your precious zocrum—so predictable."

It was one thing to spend months awaiting a showdown like this, but now that absolutely nothing was going according to plan, Manes found himself struggling to calm a racing mind. He wanted to be angry—he *was* angry—but losing his temper would be the least productive course of action. As much as he'd like to take offense at the fact that Tobias had accused him of being predictable, the bigger question was how the man had predicted anything at all. How had he known the zocrum was the priority?

Matia would know. The attack on Panuco, the breach of his defense systems, the sabotage of his development projects, the presence of the bariine ammo here on Delatori, the presence of the *Niiosians* here on Delatori...suddenly every ounce of it made perfect sense. His intuition had been right all along. He'd been played worse than he thought.

"You don't know anything, old man," he replied with a wag of his head.

Before either of them could say anything further, an explosion somewhere outside the facility rocked the building. The lights flickered and dust and rubble rained down around them. Manes saw his opportunity and pivoted, ducking low and yanking a flashbang grenade from the supply belt of one of his men. He flipped the primer switch and lobbed the device toward the Niiosians. Recognizing the effort, another soldier followed up with a smoke grenade. Both devices detonated within a split second of each other, sending tremors and echoes reverberating up and down the metal structures. The last thing he saw were several Niiosian thugs moving to shield Tobias before the smokescreen enveloped them.

Manes turned and plunged back down the stairs as plasma bolts began to fly.

Chapter 30
Zocrum Repository - Delatori

Nobody moved as they watched Alastair Manes and his entourage head across the clearing toward the repository's main entrance. Or at least Aroska assumed it was Manes—the thought occurred to him that he'd never seen the man in person. But based on the way Ziva's face hardened and her focus zeroed in on this newcomer, his assumption was correct. The Ibarra leader was tall, handsome, and well-dressed; Aroska had taken to picturing him older, almost as a carbon copy of Tobias considering his reputation.

Manes and the soldiers with him disappeared through the front doors. Voices could still be heard on the far side of the clearing, closer to where the landing craft had touched down, but the people to whom they belonged were impossible to see from this vantage point. None of the craft were large, probably shuttles belonging to Manes's flagship, so regardless of how many people total had been aboard, the Niiosians had more than enough ground forces to subdue them.

A couple of minutes passed before several people appeared from the direction of the voices. They were led by a tall blonde woman— Aroska could have sworn she was Haphezian—and moved at a rapid clip toward the facility. A quiet scraping sound drew his attention back to Ziva. He wasn't sure if he'd ever seen her features so cold as she stood there unscrewing the long barrel of her rifle, preparing the weapon for closer quarters combat without removing her eyes from the woman.

For a moment, he feared he'd have to hold her down to keep her from springing forward and starting something. "Who is she?" he whispered.

Her lips barely moved. "Not now."

They fell silent again, though this time the quiet barely lasted a minute before the blonde woman burst back out the front door, comm in hand, and took off at a full sprint across the clearing.

"*Sheyss*," Skeet murmured, "she'll get out of jamming range and get a call out."

It was at that instant that a dull roar filled the air. Nothing could be seen through the trees and cloud cover, but the sound of more ships descending was unmistakable.

"The fleet has sprung its trap," Ken announced, listening to his earpiece for another couple of seconds. "Several Ibarra vessels immediately broke away and are headed down here. We have forces in pursuit." Then, over the wide channel: "Fan out. Prepare for reinforcements on both sides."

He could be heard gathering more information from his contact within the fleet as he moved away. The four Haphezians began to heed his instruction and spread out, but Aroska hadn't taken two steps before another strange sound drew his attention to the sky. With the clouds preventing any visual confirmation, it took him an extra split second to recognize the whine of an approaching small aircraft.

The first bomb fell less than twenty meters away.

Zinni wasn't sure how much of her movement was of her own accord and how much was the result of the blast. She staggered sideways, miraculously maintaining her footing while others around her fell, thanks in large part to the tree beside her that had absorbed the brunt of the shockwave. Through the ringing in her ears, she could hear the bomber craft tear away over the clearing, followed by the growl of a second engine and the rapid spit of large-caliber plasma fire as a Niiosian fighter swooped in to engage.

It was tempting at that point to make a rush for the repository—she was almost positive she heard another explosion of some sort inside as well. But the squad of troops Tobias had taken with him was sufficient to deal with the squad accompanying Manes, so if Niio's ultimate goal was to reclaim this facility, then their best bet was to remain outside and act as a barrier to keep Ibarra forces out.

"Listen up," she called over the team comms, opting to cut to the chase and take matters into her own hands, "all Niiosian ground forces take defensive positions immediately. Protect the repository from Ibarra incursion at all costs."

She almost hated herself for speaking the words. This certainly wasn't what she'd bargained for when she and Skeet had offered to retrieve Starcer's specs, and she was well aware of how easily they could —and probably should—walk away from this battle before it escalated any further. The problem at this point was she wasn't convinced Ziva would agree to leave with them, and she wasn't prepared to leave her old friend behind again without some sort of discussion on the matter.

Her focus returned to the present as she moved through the trees toward the loading docks. She was vaguely aware of Skeet following close behind her, and of Ken directing some of his people to take overwatch positions on the roofs of the repository's outbuildings. The roar of another explosion filled the air, and she glanced across the clearing in time to see a fireball consume Manes's shuttle. A pair of Niiosian fighters whizzed by overhead, the treetops swaying in their wake.

She skidded to a stop along the edge of the loading dock nearest the facility, somewhat concealed under the large vacuum tubes. One of them was still smoking from the explosive Ken had placed earlier. Through the haze of the smoke and clouds, she could make out the silhouettes of numerous ships moving in for a landing. She swallowed and checked the plasma charge in her weapon; even after everything they'd already been through that morning, it seemed the real fight was just beginning.

"Tobias is mine, do you understand me?" Manes growled. He doubted any of his people would be stupid enough to deprive him of the privilege of killing the man, but at this point, after so much else had gone wrong, he wasn't about to take any chances.

He couldn't see Tobias from where he stood, taking cover just inside an alcove full of control stations a level below the landing where the old mobster ambushed him. But he had a strong suspicion the man would come down this way, if for no other reason than that there was more room to maneuver than if he headed for the more damaged areas on the upper levels. Separating him from his troops would be key; the Ibarra crew was outnumbered but undoubtedly had superior firepower. If Manes could lure Tobias to the lower levels, he was confident his men would be able to deal with the Niiosian crew.

He relayed this information to the soldier nearest to him, who began to signal the others. They spread out along the edges of the landing outside the control center, their personal shields absorbing the stray plasma bolts that managed to reach them through the catwalks and platforms above. Several of them primed fresh smoke grenades, and two of them removed heavier weaponry from the harnesses on their backs. At one's signal, those holding the grenades lobbed them upward. The devices detonated, filling the mineshaft with smoke. The opposing fire became more sporadic as the Niiosians lost sight of their targets. Then, with nearly perfect synchronization, the two men with heavy arms fired; each of their bulky, three-barreled weapons discharged a trio of heat-seeking explosive projectiles that snaked up through the smoke and impacted on the landings above.

The screams of Niiosian soldiers filled the air. A couple of bodies tumbled—in flames—over the catwalk railings and crashed onto the platform just meters from Manes. If the playing field hadn't become totally balanced just now, it was a good start. The Niiosians on the upper landings where Tobias had been would have no choice but to come this way if they wanted to engage, and having the higher ground didn't mean much when they couldn't see the enemy they had pinned down.

Conventional plasma fire resumed, and it took only a few moments for the Niiosians to appear out of the haze. The first ones through were mowed down before they knew what hit them. Their comrades wised up and took a more cautious approach, picking off a few Ibarra men who'd gotten too close to the stairs as they descended.

A blinding volley of plasma bolts lit up the platform, accompanying the emergency strobes that had begun flashing throughout the facility.

Manes leaned out and squeezed off several shots, taking the Niiosians by surprise while they had their attention on the more immediate threat his men posed. He ducked back into cover when a spray of plasma came his way, taking the opportunity to search the fray for his nemesis. Tobias would have to be bold to accompany his soldiers directly, though the man had already displayed such a degree of tenacity simply by being here that Manes wouldn't put it past him. But a cursory look into the lingering haze revealed no sign of him. Perhaps he was still lurking like a coward up top, waiting for his men to do his dirty work—

Movement in the distance drew Manes's attention, and he looked across the massive mineshaft to see Tobias and two Niiosian soldiers slinking down a curving stairway against the opposite wall. The walkways required to get over there were in bad shape, so he'd written them off as a means of traversal for Niio's forces. But it seemed a mere three people had managed to navigate them successfully.

Gritting his teeth, he burst from cover and seized a rifle from one of his soldiers just as the man finished loading a fresh plasma cell. He sighted up the three figures across the way, firing off several rounds in quick succession that took out one of the Niiosian bodyguards. The second man threw himself in front of Tobias, but not before another burst of shots cut across the shaft wall, striking the mobster in the upper arm. Both of them hurried downward without looking back.

Manes cast the rifle aside, recovered his pistol, and rushed down the nearest stairs after them.

The growl of dozens of vehicle engines now contributed to the noise and chaos surrounding the repository. Ziva had counted at least ten small ATV-style vehicles exiting the Ibarra drop ships, each occupied by a driver and a marksman. Then there were a handful of hoverbikes and open-top groundcars with mounted weapons. And that was all in addition to the fresh foot soldiers the ships had brought in. The Niiosians had contributed additional numbers as well; the clearing in front of the facility now hosted hundreds of troops, all gladly unleashing hell upon each other.

Tobias had been right in that Niio didn't exactly represent a true military force. Ibarra didn't, either, but even an unorganized battalion could do some damage with the amount of ordnance they were packing.

She ducked behind a tree, bagging a pair of Cartel thugs as she opened a transmission on the team channel. "Your friendly neighborhood Haphezians will handle the Ibarra heavy weaponry. All remaining ground forces, pick on somebody your own size."

"Acknowledged," Skeet said. He heard similar affirmations from Zinni and Aroska, as well as a few devilish chuckles from Niiosian soldiers who seemed to be downright enjoying themselves in the midst of this bloodbath.

He dashed forward, dropping to one knee and sliding through the softening mud to put himself directly in the path of one of the Ibarra hoverbikes. Two shots were all it took to send the pilot toppling off. As the machine slowed, he stood, slinging his rifle around to his back and seizing the bike's handlebars. He leaped on, wrenched the controls around, and took off in the direction from which it had come.

The groundcars that had arrived on the scene were quite possibly doing the most damage out of all of Ibarra's armament, slicing through the chaos with their high-caliber mounted guns and running over anyone—sometimes even their own troops—unfortunate enough to get in their way. He steered the bike toward one that had strayed out into the trees and was weaving about looking for space to turn around. The gunner glanced his way but didn't seem to realize an impostor was piloting the Ibarra bike until he was right up alongside them. The mounted gun hadn't quite swiveled in his direction when he drew his sidearm and put a round through the operator's forehead.

In a panic, the pilot swerved and slowed, giving Skeet the opportunity to leap from the bike to the tail of the vehicle. He flailed for purchase for a moment then flung himself over the side and fell in, taking up the gun controls and turning the weapon on the nearest identical groundcar. The heavy rounds slammed into the other vehicle, shredding the gunner, the pilot, the chassis, and the windshield. Out of control, the car hurtled full speed into a large tree and went up in flames.

A plasma bolt whizzed past his face, so close he could feel its heat against his skin. He turned his attention back to his own vehicle, where the pilot had managed to pull a pistol and was lining up a second shot while attempting to keep the car under control. Skeet shot him in the head, then turned and leaped out just as the vehicle hit an embankment and rolled. He tumbled several meters and scrambled to his feet, already running by the time he got upright.

Two down, and a seemingly infinite number to go.

Zinni ran at a full sprint toward a third groundcar that had just been upended by a stray blast from one of the fighters that continually screamed by overhead. The vehicle had landed upright and appeared to still be functional, but the gunner and pilot had both been thrown from it on impact. She could see them on the far side, struggling back to their feet. They would not be allowed to regain control of the car.

Quickening her steps for the final few strides, she threw all her forward momentum into a leap, vaulting off the edge of the open car and jumping out the other side. She latched onto the gunner's shoulders just as he managed to stand, her weight forcing him toward his companion and putting her in prime position to throw a kick at the second man's head. He staggered backward as the gunner collapsed beneath her. She rolled off him and rose up on one knee, drawing her pistol and delivering a double tap to the pilot's center of mass. She swiveled and did the same to the gunner, sending a third round through his head that put a permanent stop to his attempts at getting up again.

Then her eyes were roving over the clearing, searching for any nearby Niiosians. She placed her fingers in her mouth, letting out a shrill whistle that managed to cut through the din of battle and capture the attention of a trio of Mob soldiers. With a wave of her hand, they were moving in her direction, their eyes fixed hungrily on the abandoned Ibarra car. One of them even offered her a nod of thanks.

She took off at a jog, hunting for her next target. "All forces, be advised a Cartel groundcar is now under Niiosian control."

"Nice work!" Aroska said, firing off several shots that put a halt to a pair of Ibarra soldiers' journey toward the repository entrance. Following Ziva's instruction to target the Cartel's heavy ordnance, he hadn't seen any of his teammates—even from a distance—for at least several minutes. But simply hearing their voices and knowing they were making valuable contributions to this fight was reassuring.

The next two rounds he fired were hardly more than sparks, indicating an empty plasma cell. He abandoned the rifle and snatched a new one up from a corpse on the ground without breaking stride. There was no shortage of either—corpses *or* weapons—around here. The air was thick with the hot scents of smoke and plasma, but through all of that, the area reeked of gore and death. And somehow the fact that everything was wet made it all worse. The skies had opened up and the light drizzle had evolved into full-blown rain. The frozen ground he'd grown accustomed to early that morning had been transformed into a mud pit after being trampled, driven over, and blown up.

He could genuinely say he'd never seen such a mess.

As he continued forward, his gaze fell on a pair of Ibarra engineers who were attempting to set up some sort of mobile turret a little too close to the repository's front doors for his taste. He swept his commandeered carbine across the space in front of him, picking off a couple of Cartel thugs who crossed his path. *Ah, projectile weapon.* Two more shots. And... empty.

He was partway through the motion of turning to look for a re-placement weapon when a burly Ibarra soldier barreled into him at full speed, knocking him cleanly to the ground. The thug's shadow—holding some sort of long, straight weapon—rose up over him. Aroska flipped onto his back, bringing the rifle up horizontally to block a blow from some sort of...five moons, an axe? *Sheyss.*

He shied to one side and then the other as the axe came down again and again, embedding itself in the sticky mud. A solid kick to the brute's kneecap sent him staggering one precious step backward, giving Aroska the two seconds needed to roll away and grab a fresh pistol from another man who'd just fallen. He flung himself back around and unloaded on the Ibarra thug just as the axe blade came free from the mud, shimmying away to avoid the grisly weapon as the man collapsed.

His attention was drawn back to the Niiosian who'd just died beside him. A single grenade remained on the man's belt. He plucked it off, flicked the primer switch, and rolled, hurling it toward the turret. The machine had just started firing when the device detonated, consuming it in a ball of fire and sending the two men operating it flying.

"Watch for teams setting up turrets," he advised over comm.

Movement in his peripheral vision drew his gaze to the repository entrance, where a tall figure with a mop of blonde hair was just slipping inside.

Ziva came up behind one of the very turrets Aroska spoke of, putting a trio of her bariine rounds into its operator's back before he knew what hit him. The machine was automated, firing on Niiosian troops based on some sort of targeting algorithms. She slung her rifle over her shoulder and grasped the turret's head with both hands. Servos whined as the device struggled against her hold, but she managed to angle the barrel away to avoid a cluster of Mob soldiers, then bring it back up again to target one of Ibarra's hoverbikes. The vehicle crashed into the mud, flinging its pilot off to one side.

As far as she could tell as she continued to sweep the weapon over the scene, the Niiosians were holding, thanks in no small part to her team's efforts. Two of the Ibarra groundcars with the mounted guns remained, though one was currently being pursued by the vehicle Zinni had freed up for Niiosian use. No additional ground forces had arrived for either side for some time now. Not that either side had that many troops at their disposal in the first place. At this point, any remaining personnel were needed aboard the ships that continued to engage each other in high orbit. She looked up, blinking the pouring rain out of her eyes, only able to imagine what was going on beyond the dense clouds.

She turned the turret on a pair of Cartel soldiers who'd begun to fire toward her upon realizing the gun was no longer under their side's control. Satisfied for the time being, she stepped back, putting a round through the machine's control panel and rendering it inoperable.

She by no means considered herself an expert on battle strategy, but it didn't take a genius to tell some gaps had started to open in Niiosian ranks closer to the repository. If enough Ibarra troops noticed and got inside, it would be far too easy for Niio to lose whatever advantage it had.

"All available Niiosian forces," she called over comm, "reconvene as close to the facility as possible. Hold that line."

This far down in the mine, the noise of all the automated machinery was almost deafening, the sound waves bouncing off the rounded walls with nowhere to go. Manes wasn't even sure which level he was on; the lower he went, the farther apart the landings and platforms were to make way for the larger diggers and drills. None of those things were functional right now with nobody down here to operate them, but all the conveyors and lifts continued moving like normal, carrying empty containers to the surface.

His feet hit the next landing and he paused. Only darkness remained below him. This must be the end of the primary workspace;

anything lower was done entirely by machinery controlled by workers on this level. He turned to his left and studied his surroundings. A long hallway had been cut into the mine wall, following the curve of the shaft. Several rooms branched off from that, maintenance spaces and control centers for the digging equipment. The infrastructure was intact here, but the massive shovel and drill down below were both damaged. This and the partially caved-in processing center upstairs were why he didn't have the zocrum he needed yet. Why he hadn't been ready to take on Tobias before now. Why he was *here* now.

Manes turned and moved to his right. A long metal bridge led across the shaft to an identical bank of mechanical rooms, as well as the control centers for the diggers that were still functional. If Tobias had made it down this far, he was bound to be over there. And if he hadn't, Manes would intercept him, forcing him to either risk going back up toward the battle or stay and fight.

No sooner had the thought crossed his mind than the ear-shattering report of a projectile weapon echoed all around him. A bullet struck the bridge railing as he sprinted forward. The sound of a second shot filled the air. Something tugged at the clothing on the back of his shoulder, and he felt the burn of friction against his skin. Too close.

He reached the other side and ducked into the cover of the hallway, adequately shielded from the shooter above. With his attention directed upward, he didn't see the handheld shovel swinging toward his face until it was too late. The blow was a glancing one but sent him reeling back nonetheless. His pistol flew from his hand, and blood streamed from a long cut across his cheek where the metal had sliced through flesh. He looked up, his vision righting itself just in time to avoid a second blow, and he found himself staring at Tobias.

"You're beaten, Alastair. Your transport fleet is mine. Your ships are pinned down. We have superior numbers. Surrender now and I will allow you to walk away from this."

Manes dragged a hand across his face and leaned over to spit. "A likely story."

The corners of Tobias's mouth curled upward, and the eyes behind those antique spectacles were frigid. "No, I didn't think you'd believe that bit. But it was worth a try."

Footsteps thundered down the stairs outside. Both men dove for the fallen gun. To Manes's dismay, Tobias reached it first; the mobster was surprisingly quick for his age and stocky build. Manes rolled away from the flurry of shots he unleashed, pivoting around to take out the bodyguard's legs as the man arrived on the scene. The Mob thug sprawled out beside him, and Manes hooked an arm around his throat, yanking him up to form a human shield just as Tobias fired several more shots. The man's body spasmed as the plasma bolts burned into his chest. Manes didn't wait for him to fall still before relieving him of his projectile weapon and returning fire. One of the rounds struck flesh; Tobias let out a grunt and ducked away. The rest hit a series of pipes running up the wall, rupturing them and filling the hallway with hot steam. The mobster disappeared on the other side of the cloud.

Manes shoved the dead Niiosian off him and scrambled to his feet, checking the mag in his new weapon. The few rounds remaining would be adequate to do what he'd come here to do. Raising a hand to shield his face, he plunged through the steam, growling in pain as it seared his skin. Wherever Tobias had gone, whatever he thought he was accomplishing here...this wasn't over, and it wouldn't be until he was dead.

"All available Niiosian forces, reconvene as close to the facility as possible. Hold that line."

"Gladly," Skeet replied, though as soon as the word was out of his mouth, it struck him as an odd thing to say in response to a call for Niiosian troops. No matter—he might as well be one at this point anyway. After all of this, he was beginning to commiserate with what Ziva had once said about selling her soul to the Niiosian Mob. If you offered to do anything for Tobias Niio, he owned you until it was done. And, apparently, long after.

The team should have known better than to get involved, but now that they were here, he couldn't help but feel the need to see this through to the end. Part of it was just how he was wired; he was trained to be thorough, to finish what he started. But after some reflection, he could also say he was doing this for Ziva. As put out as he still was with her, he sincerely did want to help her find some closure after the hell she'd been through. And her finding closure could lead to all of them finding closure. If winning this battle was what it took to free her from these absurd obligations and return to a sense of normality, well then, he supposed he should do his damndest to win it.

He came up on the rear side of the loading docks, jogging alongside several other Niiosians who'd answered Ziva's call. Some of the fighting had migrated farther out into the woods as these rival gang members focused more on destroying each other than claiming this crucial piece of turf. The clearing was no less chaotic for it though; as ammunition ran low and Ibarra's superior firepower was stripped from them, people had taken to using melee weapons or even brawling hand to hand.

Zinni arrived momentarily, breathing hard but shooting him a look of reassurance nonetheless. They continued moving along the tree line toward the facility, crossing paths with Ziva after another few seconds. She fired off a pair of rounds, bringing down an Ibarra soldier, then fell into stride beside them.

"How long do you think we'll have to keep this up?" Skeet said, jerking his head toward the clearing.

"What, you mean you're not having fun?" Ziva replied.

He couldn't help but smirk. Movement drew his attention to his left—

The flash of light in front of him was blinding, and the sharp *bang* that accompanied it seemed to rattle his very bones. There was no ball of flames, no true explosion, but the force of the blow sent him stumbling and knocked his weapon from his grasp. He thought he heard it hit the muddy ground somewhere, but maybe that was just part of the residual crackling in his ears. He took a staggering step and tried to blink the spots out of his eyes, holding one arm up to shield his face as bits of dirt and rock that had been blown into the air began to rain back down around him. Everything felt like it was happening in slow motion, like his movements were mechanical. He pivoted, saw his gun on the ground.

Saw the Ibarra soldier three meters away, taking aim.

Not for him—for the person next to him.

Ziva. Her back was turned.

His voice didn't sound like his own. "Ziva!" He was moving without realizing it. He hit her full force just as something hit *him* full force.

Then the only thing he was aware of was the fact that they were both falling.

Chapter 31
Zocrum Repository - Delatori

"Ziva!"

She'd managed to avoid the brunt of the flashbang's impact, but it still left her reeling. She began to pivot, vaguely aware someone had her in their sights before Skeet tackled her to the ground. Something wet splattered her face—warm and metallic, unlike the rain—and she saw red in the edges of her vision.

Her narrow range of focus shifted back outward to the immediate threat as the Ibarra man closed in, but Zinni appeared just then and emptied half her mag into his chest before he could get another shot off. Then it became a simultaneous effort by Skeet to haul himself up and by her to scramble out from under him. He got clear and fell back into the mud, gloved hand clamped over his collarbone and dark blood pulsing out between his fingers.

"*Sheyss*," she exclaimed, leaping forward. Grasping the harness on the exterior of his stealth suit, she dragged him backward toward the nearest trees while he did his best to assist with his legs. She propped him up against the thickest trunk available and pried his hand away only to allow blood to stream steadily down his arm and chest.

"What the hell did you go and do that for?" she demanded, swearing again and keeping the pressure off just long enough to pull a small blade from her belt. She cut away at the material of the suit, granting herself a better view of the gaping wound underneath. *High-caliber slug.* She clamped one hand back down over the hole and probed the back of his shoulder with the other. No exit wound. *Damn it. Sheyss, sheyss, sheyss.*

"Couldn't...help it," he said through clenched teeth, his hoarse voice barely audible above the cacophony around them.

"It was a rhetorical question, you idiot. Hold still and don't talk. We've got to get this bleeding stopped."

"It's bad, isn't it."

Yes, it was. "What did I just say?" she hissed, putting conscious effort into keeping her voice from wavering. She probed the area around the wound again; judging by the give in his flesh, the slug had also shattered his collarbone, further contributing to the damage within. She stuck her thumb into the wound, hoping she might be able to clamp the gushing artery with her own fingers at least until help arrived, but a cursory search yielded no intact vessel to grab onto. The effort seemed to increase the flow of blood anyway. Breathing hard, she sat back and shed her jacket, wadding up the body and tying the sleeves around his shoulder as tightly as possible before pressing both palms down over the shoddy excuse for a bandage.

"What can I do?" Zinni said.

"You can make sure nobody around here does *this* again," Ziva replied, ducking low as the intelligence officer arced her rifle barrel around to take aim at an approaching Ibarra agent even as they spoke. She yanked one hand away from Skeet's shoulder just long enough to call out over the team comms: "Come in, Serenity. We need immediate medevac!"

"Copy," the woman replied after several seconds of static that seemed to stretch into eternity. "What's your position?"

A hail of plasma fire struck the tree trunk. Ziva leaned over to shield Skeet's face, forced to squint through a shower of dirt and burning wood chips to gather her bearings. "Northeast corner of the facility property," she hollered. "Make that approximately thirty degrees east of the northernmost outbuilding, behind the loading docks."

"On my way."

Hurry, she thought.

Skeet had gone pale, and his head bobbed back and forth as he took in shallow, hissing breaths through his nose. As near as she could tell, the slug had struck his subclavian artery, and the bleeding had yet to slow. For a moment, she regretted the fact that most of her anatomy expertise was from the perspective of being a more efficient killer, not for saving lives. She wondered if there was someone among the Niiosian ranks who carried some sort of clotting agent, even some basic medical supplies. But this was essentially a gang war; these people were here to kill each other and weren't operating on the type of organized level she'd always been accustomed to.

"Where the hell is Aroska?" she muttered, more to herself than anything else. She looked around, wincing against the putrid combination of rain, blood, plasma, smoke, and fog in the air, but didn't catch sight of him in the immediate vicinity.

"Skeet?"

Zinni's worried voice drew her back to the present just as she felt his torso begin to slide farther down the tree trunk.

"Hey, hey, hey, no you don't," she said through gritted teeth, bringing one bloodied palm up to tap the side of his face. His eyelids fluttered and he groaned, but his body continued to sag toward the ground.

"Skeet!" Zinni shrieked again, abandoning her post to stoop down and help lay him out flat. She clamped her own hands down over the wound, and Ziva pulled back to take in the scene from a new angle.

"You stay awake," she ordered, searching what little she could see of the sky for Serenity's shuttle.

"Get me..." he murmured, pausing to run his tongue over dry lips, "...the *Saber*."

"Now's not the time to be worried about your damn ship," she retorted. She swept her gaze around the area again, looking for a familiar face. "Where the hell is Aroska?" she repeated, this time loud enough for someone—anyone—to hear.

"No offense, sir, but this is terrible timing."

Emeri went silent for a moment on the other end of the transmission. "Lieutenant Duvo?"

"Sergeant Tarbic, sir. Skeet gave me this comm."

"And where is he?"

"I'm trying to determine exactly that." He peered out from his cover behind an outbuilding, searching the area he'd heard Ziva describe to Serenity just before he'd muted the wide channel in favor of the director's call on the comm unit from the *Saber*. Through the fog and chaos, he caught sight of Zinni with her back pressed up against a tree, laying down cover fire while Ziva knelt beside someone on the ground. As he'd feared based on what he'd heard over the wide comms, Skeet was hurt.

No time for chit-chat. "What can I do for you, sir?" he asked, ducking back into cover as stray plasma bolts zinged through the air much too close to his head.

"I've got Pahl Starcer here telling me he's just received word from some contacts on Delatori. Niio and Ibarra are at all-out war, fighting over some material that's almost guaranteed to grant one side dominance over the other."

Aroska grimaced. "I know."

"You—" Emeri hesitated. "*Sheyss*, don't tell me you're there."

"Afraid so. We all are."

The director swore again. "Damn it, I specifically told you not to get involved!"

He saw an opening and darted from his hiding place, moving quick and low over the muddy ground and squeezing off several suppressive shots as he went. "If it's any consolation, sir, we're doing it for Ziva."

"That's precisely the problem!" Emeri roared. "How the hell did a simple mission to recover Starcer's specs turn into your whole team getting caught up in this?"

The tirade continued through the earpiece, but Aroska barely heard it as he came up on the rest of the team. Both Ziva and Zinni knelt over Skeet now as he lay flat on his back; the former had stripped down to a tank top and appeared to have converted her jacket into a crude pressure bandage. She bent over and said something inaudible to Skeet before lifting her head and searching her surroundings.

"Where the hell is Aroska?" she hollered, desperation adding a hint of shrillness to her tone he'd never heard before.

"Here!" he called, skidding to a stop behind them. He took a moment to look around the scene; the Niiosians seemed to have regrouped as ordered and pushed the Ibarra soldiers back out of the immediate vicinity, and he directed his attention to what was happening on the ground. Zinni had both palms pressed against Skeet's blood-soaked shoulder, and based on Ziva's dark red hands, she'd been doing the same only moments ago. The lieutenant's chest still rose and fell, albeit in a labored, irregular pattern. Blood continued dribbling from between Zinni's fingers even through the wadded-up jacket.

Emeri's voice faded back to the forefront. "Tarbic, are you listening to me? I warned you to remain neutral and not get involved in this fight, did I not?"

Aroska had no idea what the man had been saying. He pulled the communicator itself out, switching the call to an open transmission so the two women could hear. "Lieutenant Duvo is down. I repeat, we have a man down!"

The director muttered something unintelligible, perhaps to himself, perhaps to Starcer or someone else present with him. "That's it. Sergeant, you are to assume command of the Alpha team and get your people out of there immediately. Do you hear me? You're done there. Get out *now*."

At this point Aroska had half a mind to just listen to him. They'd played their part in Tobias's game, had given the Niiosians a tactical edge in this struggle. With the extent of the havoc that raged around them, chances were slim that anyone would miss them now.

He looked down and found Zinni's wide blue eyes locked on him, waiting for a verdict. "He won't make it if we don't do something," she said, hands still pressed against Skeet's shoulder.

The lieutenant lifted his head and made an unsuccessful effort to sit up. "The...*Saber*."

Ziva shoved him back down. "I told you not to worry about your *frouchten* ship."

"No, he's right," Aroska said, devoting precisely two seconds to considering the matter. He shifted his attention back to Zinni. "Serenity's team restocked the medbay before you left the *Revenant*, right? We'll be able to get him the help he needs a hell of a lot faster than we could if we went all the way back up to rendezvous with the fleet."

Not to mention that fleet was currently engaged in the galaxy only knew what manner of turmoil far above their heads. No sense in escaping one battle only to get trapped in another.

Ziva looked to Zinni, who nodded. "Fine," she said. The roar of an approaching ship drew her attention to the sky. "Here's Serenity with transport."

"Tarbic!" Emeri's voice echoed from the comm unit, reminding Aroska the transmission was still live. "I am giving you an order! Acknowledge!"

"Message received, sir. Bugging out now." He pocketed the comm and looked up at the ship as it descended toward them. It was the same little shuttle Tobias had arrived in, with room for only a few passengers, but it would be more than adequate to get them back to the *Saber*. The repulsors sent a vibration through the air as it came in for a landing on the edge of the tree line, whipping up a fine spray of mud and rainwater that painted everything within a ten-meter radius.

"Shields are up but we don't have all day," Serenity's voice echoed over the vessel's loudspeaker before the landing gear had even hit the ground.

Aroska stooped down and hefted Skeet up under one arm while Ziva did the same on the other side. With awkward, lurching steps, they began to haul him toward the boarding ramp, his feet dragging along the ground while Zinni abandoned his wound long enough to sweep the area and cover their retreat. The ramp had become slippery in no time and the last few steps were a staggering effort, but they collapsed through the hatch and managed to get him laid out flat once more.

"Get pressure back on this," Ziva instructed, though Zinni was already moving to do just that.

Serenity threw them a glance over the back of the pilot's seat. "Status?"

"Arterial hemorrhage," Ziva answered. "Slug is still in there."

The former doctor swore. "I can call ahead, have my surgery team waiting. Can't guarantee bunk space by the time we get up there though."

"No," Aroska said, moving up to lean over the seat and look her in the eye. "Get us to the *Saber*. Rendezvous Point One."

She held his gaze for the briefest of moments, then raised a brow and shook her head. "You got it."

He tapped the seat in thanks and turned, ready to tell her to take off until he realized Zinni and Skeet were suddenly the only occupants of the passenger compartment. A pair of sprinting strides took him back to the boarding hatch, where he caught sight of Ziva just as her boots hit dirt.

"Where are you going?" he demanded, taking a step after her.

"Aroska, come on!" Zinni called behind him.

Ziva turned to face him but didn't stop moving away. "I'm not done here," she hollered back, her voice distorted by the vibration of the ship's engines.

"The hell you're not." He took off down the ramp, prompting her to advance toward him with her arm outstretched. Her flattened palm hit him squarely in the chest, putting a halt to his progress just before his feet touched the ground.

"I've still got a job to do!"

"You don't owe these people anything anymore!" he shouted, though even as he spoke the words, he felt a pang of regret—here was Serenity coming into the line of fire to get them out.

"I owe it to myself." She shook her head. "None of you should have been involved in this mess. I dragged you all into it and look what happened!" She flung a hand toward Skeet.

The hardened determination in her eyes was disheartening in this context, despite the fact that it was the same intensity that had bolstered his own confidence just hours before. Right now, it meant the chances of convincing her of anything were abysmal. He took hold of her shoulders, ready to order her to leave with them before realizing he had no authority to do such a thing. "Please don't do this."

Behind him, Zinni's voice barely carried over the roar of the engines. "Tarbic, let's go!"

Ziva met his gaze. Droplets of rain and mud dotted her face, and a spray of blood—no doubt Skeet's—coated one side of her neck. Her chest rose and fell in a steady rhythm, but it was impossible to miss the moment her breath hitched. "I can't come with you."

Something about the emphasis she'd put on the word 'can't' sent a wave of dread coursing through him; he got the sense she meant for reasons other than wanting to see this conflict through to the end. After all the progress they'd made, after all they'd been through…

"Partners stick together, Ziva."

"You're the one who used the word 'partner'."

Angry heat welled inside him. "*Sheyss*, tell me that's not what this is about. Tell me you're not running away from this, from me." He shook his head and ground his teeth. "I know you're scared but I've never known you to be a coward."

Something hot flared in her eyes—equal parts anger, disappointment, and desperation—and she shoved him *hard*, prompting him to take a couple of steps backward up the ramp. "This is about keeping you safe!" she shouted, the first signs of tears making an appearance. She pushed him again, stepping forward and blocking his path before he could try to come back down. Her features softened. "Please don't fight me."

"Tarbic!" Zinni shrieked in what sounded like the very far distance, igniting a spark of guilt in the pit of his stomach. An invisible force threatened to tear him in half, a sense of love and duty pulling him nearly as strongly back into the ship as it did down the ramp. He sincerely hoped Ziva wasn't intentionally playing on those divided loyalties right now.

She peered behind him, brows turned upward in concern, before rapidly closing what little distance remained between them. She wrapped a hand around the back of his neck and pulled him toward her, pressing his forehead against hers just as she had done in the cabin aboard the *Revenant*. "Go," she said quietly. "Go take care of your team."

She began to step away, but he pulled her back to him, drawing her in for an all-too-brief kiss. She tasted and smelled of earth and rain and blood, a mixture he had no doubt would be seared into his memory for the rest of eternity.

Damn it, Ziva. He gripped the sides of her face a moment longer to ensure he had her attention. "You keep your ass alive, you hear me?" he hollered, fending off a fresh wave of anger lest it completely take control. It was all he could do to pry his hands away from her and force his feet to begin moving up the ramp again.

A sickening lump formed in his gut as he came to a stop in the hatch, equal parts due to the thought of leaving her and the thought of delaying Skeet's care any longer. He looked back down at her once more before stepping through the opening.

"I didn't want to lose you again," he called, willing his voice to remain steady for her sake. Behind him, he was aware of Zinni screaming for Serenity to take off.

Ziva moved to the edge of the ramp and turned to face him as the little ship began to rise from the ground. With the rainfall, it was impossible to tell whether she was truly crying, but the look on her face was indescribable. Her features were rock-solid, but in her eyes, he saw everything from sadness to hope, from pity to determination.

She shook her head. "You never did."

And in that instant, she stepped backward off the ramp and disappeared.

CHAPTER 32
ZOCRUM REPOSITORY · Delatori

She trudged forward, putting one heavy foot in front of the other as she directed herself back toward the main repository. Realistically, she knew it was impossible for her to actually trudge given the environment and circumstances—her body and senses were too well-honed, acting of their own accord to keep her moving even though the fog in her head felt nearly as thick as the cloud cover above. The repulsion system on Serenity's shuttle doused her in rain and mud spatter. She was cold, or certain she *should* be cold considering how wet and filthy she was, but that was a trivial detail thanks to the fresh rush of adrenaline surging through her veins. That's all anything around her was now: trivial details. Nothing mattered anymore, and the reason nothing mattered was—

—closed off in the back of her mind before she could allow herself to fixate on it. There was only *forward*. Onward. Forward. Continue. Forward.

Despite feeling like she was moving in slow motion, she was back within the trees in seconds, gathering up her rifle from where it had fallen as Skeet tackled her. She swiveled and sighted up an Ibarra soldier who happened to be running by, gunning him down in addition to the man who followed closely behind him. That one might have been Niiosian; she no longer cared. The Niiosians were why she was here in the first place, why her team had been here, and thus why they'd had to leave. She set her sights once more on the repository's front doors, where both Tobias and Manes had disappeared what felt like years ago. All she wanted was to end this.

She plunged forward, drawing little attention from anyone in the vicinity, intent as they were on slaying each other. Those who got too close were shot before they even realized a third party was upon them. She ducked and wove, her legs and arms working almost reflexively as her mind struggled to prioritize everything she was seeing through the haze. She was aware of herself diving and rolling to avoid a hail of plasma fire, of lunging to one side and getting thrown off balance as a stray bolt from one of the fighters overhead struck the earth. The front door loomed ahead, left open by whoever had last gone inside and seemingly no closer than it had been when she'd started. Her own heartbeat hammered in her ears. Her breath hitched in her throat.

Agent Payvan.

The voice sounded so impossibly distant that it took her a moment to realize the words had even been spoken. She turned, back-pedaling the final few steps to the repository entrance, and swept the scene behind her. The battle raged on, the massive clearing a sea of mud and bodies and blood and running feet.

"Agent Payvan!"

Everything around her—sounds, smells, sights—sharpened and solidified. Her head whipped toward the voice. Ken appeared from the opposite side of the clearing; a trio of Niiosian soldiers who trailed behind him continued to provide cover fire as he moved closer to talk.

"Going inside?"

She managed a nod.

"Can't raise Tobias on comms. Find him! Make sure he's safe."

He and his squad moved on without stopping, leaving her to continue through the repository doors. She shut them behind her. The change in noise level was immediate; deeper within the facility, she could hear fights continuing among the smaller groups who had entered initially, but here in the expansive foyer, all was relatively silent.

And in the quiet, she could hear herself think, which was the last thing she needed right now. She allowed herself the luxury of pausing for precisely five seconds, drawing a deep breath with more tremor in it than she would have liked. *Forward*, she reminded herself. *Forward.*

There was no telling where Tobias—or Manes, for that matter—had ended up. She'd set foot in this facility on two previous occasions while working here as Matia, though neither visit had exactly been a grand tour. Still, she had a basic idea of the layout. She opted to stick to these upper levels for now; if the men weren't somewhere in the final processing areas, she'd know soon enough, and she'd work her way back down.

The problem, however, was that previous battle damage had rendered much of the ground level impassable, and based on the scent of smoke in the air, who knew what greater destruction lay ahead. She pressed on, staring intently down the barrel of her rifle as she angled toward the primary corridor that led down to the mineshaft.

What she found when she reached the mine entrance gave her pause. Bodies littered the stairways and landings both above and below her. The next platform up was blackened like some kind of explosive had gone off. Niio and Ibarra must be truly desperate to destroy each other if they were setting off charges in here, even small ones. It was a good thing there wasn't any product being moved at the moment; the raw zocrum was unstable, hence the reason the mine utilized drills and augers over lasers. The last thing anyone needed was to lose this entire facility because someone got careless with a grenade, especially after so many pains had been taken to claim it.

She peered down the shaft. It extended deeper than she could see from where she stood, and catwalks, platforms, and conveyors obscured much of the view. Muzzle flashes still penetrated the shadows below at intervals, but other than that, it was difficult to differentiate between the racket of battle and that of mining machinery.

Turning her gaze upward, she fixated on the nearest set of mostly intact steps leading to the final processing area on the uppermost level. She took the stairs two at a time, stumbling as a blast somewhere outside shook the building...then grasping the railing for dear life as the section of steps on which she stood detached from the wall. Her rifle strap slipped from her shoulder. She lunged for it. Her fingers brushed metal, but she could only lie there and watch helplessly as her beloved weapon fell, bouncing off the railing of the landing beneath her and disappearing in the chasm below.

A brief sense of panic transformed into fury as she added the gun to the ever-growing list of things that had been stripped away from her thanks to this battle. *Get the hell up*, her mind ordered as she clenched her teeth. *Forward. Onward. End this.*

Despite no longer being supported by the wall, the stairway remained in one piece. The steps buckled and groaned under her weight as she got to her feet and continued upward as quickly as caution would allow. Bright orange emergency strobes flashed around her, no doubt indicating a new mishap caused by all the fighting, but they went ignored. She wondered if the entire repository might blow at any second.

Blood, shell casings, and plasma scoring on the walkway indicated that someone had been engaged in combat up here at some point, but all was still now. No sooner had that thought crossed her mind, however, than a pained shout sounded from somewhere ahead, followed by what seemed to be a man begging for his life. She quickened her pace and drew her sidearm, rounding the corner toward what would have been a bank of offices if that section of the building hadn't been destroyed.

Her mind—sharp and clear now—processed the scene in a split second. Kimbra. The sound of vertebrae cracking. A man sliding from her hands into a limp heap on the floor. A second man already lying there, twitching and gurgling with the blade of a long knife jammed into his throat.

Kimbra stood and admired her grisly handiwork for a moment before turning. Her neck, chest, and bare shoulders were splattered with blood—not her own—and the faint smile on her lips indicated she was proud of it. That smile vanished as her attention settled on Ziva, and a brief look of indifference preceded a clear moment of recognition.

The woman had her own sidearm drawn in an instant. With no cover to speak of in the hallway, Ziva took immediate aim for Kimbra's weapon, blowing it out of her hand...and was startled when her own pistol simultaneously exploded in a cloud of sparks as the other woman got a shot off. Each of them spared their mangled weapons a wide-eyed glance before tossing them aside. It seemed they had more in common than they thought.

Ziva straightened, shifting her weight to the balls of her feet and shaking her arms out, preparing them for action. Kimbra did the same, wiping the back of her hand across her mouth. When it came away, her lips had parted in a wicked grin.

"Oh, I've been looking forward to this," she said, reaching down and yanking the knife free from her victim's neck.

She lunged forward.

By now the rhythmic growl of the mining machinery had become so mundane that Manes hardly noticed it. Or maybe it had just faded to the back of his mind, focused as he was on the sight of Tobias gimping back across the bridge. The man kept a bloodied hand pressed against his abdomen but was still moving faster than Manes would have expected. In fact, so far nothing about Tobias had been exactly as he'd expected. The mobster wasn't as old, wasn't as feeble, despite his reputation for being somewhat old-fashioned. But he was certainly *older*, and *more* feeble. Manes had the objective physical advantage here, and he was assuredly better versed with weaponry. He wasn't afraid to get his hands dirty, while the other man seemed the type to always have someone else do his dirty work.

Only the strong survive.

It was tempting to just shoot Tobias in the back as he hobbled away and be done with it. Manes had no qualms about doing such a thing, but it would certainly take some of the fun out of this encounter. After everything that had happened, after all the ways the mobster had quietly beaten him already, he wanted to savor this. Wanted to stand over Tobias and look him in the eye. Make sure the man knew he'd lost.

Tremors from the battle on the surface rippled down the shaft every so often, but one in particular rocked everything so violently that Manes was forced to steady himself against the bridge railing. A low hiss grew louder behind him, and he glanced back just as the ruptured pipes in the corridor burst open entirely. Rocks and rubble blew out of the wall, exploding into the shaft in a great cloud of dust. The bridge rocked under Manes's feet as he put an arm up to shield his head from the falling chunks of stone. A pair of larger boulders came crashing down behind him. Off balance, he dove onto his stomach and grasped the railing as the entire walkway tilted. His weapon clattered to the floor somewhere, invisible behind the veil of smoke and dust. He felt around for it. Couldn't see it.

But what he *could* see was Tobias sprawled on the ground several meters away, struggling to regain his footing. No time to waste. Manes rose to his feet, staggering forward as the bridge continued to quake and debris rained down around him. The mobster turned and took aim with his pistol, but the single shot he fired petered out in mid-air. He hurled the empty weapon at Manes and crawled on his hands and knees, making a desperate beeline for the safety of the more stable platform ahead.

Manes closed the distance between them, catching the man hard in the stomach with a powerful kick. Tobias cried out and tumbled away onto the landing, the blood stain on his side enlarging as he went. He flopped over and continued crawling, lunging for a bulky wrench someone had left lying nearby. He would not be granted the privilege of raising it up to use as a weapon.

But apparently he didn't need to. He whipped around, flinging the wrench toward Manes, as well as the length of heavy chain attached to it. The wrench striking his shins hurt badly enough, but the chain ensnared his ankles, sending him crashing to the floor. Tobias pounced, slamming a fist into his kidneys. Manes managed to get one leg loose and kicked upward, driving a knee into the other man's ribs. The mobster scrambled away again. He'd barely gotten upright before Manes sprang after him, seizing him around the waist and bringing him back down.

Fists, elbows, knees, and feet flew as the two of them rolled into the corridor. Tobias was fading, his movements slowing, his breathing ragged. Still, he finagled another solid strike against the side of Manes's head that left his ears ringing. The man made it to his feet again, angling for a mechanical room along the corridor.

Manes stood, spitting out a gob of bloody saliva before kicking the chain away for good and striding after him. To hell with savoring the moment. This had gone on long enough. Surely Tobias had to know he was beaten; now here he was allowing himself to be cornered. Was this a silent form of surrender? There'd be more dignity in his death if he'd simply admit his situation.

He entered the room and found the mobster standing amid an array of gauges, pipes, tanks, and their corresponding control terminals. A long workbench sat against the far wall. An assortment of hand-held tools—hammers, chisels, and picks for precision mining, as well as more wrenches, ratchet sets, and other implements for effecting repairs—hung above and beside it, ready for use. On the floor, several thick power cables lay coiled at the base of what appeared to be some sort of large, manually guided drill. A gleaming, razor-sharp drill bit a meter long jutted from the front of it.

Tobias straightened as well as he likely could, which wasn't saying much. He reached up and tore off his bent spectacles, the lenses of which had long since been shattered. The blood stain had spread across most of his stomach now. Nevertheless, he watched Manes with a surprisingly keen gaze considering his deteriorating state. So delusionally bold.

Manes charged forward, seizing Tobias by the throat and pinning him back against the wall. He towered over the older man, reveling in the sight of those wide, desperate eyes. Killing Tobias Niio with his bare hands hadn't originally been on the docket, but now that the opportunity presented itself, it was too good to pass up.

"You're finished, Niio," he said through gritted teeth, enjoying the sensation of Tobias's windpipe caving under the pressure of his thumbs. "You had to know it was always going to end this way."

The man's arms began to flail, but it was only *after* something hard and heavy impacted Manes's ribs that he realized one of those flailing arms had managed to get ahold of a hefty hammer from the wall. He sputtered and released Tobias, reflexively doubling over to clutch his midsection...and putting himself in prime position for a second blow to the jaw, driven by more force on the mobster's part than he thought possible.

For a brief moment, his vision went completely black. When it returned, he was seeing double. Thought he might be sick. Reached out to steady himself against the workbench.

It was almost as though he could feel the individual bones in his elbow shattering as the hammer came down once more against his outstretched arm. He screamed in agony, aware of a shard of bone tearing through his skin inside his coat sleeve. He lashed out at Tobias with his good arm, anything to close the distance and leave too little room for another strike. The primal desire to kill this man propelled him forward. The room around them faded away as his focus zeroed in on only what was in front of him. Everything he'd striven for over the past several years had led to this moment.

Manes summoned all his remaining strength and lunged.

His fist, driven by the full force of his forward momentum, came within a centimeter of Tobias's head as the man sidestepped.

Manes swiveled, fighting to slow himself as he prepared to reverse course and try again.

His heel struck one of the coiled-up cables. His stomach lurched as his brain told him he was off balance. Another solid hit to the chest from the hammer sent him reeling.

The blow to his back punched all the air from his lungs. Or at least a blow was what his nerves insisted had happened. It didn't make any sense, considering there was no one else present in the room. He couldn't move. Could only feel a throbbing ache around the impact site.

And then he looked down and found the tip of that big drill bit protruding from his abdomen.

He wasn't sure then whether the chill that washed over him was an actual change in the stuffy little room's temperature, or simply his body's reaction to his newfound predicament. The bit was relatively smooth, and the angle upon which he'd hit it was such that even the slightest movement drove it further through him. He reached behind him, bracing his good arm against the machine in an attempt to hold himself steady.

The sharp *clang* of the hammer falling to the floor drew his attention back to Tobias. The mobster stood a couple of meters away, his hand once again pressed against the bullet wound on his side. His shoulders sagged, but the smug twinkle in his eye was clear as day.

"Oh, Alastair," he said, shaking his head. "Once again, so predictable. I *did* know it was going to end this way. Your arrogance—your impulsive desire for vengeance—was always going to be your downfall."

Tobias heaved a sigh of satisfaction. Then he collapsed to the floor.

The bloodied blade of the knife cut through the air, propelled by Kimbra's powerful arm. Ziva pivoted, dropping lower as she turned, fully aware of the breeze tickling her skin as the blade came within millimeters of slicing into her shoulder. She slammed a fist into Kimbra's gut, followed by the sharp end of a broken pipe she'd picked up. Kimbra staggered, slashing downward and catching the top of Ziva's thigh with the knife tip. Ziva ducked and rolled, bringing the pipe down hard against the backs of Kimbra's knees just as the blade came sailing past her head again.

She righted herself and stood, using the pipe to block another jab before switching it to her opposite hand. Kimbra slashed again. Ziva caught her wrist, turning the blade downward as she stabbed the pipe toward Kimbra's head. The woman blocked that blow with her own free hand. They each let out a growl, gazes locked as they stood there struggling to break free from each other. Ziva moved first, sliding forward far enough to drive her knee up into Kimbra's stomach. Kimbra yanked her arm free, bringing the knife up into a backhanded slice through the space where Ziva had been a fraction of a second earlier.

As far as hand-to-hand opponents went, the two of them were probably some of the most evenly matched on this planet. Ziva had never considered herself overly quick, at least not like Zinni or an agile operative like Ken. Meticulous training over the years had honed her reflexes sufficiently to perform well for the agency, but someone of her size was objectively designed more for straight combat and brute strength. Still, she was quicker than Kimbra, though the other woman seemed to have the strength advantage. She hated to spend this whole fight on the defensive, but wearing Kimbra down might be the only option to win it.

She took several steps backward, both to put some distance between them and to draw Kimbra out of the enclosed space they'd found themselves in. She kept her body low, her weight evenly distributed. Blocked a blow with the pipe. Blocked another with her elbow. Got a good jab of her own in, catching Kimbra in the chin with the sharp end of the pipe and drawing blood. The other woman spat some sort of curse through gritted teeth and came at her with renewed fervor.

The texture of the floor beneath her boots changed, and without removing her eyes from her opponent, Ziva knew they were back above the mineshaft. Here on the upper level, many of the catwalks had cage-like walls that ran floor-to-ceiling for safety reasons, but the way the metal walkway shuddered in response to every sizable blast outside didn't bring her much comfort. She continued shuffling backward, dodging, ducking, striking out when she could. The next successful hit she landed with the pipe was followed immediately by a hard right hook from Kimbra that struck her squarely in the cheek. She took a staggering step back, seeing spots. The knife came flying toward her again and she feinted left. An abrasive, metallic screech filled her ear as the blade hit metal instead of her face.

Kimbra was already growing frustrated; the speed and force of her attacks increased while her control deteriorated. Ziva's arms moved as though they had minds of their own, blocking, jabbing, anticipating. A particularly reckless slash from Kimbra left an opening. Ziva darted behind her and moved in, hooking her arm up under the other woman's and locking her shoulder back. With her free hand, she blocked further stab attempts, moving in a slow circle and keeping Kimbra off balance.

The blonde woman let out a growl of rage and leaped backward, her weight sending them both crashing to the floor. Ziva gasped for air, for a moment so preoccupied with getting a breath that she didn't realize the burning sensation she now felt was the knife plunging into her thigh. She yelped and rolled; the blade ripped free as she went. She'd dropped the pipe. Wasn't sure where it went. Needed to move. Reset. Get into a better position.

The sole of Kimbra's boot hit her squarely in the back, propelling her down the very stairway she'd used to get up here. It was hard to tell with all the tumbling, but she was reasonably sure she caught air before crashing down against the section of stairs that had broken on the way up. Every aching muscle in her body protested, but the adrenaline had her up and crawling over the busted steps before she even realized she could move. Metal creaked as Kimbra descended behind her. The heavy footfalls came within a meter before she got to her feet and managed to leap to the relative safety of the intact steps below, her injured leg quivering under the impact of the landing.

The reverb of her jump rocked the top set of stairs. A metallic groan filled the air as the entire upper staircase began to tear loose from the wall the same way the middle section had. Kimbra stumbled and leaped for the lower steps as well. The knife flew from her hand, clattering off somewhere across the platform. They both tumbled to a stop on the stable surface just as the remaining stairs broke away, crashing down to the next platform at least three levels below.

And then they were on their feet again, arms, legs, fists, and elbows all a blur of movement. Blood filled Ziva's mouth, and she could tell her cheek was already swelling from the hit Kimbra had landed up top. The other woman was bleeding, too; red flecks dotted her blonde hair, and her nose turned at an odd angle.

Ziva shuffled sideways to avoid a blow and let out a grunt as her back hit the thick railing around the platform, immediately bringing her elbows up to block a second swing. She braced a hand on Kimbra's dominant shoulder, but the other woman seized fistfuls of her shirt, slamming her back once more against the railing. They struggled for a moment, stuck in a gridlock with hands pushing against each other's shoulders. Ziva slid a hand down Kimbra's arm, grasping her wrist and wrenching that arm away. That opened up some room to maneuver, but Kimbra took advantage of the space as well and lashed out with a high kick, squarely hitting Ziva's freed hand. She followed it up with a kick to the jaw; even the glancing blow sent Ziva stumbling backward.

She ducked under the punch that followed and sprang forward, driving her own fist into Kimbra's ribs. The blonde woman pivoted, throwing a jab with one arm and then the other. Ziva caught the second attempt, pinning the woman's forearm in the crook of her elbow. Turning to place her body perpendicular to Kimbra's, she hooked a leg behind the other woman's ankle and threw with all her might. Immobile with her foot locked in place, Kimbra tumbled to the floor.

Ziva turned, prepared to run—where had that damn knife landed?—but her legs were swept out from beneath her, sending her sprawling. She barrel-rolled back toward Kimbra immediately, using the momentum to drive her elbow into the woman's face once, then twice, before she could even get up. She lunged away again, catching sight of something glinting in the light of the emergency strobes. The knife lay maybe three meters away, dangerously close to the edge of the platform. It was the key to putting an end to this.

She dove forward, covering about half of that distance before Kimbra's full body weight came down on her. A knee dug into her lower back as the woman sprang off her in a desperate bid to reach the knife herself. Ziva pushed upward, her most primal instincts kicking in as she saw Kimbra's hand come to rest on the weapon. She summoned all her strength to leap forward and pin the other woman down. She seized the arm that held the knife, wrenching it back and rolling away in the opposite direction. The satisfying sound of a shoulder dislocating wasn't quite drowned out by Kimbra's scream, and the knife went flying across the platform again.

Ziva released her and pounced after it. Kimbra's hands latched onto one of her ankles. She kicked out with her free leg; the woman's head snapped backward as Ziva's boot collided with her face. The knife was nearly within reach. She went for it again. Felt Kimbra's hands on her legs. Heard the woman shriek in rage.

Her fingers closed around the weapon and she turned, jamming the blade into Kimbra's stomach just as much as Kimbra fell onto it in the midst of one final push to grab it. The woman let out a strangled cough as her eyes went wide. Ziva gave the blade another good shove, ensuring it was buried up to the hilt before yanking it free with no regard whatsoever for what further damage the movement might cause. She shoved Kimbra off, waiting until the woman sank the rest of the way to the floor before collapsing onto her own back, her ears ringing, head throbbing. The knife slid from her hand and came to rest on the platform between them.

For several seconds, it almost felt quiet, even with all the noise of the mining equipment. Distant rumbles could be heard outside, but there was no longer any sign of fighting throughout the rest of the mineshaft. Ziva drew in several deep breaths, relishing the feeling of simply *holding still*. But with that stillness came increased awareness of details her mind had deprioritized in favor of self-preservation over the past number of minutes, such as the gash in her leg and a new pain she suspected was a fractured wrist.

She turned and looked at Kimbra, who also lay flat on her back about two meters away. Her chest continued to rise and fall, but her breathing was gurgly and uneven. The hand she kept clamped down over her abdomen seemed to have no effect on the blood streaming steadily from it.

"It was never personal," Ziva muttered, lying back and allowing her eyes to close for just a couple of seconds.

Kimbra let out some cross between a scoff and a cough. "I told him from the beginning...something wasn't right about you," she sputtered. "I told him we should have turned you over to the Federation." She wheezed as she struggled to prop herself up on one elbow. "You destroyed our entire operation. You destroyed *him*. I can't let you get away with that."

The first thing that crossed Ziva's mind was how pathetic it was that Kimbra still felt compelled to defend and avenge Manes even as she lay there bleeding to death. In that sense, her veiled threat meant nothing. But then she couldn't help but fixate on what the woman had said before that: they *should have* turned her over to the Feds? Did that mean they hadn't, despite having seen the copy of the Federation bulletin listing her as a Nosti? She wasn't sure why they might have chosen not to alert anyone, though maybe it didn't really matter. The idea that she could be—dare she say it—*safe*, at least from the Feds...

The sound of increased movement in Kimbra's direction quashed that train of thought. She turned and found the woman trying to roll over, abandoning her wound in favor of using her good arm to push herself forward. Blood gushed from the injury; with a stomach wound like that, she wouldn't last long. But her gaze was fixed squarely on the knife where it lay between them, and fueled as she was by anger, she could still do plenty of damage if she managed to get ahold of it.

"Stay down, Kimbra," Ziva muttered, struggling to sit up herself. "It's over."

The weapon was nearer to her by a long shot. Any attempt Kimbra made to reach it would have to be one of pure desperation, yet she appeared ready to do it anyway.

"It's over when I say it's over," she hissed, dragging herself closer.

Kimbra gritted her teeth and closed the distance with more of a frantic flop than a lunge, her fingers coming within centimeters of the knife's hilt before Ziva snatched it up. Kimbra collapsed onto her stomach, and Ziva thought she glimpsed a look of true defeat on her face just before she drove the blade into her back.

The woman gasped and writhed for a moment. Ziva leaned down closer, using her body weight to force the knife in to the hilt; bones cracked somewhere beneath her, and Kimbra fell still.

"That's *enough*," she said into her adversary's ear, not caring whether she could even hear her anymore.

Leaving the blade embedded, she rolled away again and lay back, reveling in the stillness as she closed her eyes.

CHAPTER 33
ZOCRUM REPOSITORY · Delatori

There was no way she'd been lying there long enough to truly fall asleep, but when she opened her eyes, the moment of disorientation was noticeable. Everything hurt. *Sheyss*, how she wished she could just stay right there. But her battered body was demanding her attention, and this wasn't over. Not quite yet.

She pushed herself up into a sitting position, watching Kimbra's corpse for another few seconds to ensure the woman was down for good. Then her focus shifted to her own legs and the stab wound on her thigh. It was on her outer leg, well away from her femoral artery, and didn't appear as deep as she'd initially suspected, but it was still plenty bloody and plenty painful. She'd need treatment soon if she didn't want permanent muscle damage.

With a sigh, she went to work tearing off a strip of material from the bottom hem of her tank. She wound it around her leg, tying a knot as tight as she could stand over the gash; that should hold for at least a little while. Using the platform railing for support, she hauled herself to her feet, waiting for a bout of lightheadedness to pass before retrieving the knife from Kimbra's back and angling for the stairs.

She descended slowly, favoring her sore leg as she took stock of her surroundings and searched for any signs of remaining danger. Smoke curled upward from blackened sections of the walls and platforms where more explosives had gone off. Bodies—Mob and Cartel alike—lay strewn in the stairways and draped over railings. But these were all mere soldiers; there was no sign of Tobias or Manes among them. She picked up a discarded plasma pistol, pleased to find it still half-charged, and tucked the blade away in favor of the gun.

The search proved fruitless until she reached the bottom of the mineshaft. She was just starting to wonder if there was some way the two men could have made it back outside without anyone noticing when she caught sight of blood on the platform. A trail of droplets led into a corridor off to her left, where a dark red smear indicated recent movement into a nearby room.

The amount of blood splattered across the grate in front of the doorway told her she'd reached her destination. She paused for a moment, able to detect the scent of human sweat and body fluids even amid the hot mustiness of the mine. She adjusted her grip on the pistol as she steeled herself for what she might find inside. Whatever it was, it potentially signaled the end of all this, a concept she found herself simultaneously dreading and welcoming with open arms.

She took one last deep breath before stepping through the opening, leveling her weapon as she took in all the details of the scene. The room reeked of blood; both Manes and Tobias were present, something she hadn't quite expected. The two men lay a couple of meters apart in various states of impairment. A series of tools and machine parts lined the far wall; at first glance, it appeared Manes was leaning against a large manual drill, supporting himself with one bloodied arm while the other hung limply and obviously broken at his side. As she moved closer, however, she took note of the amount of blood running down the front of his shirt and noticed the tip of the ultra-sharp drill protruding from his torso. The quivering arm braced against the machine itself was the only thing keeping him from sliding backward and impaling himself further. For just a moment, something prickled inside her, insisting she should help him. Protect him. It made her want to vomit.

She drew out her communicator, her earpiece lost beyond hope. "Come in, Ken. Found him. Bottom sublevel maintenance room."

Tobias's eyelids had been drooping, but the sound of her voice seemed to draw him back to the present. He struggled to sit up straighter, teeth clenched as he kept one hand pressed against a gushing wound on his side. The clothing around his shoulder also appeared to be scorched by a plasma blast. His spectacles were nowhere to be found, rendering his twisted, angry features even more foreign.

"Payvan," he growled, still floundering, "help me."

Ziva spared him only the briefest of glances before holstering her pistol and zeroing in on Manes. The younger man had also appeared to be fading, but his eyes brightened with renewed fury as he focused on her. There was recognition there as he studied her true face, the face he'd only ever seen via hologram. Surely he had put the pieces together by now, had figured out Matia Moryi was Tobias Niio's asset, but the shaky glance he cast toward the old mobster just then told her he was at least getting some confirmation, if not making the connection for the first time. The fact that Tobias not only knew her but was demanding her help was telling.

She moved closer and bent down, her face just centimeters from Manes's as she stared silently into those hateful eyes. There was something new there that sent a tingle of satisfaction curling up her spine: fear. He was done. He had no more control over the situation, and he knew it. Imagining what must be going through his mind, as well as the knowledge that her face was the last thing he'd ever see, made her skin crawl in pleasure. It was tempting to smile, but the memory of everything he'd put her through left her jaw set. She may have told Kimbra it was nothing personal, but this? This felt pretty personal.

In her experience, it was certainly possible for sheer rage to sustain someone who was otherwise mortally wounded, but at this point, Manes objectively wouldn't last more than a few minutes. Content to leave him there to suffer, she pulled back and straightened...then tensed when she sensed him wind up to strike. His broken arm still dangling, he released his grip on the drill long enough to swipe at her. His bloody hand came within a hair's breadth of grazing her neck before falling away abruptly. Without the arm braced against the machine, he began to slide backward on the slick drill bit.

Now the corners of Ziva's mouth did curl upward as she saw the realization of what he'd just done dawn on him. Not that there'd been any saving him anyway, but his final attempt to lash out had sealed his fate. She placed a palm against his chest, pushing him backward ever so gently. He grunted and sputtered something as blood dribbled anew from his mouth. His arms—even the broken one—flailed desperately for purchase, but the excess motion only worsened his predicament. Eyes wide, he twitched violently a couple more times before falling still.

She shifted her attention back to Tobias, who by this time lay nearly flat on the floor. His bleary gaze shifted between her and his rival's limp form, and he sucked in increasingly ragged breaths. "Help me," he wheezed as she stepped toward him. "I demand that you help me."

Even as he spoke, she saw his eyes widen as it struck him that she wasn't necessarily approaching with friendly intentions. He pushed against the floor with one arm, sliding away and risking a look around him. Some sort of hammer lay another half meter out of his reach.

She watched this unfold as she slowly advanced, feeling no need to rush. His awkward crawl evolved into a desperate scramble as her shadow crossed over him, and he abandoned his wound in favor of using both arms to make a final push for the hammer. One hand came to rest on the tool at the exact moment the sole of her boot settled over his fingers.

He groaned in pain and collapsed onto his back again as she shifted her weight forward, crushing his fingers between the hard floor and the weapon's handle. In that moment, he was nothing more than a feeble old man, recognizing his own defeat just as Manes had. Her attention was drawn to his stomach wound, which had begun to gush more profusely thanks to the frenzied movement. As tempting as it was to simply finish him then and there, some deep part of her didn't want to. Despite what he'd told her four years prior about wanting to face Manes man-to-man, she had always imagined potentially killing the Ibarra leader herself whether he liked it or not. But not once had the thought of killing the prestigious Tobias Niio ever crossed her mind. Now that the opportunity presented itself, it felt...not necessarily wrong, but so alien as to give her pause. He *had* helped her, had taken care of her, had even been an ally, if a somewhat tenuous one. But after deceiving her and using her the way he had?

She lowered herself into a squat, keeping her foot planted firmly over his hand and noting the amount of blood pooling around him. He wouldn't last long. Funny that he and Manes had both wanted nothing more than to kill the other, and then they'd each done just that. While she'd delivered somewhat of a final blow to Manes, she felt no immediate need to do the same to Tobias. He was clearly a fan of playing the long game; perhaps leaving him to suffer was more befitting anyway. If nothing else, it was objectively the most neutral response possible, which was ideal given the odd sense of conflict churning through her stomach.

There was one thing she did know for certain. She reached down and placed a hand under his head, lifting him closer and turning his face toward her to ensure he met her gaze. His eyes were blue, something she'd never given any special consideration before now.

"Our business is concluded," she said.

His shallow breathing hitched as she released him, and he fell back to the floor. She found herself once more entertaining the idea of simply putting him out of his misery, but the sounds of hurried footsteps descending the metal stairs outside reached her ears. She tensed, ready to pull her weapon, but then recognized Ken's voice. Rising to her feet, she nudged the hammer out from under Tobias's crushed hand and sent it skidding off to disappear under another piece of equipment.

When Ken entered the room, she was once more kneeling at the mobster's side, analyzing his injuries as if she'd always been doing exactly that. She looked up and was surprised to see Serenity there too, her medical bag slung over her shoulder. Ken paused, taking a prolonged look at Manes's corpse with his weapon drawn, while the doctor spared the dead man only a brief glance before making a beeline for her husband.

Ziva stood and gave the woman some space, watching as she performed a quick assessment of the injuries before getting to work as best she could with the limited supplies she had at her disposal. She patted Tobias's face and murmured his name, her voice uncharacteristically despairing.

"There was nothing I could do," Ziva said.

The way she saw it, that wasn't completely false. Granted, she hadn't *tried* to save him, but she firmly believed he was beyond saving.

Ken pried his attention away from Manes to study her quizzically, his dark, calculating eyes boring into her, searching for sincerity. His face hardened briefly as though he could sense the lie—after their conversation upon arriving on Delatori, she couldn't blame him—and he left his gaze locked on her for another couple of seconds, perhaps to ensure she knew that *he* knew. But then he shifted his focus to Serenity without comment.

The two of them stood there in silence for another minute, watching the woman work. Neither of them offered any assistance, but neither did she ask for any help. The pool of blood under Tobias's body continued to spread. Serenity's palms were coated in red as she alternated between putting pressure on the wound and trying to keep him coherent.

Finally, she sat back on her heels and drew a deep breath before wiping a clean section of the back of her hand across her mouth. It struck Ziva that the man had stopped moving entirely; all three of them stared silently at his inert form, watching with bated breath for any signs of life until Serenity checked fruitlessly for a pulse and laid his hands across his chest. "He's gone."

While quiet, her voice was strong, not at all like any true wife grieving over a dead husband. Still, objectively speaking, Ziva imagined this must be strange for both Niiosians in the room. Hell, it was a little strange for her—everything she'd been through aside, Tobias was a figurehead in Fringe Space, and while she'd never particularly trusted him, she'd worked with him and relied on him, which wasn't *nothing*. Now he was no more, and strangely enough, even his two closest advisors didn't seem too broken up about it.

In the silence of the room, the weight of everything that had just occurred began to creep to the forefront of her mind. She fixed her gaze on Tobias for a moment, then shifted it to Manes. Both bloodied, both wounded by their own pride. Both dead. *Dead.* It was over. Everything she'd been through, everything she'd done, everything that had been done to her—it was all finished.

A wave of emotion crashed over her at the thought, and she sucked in a breath and turned away before that emotion could fully take root. *It's over.* Her mind could only repeat that single thought, almost as though it wasn't sure how to respond to that fact. She began to spring forward, ready to rush outside to find her team and share this moment with them, but the realization that they were gone hit her like a fresh blow from Kimbra. If Serenity was here, it meant they must have gotten safely back to the *Saber*, which was a relief no matter which way you looked at it. But even if they hadn't departed the planet yet, she couldn't go with them. Couldn't delay Skeet's care any longer. A dull ache settled in her chest as she found herself wishing desperately they could still be here.

Ken and Serenity were discussing something quietly, but their voices were hardly more than an echo in the background. If they were talking to her, whatever they had to say could wait. She was done here.

She pivoted and strode from the room, leaving Tobias Niio and Alastair Manes behind for good.

Chapter 34
SABER · Deep Space

Multiple voices reached Zinni's ears as she made her way down the corridor in the direction Aroska had disappeared not long ago. *Sheyss*, he must already be on comm with the director. She'd known he was planning on reporting in at some point during the journey home but hadn't expected him to do it so soon. Of course, considering how anxious Emeri and the Royal House were to get this whole mess cleared up, he might not have had much say in regard to the timing. She'd just hoped to catch him with an update on Skeet's condition before he started.

She wanted to be angry—and maybe still was, at least a little—about what happened at the repository. His reluctance to leave could very well have cost Skeet his life. No offense whatsoever to Ziva, but the lieutenant's well-being had been Zinni's primary concern at the time, and it hurt to see her teammate devote his attention elsewhere in the heat of the moment. But Skeet was alive, thanks in no small part to the full stock of Niiosian medical supplies and the work Serenity had done to stabilize him before they got underway. Now that she'd had a chance to cool off and reflect, she couldn't completely fault Aroska for his behavior. But still. They were all lucky things had turned out okay.

As she drew nearer to the comm room, she recognized one of the voices within as Emeri's; the other sounded like Jan Ganten, the Royal Officer in Haphor. She didn't hear Aroska speaking at all, and she could picture the other two men launching into an argument and forgetting he was even standing there.

Curiosity ate at her, but it wasn't her place to pry. Still, she found herself lingering a moment outside the room, then going so far as to steal a peek through the doorway. Aroska stood on the comm pad, hands clasped behind his back. It was difficult to tell whether the sag in his shoulders was due to exhaustion or exasperation; she knew the former was true, but given that her theory about Emeri and Ganten's conduct appeared to be accurate, the latter was plausible, too. The holograms of the two men faced each other, tersely referencing Haphezian law under the guise of formality. It sounded as though the argument had only just started.

Aroska heaved a sigh and lowered his head, catching sight of her in his peripheral vision. She held up a hand in apology when he glanced her way and began to shrink away from the door, but he gave her a subtle jerk of his head, inviting her to enter. She still wasn't sure if she should, though the thought occurred to her that he might not mind having a teammate there for support, even if she remained silent for the duration of the conversation.

"On to the topic at hand," Emeri growled, prompting her to scurry into the room and slide into a chair in the back corner.

"Indeed," Ganten said, voice just as low and rough. "Sergeant Tarbic, we received word from Director Arion after your initial briefing and understand that you are *refusing* to testify against Matia Moryi. Further, you married her and are attempting to invoke spousal privilege to avoid being compelled to testify. You realize Haphez has no such provisions, yes? Do you have anything more to say for yourself?"

Aroska merely shrugged. "I think that just about covers it."

"Sergeant, do not test me."

Zinni crossed one leg over the other and bit the inside of her lip to keep from grinning.

"Haphezian law also has no specific constraints *against* a union between two Haphezian citizens facilitated by a foreign entity," Aroska said.

Ganten's mouth hung open for an extra split second as though his planned response had been curbed by that piece of information. He knew the law; as Royal Officer, he essentially *was* the law. But based on this slight falter, it was quite possible he'd been so caught up in his quest to apprehend Matia that he'd overlooked this detail.

"Do you seriously expect that argument to hold up?" the man said, regaining his composure. "You'll only be wasting everyone's time. You *will* eventually testify, and we will have Moryi."

"Respectfully, sir, wasting time was the point."

The Royal Officer's eyes were shrouded in the shadows cast by his furrowed brows. "Explain."

Zinni drew in a breath and held it as Aroska hesitated and heaved a sigh. Emeri had informed them he was working on a solution on his end, but they had no details. Any explanation Tarbic gave now would have to be pulled out of nowhere.

Just as he opened his mouth to respond, the director cut him off. "New information came to light regarding Moryi's identity. I instructed the team to hold off on giving any official statements until we could resolve the situation."

On the comm pad, Aroska froze, eyes fixed solidly on Emeri's hologram. Zinni's throat went dry, and she gripped the arm of her chair to keep herself from leaping to her feet. Surely the director wouldn't betray Ziva's identity now, not after all he'd done for them. Besides, if he was going to do such a thing, he could have easily done it in the intervening days since Ziva revealed herself to him.

Ganten's hologram twisted toward Emeri's, and the man crossed his arms. "And who exactly is Moryi?"

"I'm not at liberty to disclose all the details of the operation. In short, Matia Moryi is an alias used by a Haphezian agent taking part in a long-term, deep-cover operation investigating the presence of niobi crystals within the Ibarra Cartel."

Zinni's grip on the chair arms relaxed, but her eyes remained fixed on the hologram. Technically, nothing Emeri had just said was an outright lie, and what better way to hide the truth from Ganten than with the truth itself? Ziva may not have been on Panuco looking directly into the use of niobi technology, but she'd known it was there, and it *had* been a long-term undercover mission, just not on behalf of the agency.

Ganten tilted his head and returned his attention to Aroska, regarding him from behind those furrowed brows. "And this marriage?"

"When Moryi shot me, it was an act designed to convince the Ibarra leader that she was still loyal to him. She…did not intend to hurt me."

Again, all true, even if they hadn't realized it was true at the time. Even now, she could sense the pain in Aroska's tone as he recounted the incident on the beach. But she allowed herself to ease back in the chair, confident he could roll with the scenario Emeri had just introduced.

"After it became clear that the Royal House wanted my testimony regarding these events," he continued, "we knew something needed to be done to protect the operative's identity, even temporarily, and allow both her and our team to complete our respective missions. I realize the marriage seems like an odd choice, but it was the first solution that came to mind."

"An odd choice," Ganten echoed with a scoff. "That is an understatement. And this union was facilitated by Tobias Niio of all people. Where the hell does the Niiosian Mob factor into all of this?"

Emeri cleared his throat. "The Niiosians have been at war with the Ibarra Cartel for some time now. This team has associated with Tobias on several occasions in the past, so he turned out to be an unlikely ally in these circumstances. And surely you remember his contribution to the battle against Ronan's fleet four years ago."

The Royal Officer hummed in thought, but given his obvious displeasure for the entire situation, the sound came across as more of a growl. "Indeed," he muttered, glancing between Emeri and Aroska for a moment as though trying to decide whether he should believe this tale. Finally, his focus settled on the director. "What I want to know now is how *you* lost track of this agent and her operation to the extent that the team went into this mission without realizing who they were dealing with."

It was all Zinni could do to keep from cringing, and she saw Aroska shift his weight ever so slightly on the comm pad. This meeting was supposed to be about him and his actions, and now here Emeri was taking the heat, all because of the story he'd concocted to cover for them in the first place. It felt like an entirely different form of punishment.

"Past correspondence indicates it was a Black Op," the director answered without missing a beat.

He was good. And once again, it wasn't a complete fabrication.

Once upon a time, Ziva had been one of the Black Agents who would've carried out this exact sort of mission—highly skilled, unattached to the agency, accountable to no one.

"The operation had evidently been ongoing since the incident with the Red Ring mercenaries in Argall," Emeri continued, the first blatant lie of the conversation rolling from his mouth as smoothly as ever. "The unit captain who initially sanctioned the mission has since been killed in action, and without that connection to the agency, the operative took it upon herself to continue her assignment independently. I will admit that the situation was somewhat out of control, but the marriage between this agent and Sergeant Tarbic gave us the opportunity to resolve it to the best of our ability without unduly involving the Royal House."

"And what is the true identity of the agent?"

"With respect, that information is classified."

Emeri was one of the most refined, collected people Zinni had ever met. To someone who didn't know any better, his reply might have sounded perfectly reasonable. But if she knew the man—and after fourteen years, she liked to think she did—then it was safe to assume his response could accurately be translated to 'kiss my ass.'

Ganten drew a deep breath as though preparing to launch into a fresh tirade, but he released it in the form of an exasperated sigh and sent Emeri a glare Zinni could feel through the virtual comm interface and across the vastness of space. "Director Arion, we will discuss your apparent inability to monitor your own agency personnel in a different forum. Sergeant Tarbic, the Royal House will continue reviewing your case, taking this...*new information* under consideration. Suffice it to say you have complicated matters." He watched Aroska in silence for a moment, as though waiting for some form of reaction, and when nothing happened, he cleared his throat. "That will be all."

The hologram fizzled away, leaving only Emeri's rendered on the projection pad. Zinni lifted a brow and huffed a quiet breath; she'd known Jan Ganten to be brusque in the four years he'd served as Royal Officer, and she didn't envy Aroska—or Emeri—for being on the receiving end of his ire. She hoped he at least half-believed everything he'd just been told, lest she and Skeet end up coming under fire as well.

"That was quite a story, Director," Aroska ventured.

"Yes, well, I've learned from the best," Emeri muttered, the corners of his mouth curled upward in more of a sneer than a smile. He sighed and lowered his head, pinching the bridge of his nose between his thumb and forefinger for several long seconds before recomposing himself. "How is Lieutenant Duvo?"

A soft, involuntary tingle crept over Zinni's skin at the mention of Skeet's name, and she fought off an image of him—bruised and bandaged and heavily medicated—lying in the *Saber's* medbay. She offered an affirmative nod when Aroska looked to her for an answer.

"He's stable," he replied. "We're lucky we had extra supplies from the Niiosian doctor. But we've done all we can for him. He'll need immediate attention when we get home."

"How far out are you?"

Zinni held up two fingers.

"Couple of days, at least."

"And Ziva? May I speak with her?"

"She's not here," Aroska answered. The response was gruffer than Zinni expected, but maybe that was because it had been forced. "She stayed behind on Delatori."

"I see." The director watched him with something that almost appeared to be pity for a moment before sighing again. "Well, I suppose I will wish you safe travels and let you be on your way. Meanwhile, I will be off cobbling together something that gives the load of *sheyss* I just shoveled at Ganten a semblance of plausibility."

"We appreciate it, sir. I hope you know that."

"And I hope you know nothing like this will ever happen again." Emeri's lips parted as though he wanted to say more, but then his features softened a bit, like a disappointed father still concerned about his children's well-being. "Please contact me if your plans change."

"We will."

The man offered a respectful nod before his hologram faded away as well, leaving Zinni and Aroska alone in the silent comm room.

For a full minute, neither of them spoke. Tarbic stood motionless, staring at the empty projection pads with folded arms while Zinni stared at him. His entire demeanor spoke of pain. His shoulders had straightened out while he was on the defensive speaking with Ganten, but they were starting to droop again now that he was no longer under scrutiny. Some of it was anger. Some of it was sorrow. Some of it was still exhaustion. His movements were stiff, mechanical.

"How are you doing?" Zinni ventured. They'd already been traveling for two days since leaving Delatori, but the two of them had spent that time trading off maintaining the *Saber*, tending to Skeet, or occasionally catching some much-needed shut-eye, which left little opportunity to talk, at least not one-on-one like this. Now that the lieutenant was in moderately better shape, that freed up time for some long-overdue personal inquiries.

He briefly glanced her way before shaking his head and tossing up one hand in a gesture she interpreted as a dejected shrug. It could just as easily mean 'I don't know' or 'terrible'; either way, it was enough to answer her question.

To say he and Ziva had made a remarkable impact on each other's lives was an understatement, but it seemed as though the biggest strides in their extraordinary relationship had been taken while she wasn't around to witness them—on that Dakiti landing pad, on Chaiavis, while she'd been incapacitated by Ronan's agents. In that respect, it had been a shock to see the recording of their emotional farewell in the HSP holding room just before Ziva's disappearance, but after four years of watching Aroska fight so hard to find her, everything made a little more sense. Still, it was strange to have finally gotten a closer, firsthand look at this connection they shared. And then to have all of that taken away again?

"I keep thinking about what I said to her before we took off," he said quietly, stroking his jaw as he turned and leaned against the short railing separating the comm pad from the larger projectors. "I was being selfish, only thinking about what I wanted." He snorted in disgust. "I called her a coward."

Zinni had heard, though at the time she'd been too focused on keeping Skeet from bleeding out to really dwell on the significance of the statement.

"And the worst part is I don't know whether I'll ever get the chance to apologize for it." He stared at the floor in silence for a moment before looking her way again. "Do you think I was wrong? For wanting her to abandon her mission and come with us? Come with *me*?"

"No, I don't," Zinni answered without hesitation. When it came down to it, she'd wanted—and *still* wanted—the same thing, but perhaps she'd simply come to terms with the fact that it couldn't happen better than he had. "And I don't think it was selfish."

"For the past four years, I had to remind myself there was a chance the surveillance footage was a fluke, that we'd never find her because she'd actually died when the *Intrepid* blew. I was so indescribably happy to know she was alive, but now, knowing she's still out there and out of reach..." He swallowed and shook his head.

"Hurts the most," Zinni finished for him.

He nodded and ran a hand across his forehead. "And now I don't even know for sure if she *is* still out there. She could have gotten killed when she went back out into that fight, and we'd never know."

"You can't think like that." She knew he was probably aware of that, but a pang of guilt rolled through her own stomach in response to his words. She'd imagined Ziva going back out there and seeing the battle through to the end—whether that meant a victory for Niio or Ibarra—and she'd never even considered a bleaker alternative.

"After everything we went through, I thought she would have come with me," he continued, staring across the room at nothing in particular. The muscles in his jaw flexed as he ground his teeth. "So maybe she was right all this time. Maybe I didn't know her like I thought I did. I was getting ahead of myself, too focused on what I felt, and she just played along."

There was plenty of evidence to the contrary, such as the way Ziva had once broken out of HSP custody to go find him on the Resistance flagship. But Zinni recognized that he was merely venting, allowing the pain to take over in a secure environment in the company of a trusted friend, even if it meant spouting nonsense. She remained silent.

"And then she had the nerve to act like her leaving again was somehow for our benefit. *Sheyss*, the woman is insufferable."

"You don't mean that."

Aroska's gaze remained fixed on the far wall a moment longer before he blinked and shook his head as though realizing what he was saying. "No, you're right, I don't." He waved a finger and forced a stiff chuckle. "I do, but I don't."

Zinni dipped her head, all too aware of what he meant. Ziva was objectively one of the most difficult people she'd ever dealt with, and that was even after nearly fifteen years of friendship. But she wouldn't have it any other way; it was part of what made the woman unique *and* great at her job.

"So why the hell am I so drawn to her?" he asked, almost to himself.

"Welcome to our lives," she replied with a scoff. "If you ever figure it out, let me know."

The room fell awkwardly silent for a solid couple of minutes. She studied him as he stood there, eyes closed, resting his forehead in his open palm, certain he had more to say but unwilling to press him on it. The extent of this connection he'd formed with Ziva in a relatively short period of time was fascinating, and the fact that Ziva had allowed it to form even more so. She loved Ziva, no question about it; when you spent ten years working so closely with someone and backing each other up in life-and-death situations, it was all but inevitable. But whatever Aroska felt went beyond that, namely in that a romantic element had emerged in addition to the camaraderie. She considered him her friend just as much as Ziva was, so in that sense she couldn't help but be pleased her two companions had bonded with each other in this manner. Ziva's latest disappearance stung, though perhaps a bit less than it had four years ago thanks to the reconciliation—however brief—that had taken place. But that was merely from her own perspective. Given the differences in Aroska's relationship, she couldn't imagine what he must be feeling right now.

"She showed me her scars," he murmured, breaking the silence.

Zinni straightened and mentally ran back through what he'd just said to ensure she'd heard him correctly.

"We had what I guess you'd call a...moment of clarity. Completely raw. I told her what I wanted, asked her what she wanted. She ran at first—I think she just didn't know how to react. But she came back. We spent..."

His voice trailed off and his gaze went out of focus as though his mind was back aboard the *Revenant* instead of here in the *Saber's* comm room. The details of whatever else may have transpired between them were none of Zinni's business, though she couldn't help but be curious. The scars alone were a big deal; it was no secret they existed, but not even she and Skeet had ever gotten a good look at them.

He shook his head and continued. "Zinni, I lay there and held that woman in my arms while she wept and confessed thing after thing after thing that she did and endured in the past four years. I don't know that it's possible to truly describe that experience."

It wasn't a scene she had ever anticipated picturing, but after seeing how broken Ziva had become, she found that the image formed in her head without much trouble. Frankly, she was pleased Ziva had been willing to open up to someone in such an intimate manner, and even more so that she'd entrusted Aroska with all of her ordeals. It was encouraging, to say the least, a positive step toward normalcy. Now if only the two of them could be allowed to continue taking those steps.

Aroska sighed. "I've been thinking a lot about something Skeet told me. He said it was almost easier to pretend she died on the *Intrepid* than be stuck dwelling on the fact that she was out there somewhere. Part of me is beginning to think he had the right idea." He dragged a hand down his face. "Her leaving again...maybe this is what's best."

"You don't mean that, either," Zinni said.

"I don't want to, but I may not have a choice."

She rose from her seat and moved across the little room, sidling up to him and wrapping an arm around his back. He was a strong man, stout in both body and mind; it was still uncanny to see someone so broken up about Ziva of all people, let alone someone like him. And yet, she was glad to know he cared so much. Glad to have witnessed his tireless pursuit of her old friend. Ziva needed someone like him in her life, whether she liked it or not.

"I don't know what to say that will help," she murmured, patting him on the shoulder and running her hand back and forth across his back.

"I know," he said, sighing again. He slid his own arm around her shoulders and gave her a squeeze. "I...thank you for listening to my angst-filled ramblings."

She opened her mouth with every intention of chastising him for the self-deprecating comment but decided he deserved the luxury of a little angst, at least until they returned to Haphez. Now that his debrief with Ganten was out of the way, he could afford it, so long as it didn't somehow jeopardize Skeet's well-being or their ability to travel.

"Come on," she said, giving him one last solid pat before breaking away. "I'll see what I can do about shaving a little time off the rest of the trip. We'll get home and—" she had to force herself to believe the words "—everything will be okay."

She moved toward the door, her mind focused on Skeet's vitals while simultaneously running through the various FTL routes that would carry them to Haphez. She paused one last time in the doorway and turned back. "You'll be all right?"

The dullness in Aroska's amber eyes was a testament to the pain he was still in, but when he spoke, there was more conviction in his voice than she'd expected. "Yeah."

Chapter 35
Warehouse District - Niio Spaceport

A grinding screech echoed up and down the ill-lit warehouse corridor as Ziva lifted the storage unit's overhead door. She coughed and waved a hand in front of her face to ward off the dust that rained down from the door's tracks. Technically, that much dust buildup was a good thing, as it likely meant nobody had touched this unit since she'd sealed it up before departing for her foray into Ibarra territory. A quick glance around the interior revealed nothing out of the ordinary.

Part of her had given up on the idea of all her belongings still being intact upon her return to Niio, so in that sense, the sight of all the neatly stacked storage canisters was a pleasant surprise. But the other part wasn't sure how much she even cared about any of this stuff anymore. It had all been confiscated from her house following her wrongful arrest for Tachi's murder, then returned to her after her rehab and trial at the Na Facility. It had sat untouched aboard the *Zenith* throughout that whole fiasco with Ronan and the Resistance, and there it had remained as she'd staged her death and escaped Haphez. Anything crucial—namely weapons—had come with her as the *Zenith* transformed into the *Talon* and she transformed into Matia Moryi. Nothing left here had been missed in the intervening years.

And yet, it *was* her stuff. Sometime during the journey back here from Delatori, the realization had struck her: there was no longer anywhere in the galaxy she truly belonged, especially now that this operation was over. Once upon a time, that notion would have been rather liberating—she could go where she wanted, do what she wanted, and was responsible for nothing and no one. But after leaving home four years prior, and after spending the past several days being constantly reminded of everything she'd left behind, she felt...'lost' was the first word that came to mind, or perhaps 'unsure.' As such, she found herself taking an odd amount of comfort in this pile of containers, these few things that belonged to her in a universe where she otherwise had nothing.

The room's single lighting panel flickered and fizzled when she turned it on, so she pulled out the little spotlight she carried and focused the beam of light on the storage canister nearest to the door. As she'd suspected based on her own old habits, the first item sitting at the top of the container was the data pad with the full inventory of items HSP had catalogued—all the items in this room, minus what she'd taken out previously. She silently thanked her past self for leaving it somewhere accessible and shone the light on it to take a closer look at the list. Maybe the first step would be to go through all this stuff and account for what she could, then pick out what mattered most and sell the rest.

Unable to remember specifically what any of these boxes contained, she took a seat on the one from which she'd retrieved the data pad and flipped the latches on the next three down the row. A cursory glance through the first one revealed several small pistol cases from her old stash that she simply hadn't bothered to take with her. They could probably go—the galaxy only knew how many more she'd accumulated since leaving them here.

The second canister contained parts from her old personal comm system. Her first instinct was to keep it, but what would she even use it for? She didn't have anyone to talk to. The joke was on the agency for even confiscating it in the first place; she knew better than to transmit anything of consequence over a personal system, and it wasn't like she'd ever used it to talk to anyone besides her team or Marshay and Ryon anyway. There'd never been anyone else who mattered to her.

A cold tingle crept through the back of her mind, and she rushed to quash that train of thought before it could take off—something she'd become very adept at over the last few years.

And then just like that, what she found in the third box sent her back to square one. She sat and just stared for a moment, one hand poised to slam the lid shut, the other keeping the spotlight aimed steadily at the contents. It had taken her a second or two to realize what she was looking at; the jet suit looked so plain without the repulsion pack attached. But the dirty black material and the crusted, burnt parts were unmistakable.

She hadn't given this suit a second thought over the past couple of years. Looking at it now, she remembered peeling the ruined garment off sometime during the initial journey from Haphez to Niio and having to cut away pieces that had melted and adhered to her skin. She'd stuffed it into a random container—this one, apparently—and forgotten it as she'd focused on treating her wounds and getting herself somewhere safe.

She lifted part of the suit out of the box and ran her fingers over the material. The feeling of the burnt cloth sent her right back to that fateful day; it was something she'd worked hard to forget, so these all-too-familiar images forming in her mind left her numb as she sat there. She remembered saying goodbye to her team and regretted the way she'd been so distracted as she mentally ran through her escape plan. The ascent into Noro airspace from the HSP landing pad was a blur at this point. She'd been in the cargo hold for most of that time anyway, frantically trying to get into this very suit while ignoring the comm attempts from Skeet. She did remember pulling this suit down from the middle hanger—another large one on its left, Zinni's smaller one on its right—and the thought prompted her to examine what was left of the material on the right sleeve.

The patch on the shoulder had been burned, but enough of it remained intact that she could make out the information she was looking for. She hadn't noticed at the time, but this suit was designated Alpha Two. Aroska's suit.

Her breath caught in her throat as a new, sharp pain began to throb in her chest, and for several minutes, she could only sit there in silence. It felt oddly poetic that his suit had saved her life in the midst of the plan she'd set in motion to save *his* life, as well as everyone else's. And then she'd had it here this whole time without realizing it, while the other two suits and the rest of the *Intrepid's* cargo had been vaporized when the ship blew. She wasn't exactly sure what to do with that information, but it somehow felt significant.

She ran a hand over the suit's front clasps and lifted the garment to her nose, closing her eyes as she drew in a deep breath. It still smelled of smoke and burned cloth, now with a musty undertone from being in storage. These suits would have been aboard the *Intrepid* during the team's hunt for Ronan while she was at the Na Facility. She had no idea if they'd even been used during that time; for all she knew, she was the only one who'd ever worn this thing. And yet, she was almost positive she could smell Aroska in the material.

Realistically, even if he'd worn it multiple times back then, the likelihood of his scent remaining after all these years and after the *Intrepid's* destruction was low, so it was probably just her imagination. But for once, she didn't care. For just a moment, he was right here in this filthy little storage room with her, and she let herself believe it for those few precious seconds. Then suddenly they were both back in that tiny lav in Ken's cabin, where she'd finally elected to cease the hopeless fight she'd always put up against him. She could feel his hands on her skin, could see the individual gold flecks in his eyes, could hear his voice.

"Now, you're Ziva Payvan. You don't need anyone, right? But what do you want?"

The truth was she'd never put much thought into what she wanted. He was right; so much of the time, she simply did things because she'd been ordered to, or out of necessity. Nothing was ever personal. Now, for the first time in recent memory, she had a pretty clear idea of what she wanted, and it was the one thing she couldn't have.

Sheyss, she hated this. Had she become so weak and undisciplined as to be unable to fend these thoughts away and move on? She'd done it before, despite the pain—surely she could do it again.

Of course, back then, she'd needed to move on in order to protect both herself and him. There it was again, the issue of need versus want. *What do you want?*

Once, she might have worried that feeling this way about another person would result in compromised missions and poor judgment. But they were both so damn far past the point of no return on that front, deviating from mission plans on multiple occasions to save each other, and thus it seemed like a waste of energy to keep being concerned about it. So here she was, drawn to this man—it felt odd to be freely admitting it, even to herself—who was still a relative stranger despite everything they'd experienced together. That was the part she didn't like, the feeling of longing. It made her feel vulnerable, like he was ruining her, just like she'd told him. It was strange. Different. Confusing.

And above all, she hated the fact that no matter how hard she tried, she couldn't stop herself from thinking this way.

She sat quietly for a moment. What *exactly* was preventing her from returning to Haphez? The whole reason she'd staged her death and left in the first place was to keep the Federation from hounding her world and her friends for the rest of their lives. While the circle of people who knew she was alive had grown substantially in the past week or so, as far as she knew, the Feds still believed she'd died that day. At the very least, they weren't actively looking for her, especially not after four years.

But the whole point of not going home at any point more recently —the Ibarra operation aside—was to stay away from anything familiar. She sincerely doubted any Haphezian in their right mind would go running to the Feds to report her presence, but there was still a risk. If they discovered she was alive, Haphez could very well be done for, whether anyone there had actively aided her or not. Returning would mean living a life of complete secrecy. Always looking over her shoulder.

She snorted to herself. As if that was much different than how she'd been living out here. If she went home, she'd at least be able to live that way in the presence of the few people in this whole galaxy she cared about.

The chirp of her communicator put an abrupt end to that line of thought—it was probably crazy anyway. She picked up the device and examined the text-based message it displayed: a summons from Ken. She'd spoken neither to him nor Serenity since arriving back at Niio Spaceport the day before yesterday. Interesting that he would reach out now.

Unsure whether to dread or welcome whatever he might have to say, she laid the old jet suit back in the canister she'd taken it from and went to leave. She paused one last time in the doorway of the little room, heaving a sigh as she looked back at her neat stacks of belongings and all the memories they brought with them.

Then she shut the door and locked it behind her.

BUSINESS DISTRICT - NIIO SPACEPORT

"How's the leg? The wrist?"

Ziva had barely set foot in the room when Serenity posed the questions. The woman leaned against the edge of the desk in Tobias's spacious office while Ken stood upright a couple of paces away, arms crossed. Ziva had only been in here twice; usually she'd met with the mobster at more discreet meeting locations around the city, or even at the old restaurant he always frequented. It was odd not having him present.

"Fine," she answered, somewhat caught off guard by the inquiry. She held up her arm, flexing her hand within the small bio brace she wore on her wrist, then glanced down and rubbed at her thigh, able to feel the medical wrap under her pants. "Treatment seems to be doing its job."

Despite her abrasive demeanor, there'd often been an element of kindness in Serenity's face, but it was more subdued today. Her eyes were dull, and the lines around her mouth seemed to have deepened. She *had* just lost her husband, however artificial their relationship may have been, but she seemed particularly solemn right now.

Awkward silence lingered in the room for a moment before Ken shifted and cleared his throat. "We wanted to discuss what comes next."

Ziva bristled, doing her best to suppress the defensive instincts she felt come alive in response to his words. She allowed her brows to slide into a half-scowl, a challenge, a warning to the two of them that she wouldn't yield easily and that they should tread carefully. "What *does* come next?"

He offered a conciliatory tilt of his head. "There's a wake scheduled for the day after tomorrow. I imagine half the city will be there, and we've already received numerous messages from off-world allies who wish to pay their respects."

While she was certain such an event would be quite the spectacle, he hadn't answered her question, at least not in the way she wanted. As strange as Tobias's absence felt, she couldn't bring herself to mourn his passing and had no desire to attend.

"And then?" Serenity said with a shrug. "Frankly, we're not sure yet. There are hundreds of matters to attend to—accounts to settle, operations to oversee, supply lines to reestablish after they were disrupted by Ibarra. Handling each will be...complex, to say the least. Tobias was the last blood Niio. This is hardly the Niiosian Mob anymore."

Now *that* was a strange concept. Even if her team hadn't associated with Tobias a few times in the past, the Niiosian Mob was well-known by the HSP ops divisions. Hell, it was a household name on most Fringe worlds. Ziva had dreaded the thought of the Mob gaining too much power and influence across the Fringe, but the idea of it ceasing to exist entirely was almost uncomfortable. Even with Manes and many of his top lieutenants gone, Ibarra would almost certainly still exist, though perhaps confined to its original territory. She'd just imagined the Mob would do the same.

"But," the woman went on, "this is and will continue to be Niio Spaceport. And I'm technically a Niio by name."

"Serenity has already received no less than a dozen endorsements from Mob affiliates," Ken said. "Regardless, she'd be well within her rights to take over."

Ziva raised a brow. It did make sense, she supposed, though she was still having trouble picturing this elaborate crime network under any leadership besides Tobias's. But as she watched Serenity's lips turn down in response to Ken's words, she understood the nuances behind the woman's melancholy; this was all an outcome she'd already taken into consideration, and she wasn't a huge fan of the concept.

"The current plan is for the two of us to double-team things for a while, until everything stabilizes," Ken went on. "We'll get Delatori back in commission, perhaps see if we can still get some use out of Pahl Starcer's schematics, and then…"

"And then we'll see," Serenity murmured, heaving a sigh and rubbing her forehead as though the mere thought was giving her a headache.

Ziva crossed her arms. "You don't want the job?"

"Let's just say I hoped to never be faced with such an under-taking," the woman answered. "But this is my home. This is what I do, what I know. Wouldn't be the first time I've had to make sacrifices and go to painful lengths to preserve it all."

That was something they had in common. Despite wanting no-thing further to do with the Mob, the thought occurred to Ziva that if Serenity and Ken took over operations, it could be beneficial for her to have a good rapport with people who held that much power and influence in the Fringe. Of course, that's what she'd once thought about Tobias, and that hadn't turned out so well.

"But enough about me." Serenity straightened and brought her hands to rest on her hips, her squared shoulders giving her a command-ing presence befitting of this office. "Let's talk about you."

This was the part Ziva had wanted to hear, but she couldn't help but stiffen again.

"Tobias's request was that you stay in his service until the conflict with Ibarra was resolved," Ken said. "Suffice it to say things didn't turn out the way he'd planned—" his eyes narrowed as though he was still trying to ascertain what exactly had occurred in that maintenance room "—and we still have a bit of housekeeping to do on that front, but I for one would consider your role complete."

Serenity nodded. "We know it would be a tremendous waste of time to try to contain you against your will anyway, so as of this mo-ment, we're offering you a formal release from the Mob's service."

Ziva's heart leaped into her throat, though she forced her coun-tenance to remain unchanged. She'd planned on leaving whether they liked it or not, but to receive their blessing without even asking for it?

The weight that lifted from her shoulders just then was as liberating— if not more so—as what she'd felt when it struck her that both Manes and Tobias were dead.

The former doctor sobered abruptly, and based on the dark quality that fell across her face, Ziva wondered if Ken had shared his theory about Tobias's fate with her. "You've done us a great service over the past four years, but I would tend to vote for quitting while we're ahead. We'll take a look at your records and arrange for any final payments to be processed. Consider the ledger balanced—I've always liked to part ways amicably whenever possible."

Damn, the woman was a Niio, all right. Ziva couldn't help but smirk in response to the poise and cool composure she was already displaying. "Deal."

Serenity moved over and stood before her, studying her with a keen eye. "A little unsolicited advice before you leave: I don't know where you'll go or what you'll do now, and I can't tell you where to go or what to do, but I think *you* know what you *should* do, and I agree."

Ziva's heart rate quickened as everything she'd been mulling over in the storage unit came flooding back at once. Five moons, it was like the woman could read her mind. She steeled herself and met her gaze, somewhat surprised to find absolute sincerity there.

After a beat, one corner of Serenity's mouth twitched upward, and in that moment, she was the quirky caregiver Ziva remembered. She winked. "But that's none of my business."

CHAPTER 36
5 DAYS LATER – RESIDENTIAL SECTOR · NORO, HAPHEZ

There was something about the sound of the security gate clanging shut behind him that always brought Emeri a sense of comfort. His house wasn't large—comfortable and luxurious in its own right, certainly, but nowhere near as grand as the gaudy fortresses in Haphor's Royal City or even some of the others in his own upscale neighborhood. Still, it was set back a good distance from the street, nestled amid some sturdy trees on a large piece of property, and when that gate shut, locking out anyone or anything that might cause him trouble, this place became his sanctuary.

The sleek town car pulled up and deposited him at his front door. As always, he bid his driver a good night—though by now it was the wee hours of the morning—and specified the following day's pick-up time. A guard greeted him at the door, one of several members of a personal security detail patrolling his property at all times. He'd never had any need for them, not here at home, anyway, but they came with the job.

The sound of the front door closing added an extra sense of finality, one more layer of security to shut out the rest of the world, even if for just a few hours. The interior of the house was silent, as usual. His housekeeper, a kind woman who probably spent more time here than he did, had long since finished for the day, but in all her wisdom and experience working for him, she'd left a dim lighting panel on in the entry hall. Bless her.

Emeri moved to disarm his internal security system before the alarm tripped. The last thing he needed was a screeching klaxon disrupting his glorious silence, especially with the headache that had set in shortly before he finally left his office. But upon examining the control panel, it appeared the alarm had already been disabled. He frowned. It should have been set when the housekeeper left. For a brief moment, his tired mind awakened enough that he considered calling to the guard outside, but then he paused to weigh the possibilities. One of the members of his home detail was newer; perhaps he had simply forgotten to reactivate the system. Such an error would need to be addressed, but there was no real point in doing it now. It would only make the long night even longer. Regardless of what had occurred, it wasn't like there hadn't been multiple guards posted outside in the meantime. When it came down to it, the internal alarm system was merely a redundancy. He was certain everything was fine.

Unbuttoning his dress jacket as he went, Emeri continued down the hall, angling for the kitchen. No matter how tired he was, sleep would almost certainly not be forthcoming thanks to the twinge of hunger currently gnawing at him. The room was dark, but he opted to leave the lights off to quell his headache. Just a quick snack, and then his bed called to him. After the last couple of days he'd had, he had half a mind to not go into the office tomorrow. Unfortunately, all the same issues that had been plaguing him continued to require his attention.

Something hit him as he went to open the cooler: a scent, somehow familiar but simultaneously like a distant memory. The hairs on the back of his neck stood on end as long-buried instincts came alive. He drew his concealed sidearm. Someone was there. His mind articulated that thought and managed to connect it to the disabled alarm just as he caught sight of a shadowy figure in his peripheral vision. He whirled toward the person and took aim.

An odd sense of familiarity kept him from firing or even calling out to the figure, and the defensive hostility that had briefly overtaken him dissolved instantly as recognition dawned on him. He lowered his weapon and heaved a sigh, giving his racing pulse a moment to slow. There was no doubt in his mind now that the security system had been intentionally disabled, and of all the people to make it past the guards and get inside undetected—

Ziva leaned against the kitchen's far wall, unmoving. A shaft of dim ambient light from outside fell across her face, revealing tired but ever-wary eyes. She seemed unbothered by having a weapon drawn on her; when it came down to it, she'd probably been expecting it.

"Dare I ask what you're doing here?" Emeri finally managed as he drew closer.

She said nothing for another couple of seconds. "I thought we should talk."

His first instinct was to argue that this was hardly the time, but seeing her here—not only alive and in the flesh but *here* on Haphez after the team said she'd remained on Delatori—prompted him to keep his mouth shut. His weary mind was beginning to process how surreal this whole situation was, and though all the fires he'd spent the past few days putting out could inarguably be traced back to her, now that she was here, he was more inclined to set all the grief she'd caused him aside and just let himself be relieved to see her in one piece.

Relinquishing the idea of going to bed anytime soon, he motioned for her to take a seat at the tall serving counter and went about fishing out the leftovers he'd been after in the cooler. Ziva had always been reclusive; if she was initiating contact now, whatever she had to say must be important.

He spooned some food into a bowl for himself and held the container up to her. "So, what would you like to talk about?"

She shook her head in response to his offer and steepled her hands in front of her mouth, remaining silent for a moment. "What happens now?"

That was the big question, wasn't it? He set his bowl down, unsure if he'd even get the chance to eat, and studied her. He'd never viewed Ziva Payvan as a particularly selfish person; one had to possess a certain measure of selflessness in order to put one's life on the line time after time, mission after mission. But he also knew she possessed exceptionally strong self-preservation instincts, and despite being separated for four years, he recognized those instincts were driving her current question.

"You want to know what comes next for you, what can be done to protect you."

She didn't respond immediately, perhaps not wanting to admit to that feeling of uncertainty. Then she offered him a single nod.

"For starters, you may be pleased to know you're in the clear as far as Ganten and the Royal House are concerned."

"What do they know?"

"The short version? They believe Matia Moryi was an alias used by a deep-cover Haphezian agent operating independently within Ibarra-controlled space, and that Sergeant Tarbic married her to safeguard her identity and buy both her and the Alpha Team enough time to complete their respective missions."

She lifted a brow.

"After *multiple* days of hearings, interrogations, and more song and dance than I've had to perform throughout the rest of my career combined, I believe the issue has been put to rest. As far as the Royal House is concerned, the operator who took on the Moryi mantle was a Black Agent whose true identity is not authorized to be disclosed to anyone but her handler, so that should be enough to bring their questioning to a reluctant close. This ridiculous 'marriage' between Sergeant Tarbic and yourself is technically still intact, though it can be dissolved at any point. You're damn right in that the only thing it was good for was buying time—there's no way in hell it would have held up in a court setting if it came down to it. Consider yourselves lucky I went to the wall for you."

Even in the semi-darkness, he caught a glint of something in her eyes, a certain emotional sincerity that was completely foreign compared to the fire he'd always seen there. Her time away must have taken an untold toll on her. Despite having always been somewhat of a loner, and despite the danger she was putting herself in by being here, he could only imagine how nice it must feel to be in the presence of a familiar face.

"Thank you," she murmured, her melancholy tone multiplying the weight of the simple phrase tenfold.

"Yes, well, don't thank me yet. There's a high probability I'll be facing some form of disciplinary action myself for 'allowing' an operative to go rogue in the first place, thus causing said operative to threaten the integrity of an active team. They tell me the Prime Director of HSP should be able to keep his agency under control."

Of course, all of that was the result of this story he'd woven and wasn't based on factual events. Ziva's lips flattened into a thin line, indicating to him that she understood that.

"So why bother?" she asked. "You didn't have to do any of this."

"I seem to recall you asking me a question like that once before. Call it a protective instinct." He placed his palms on the countertop and stared down at the swirling designs in the marble for several seconds. "Though to be perfectly honest, I'm not sure if I know exactly who it is I'm protecting. I've always known you to be brutal, Ziva, but I don't like a lot of what I heard about Moryi."

Her exhausted, vulnerable demeanor hardened into an eerily familiar cold stoicism that might have given him pause if he hadn't spent ten years dealing with it before her disappearance. She watched him in silence, jaw set, eyes calculating, and he would have been lying if he said it didn't make him a little uncomfortable given the context. But then she swallowed hard, quashing his concern that she might try to defend her actions.

"I did some things," she said, voice low and steady. "I'm not proud of that, but I did what I had to do to survive. I'm not trying to make excuses, just stating facts. The past is the past, and nothing can change it."

That was true, Emeri supposed, though some of the atrocities he'd heard Moryi was responsible for still made him uneasy. When it came down to it, much of what she'd done was hardly different from the type of work she'd always done for the agency. The only distinction was that the agency jobs were disciplined. Sanctioned through official channels. Did that somehow make it better?

"This is all I know," she continued. "I don't know what comes next for me. The galaxy thinks I'm dead. Even if it didn't, I could never settle down and live a 'normal' life. All this chaos? It's my definition of normal. Surviving is all I know how to do."

It had been decades since he'd done any field work, but Emeri could at least partially relate. Even from the comfort of his office and the HSP campus, there was still a measure of chaos about his day-today life, thanks in no small part to agents like Ziva and her former team. He may have been looking forward to coming home and enjoying a few hours of rest and solitude, but late nights and even all-nighters at the office weren't uncommon, and, frankly, he wasn't sure what he'd do with himself if he didn't have that turmoil driving him.

He drew a deep breath as the wheels inside his head began to spin rapidly. He didn't think she was here looking for handouts; she wasn't someone who did that sort of thing. She was merely reaching out, venting, seeking advice and closure from a trusted source, something he viewed as a big step for her.

Considering those things, he wasn't sure what compelled him to say what he was about to say. "Your personnel file has been wiped from agency records. It began with simply ensuring your arrest bulletin was removed, and...I suppose I got carried away."

That got her attention. Her piercing gaze settled squarely on him, though something else glistened in her eyes. Hope, maybe. In that moment, she wasn't a lethal killer or even one of his former agents, but merely a woman with no place in the galaxy. She'd lost her home in every sense of the word—her job, her physical house, her *world*—and now even the precarious niche she'd carved for herself with the Niiosians was no more. He almost felt sorry for her, and he feared that sense of sympathy was steering the conversation.

"It should come as no surprise that I don't believe there is any feasible way you could ever have a direct role within the operations divisions again," he continued. *Sheyss*, was he crazy for saying this? "But there's also no sense in letting years' worth of agency skill go to waste."

Ziva's gaze didn't waver. "What are you saying?"

He massaged his jaw for a moment as he wondered that very same thing, painfully aware of the fact that he was past the point of no return in terms of broaching this topic. He'd admonished the team for going out of their way to make sacrifices for Ziva, yet here he was on the verge of doing the same thing. And not for the first time.

"I would have no immediate objections to the idea of you serving as an indirect agency asset, if you're interested," he replied. "There's very little—if anything—I can do to protect you personally, but your former team could serve as your collective handler."

Now that he'd articulated the thought aloud, it struck him how lame the offer sounded. Such a role would make her nothing more than a glorified CI, but with her experience and skill set, she could be the most valuable CI the agency had.

That little spark of hope faded from her eyes, and her already-grave features darkened further. "And what of the team now? How are they? How...how will all of this affect their status?"

Emeri sighed; they must have explained their predicament to her. "Returning from an independent service term under emergency orders is not the same as failing or not completing a mission, so that will be taken into consideration when it comes time for evaluations.

"Lieutenant Duvo arrived home in stable condition, but the agency physicians who have been working on him are concerned about permanent nerve damage after he lost so much blood and circulation in his arm."

She shut her eyes and lowered her head.

"However," he continued, prompting her to immediately look back up in anticipation, "they've sent him up to the Na Facility for a couple of weeks to look at rehab options, after which they will reevaluate and decide how to move forward. Meanwhile, Sergeant Tarbic and Officer Vax are lying low. I truthfully don't know where either of them went during this furlough. The hope is that all three of them will be able to go out and complete their deployment after this two-week intermission. But..."

He allowed himself to trail off, unsure how to address an issue he himself dreaded dealing with. He knew good and well he shouldn't—and couldn't—show favor toward any one operations team, but damn if these agents hadn't imprinted on him in a certain way very few others ever had. He didn't envy his people when they were out there risking their lives, but there were times when he found himself sitting in his cushy office wishing he could do more to protect them. Understanding the stakes of this latest mission from a bureaucratic standpoint and then helplessly watching it fall apart from a distance had been more difficult than he'd ever anticipated.

He moved around the serving counter to directly face the barstool she sat on. "Ziva, the truth is there's no way for me to predict how their status will change thanks to this whole mess. The situation is incredibly delicate. I admit that at this point, it might be simpler for them to accept a downgrade than try to cling to Alpha status and dig themselves deeper into the lies."

Based on her steely expression and the subtle sigh she heaved, she recognized that as well. But that in no way made it any easier to hear.

"I wish it hadn't come to this," she said, swiveling toward him and looking more defeated than he'd ever seen her. "I never meant for things to get this bad. I'm sorry."

Emeri couldn't pinpoint what force in the galaxy propelled him forward, but he didn't fight it. "Come here," he said, taking her by the shoulders and wrapping his arms around her. Never in his life would he have imagined himself embracing one of his agents, least of all this one, but he had to remind himself she no longer fell into that category. She was supposed to be dead. Technically, she didn't even exist anymore.

Besides, even though she'd always maintained such a cold and aloof demeanor, it simply seemed like she could use a hug right now.

He pulled back and found that her features had softened into a vaguely amused look as though she could sense the awkwardness but appreciated the gesture anyway. He left his hands on her shoulders and studied her a moment longer, this legendary woman. She had made his life a living hell at times, but he doubted anyone would ever truly replace her.

"Despite the fact that the past few years objectively did more harm to you than good, you did the right thing by leaving," he told her.

Unless it was his imagination, she perked up ever so slightly in response to the positive reinforcement.

"When the *Intrepid* was destroyed and we all thought you were gone, I took solace in the fact that you'd at least managed to go out on your own terms rather than fall into the Federation's hands. So—" he stepped back, giving her the space to leave "—regardless of what you decide to do now, know that it is a relief and a privilege to see you alive."

Ziva stood and offered him a subtle nod as she began to walk away, but she hesitated a moment in the kitchen doorway before turning back to look at him. Emeri had allowed his words to carry a questioning tone—what *would* she do now?—and based on the way her eyes narrowed as she watched him, she was trying to decide how or if to answer that question.

"I don't know if I could stay in any capacity where I'm not leading a team," she said quietly, a pained expression on her face as though she were coming to this conclusion for the first time. "That's all I've ever known."

"Well then, it seems you've got a choice to make."

It wasn't a particularly helpful response, but the decision to stay or leave would ultimately be up to her and her alone. Emeri found himself hoping she would at least consider staying, though he couldn't fault her for leaving again, either. There were a number of things—or people, perhaps—aside from the agency that might compel her to remain, but she'd walked away from those things once before.

Her gaze remained fixed on him for a few more seconds, her crimson eyes rendered black by the shadows of the dark kitchen. Then she turned and vanished through the doorway, departing just as quickly and silently as she had no doubt arrived.

CHAPTER 37
SEA OF HAPHEZ - MAIRO REGION, HAPHEZ

The cold. The chill. The steady, dull rumble.

Aroska did everything in his power to focus on these things, letting them consume him, numb him. He sat on an old piece of driftwood, its surface smooth under his fingertips, staring out at the expanse before him. Fifty or so meters away, across a stretch of black pebbles and a limited amount of coarse sand, the Sea of Haphez roared, the white caps of the crashing waves barely perceptible in the dark. Combined with the chill of the briny ocean breeze, the growl of the water reverberating in his ears sufficiently enveloped his mind. No thoughts, no concerns. Only cold, only noise.

Or so he told himself.

He looked to the horizon, where a sliver of gray was finally beginning to separate the void of the sea from the void of the night sky. He wasn't sure how long he'd been sitting there—long enough for his fingers to be half frozen. Being placed on leave pending Skeet's recovery had left him feeling useless, and trying to escape that feeling by coming out here to Mairo had only left him alone with his thoughts, which was somehow worse. The silence of his hotel room had driven him outdoors in the dead of night, seeking any form of distraction. And here he found himself.

The problem was that it wasn't very relaxing to sit there wrestling with his thoughts, trying to forget, and it was disappointing that all his attempts at forgetting were proving to be ineffective. He was tired. Dwelling on everything that had occurred over the past few days was exhausting, but expending so much energy trying to block it all from his mind was equally so.

So screw it. A chill—more abstract than the chill of the wind—ran down his spine as he opened himself up to this previously unwelcome flood of thoughts and did his best to sort them all out. It was infuriating how trying *not* to think about Ziva always resulted in *constantly* thinking about her. It had been this way since the beginning, even since before the Dakiti mission when he'd been hell-bent on exacting his revenge for Soren's death. He supposed the wounds created by her absence would sting less over time, just as they had the last time she fell from his grasp. He didn't want to purge all memory of her, didn't want to forget her, but if that was what it took to function, to move on—

He scoffed. *Sheyss*, he was starting to sound just like her.

This wasn't the first time he'd found himself wishing he was gifted with the same detached temperament she often exhibited. The problem was that he'd come to realize that demeanor was sometimes a farce, a mere coping mechanism she deployed to hide the pain when she did truly care, so there was no real point in being envious of it. Still, he'd take that false sense of security over this ache in his gut any day.

The gray on the horizon was beginning to turn pink. He fixed his gaze on that band of color, watching as it widened and gradually took on more orange and yellow hues. Something she'd said just before they parted ways had stuck with him for the past several days—he hadn't given it a second thought in the moment, but she'd told him to go take care of his team. The first few times he'd replayed their final exchange in his mind, he'd assumed she was simply acknowledging the fact that Emeri had put him in command following Skeet's incapacitation. She couldn't have known it at the time, but the word was the lieutenant would eventually make a full recovery, though the extent of the effort needed to repair his shoulder remained to be seen. So regardless of what status the team held once everything returned to normal, Skeet would still be in charge. Aroska's tenure as team leader had been short-lived.

Then it had eventually occurred to him...what if, rather than referring to the team as *his*, she'd simply been signifying that it was no longer *hers*? He recalled what she'd said in the medbay aboard the

Revenant, calling them her pride and legacy. There was no denying those things; hell, she was the reason the three of them were a team in the first place. By telling him to take care of his team, she was relinquishing control. The concept struck him as significant, as it demonstrated a measure of personal growth on her part. But it also saddened him, because that sort of concession was the exact thing someone might do if they thought they'd never see you again.

And *sheyss,* that hurt.

A noise off to his right drew his attention. He turned to look, but the majority of the beach was still shrouded in darkness. The tall grasses behind him rustled in the breeze, and some sea birds called to each other high above, nothing more than dark silhouettes as they rode the wind, wings spread. He shook his head and turned back to face the water. Ziva had been totally correct in her assessment of how spec ops had changed him. He had learned to embrace the chaos, had begun to thrive on the thrill of it all. The problem was that it was a package deal that included things like a newfound measure of paranoia he could do without. He'd come out here to get lost in the noise, and now he was worried about hearing things.

He drew a deep breath of salty air in through his nose. The moment the sun crested the horizon was noticeable; he closed his eyes, relishing the feeling of the golden light on his face. Maybe it was just his imagination, but he was almost positive he could feel its heat cutting through the cold, tearing through the dark, warming him even from so far away.

It was a new day, a new start. Moving on was going to take a series of baby steps, and this might as well be one of them.

...and even as he processed that thought, he found himself wishing she could be here sharing this moment with him.

So no, he decided then and there, he wasn't going to go through this again. He'd found her once. He could do it again, the consequences be damned. He'd hunt her down, cross the galaxy if he had to—

Another noise—this one sharper, clearer—put a halt to his train of thought. His eyes snapped open and he whipped his head to the left, sensing another presence.

There she stood, several meters away and slightly behind him, staring out at the sunrise without acknowledging him. She was bundled in a leather jacket and scarf, her hands stuffed firmly into her pockets. A series of short hairs had come loose from her still-ragged ponytail and whipped across her face in the wind. Otherwise, she didn't move.

Aroska found himself frozen in return, unable to peel his eyes away from her as he tried to determine whether she was simply a figment of his imagination. Then she took a step, looking down and moving slowly over the rocky beach as she came around to sit beside him. She still didn't look at him, squinting slightly as she returned her attention to the sun. The way the dawn light reflected in her crimson eyes gave them the appearance of pure fire.

He swallowed, so many thoughts and questions swirling through his head that it was impossible to make sense of them all. He settled on the first one he was able to articulate. "Are you home?"

For the longest time, she said nothing, the brilliant light illuminating her striking features. Finally, she drew a breath, glancing down for a moment at the log upon which they sat.

"Yeah," she said. She removed her hand from her pocket and slid it over his. The heat of her fingers seemed to radiate up his arm, warming his entire being. She once more lifted her gaze to the sun. To the new beginning.

"I'm home."

EMBERS

I hope you enjoyed the conclusion of this series.
I certainly enjoyed crafting it for the characters!
While this chapter of their story has indeed
come to a close, I have a feeling we haven't
seen the last of Ziva, Aroska, & Co.

*Visit **ejfisch.com** and subscribe to my newsletter,*
Updates From EJ, for all the latest info on what
else might be coming from the Ziva Payvan universe!

- EJ

Like what you read? Tell someone about it!
Taking the time to leave an honest review is immeasurably helpful
for any author, new or established. Your opinion helps other
people make informed decisions about their reading options and
allows the book to reach its target audience.

Your ratings and reviews are greatly appreciated!

About The Author

EJ Fisch is a long-time action junkie and fan of the science fiction genre. She'll readily admit that she has a vivid imagination, which can be both a blessing and a curse. She has been writing as a hobby since junior high and began publishing in the spring of 2014.

When she's not busy writing or working her day job as a data analyst in the medical field, she enjoys listening to music, working on concept art, reading, gaming, and spending time with her animals. She currently resides in southern Oregon.

Embers is her fifth novel, Book 5 in the Ziva Payvan series and Book 2 of the Ziva Payvan Legacy duology.

Find EJ Fisch on your favorite social media site!

Keep up with news, catch sneak peeks, and more at:
www.ejfisch.com

Questions? Comments? Use the resources above or email at:
ej@ejfisch.com

Your thoughts about the characters and storylines are always welcome and appreciated!